FROM THE DEEPEST RECESSES OF
THE HUMAN MIND . . .
TO THE FARTHEST REACHES
OF THE UNIVERSE . . .

ENTER AN AWESOME REALM OF
EYE-OPENING WONDERS!

—A battle of the bands is judged by extraterrestrial music lovers on the darkest night of the '60s . . .
—In a world of robotic card sharks, a cybernetic con man takes the most desperate gamble of his life . . .
—A young woman in love forgets one inescapable truth: a girl's best friend is her plant . . .
—A machine that enables loved ones to access hours from the past lives of their dearly departed develops a strange and disturbing glitch . . .
—A group of intergalactic smugglers faces disaster when it crosses the path of man-made instruments of destruction en route to devouring a planet . . .
Plus twelve more masterpieces of the imagination by Edward Bryant, Pat Cadigan, George R. R. Martin, Bruce McAllister and others from the pages of OMNI magazine.

THE FINEST IN FICTION
FROM ZEBRA BOOKS!

HEART OF THE COUNTRY   (2299, $4.50)
by Greg Matthews
Winner of the 26th annual WESTERN HERITAGE AWARD for
Outstanding Novel of 1986! Critically acclaimed from coast to
coast! A grand and glorious epic saga of the American West that
NEWSWEEK Magazine called, "a stunning mesmerizing perfor-
mance," by the bestselling author of THE FURTHER ADVEN-
TURES OF HUCKLEBERRY FINN!
      "A TRIUMPHANT AND CAPTIVATING NOVEL!"
        –KANSAS CITY STAR

CARIBBEE   (2400, $4.50)
by Thomas Hoover
From the author of THE MOGHUL! The flames of revolution
erupt in 17th Century Barbados. A magnificent epic novel of
bold adventure, political intrigue, and passionate romance, in the
blockbuster tradition of James Clavell!
     "ACTION-PACKED . . . A ROUSING READ"
      –PUBLISHERS WEEKLY

MACAU   (1940, $4.50)
by Daniel Carney
A breathtaking thriller of epic scope and power set against a
background of Oriental squalor and splendor! A sweeping saga
of passion, power, and betrayal in a dark and deadly Far Eastern
breeding ground of racketeers, pimps, thieves and murderers!
        "A RIP-ROARER"
      –LOS ANGELES TIMES

THE SEVENTH
OMNI
BOOK OF
SCIENCE FICTION

**EDITED BY
ELLEN DATLOW**

**ZEBRA BOOKS
KENSINGTON PUBLISHING CORP.**

ZEBRA BOOKS

are published by

Kensington Publishing Corp.
475 Park Avenue South
New York, NY 10016

First printing: June, 1989

Printed in the United States of America.

CONTENTS

Introduction to The Omni Book of Science Fiction #7

Short fiction is rarely assigned, because commissioning *anything* is a very risky proposition—you may be stuck with a story completely unsuited to your magazine or anthology. As OMNI's Fiction Editor, I have, however, commissioned several special projects. The first was a group of six humorous short-shorts by regular OMNI contributors. The successful result was *"Double Treble,"* which appeared in OMNI's November 1983 issue. Two of those short-shorts are included in this volume, Edward Bryant's "Bean Bag Cats" and Thomas M. Disch's "The Wandering Jew."

The second project that I assigned was inspired by Barry Malzberg's mini-play, "To Mark The Times We Had." I received the story, loved it, but had no idea how to fit it into OMNI's format. I finally decided to commission five other short-shorts around it—on a political theme. These results, too, were successful, and appeared in the November 1984 OMNI as *"Poly-Sci-Fi."*

Good hard-science stories—those with depth of character as well as strong themes and interesting ideas—may be the most difficult kind of science fiction to write. But anyone who says hard-science-fiction stories are boring just hasn't been paying attention to what's been happening in the field these last years. There has been a hard science renaissance of sorts. People like William Gibson, Bruce Sterling, Pat Cadigan, and Greg Bear have been writing high-tech or hard-science stories that are unlike anything that has been previously published. They have each developed their own unique vision of a very plausible future.

A new voice in this subgenre, Tom Maddox, had his first story published in OMNI. That story, "The Mind Like a Strange Balloon," appears here. Michael Swanwick, not normally known for writing hard-science short stories, is represented in this volume by "Trojan Horse," a novelette combining hard science, strong characterizations, good plotting, and theology. It's a combination that creates what I think is an almost perfect hard-science story. Pat Cadigan's "Variation on a Man" is one of a series on the character Deadpan Allie, a "Pathosfinder" hired to delve into troubled client's minds in a rather bizarre future therapy. Her novel *Mindplayers* (Bantam 1987) incorporates these stories.

Two selections in this volume are time-travel stories. They are both memorable. George R. R. Martin's "Under Siege" is made so by its great attention to historical detail. Bruce Sterling and Lewis Shiner's "Mozart in Mirrorshades" will leave the reader with an indelibly delicious image of Marie Antoinette as you've never seen her.

Also included in THE SEVENTH OMNI BOOK OF

SCIENCE FICTION are top-notch stories by William F. Wu, Roger Zelazny, Bruce McAllister, Howard Waldrop, Karl Hansen, David Bischoff, Kate Wilhelm, and John Crowley. And finally, an original novelette by the late grand master of science fiction, Alfred Bester.

Ellen Datlow
Fiction Editor

Mozart in Mirrorshades

By Bruce Sterling and Lewis Shiner

From the hill north of the city, Rice saw eighteenth-century Salzburg spread out below him like a half-eaten lunch.

Huge cracking towers and swollen, bulbous storage tanks dwarfed the ruins of the St. Rupert Cathedral; thick, white smoke billowed from the refinery's stacks. Rice could taste the familiar petrochemical tang from where he sat, under the leaves of a wilting oak.

The sheer incongruity of it delighted him. Like the phallic pumping station lurking in the central square of the convent, or the ruler-straight elevated pipelines ripping through Salzburg's maze of cobbled streets. A bit tough on the city, maybe, but that was hardly Rice's fault. The temporal beam had focused at random on a point in the bedrock below Salzburg, forming an expandable bubble connecting this world to Rice's own time.

High, chain-link fences surrounded the square mile of the complex. Rice had been inside them for two years, directing teams all over the planet as they ordered Nantucket whalers caulked up to serve as tankers, or trained local pipe fitters to lay down line as far away as the Sinai and the Gulf of Mexico.

Now, finally, he was seeing it all from the outside, despite the objections of Sutherland, the company's political liaison. His mere presence, she claimed, would only worsen the future shock that had left the city reeling.

Rice had no patience with her attitude. The plant was up and breaking design records, and Rice was due for a little R and R.

A moped sputtered up the hill toward him, wobbling crazily. The rider couldn't keep his high-heeled, buckled pumps on the pedals while carrying a huge portable stereo in the crook of his right arm. The moped lurched to a stop at a respectful distance, and Rice recognized the music from the tape player: Symphony 40 in G minor.

The boy turned the volume down as Rice walked toward him. "Good evening, Mr. Plant Manager, sir. I am not interrupting?"

"No, that's okay." Rice glanced at the bristling hedgehog cut that had replaced the boy's outmoded wig. He'd seen the kid around the gates; he was one of the regulars who waited day and night outside the fence, begging for radios, nylons, jabs of penicillin. But the music had made something else fall into place. "You're Mozart, aren't you?"

Wolfgangus Amadeus Mozart, your servant."

"I'll be goddamned. Do you know what that tape is?"

"It has my name on it."

"Yeah. You wrote it. Or would have, I guess I should say. About fifteen years from now."

Mozart nodded. "It is so beautiful. I have not the English to say how it is to hear it."

By this time most of the other gate people would have been well into some kind of pitch. Rice was impressed by the

12

boy's tact, not to mention his command of English. The standard native vocabulary didn't go much beyond, *radio, drugs,* and *fuck.* "Are you headed back toward town?" Rice asked.

"Yes, Mr. Plant Manager, sir."

Something about the kid appealed to Rice. The enthusiasm, the gleam in the eyes. And, of course, he did happen to be one of the greatest composers of all time.

"Forget the titles," Rice said. "Where does a guy go for some fun around here?"

At first Sutherland hadn't wanted Rice at the meeting. But Rice was the company expert on temporal physics, and Jefferson had been pestering the American personnel with questions about time holes and parallel worlds.

Rice, for his part, was thrilled at the chance to meet Thomas Jefferson, the first President of the United States. He'd never liked Washington, was glad the man's Masonic connections had made him refuse to join the company's "godless" government.

Rice squirmed in his Dacron double knits as he and Sutherland waited in the newly air conditioned boardroom of the Hohensalzburg castle. "I forgot how greasy these suits feel," he said.

"At least," Sutherland said, "you didn't wear that goddamned hat today." The VTOL jet from America was late, and she kept looking at her watch.

"My tricorn?" Rice said. "You don't like it?"

"It's a Masonista hat, for Christ's sake. It's a symbol of antimodern reaction." The Freemason Liberation Front was another of Sutherland's nightmares, a local politico-religious group that had made a few pathetic attacks on the pipeline.

"Oh, loosen up, will you, Sutherland? Some groupie of

13

Mozart's gave me the hat, Therese-Maria-Angela something-or-other, some broken-down aristocrat. They all hang out together in this music dive downtown. I just liked the way it looked."

"Mozart? You've been fraternizing with him? Don't you think we should just let him be? After everything we've done to him?"

"Bullshit," Rice said. "I'm entitled. I spent two years on start-up while you were playing touch football with Robespierre and Thomas Paine. I make a few night spots with Wolfgang and you're all over me. What about Parker? I don't hear you bitching about him playing rock and roll on his late show every night. You can hear it blasting out of every cheap transistor in town."

"He's propaganda officer. Believe me, if I could stop him I would, but Parker's a special case. He's got connections all over the place back in Realtime." She rubbed her cheek. "Let's drop it, okay? Just try to be polite to President Jefferson. He's had a hard time lately."

Sutherland's secretary, a former Hapsburg lady-in-waiting, stepped in to announce the plane's arrival. Jefferson pushed angrily past her. He was tall for a local, with a mane of blazing red hair and the shiftiest eyes Rice had ever seen.

"Sit down, Mr. President." Sutherland waved at the far side of the table. "Would you like some coffee or tea?"

Jefferson scowled. "Perhaps some Madeira," he said. "If you have it."

Sutherland nodded to her secretary, who stared for a moment in incomprehension, then hurried off. "How was the flight?" Sutherland asked.

"Your engines are most impressive," Jefferson said, "as you well know." Rice saw the slight trembling of the man's hands; he hadn't taken well to jet flight. "I only wish your political sensitivities were as advanced."

"You know I can't speak for my employers," Sutherland said. "For myself, I deeply regret the darker aspects of our operations. Florida will be missed."

Irritated, Rice leaned forward. "You're not really here to discuss sensibilities, are you?"

"Freedom, sir," Jefferson said. "Freedom is the issue." The secretary returned with a dust-caked bottle of sherry and a stack of clear plastic cups. Jefferson, his hands visibly shaking now, poured a glass and tossed it back. Color returned to his face. He said, "You made certain promises when we joined forces. You guaranteed us liberty and equality and the freedom to pursue our own happiness. Instead we find your machinery on all sides, your cheap manufactured goods seducing the people of our great country, our minerals and works of art disappearing into your fortresses, never to reappear!" The last line brought Jefferson to his feet.

Sutherland shrank back into her chair. "The common good requires a certain period of, uh, adjustment—"

"Oh, come on, Tom," Rice broke in. "We didn't 'join forces,' that's a lot of crap. We kicked the Brits out and you in, and you had damn-all to do with it. Second. If we drill for oil and carry off a few paintings, it doesn't have a goddamned thing to do with your liberty. We don't care. Do whatever you like, just stay out of our way. Right? If we wanted a lot of back talk we could have left the damn British in power."

Jefferson sat down. Sutherland meekly poured him another glass, which he drank at once. "I cannot understand you. You claim you come from the future, yet you seem bent on destroying your own past."

"But we're not," Rice said. "It's this way. History is like a tree, okay? When you go back and mess with the past, another branch of history splits off from the main trunk.

15

Well, this world is just one of those branches."

"So," Jefferson said. "This world—my world—does not lead to your future."

"Right," Rice said.

"Leaving you free to rape and pillage here at will! While your own world is untouched and secure!" Jefferson was on his feet again. "I find the idea monstrous beyond belief, intolerable! How can you be party to such despotism? Have you no human feelings?"

"Oh, for God's sake," Rice said. "Of course we do. What about the radios and the magazines and the medicine we hand out? Personally I think you've got a lot of nerve, coming in here with your smallpox scars and your unwashed shirt and all those slaves of yours back home, lecturing us on humanity."

"Rice?" Sutherland said.

Rice locked eyes with Jefferson. Slowly Jefferson sat down. "Look," Rice said, relenting. "We don't mean to be unreasonable. Maybe things aren't working out just the way you pictured them, but hey, that's life, you know? What do you want, *really?* Cars? Movies? Telephones? Birth control? Just say the word and they're yours."

Jefferson pressed his thumbs into the corners of his eyes. "Your words mean nothing to me, sir. I only want . . . I want only to return to my home. To Monticello. And as soon as possible."

"Is it one of your migraines, Mr. President?" Sutherland asked. "I had these made up for you." She pushed a vial of pills across the table toward him.

"What are these?"

Sutherland shrugged. "You'll feel better."

After Jefferson left, Rice half-expected a reprimand. Instead, Sutherland said, "You seem to have a tremendous faith in the project."

"Oh, cheer up," Rice said. "You've been spending too much time with these politicals. Believe me, this is a simple time, with simple people. Sure, Jefferson was a little ticked off, but he'll come around. Relax!"

Rice found Mozart clearing tables in the main dining hall of the Hohensalzburg castle. In his faded jeans, camo jacket, and mirrored sunglasses, he might almost have passed for a teenager from Rice's time.

"Wolfgang!" Rice called to him. "How's the new job?"

Mozart set a stack of dishes aside and ran his hands over his short-cropped hair. "Wolf," he said. "Call me Wolf, okay? Sounds more . . . modern, you know? But yes, I really want to thank you for everything you have done for me. The tapes, the history books, this job — it is so wonderful to be around here."

His English, Rice noticed, had improved remarkably in the last three weeks. "You still living in the city?"

"Yes, but I have my own place now. You are coming to the gig tonight?"

"Sure," Rice said. "Why don't you finish up around here, I'll go change, and then we can go out for some Sacher torte, okay? We'll make a night of it."

Rice dressed carefully, wearing mesh body armor under his velvet coat and knee britches. He crammed his pockets with giveaway consumer goods, then met Mozart by a rear door.

Security had been stepped up around the castle, and floodlights swept the sky. Rice sensed a new tension in the festive abandon of the crowds downtown.

Like everyone else from his time, he towered over the locals; even incognito he felt dangerously conspicuous.

Within the club Rice faded into the darkness and relaxed. The place had been converted from the lower half of some young aristo's town house; protruding bricks still marked the lines of the old walls. The patrons were locals, mostly, dressed in any Realtime garments they could scavenge. Rice even saw one kid wearing a pair of beige silk panties on his head.

Mozart took the stage. Minuetlike guitar arpeggios screamed over sequenced choral motifs. Stacks of amps blasted synthesizer riffs lifted from a tape of K-Tel pop hits. The howling audience showered Mozart with confetti stripped from the club's hand-painted wallpaper.

Afterward Mozart smoked a joint of Turkish hash and asked Rice about the future.

"Mine, you mean?" Rice said. "You wouldn't believe it. Six billion people, and nobody has to work if they don't want to. Five-hundred-channel TV in every house. Cars, helicopters, clothes that would knock your eyes out. Plenty of easy sex. You want music? You could have your own recording studio. It'd make your gear on stage look like a goddamned clavichord."

"Really? I would give anything to see that. I can't understand why you would leave."

Rice shrugged. "So I'm giving up maybe fifteen years. When I get back, it's the best of everything. Anything I want."

"Fifteen years?"

"Yeah. You gotta understand how the portal works. Right now it's as big around as you are tall, just big enough for a phone cable and a pipeline full of oil, maybe the odd bag of mail, heading for Realtime. To make it any bigger, like to move people or equipment through, is expensive as hell. So expensive they only do it twice, at the beginning and the end of the project. So yeah, I guess we're stuck here."

Rice coughed harshly and drank off his glass. That Ottoman Empire hash had untied his mental shoelaces. Here he was opening up to Mozart, making the kid want to emigrate, and there was no way in hell Rice could get him a Green Card. Not with all the millions that wanted a free ride into the future—billions, if you counted the other projects, like the Roman Empire or New Kingdom Egypt.

"But I'm really *glad* to be here," Rice said. "It's like . . . like shuffling the deck of history. You never know what'll come up next." Rice passed the joint to one of Mozart's groupies, Antonia something-or-other. "This is a great time to be alive. Look at you. You're doing okay, aren't you?" He leaned across the table, in the grip of a sudden sincerity. "I mean, it's okay, right? It's not like you hate all of us for fucking up your world or anything?"

"Are you making a joke? You are looking at the hero of Salzburg. In fact, your Mr. Parker is supposed to make a tape of my last set tonight. Soon all of Europe will know of me!" Someone shouted at Mozart, in German, from across the club. Mozart glanced up and gestured cryptically. "Be cool, man." He turned back to Rice. "You can see that I am doing fine."

"Sutherland, she worries about stuff like all those symphonies that you're never going to write."

"Bullshit! I don't want to write symphonies. I can listen to them anytime I want! Who is this Sutherland? Is she your girlfriend?"

"No. She goes for the locals. Danton, Robespierre, like that. How about you? You got anybody?"

"Nobody special. Not since I was a kid."

"Oh yeah?"

"Well, when I was about six I was at Marie Theresa's court. I used to play with her daughter—Maria Antonia. Marie Antoinette she calls herself now. The most beautiful girl of the age. We used to play duets. We made a joke that we would be married, but she went off to France with that swine, Louis."

"Goddamn," Rice said. "This is really amazing. You know, she's practically a legend where I come from. They cut her head off in the French Revolution for throwing too many parties."

"No they didn't. . . ."

"That was *our* French Revolution," Rice said. "Yours was a lot less messy."

"You should go see her, if you're that interested. Surely she owes you a favor for saving her life."

Before Rice could answer, Parker arrived at their table, surrounded by ex-ladies-in-waiting in spandex capris and sequined tube-tops. "Hey, Rice," Parker shouted, serenely anachronistic in a glitter T-shirt and black leather jeans, "where did you get those un-hip threads? Come on, let's party!"

Rice watched as the girls crowded around the table and gnawed the corks out of a crate of champagne. As short, fat, and repulsive as Parker might be, they would gladly knife one another for a chance to sleep in his clean sheets and raid his medicine cabinet.

"No thanks," Rice said, untangling himself from the miles of wire connected to Parker's recording gear.

The image of Marie Antoinette had seized him and would not let him go.

Rice sat naked on the edge of the canopied bed, shivering a little in the air conditioning. Past the jutting window unit, through clouded panes of eighteenth-century glass, he saw a lush, green landscape sprinkled with tiny waterfalls.

At ground level, a garden crew of former aristos in blue-denim overalls trimmed weeds under the bored supervision of a peasant guard. The guard, clothed head-to-foot in camouflage except for a tricolor cockade on his fatigue cap, chewed gum and toyed with the strap of his cheap, plastic machine gun. The gardens of Petit Trianon, like Versailles itself, were treasures deserving the best of care. They belonged to the Nation since they were too large to be crammed through a time portal.

Marie Antoinette sprawled across the bed's expanse of pink satin, wearing a scrap of black-lace underwear and leafing through an issue of *Vogue*. The bedroom's walls were crowded with Boucher canvases; acres of pert, silky rumps, pink haunches, knowing pursed lips. Rice looked dazedly from the portrait of Louise O'Morphy, kittenishly sprawled on a divan, to the sleek, creamy expanse of Toinette's back and thighs, took a deep, exhausted breath. "Man," he said, "that guy could really paint."

Toinette cracked off a square of Hershey's chocolate and pointed to the magazine. "I want the leather bikini," she said. "Always, when I am a girl, my goddamn mother, she keep me in the goddamn corsets. She think my what-you-call, my shoulder blade stick out too much."

Rice leaned back across her solid thighs and patted her bottom reassuringly. He felt wonderfully stupid; a week and a half of obsessive carnality had reduced him to a euphoric animal. "Forget your mother, baby. You're with *me* now. You want ze goddamn leather bikini, I get it for you."

Toinette licked chocolate from her fingertips. "Tomorrow we go out to the cottage, okay, man? We dress up like the peasants and we make love in the hedges just like noble savages."

Rice hesitated. His weekend furlough to Paris had stretched into a week and a half; by now security would be looking for him. To hell with them, he thought. "Great," he said. "I'll phone us up a picnic lunch. Foie gras and truffles, maybe some terrapin . . ."

Toinette pouted. "I want the modern food. The pizza and

21

burritos and the chicken fried." When Rice shrugged, she threw her arms around his neck. "You love me, Rice?"

"Love you? Baby, I love the very *idea* of you." He was drunk on history out of control, careening under him like some great black motorcycle of the imagination. When he thought of Paris, take-out quiche-to-go stores springing up where guillotines might have been, a six-year-old Napoleon munching Dubble Bubble in Corsica, he felt like the archangel Michael on speed.

Megalomania, he knew, was an occupational hazard. But he'd get back to work soon enough, in just a few more days . . .

The phone rang. Rice burrowed into a plush house robe formerly owned by Louis XVI. Louis wouldn't mind; he was now a happily divorced locksmith in Nice.

Mozart's face appeared on the phone's tiny screen. "Hey, man, where are you?"

"France," Rice said vaguely. "What's up?"

"Trouble, man. Sutherland flipped out, and they've got her sedated. At least six key people have gone over the hill, counting you." Mozart's voice had only the faintest trace of accent left.

"Hey, I'm not over the hill. I'll be back in just a couple days. We've got what, thirty other people in Northern Europe? If you're worried about the quotas . . ."

"Fuck the quotas. This is serious. There's uprisings. Comanches raising hell on the rigs in Texas. Labor strikes in London and Vienna. Realtime is pissed. They're talking about pulling us out."

"What?" Now he was alarmed.

"Yeah. Word came down the line today. They say you guys let this whole operation get sloppy. Too much contamination, too much fraternization. Sutherland made a lot of trouble with the locals before she got found out. She was organizing the Masonistas for some kind of passive resistance and God knows what else."

"Shit." The fucking politicals had screwed it up again. It wasn't enough that he'd busted ass getting the plant up and online; now he had to clean up after Sutherland. He glared at Mozart. "Speaking of fraternization, what's all this *we* stuff? What the hell are you doing calling me?"

Mozart paled. "Just trying to help. I got a job in communications now."

"That takes a Green Card. Where the hell did you get that?"

"Uh, listen, man, I got to go. Get back here, will you? We need you." Mozart's eyes flickered, looking past Rice's shoulders. "You can bring your little time-bunny along if you want to. But hurry."

"I . . . oh shit, okay," Rice said.

Rice's hovercar huffed along at a steady 80 kph, blasting clouds of dust from the deeply rutted highway. They were near the Bavarian border. Ragged Alps jutted into the sky over radiant green meadows, tiny, picturesque farmhouses, and clear, vivid streams of melted snow.

They'd just had their first argument. Toinette had asked for a Green Card, and Rice had told her he couldn't do it. He offered her a Gray Card instead, that would get her from one branch of time to another without letting her visit Realtime. He knew he'd be reassigned if the project pulled out, and he wanted to take her with him. He wanted to do the decent thing, not leave her behind in a world without Hersheys and *Vogue*s.

But she wasn't having any of it. After a few kilometers of weighty silence she started to squirm. "I have to pee," she said finally. "Pull over by the goddamn trees."

"Okay," Rice said. "Okay."

He cut the fans and whirred to stop. A herd of brindled cattle spooked off with a clank of cowbells. The road was deserted.

Rice got out and stretched, watching Toinette climb a wooden stile and walk toward a stand of trees.

"What's the deal?" Rice yelled. "There's nobody around. Get on with it!"

A dozen men burst up from the cover of a ditch and rushed him. In an instant they'd surrounded him, leveling flintlock pistols. They wore tricorns and wigs and lace-cuffed highwayman's coats; black domino masks hid their faces. "What the fuck is this?" Rice asked, amazed. "Mardi Gras?"

The leader ripped off his mask and bowed ironically. His handsome Teutonic features were powdered, his lips rouged. "I am Count Axel Ferson. Servant, sir."

Rice knew the name; Ferson had been Toinette's lover before the Revolution. "Look, Count, maybe you're a little upset about Toinette, but I'm sure we can make a deal. Wouldn't you really rather have a color TV?"

"Spare us your satanic blandishments, sir!" Ferson roared. "I would not soil my hands on the collaborationist cow. We are the Freemason Liberation Front!"

"Christ," Rice said. "You can't possibly be serious. Are you taking on the project with these popguns?"

"We are aware of your advantage in armaments, sir. This is why we have made you our hostage." He spoke to the others in German. They tied Rice's hands and hustled him into the back of a horse-drawn wagon that had clopped out of the woods.

"Can't we at least take the car?" Rice asked. Glancing back, he saw Toinette sitting dejectedly in the road by the hovercraft.

"We reject your machines," Ferson said. "They are one

24

more facet of your godlessness. Soon we will drive you back to hell, from whence you came!"

"With what? Broomsticks?" Rice sat up in the back of the wagon, ignoring the stink of manure and rotting hay. "Don't mistake our kindness for weakness. If they send the Gray Card Army through that portal, there won't be enough left of you to fill an ashtray."

"We are prepared for sacrifice! Each day thousands flock to our worldwide movement, under the banner of the All-Seeing Eye! We shall reclaim our destiny! The destiny you have stolen from us!"

"Your *destiny?*" Rice was aghast. "Listen, Count, you ever hear of guillotines?"

"I wish to hear no more of your machines." Ferson gestured to a subordinate. "Gag him."

They hauled Rice to a farmhouse outside Salzburg. During fifteen bone-jarring hours in the wagon he thought of nothing but Toinette's betrayal. If he'd promised her the Green Card, would she still have led him into the ambush? That card was the only thing she wanted, but how could the Masonistas get her one?

Rice's guards paced restlessly in front of the windows, their boots squeaking on the loosely pegged floorboards. From their constant references to Salzburg he gathered that some kind of siege was in progress.

Nobody had shown up to negotiate Rice's release, and the Masonistas were getting nervous. If he could just gnaw through his gag, Rice was sure he'd be able to talk some sense into them.

He heard a distant drone, building slowly to a roar. Four of the men ran outside, leaving a single guard at the open door. Rice squirmed in his bonds and tried to sit up.

Suddenly the clapboards above his head were blasted to

splinters by heavy machine-gun fire. Grenades whumped in front of the house, and the windows exploded in a gush of black smoke. A choking Masonista lifted his flintlock at Rice. Before he could pull the trigger a burst of gunfire threw the terrorist against the wall.

A short, heavyset man in flak jacket and leather pants stalked into the room. He stripped goggles from his smoke-blackened face, revealing Oriental eyes. A pair of greased braids hung down his back. He cradled an assault rifle in the crook of one arm and wore two bandoliers of grenades. "Good," he grunted. "The last of them." He tore the gag from Rice's mouth. He smelled of sweat and smoke and badly cured leather. "You are Rice?"

Rice could only nod and gasp for breath.

His rescuer hauled him to his feet and cut his ropes with a bayonet. "I am Jebe Noyon, Trans-Temporal Army." He forced a leather flask of rancid mare's milk into Rice's hands. The smell made Rice want to vomit. "Drink!" Jebe insisted. "Is koumiss, is good for you. Drink, Jebe Noyon tells you!"

Rice took a sip, which curdled his tongue and brought bile to his throat. "You're the Gray Cards, right?" he said weakly.

"Gray Card Army, yes," Jebe said. "Baddest-ass warriors of all times and places. Only five guards here, I kill them all! I, Jebe Noyon, was chief general to Genghis Khan, terror of the earth, okay, man?" He stared at Rice with great, sad eyes. "You have not heard of me."

"Sorry, Jebe, no."

"The earth turned black in the footprint of my horse."

"I'm sure it did, man."

"You will mount up behind me," he said, dragging Rice toward the door. "You will watch the earth turn black in the tireprints of my Harley, man, okay?"

From the hills above Salzburg they looked down on anachronism gone wild.

Local soldiers in waistcoats and gaiters lay in bloody heaps by the gates of the refinery. Another battalion marched forward in formation, muskets at the ready. A handful of Huns and Mongols, deployed at the gate, cut them up with orange tracer fire and watched the survivors scatter.

Jebe Noyon laughed hugely. "Is like siege of Cambaluc! Only no stacking up heads or even taking ears anymore, man, now we are civilized, okay? Later maybe we call in, like grunts, choppers from Nam, napalm the son-of-a-bitches, far out, man."

"You can't do that, Jebe," Rice said sternly. "The poor bastards don't have a chance. No point in exterminating them."

Jebe shrugged. "I forget sometimes okay? Always thinking to conquer the world. He revved the cycle and scowled. Rice grabbed the Mongol's stinking flak jacket and they roared downhill. Jebe took his disappointment out on the enemy, tearing through the streets in high gear, deliberately running down a group of Brunswick grenadiers. Only panic strength saved Rice from falling off as legs and torsos thumped and crunched beneath their tires.

Jebe skidded to a stop inside the gates of the complex. A jabbering horde of Mongols in ammo belts and combat fatigues surrounded them at once. Rice pushed through them, his kidneys aching.

Ionizing radiation smeared the evening sky around the Hohensalzburg castle. They were kicking the portal up to the high-energy maximum, running cars full of Gray Cards in and sending the same cars back loaded to the ceiling with art and jewelry.

Over the rattling of gunfire Rice could hear the whine of VTOL jets bringing in the evacuees from Africa, and the U.S. Roman centurions, wrapped in mesh body armor and carrying shoulder-launched rockets, herded Realtime personnel into the tunnels that led to the portal.

Mozart was in the crowd, waving enthusiastically to Rice. "We're pulling out, man! Fantastic, huh? Back to Realtime."

Rice looked at the clustered towers of pumps, coolers, and catalytic cracking units. "It's a goddamned shame," he said. "All that work, shot to hell."

"We're losing too many people. Forget it. There's plenty of eighteenth centuries."

The guards, sniping at the crowds outside, suddenly leapt aside as Rice's hovercar burst through the gates. Half a dozen Masonic fanatics still clung to the doors and pounded on the windscreen. Jebe's Mongols yanked the invaders free and axed them while a Roman flamethrower unit gushed fire across the gates.

Marie Antoinette leapt out of the hovercar. Jebe grabbed for her, but her sleeve came off in his hand. She spotted Mozart and ran for him, Jebe only a few steps behind.

"Wolf, you bastard!" she shouted. "You leave me behind! What about your promises, you *merde,* you pig-dog!"

Mozart whipped off his mirrorshades. He turned to Rice. "Who is this woman?"

"The Green Card, Wolf! You say I sell Rice to the Masonistas, you get me the card!" She stopped for breath and Jebe caught her by one arm. When she whirled on him, he cracked her across the jaw, and she dropped to the tarmac.

The Mongol focused his smoldering eyes on Mozart. "Was you, eh? You, the traitor?" With the speed of a striking cobra he pulled his machine pistol and jammed the muzzle against Mozart's nose. "I put my gun on rock 'n' roll, there nothing left of you but ears, man."

A single shot echoed across the courtyard. Jebe's head rocked back, and he fell in a heap.

Rice spun to his right. Parker, the DJ, stood in the doorway of an equipment shed. He held a Walther PPK. "Take it easy, Rice," Parker said, walking toward him. "He's just a grunt, expendable."

"You *killed* him!"

"So what?" Parker said, throwing one arm around Mozart's frail shoulders. "This here's my boy! I transmitted a couple of his new tunes up the line a month ago. You know what? The kid's number five on the *Billboard* chart! Number five!" Parker shoved the gun into his belt. "With a bullet!"

"You gave him the Green Card, Parker?"

"No," Mozart said. "It was Sutherland."

"What did you do to her?"

"Nothing! I swear to you, man! Well, maybe I kind of lived up to what she wanted to see. A broken man, you know, his music stolen from him, his very soul?" Mozart rolled his eyes upward. "She gave me the Green Card, but I guess that still wasn't enough. She couldn't handle the guilt. You know the rest."

"And when she got caught you were afraid we wouldn't pull out. So you decided to drag *me* into it. You got Toinette to turn me over to the Masons. That was *your* doing."

As if hearing her name, Toinette moaned softly. Rice didn't care about the bruises, the dirt, the rips in her leopard-skin jeans. She was still the most gorgeous creature he'd ever seen.

Mozart shrugged. "I was a Freemason once. Look, man, they're very uncool. I mean, all I did was drop a few hints, and look what happened." He waved casually at the carnage all around them. "I knew you'd get away from them somehow."

"You can't just *use* people like that!"

"Bullshit, Rice! You do it all the time! I *needed* this siege so Realtime would haul us out! For Christ's sake, I can't wait fifteen years to go up the line. History says I'm going to be *dead* in fifteen years! I don't want to die in this dump! I want that car and that recording studio!"

"Forget it, pal," Rice said. "When they hear back in Realtime how you screwed things up here—"

Parker laughed. "Shove off, Rice. We're talking Top of the Pops, here. Not some penny-ante refinery." He took Mozart's arm protectively. "Listen, Wolf, baby, let's get into those tunnels. I got some papers for you to sign as soon as we hit the future."

The sun had set, but muzzle-loading cannons lit the night, pumping shells into the city. For a moment Rice stood stunned as cannonballs clanged harmlessly off the storage tanks. Then, finally, he shook his head. Salzburg's time had run out.

Hoisting Toinette over one shoulder, he ran toward the safety of the tunnels.

Variation on a Man

By Pat Cadigan

I was convinced (still am) that it was the pearl-necklace episode that caused Nelson Nelson to give me the Gladney case.

All mindplayers can pretty much count on getting pearl necklaced sooner or later, but it's a far more vivid experience for pathosfinders than it is for neurosis-peddlers, say, or belljarrers, who don't spend as much time in direct mind-to-mind contact with their clients as we do.

It seems the more time you spend working as a disembodied mind, the more intensely you get pearl necklaced.

My pearl necklace came during a routine reality affixing. Reality affixing is mandatory for mindplayers by federal law, though I don't really believe we're more prone to delusional thinking than anyone else. And there's something about having to have my perceptions stamped ACCEPTABLE PER GOVERNMENT REGULATORY STANDARDS that makes me a touch uneasy. On the other hand — or lobe, if you will — a mindplayer who is convinced everybody must accept the

31

water buffalo as a personal totem is not someone you'd want fooling around in people's minds.

Still, I didn't look forward to having my reality affixed, in spite of Nelson Nelson's reassurance that government standards were broad enough to encompass all the varieties of normal. I always wanted to ask him what made him so sure about that. But there was no room for argument — either I had my reality affixed or I lost my job at the mind-play agency and my license to practice pathosfinding.

All I had to do was go headfirst into the agency's system and let it probe me for perhaps ten minutes, if that. Of course, it can seem like days when you're lying on the slab with your eyes out and the system hooked into your mind via the optic nerves, body awareness blocked off so that you're completely alone with yourself. NN was always telling me that I should look at it as a particularly intense kind of mediation and that as long as I was myself, I certainly had nothing to feel uneasy about.

As long as I was myself. And who else would I be? The system had apparently stimulated this particular question, and out came the pearl necklace. That was exactly how it appeared to my inner eye, as a long, long line of pearls, each one holding a moment in the life of Alexandra Victoria Haas, a.k.a. Deadpan Allie, separate, self-contained, unrelated to those on either side of it. The connecting thread running through them was suddenly gone, and I was looking at a series of strangers who shared my face but nothing more, as though I had popped in and out of being every moment I had been alive instead of existing continuously. The realization flared like sudden pain: *I have not always been as I am now.*

I couldn't remember being any different. Nor could I conceive of what I would be like in the next moments — the future me was as much a stranger as the past one.

The pearls began moving away from one another, the sequence going from ordered to random. I lunged to gather them up, and panic sent them flying apart as I fell toward disintegration.

The next thing I knew, I was fine again, and the pearl necklace was gone. The foundation of everything I'd lived was under me again; I was no longer a stranger to myself. The system ran through the rest of the affixing procedure and then disengaged. I put my eyes back in and went off to have a nap.

Naturally, the crisis was reported to Nelson Nelson. I knew it would be, but he never mentioned it. Instead he called me into his office to give me an assignment.

"In your work with artists," he said, while I lay on the gold-lamé interview couch and tried not to be obvious about the rash the tacky upholstery was giving me, "what would you say your primary objective as a pathosfinder is?"

I rested my cheek on my left hand and thought it over. "To assist them in reaching a level where inward and outward perceptions balance well enough against each other so that—"

"*Allie.*" He gave me a look. "This is *me* you're talking to."

"Help them move past irrelevant and superficial mental trash."

NN raised himself up on one elbow, his own couch creaking and groaning, and actually shook his finger at me. "Never, never, *never* essay-answer me."

"Sorry."

His eyes narrowed. He had brand-new pink-jade biogem eyes, and they made him look like a geriatric rabbit. "Don't be sorry. In spite of your initial choice of words, you're right." The wrinkled old face took on a thoughtful expression. "Would you say that in many cases the pathosfinder is responsible for helping an artist locate the creative generator's ON button as well as helping to enhance the soul in the work?"

For someone who didn't like essay answers, he was pretty fond of essay questions. "In many cases, sure."

Now he looked satisfied. "That's why I'd like to put you on the Gladney case."

"Rand Gladney? The composer? I thought he'd been sucked."

"He was. But he's out of full quarantine now, and his new personality's grown into mature form. He's lucky his old recording company had regeneration insurance on him. Of course, he's not really Gladney anymore and never will be again."

"Have they told him who he used to be?"

"Oh, yah. Every detail. He wanted to know. Most victims of involuntary mind-suck do. They're all intensely curious about their former lives, and the doctors figure honesty is the best policy. Better for them to hear about it in a sheltered environment where they can learn to deal with it. Anyway, I thought this would be a good opportunity for a pathos-finder to work with an adult who has no history whatsoever and help him become an artist."

For the millionth time, I thought about the career in neurosis-peddling I'd given up. NN had promised (sort of) that someday he'd let me go back to it.

I'd never thought peddling things like compulsive cleanliness to wealthy people who enjoyed feeling a little more unstable than usual was easy work until NN had made a pathosfinder out of me.

But I didn't have to tell him I'd take the job. He knew I would.

I ran through the bare minimum of information on Gladney that NN had dumped into the data-keep in my apartment while the portable system I used for mind-to-mind contact with clients was being overhauled. Prior to having his mind stolen, Rand Gladney had been a composer of middle-high talent with a fair number of works that had settled into the cultural mainstream. At the time of his erasure, he'd been approaching a turning point in his career where he would have either ascended to greater ability and prominence or settled slowly into repetition and, eventually, semioblivion. In seven years, he had peaked twice after his breakthrough. And that was just about all NN wanted me to know about the Gladney-that-had-been. I could have easily found out more, but I trusted NN's judgment as to how much information on Gladney's previous incarnation I should bring with me to the job.

The Gladney-that-was-now had been out of full quarantine for a month, though he was still hospitalized and his movements were restricted. Rehabilitating mindwipes is a precarious business, like trying to stand with your hands both on and off someone's shoulders. Personality regrowth begins with the restoration of language, first by machine, then by humans. If humans don't replace the machine at precisely the right moment, you end up with a person unable to think in anything but a machine-type mode. People like that may be great logicians, but they're lousy on theory. Most often they resolve the conflict between the definite and the gray in their lives by suicide or voluntary mindwipe, which is pretty much the same thing. There are very few brains hardy enough to redevelop a mind after a second erasure, the myelin sheathing on the axons just won't stand up to that kind of abuse.

In any case, Gladney (who was apparently still going by that name for the sake of convenience) had passed all the critical points in redevelopment and had become a person, again or for the first time, depending on your point of view.

He was certainly not the same person—the man who had emerged from the blank brain was reminiscent of his former self but no more that self than he was anyone else.

The extreme convolutedness of such a situation was one reason why I chose not to go into rehabing mindwipe as a profession when I'd had the chance. Still, it was a fascinating field, easier to succeed in if you have a bit of a mystic bent, or so I've been told. I'd never thought of myself as particularly mystical, but I suppose all mindplayers are to a certain extent, if you accept the mind as the ghost in the biological machine or something like that.

I filed the idea away for later meditation and went over Gladney's aptitude tests. His new personality had grown in with a definite talent for music and more—I was startled to find that he now had perfect pitch. The previous man did not. It made me wonder. Was the perfect pitch something that had shown up due to some alteration in Gladney's brain chemistry brought about by the mindsuck? Or was it just due to a different brain organization? Possibly it was a combination of both.

Whatever it was, I didn't really have to worry about it. I was supposed to treat Gladney as I would any other client, which is to say as though he had never been anyone else but who he was now.

"Truth to tell," said the woman with the carnelian eyes and the too-short apple-red hair, "we ended up selecting you for your business name. Anyone operating as Deadpan Allie must have quite a lot of control over herself." She smiled brightly. Her name was Lind Jesl, and she looked less like the chief doctor on the Gladney case than she did someone finishing up her own recovery. Except for the carnelian eyes and the hair, she was as plain as possible, her stout body concealed in a loose, gray sacksuit. The office we were sitting in was even more austere, a cream-colored box with no decorations. Even the computer desk was all folded into a stark, bare block. The whole thing reminded me of the infamous white-room image I'd come across in certain clients' minds.

"Of course," she went on, "your self-control will be vital when you delve our boy. An involuntary wipe is supremely sensitive and impressionable, even at such an advanced stage of regeneration. Just the experience of you probing his mind is going to make quite a mark on him. Your flavor, as 'twere, will leave a bit of an aftertaste."

"I'm very careful."

"Yes, certainly you are." Her gaze snagged briefly on my equipment piled up beside me before she gave me her five-hundred-watt smile again. "And we wouldn't have hired you if we weren't as confident of his ability to think independently as we are of *your* ability to refrain from exerting too much psychic influence."

She was putting a lot of emphasis on the very thing guaranteed by the fact that I was licensed to pathosfind in the first place. "What kind of results are you looking for?"

"Ah." Five hundred watts went to six hundred. She folded her pudgy hands and plunked them on her stomach. "We're hoping you'll help him learn how to combine the various elements that make up a composer into a whole that will be greater than the sum of the parts."

I blinked.

"We know that he has a musical *bent,* as 'twere. A definite leaning toward music, an affinity for playing instruments that tends to accompany perfect pitch. But as yet, these things are fragmented in him. He's having difficulty achieving a state where they all work together. In fact, he has yet to achieve it even for a few moments."

"Isn't that just a matter of" — I shrugged — "practice and experience?"

"Usually. But I know Gladney. *This* Gladney. There are signs of a definite barrier of some kind that he just can't or won't find his way around. We don't know for certain because we haven't delved him since the very early part of the regeneration, which he does not remember. Delicate Plant Syndrome, you see—if you keep digging up a delicate plant to see how well the roots are taking, it dies." She sat forward, her hands disappearing into the voluminous cloth of the sacksuit. "We feel he's ready for mind-to-mind contact now but with a pathosfinder rather than a doctor. We want him to feel less like our patient and more like a person."

"How long *has* it been since you delved him therapeutically?"

"About nine or ten months. It's been a year since the mindsuckers got him. We're hoping to release him completely in another six months at the most. Depending on how much progress he makes with you."

"Have you let him listen to any of his old compositions? The previous Gladney's music, I mean?"

"Yes and no. Which is to say he's heard it, but he doesn't know who composed it. We removed all identification from all the recordings we've given him, not just Gladney's, to foil whatever deductions he might have tried to make."

"Does he react any differently to the Gladney compositions than he does to any of the others?"

"He reacts to all music somewhat guardedly. He puts it through some kind of mental sorting procedure, and he *can* tell with an accuracy of close to ninety percent, sometimes more, whether different pieces of music were composed by the same person. I suspect he could also arrange a composer's works in the correct chronological order as well. He's *extremely* bright. But—" Jesl spread her hands. "Something inside isn't meshing."

"Has he tried to compose?"

"Oh, yes. Some short things he won't let us hear. We had to bug the synthesizer we gave him. His work shows potential. There are moments when it *almost* breaks through, but it always stops short of achieving—well, fullness, as 'twere. You'll hear that for yourself, I'm sure." She looked at my equipment again.

She was awfully sure about a lot of things, it seemed to me. I considered the possibility that her evaluation of his music might be faulty. Perhaps the musical direction he was taking was just different from the old Gladney's, and what he wasn't achieving were her expectations. But a sight reading of her Emotional Index didn't indicate any smugness. Her certainty seemed to come from the fact that she'd been with him at every step of his regrowth. She smiled again, this time somewhat reservedly and I realized she knew I'd been taking her Emotional Index.

"When can I see him?" I asked.

"Right now, if you like. We've fixed up a room for you not far from his so you'll be within easy reach of each other. I'll take you down there, and then we'll visit our boy."

The room they'd given me was an improvised efficiency with a freestanding lavabo unit and jury-rigged meal dial. My apartment at NN's agency had spoiled me for any other kind of accommodations, no matter how temporary. The bed was a hospital bed disguised as a civilian—not very wide but, to my great relief, hard as a rock.

I'd brought only a few personal things with me, which I didn't bother to unpack. I debated taking my equipment with me to Gladney's room and decided against it. He might feel too pressured to begin work if I appeared wheeling my system with me. I wanted some extra time myself, just to see what an eighteen-month-old adult was like on the outside before I went inside.

The man lying on the bed had once had the pampered good looks found in most people of celebrity status. Over the months, he'd lost a good deal of them, the way an athlete or dancer will lose a certain amount of strength after a long period of inactivity. He was still attractive, but his appearance was changing, veering off in another direction. Typical of a regrown mindwipe. In a few months it was possible he would be so changed that no one from his previous life would recognize him.

He got up for Jesl's brief introduction, touching hands with me gingerly, as though I might be a hot iron. Something like bewildered panic crossed his face as Jesl made a quick but unhurried exit, leaving us on our own.

"So, you're my pathosfinder." He gestured at a small area arranged around an entertainment center with a few chairs and a beverage table. He'd probably set it up himself, but I could tell he wasn't completely at home with it.

"Anything you'd like to ask me in particular?" I said, sitting down. The chair I selected gave like soft clay under me, and I realized it was one of those damned contour things that will adapt a shape to complement your position. It was made of living fiber, supposedly the most comfortable kind of furniture there was, though how anyone could be comfortable with a chair that needed to be fed, watered, and cleaned up after was not within my understanding. Occasionally you'd hear horror stories about people who had sat down on one of those things and then needed to be surgically removed later. I wondered why they'd given Gladney a contour and then remembered it was also supposed to be a boon to the lonely. I was going to have a rough time being deadpan if it started any funny stuff with me. Fortunately, it seemed disposed to let me sit in peace; so I decided to tough it out rather than change seats. Gladney appeared to be watching me closely.

"I hardly ever use that one," he said as it molded itself to support my elbows. "I can't get used to it. But it's fascinating to watch when someone else is in it." He turned his attention to my face. "What kind of eyes are those?"

"Cat's-eye biogem."

"Cat's-eye." He sounded slightly envious. "Everyone here at the hospital has biogems. Even some of the other 'wipes. Dr. Jesl says that I can order some whenever I want to, but I don't feel like I can yet. *He* had biogems."

"Who?"

"Gladney. The original one, not me. After he was sucked, the hospital replaced them with these, which I guess are reproductions of the eyes he was born with." He smiled. "I remember how surprised I was when they told me almost everyone has his eyes replaced with artificial ones. It still amazes me a little. I mean, my eyes don't feel artificial — but then, I guess I wouldn't know the difference, would I?" His smile shrank. "It's strange to think of you going into my brain that way. Through my eyes. It's strange to think of anyone else in there except me." He put his hand on his chest and absently began rubbing himself. "And yet there have been a whole lot of people in there. Mindplayers. For *him*. And then the suckers. The doctors. And now you."

"Direct contact with the mind is a way of life. Not just the mindplay but many forms of higher education. People buy and sell things, too. Neuroses, memories, or —" *Nice rolling. Deadpan,* I thought. *You had to bring that up.*

"Yah. I know. People buy and sell. They steal, too." He lifted his chin with just a trace of defiance. "I made them tell me about that, and what they wouldn't tell me, I looked up. How Gladney's mind got stolen because there was some guy who admired him so much that he wanted to *be* Gladney. So he had Gladney overlaid on his own self. He went crazy. Trying to be two people at once." He slouched in his chair and rested his head on his right hand, digging his fingers into his thick, brown hair. I didn't make a move. "I asked them why they didn't just take Gladney out of him and put him back, but they said they couldn't do that after he'd already been implanted. Even if they'd found the suckers before that, it would have been impossible because this brain"—he pointed at his head and then resumed rubbing his chest—"had already begun developing a new mind. Me. There would have been too much conflict. Doesn't seem fair."

"Fair to whom?"

"Gladney." Beneath the thin material of his shirt, I could see his flesh reddening. "He just disintegrated. Evaporated when they cleaned him out of the other man. And here I am. Variation on a theme." His gaze drifted away from me to something over my left shoulder. I turned to look. He was staring at the synthesizer near the bed. It was a small one as synthesizers go, taking up about twice as much space as my portable system did when assembled. There was a very light coating of dust on the keyboard cover.

"Use it much?" I asked.

"From time to time."

"I'd really like to hear something you've composed."

He looked mildly shocked. "Ah, you would. Why?"

"Get acquainted with your music."

"So that after you get into my brain and find my music box, you'll know whether it's mine or not, huh?" He waved away his words. "Never mind. I've done nothing but short pieces, and I don't think of any of them as complete. Not when I compare them to other things I've heard."

"I would still like to hear something."

He hesitated. "Would a recording be all right? I don't like to play in front of anyone. I'm not an entertainer. Or at least not that kind of entertainer."

"A recording would be fine."

He got up and puttered around with the entertainment center for a minute, keeping his back to me.

Generally it's difficult if not impossible to sight-read the Emotional Index of someone who isn't facing you, but it was easy to tell that Gladney was dry-mouthed at the idea of my hearing one of his compositions. It was far more than stagefright or shyness. His shoulders were stiffened as though he expected someone to hit him.

Abruptly music blared out of the speakers, and he jumped to adjust the volume.

"Set it to repeat once," I told him.

He turned to me, ready to object, and then shrugged and thumbed a shiny green square on the console before sitting down again. "Just a musical doodle, really," he muttered, apologizing for it before it could offend me.

In fact, it was a bit more than that, a dialogue between piano and clarinet, admirably synthesized but too tentative. And he'd been right—it wasn't complete at all. It was more like an excerpt from a longer piece that he'd heard only a portion of in his mind. I was no musical authority, but the second time through, I could pick out spots where a surer composer would have punched up the counterpoint and let the two instruments answer each other more quickly. There might even have been the makings of a canon in it, though I couldn't be certain. Perhaps he'd been mistaking Bach for Gladney. Whatever he'd been doing or trying to do, something was definitely missing.

"How did you compose it?" I asked after the music finished.

He frowned.

"Did you just sit down at the synthesizer and fool around until you found a sequence or—"

"Oh." He laughed nervously. "That's a funny thing. I

heard it in a dream, and when I woke up, I went to the synthesizer to play it out so I wouldn't forget it. First I just played all the notes as I'd heard them. Then I put them with the appropriate instruments."

"Was that how it was in the dream — piano and clarinet?"

"I don't remember. I just remember the music itself. Piano and clarinet seemed right."

I had a feeling I knew what the answer to my next question would be, but asked anyway. "What was the dream about?"

He was rubbing again. "Gladney."

I managed to talk him into playing a few more of his incomplete compositions. When his discomfort went from acute to excruciating, I gave him a reprieve and told him I was going to get some rest. His relief was so tangible I could have ridden it out of the room and halfway down the hall.

There was a message in my phone, an invitation from Dr. Jesl to have dinner with her and the other medicos working on Gladney's habilitation. I begged off and asked her if she could supply me, without his knowing it, with dupe recordings of Gladney's recent attempts at composition, and also some of the previous Gladney's work. She could and did, and I spent most of the rest of the day and a good part of the evening in an audio-hood.

Maybe if I'd known more about music — the real hardcore stuff, mathematics of progressions and so forth — I'd have been able to pick out more similarities (or differences) between the two Gladneys' work. I called for recordings by other composers he'd listened to, and I played those as well. Our boy, as Jesl had called him, hadn't been trying to crib from Bach or anyone else. He had avoided being derivative as much as possible, admirable in a beginning talent and also evident of already well-developed control, which is a good sign only as long as it doesn't become inhibition. What he had borrowed from other composers was mostly technique — my ear was good enough to pick that up, if I listened to everything several times. The composer he seemed to have borrowed from least was, oddly enough, Gladney. Or perhaps that wasn't so odd. Perhaps the compositions sounded too familiar.

I listened to the piano-clarinet piece over and over, trying to hear some similarity between it and any of the other Gladney's music — a sequence of notes, rhythm, something. He'd been unable to tell me exactly what had happened in the dream where he'd heard it — just that he'd known the dream was about Gladney. That was somewhat unsettling and would have been more so if he had composed all his music after dreaming about that former persona. But he hadn't, and I would have found it reassuring if the piano-clarinet piece hadn't been so obviously superior to all of his other attempts. Variation on a theme, he'd called himself. It nagged at me.

I waited until Gladney had been escorted off to some kind of day-to-day culture workshop early the next afternoon and had Jesl let me into his room so I could set up for our first session. That way he wouldn't have to receive me as a guest with all the attendant awkwardness again.

The bed, I decided, would be the best place to put him; it was obviously what he gravitated to when left to himself; so he'd probably be more receptive lying down. I rolled my equipment over and assembled the eight odd-sized components. They still reminded me of a giant set of cub's blocks. With me as the giant cub, I supposed, building some kind of surreal structure, a little like a cubist idea of a skyscraper. It looked ready to topple over as most of the smaller pieces were clustered on one side of the largest one, a four-foot rectangle. In reality it would have been more trouble than it was worth to knock it over. By the time Gladney returned I had the compartmented tank for our eyes set out on the stand by the bed, the optic-nerve connections to the system primed, and a relaxation program ready to run the moment he was hooked in.

He didn't seem surprised to see me, only a little resigned and nervous. "You're not going to want to hear any more music, are you?" he asked with an attempt at a smile.

"No more recordings, no." I patted the bed. "Come get comfortable. We don't have to start immediately."

Now he did smile, stripped off his overshirt and chaps (it never fails to amaze me what will come back into style), and flopped down on the bed in his secondskins.

Rather than play one of the usual preparatory games like *What Would You Do?* or *What Do You Hear?* with him, I eased him into chatting about his habilitation. I thought I'd learn more about his state of mind from simple conversation than from games. After all, what past experience could he draw on for a game? It would only oblige him to be inventive and pull his concentration from the situation at hand. Chitter-chat was the right approach. He had some rather astute observations on modern life, as any outsider would, and I hoped he wouldn't lose them when he became an insider. He wasn't really opening up to me—I hadn't expected that—but watching him try to hide in his own talk was enlightening. He wasn't going to give a single thing away, not even in mind-to-mind contact, and if I didn't figure out a different approach, I'd end up chasing him all over his own mind.

Eventually he began winding down. I let him get away with some delaying tactics: going to the bathroom, taking his vitamins—delaying tactics can be important personal-preparation rituals, if they don't go on for too long. When he began talking about having a snack, I made him lie down again and start breathing exercises.

He was a good breather, reaching a state of physical receptiveness more quickly than a lot of more experienced clients I'd had. When the time came I removed his eyes for him; just pressed my thumbs on his closed lids and out they popped into my palms, as smoothly as melon seeds. Gladney didn't even twitch. The connections to his optic nerves disengaged with an audible *kar-chunk*. Hospital eyes are always a little more mechanical than they have to be. After I placed them in the left side of the holding tank, I slipped the system connections under his flaccid eyelids. A tiny jump in the wires told me when he was hooked in to the mental fingerpainting exercise I'd selected for him. Mental fingerpainting was about the right amount of effort for someone on his level. The system supplied the colors; all he had to do was stir them around.

I breathed myself into a relaxed state in a matter of moments, but I waited a full minute before popping my own eyes out and joining him in the system. I wanted to give him time to get acclimated. Some people experience a sense of continuous drifting when they first enter the system, a disorientation not unlike weightlessness, and they need a minute alone to right themselves before they have to get used to another presence.

My materialization was even more gradual than usual, to spare him any trauma. His perception of my entry was as another color, oozing in greenly and then transforming itself into a second consciousness. Bright lights flashed as he recognized me, some of them nightmare purple, but it wasn't me he was afraid of. There was a little fear from not having a body to feel, but he was becoming accustomed to that. He was edgy about something else entirely — quick images of traps snapping shut, closet doors slamming. But there was exhilaration, too, at being in a realm where almost nothing is impossible.

The images began to flow more continuously from him, rolling over us in a tumbling series, gargantuan confetti. Most of them were portions of dreams, scenes from books he'd read; some were strange scenes he was making up in the heat of the moment, just to see if he could do it. I stabilized myself and moved with his attention, reminding him that I was still there. The image of my own face came, followed by a series of others that gradually became more bizarre. The undertones running out of him indicated this was how he imagined everyone else in the world to be—somewhat exotic, different, mysterious, alien, existing on a plane he had only the haziest conception of.

I emphasized my presence before he could become caught up enough in his grotesquely ornamented faces to get hysterical. He steadied, his energy level decreasing. I felt him adjust something and there was a sense of balance being established, as though two large masses floating in space were settling into orbit around each other. *Space* was a good word for it. The feeling of emptiness surrounding us was enormous and almost vivid enough to induce vertigo.

This is me. So much nothingness to be filled. He was unaware that he'd said anything; it simply came out of him as everything else had. There was a brief image of Gladney—the previous Gladney—and he tensed at the thought. *Somewhere. In this big emptiness*—

The Gladney-that-had-been drifted away from us and disintegrated. The thought remained incomplete. He seemed to be at a total loss now, drifting nowhere; so I gave him a new image, a simple one: the synthesizer. As soon as I was sure he saw it, I added the music, the clarinet-piano piece.

Suspicion bristled on him for a moment, and then he was rerunning the music with me. I could hear little extra things, notes and embellishments absent from the recording. He was on the verge of rolling with it, letting it come the way it had been meant to, when hard negation chopped down like a guillotine blade. We were left in silence. If he could have withdrawn from me, he would have, but he didn't know how to.

I waited, making my presence as non-threatening as possible, while I took his Emotional Index. He registered in peculiar fragmented sensations of movement rather than visuals, because everything was movement for him. I could see that now. The universe was movement, the movement of vibration. Like a tuning fork. He was a tuning fork, and right now he was vibrating in the key of fear-sharp. One octave up I could hear a whiny echo of guilt.

The intensity of it ebbed, and I turned the music on again. This time he didn't shut it down. He just pulled back from it as far as possible and allowed it to replay as the original recording without changes. I slowed down my time sense and concentrated, tightening myself until I was small enough to slip in between the notes. At that level they thundered, no longer recognizable as music; my consciousness vibrated in sympathy. I concentrated a little more, and the thundering rumble of the notes became more ponderous. Now I could detect something else within the vibrations of the music, faint but present. I would have to concentrate even harder to find out what it was, and I was nearly to the limit of my endurance. To concentrate that forcefully is to alter the state of consciousness in such a way that one is not actually conscious in the true sense of the word — I would not be able to monitor Gladney. From his perspective it would seem as though I'd vanished into some part of his mind inaccessible to him, or gone from being real to being imaginary.

I strained, achieving it slowly. The notes swelled until I

could perceive only one at a time, and I let the nearest one swallow me up. It was a piano note, G, perfectly formed in perfect pitch, a universe created by the oscillation of a string in the air (that was how he saw it, not as synthesized piano but the real thing). Each sweep of the string through space created the universe of the note anew, the string reaching the limit of its swing before the ghost of itself opposite had disappeared. And within—

He looked up with a smile of mild interest. The face was unmistakable in spite of all the changes he'd been through in the last year and a half.

Come closer, he said.

Gladney?

The same. The smile broadened. *Well, not quite the same.* Those pampered good looks in full flower, the well-tended skin, the sculptured jawline, the hair brushed straight back and falling nearly to his shoulders. His face was the most solid thing about him. The rest had been sketched in vaguely. I could get no undertones from him, no feelings, no image.

He locked me in here, he said. *So I won't get out and take—*

The note passed away, and we were in another. Gladney was standing on a high hill in the middle of the day.

—what used to be mine. He looked around. In the distance the horizon ran wetly, melting into the sky. *I live in the music now. He can't come in unless I get out.*

It wasn't possible. If anything had been left of the old Gladney's mind after the suckers had finished cleaning out his brain, it would have shown up while he was still in quarantine. This had to be a delusion of the present Gladney, some kind of survivor guilt. Until he ceased to think of music as being a simultaneously convex and concave prison, he would never be able to compose more than a few incomplete snatches of melody.

The outdoor scene disappeared as the note went on; now we were in a vague representation of the old Gladney's recording studio. He looked up from the piano he was sitting at.

Can you prove who you are? I asked him.

You can see me as I was. Isn't that enough for you?

No. The Gladney-that-is has perfect pitch — that could easily translate to his being able to reproduce his old appearance. If you are really the Gladney-that-was, you can tell me something about yourself that the Gladney-that-is has no knowledge of.

The delusion spread his hands. *He's studied up on me thoroughly. They gave him access to vid-magazines, newstapes.*

There's still plenty he doesn't know, I said. *The private things. Certain memories. Feelings. Tell me something your family could confirm as true.*

His face took on a defiant look, but there was no more feeling from him than there would have been from a holo transmission. That in itself indicated he was a fabrication, but my merely telling Gladney that wasn't going to help. Even if I could get his intellect to believe me, his emotions probably wouldn't.

Tell me something, I prodded again.

He rose and leaned on the top of the piano. *Don't you think a man with perfect pitch would be able to interpolate the private feelings of another man who had grown from the same brain?*

The studio was gone. He was leaning on a small table in a quick-eat while I stood just outside the entrance. I could hear the drumming of his fingers on the table.

Tell me a fact, then. Just one fact he couldn't possibly know.

51

He straightened up abruptly. *The mindsuckers damaged me. I remember only what he knows.*

I'd expected him to hide behind that, but I was unsure what to do next. Arguing with the delusion was only going to strengthen its sense of presence. Even acknowledging it was giving it something to feed on. Confronting it was Gladney's job, not mine. I was going to have to get him down in the music with me.

The note passed and was replaced by a bedroom. Gladney lay crosswise on a bed with his arms folded behind his head. He was looking at me upside down.

I'm residue, he said happily. His reversed smile was grotesque. *I'm a myelin ghost. You can't get rid of me without physically damaging his brain.*

I hooked my feet under the bed and willed myself upward. His bizarre upside-down face rushed away from me as I grew through the ceiling of the phantom room, up into the emptiness to the limit of the note. The piano string swung across a sky made of the present Gladney's face. My abrupt appearance gave him a surge of alarm that nearly dislodged me.

Where were you?

You know. The piano string moved between us. I stretched out my arms. *Take my hand before that string comes back.*

No.

Why not? It's your music.

No!

From the corner of my eye, I saw the piano string return to view, slicing through space. *Please, Gladney. don't let that string put another barrier between you and your own work.*

Panic at the idea of being cut off from his music made him grab my hands; half a moment later panic at the idea of meeting his delusion head-on made him sorry he'd done it.

We were pitching and bucking in the throes of his fear, but still the piano string approached. Shortly it would pass through my wrists and fragment my concentration.

I can't pull you in, Gladney. You have to come on your own.

I'm afraid!

Why? Say it!

I'm afraid because—

Say it!

He'll get me!

Who?

Gladney!

You are Gladney.

No!

Then who are you?

There was no answer. The piano string was almost on us.

Are you a composer?

His affirmation ducked him under the string just before it would have severed my hands. He stared after it with a horrified elation, and then we were rushing down into the music together in the momentum of his admission.

The delusional image of Gladney watched us descend. The real one made a soft landing on the bed beside it, still gripping my hands. Without thinking, he tried to pull me onto the bed between himself and the other.

The bedroom vanished. We were on an underground tube, the only three in the coach. I moved around behind Gladney, and he had to let go of me. As soon as he did, the delusional image vanished. Gladney was startled, but not half as much as I was. He moved forward with his hands out in front of him, feeling the air.

He's not here, Allie. Is he?

I didn't answer. I was still trying to figure out what had

happened. Delusions didn't just go away that quickly.

Allie? He half-turned toward me, and I saw that his eyes were closed. He swung his arms back and forth awkwardly, fingers clutching at nothing. Either he was making use of a fairly sophisticated mental maneuver, a sort of sneaking up on his own blind side, or he was faking same to stay blinded to the situation. I couldn't tell which; his undertones showed only confusion.

Suddenly his hands seized on something invisible. The delusion snapped into existence again, caught in Gladney's grasp. The air around them crackled with sparks from Gladney's terror.

Allie! I can't let go!

We went from the tube to a raft in the middle of the ocean, bright sun beating down on the water. Gladney still had hold of the delusion. His eyes were open now. A shadow passed over us — a high-flying piano string.

High A sharp. Gladney said automatically, identifying the note. *We're getting close to the end of the melody. What do I do with him then?*

You're asking me? It's yours. What do you do when the music's over?

We were in the lower branches of a large tree, then back to the tube very briefly (*B flat grace note,* Gladney said), in the bedroom, on a windy rooftop several thousand feet above the ground. Gladney was plunging us to the end of the song. The images began to blend into one another, flickering and flapping. Gladney and his delusion flashed on and off in a variety of positions, Gladney still holding on, as though they were wrestling or dancing. The music went from slow-motion subsonic to recognizable melody. The background imagery faded away completely, leaving the two Gladneys in their dance/struggle. The delusion offered no resistance, but Gladney was too occupied to notice. The struggle became a tumbling, end over end over end over end. I saw Gladney's hospital room, the synthesizer, Gladney himself standing before it, staring it down as though it were an enemy. Dr. Jesl appeared briefly, carnelian eyes blind to the two figures tumbling past her through the entertainment center, where Gladney sat studying a newstape of the Gladney-that-had-been on the holo screen. The tumblers rolled on to the vision of a dimly remembered dream, that dream of Gladney, the old Gladney, lifting his head to the sight of three people, visible only from neck to thigh, rushing forward at him.

The dream-Gladney cried out, fell back, and vanished, and then the tumblers were beyond the end of the melody. But still they went on, and the music went on with them, the piano and clarinet finally making contact, playing together and opposite each other in complement.

After some unmeasurable time, the tumbling began to slow. When the music stopped, there was only one figure, not two, that stopped with it. He drifted in emptiness, excited and drained all at once. That was enough, I decided. Before he could think of doing anything else, I cued another relaxation exercise and wrapped it around him. As soon as he was completely absorbed in mental fingerpainting, I broke the contact between us and withdrew.

It took a minute or so for his vitals to calm down. I changed the exercise from fingerpainting to simple abstract visuals. He was overstimulated, in need of a passive mode. After his pulse went down below eighty, I disconnected him from the system and put his eyes back in.

As soon as he saw me, he broke into a sweat. "Don't try to talk," I told him, covering the connections and slipping them into the drawer in the largest component.

"I can talk."

"Sure. I just didn't want you to feel like you had to."

He turned his face away while I dismantled the system. His breathing was extremely loud in the room. Rhythmic. I let him be. The inexperienced are often overcome by an intense feeling of embarrassment after mindplay, particularly pathosfinding. It takes some getting over.

"Listen," he said, after a bit, still not looking at me. "You don't know what it's like. What it *was* like." He rubbed his forehead tiredly. "I was almost him. I wanted him, and I didn't want him." He paused and I knew he was staring at the synthesizer. "If I'd been him, I would have been someone. I just came out of nowhere, out of his brain. But I'm not him. Now I'm a figment of my own imagination."

I opened my mouth to say something conciliatory but neutral when the image of the pearl necklace popped into my mind. *I have not always been as I am now.* And neither was anybody else. I wanted to tell him so. I wanted to tell him he'd get over that, too, that he wasn't the only person who'd ever met the stranger in himself. Granted, his experience had been more extreme, but it was pretty much the same. I could no more tell him something like that than I could map out his life for him.

"You can't have somebody else's past," I said as gently as I could. "And there's no such thing as a ghost, myelin or otherwise. It's always just you."

"I could buy memories. People do that." His face was hard. "They even buy whole minds, remember?"

"And it drives them mad, trying to be two people at once. Remember?"

That gave him pause. "God, I'm tired," he said after a moment.

"Take a nap. I'm just down the hall if you want to talk later."

"Allie—"

I waited while he tried to settle on what it was he wanted to say. The words never came. He waved one hand, dismissing me. I let myself out, wondering how long he was going to sulk. If we prize our illusions, we are even that much more jealous of our delusions because they're so patently untrue. I was sure, though, that in a few more sessions, he'd adjust to being exactly what he was, no more and no less, and he would accept his music as his music only, to make without the fear or the desire that it came from him at the behest of something beyond his control.

Dr. Jesl phoned me sometime later, rousing me from a doze. "Our boy has a supreme mad-on for you," she said. "Thing is, I can't tell just what it's all about. I don't think he knows, either." She sounded more amused than worried.

I was still too exhausted to explain about mindplay embarrassment compounded by the loss of a self-imposed handicap. "He'll get over it," I told her.

Which he did. And I was only a little bit spooked later on when he correctly distinguished all of the old Gladney's music as having been composed by him without anyone's identifying it for him. Great minds, I told myself, think alike.

Under Siege

By George R. R. Martin

On the high ramparts of Vargön, Colonel Bengt Anttonen stood alone and watched phantasms race across the ice.

The world was snow and wind and bitter, burning cold. The winter sea had frozen hard around Helsinki, and in its icy grip it held the six island citadels of the great fortress called Sveaborg. The wind was a knife drawn from a sheath of ice. It cut through Anttonen's uniform, chafed at his cheeks, brought tears to his eyes, and froze them as they trickled down his face. The wind howled around the towering, gray granite walls, forced its way through doors and cracks and gun emplacements, insinuated itself everywhere. Out upon the frozen sea, it snapped and shrieked at the Russian artillery and sent puffs of snow from the drifts running and swirling over the ice like strange white beasts, ghostly animals all asparkle, wearing first one shape and then another, changing constantly as they ran.

They were creatures as malleable as Anttonen's thoughts.

He wondered what form they would take next and where they were running to so swiftly, these misty children of snow and wind. Perhaps they could be taught to attack the Russians. He smiled, savoring the fancy of the snow beasts unleashed upon the enemy. It was a strange, wild thought. Colonel Bengt Anttonen had never been an imaginative man before, but of late his mind had often been taken by such whimsies.

Anttonen turned his face into the wind again, welcoming the chill, the numbing cold. He wanted it to cool his fury, to cut into the heart of him and freeze the passions that seethed there. He wanted to be numb. The cold had turned even the turbulent sea into still and silent ice; now let it conquer the turbulence within Bengt Anttonen. He opened his mouth, exhaled a long plume of breath that rose from his reddened cheeks like steam, inhaled a draft of frigid air that went down like liquid oxygen.

But panic came in the wake of that thought. Again, it was happening again. What was liquid oxygen? Cold, he knew somehow; colder than the ice; colder than this wind. Liquid oxygen was bitter and white, and it steamed and flowed. He knew it, knew it as certainly as he knew his own name.

But *how?*

Anttonen turned from the ramparts. He walked with long, swift strides, his hand touching the hilt of his sword as if it could provide some protection against the demons that had invaded his mind. The other officers were right; he was going mad, surely. He had proved it this afternoon at the staff meeting.

The meeting had gone very badly, as they all had of late. As always, Anttonen had raised his voice against the others, hopelessly, stupidly. He was right, he *knew* that. Yet he knew also he could not convince them and that each word further undermined his status, further damaged his career.

Jägerhorn had brought it on once again. Colonel F. A. Jägerhorn was everything that Anttonen was not: dark and handsome, polished and politic, an aristocrat with an aristocrat's control. Jägerhorn had important connections, Jägerhorn had influential relatives, Jägerhorn had the confidence of Vice Admiral Carl Olof Cronstedt, commandant of Sveaborg. At the meeting, Jägerhorn had produced a sheaf of reports.

"The reports are wrong," Anttonen had insisted. "The Russians do not outnumber us. They have barely forty guns, sir. Sveaborg mounts ten times that number."

Cronstedt seemed shocked by Anttonen's tone, his certainty, his insistence. Jägerhorn simply smiled. "Might I ask how you come by this intelligence, Colonel Anttonen?" he asked.

That was the question Bengt Anttonen could never answer. "I know," he said.

Jägerhorn rattled the papers in his hand. "My own intelligence comes from Lieutenant Klick, who is in Helsinki and has direct access to reliable reports of enemy plans, movements, and numbers."

He looked to Vice Admiral Cronstedt. "I submit, sir, that this information is a good deal more reliable than Colonel Anttonen's mysterious certainties. According to Klick, the Russians outnumber us already, and General Suchtelen will soon be receiving sufficient reinforcements to enable him to launch a major assault. Furthermore, they have a formidable amount of artillery on hand. Certainly more than the forty pieces that Colonel Anttonen would have us believe is the extent of their armament."

Cronstedt was nodding, agreeing. Even then Anttonen could not be silent. "Sir," he insisted, "Klick's reports must be discounted. The man cannot be trusted. Either he is in the pay of the enemy or they are deluding him."

Cronstedt frowned. "That is a grave charge, Colonel."

"He is a fool and a damned Anjala traitor!"

Jägerhorn bristled at that, and Cronstedt and a number of junior officers looked plainly aghast. "Colonel," the commandant said, "it is well known that Colonel Jägerhorn has relatives in the Anjala League. Your comments are offensive. Our situation here is perilous enough without my officers fighting among themselves over petty political differences. You will offer an apology at once."

Given no choice, Anttonen had tendered an awkward apology. Jägerhorn accepted with a patronizing nod.

Cronstedt went back to the papers. "Very persuasive," he said, "and very alarming. It is as I have feared. We have come to a hard place." Plainly his mind was made up. It was futile to argue further. It was at times like this that Bengt Anttonen most wondered what madness had possessed him. He would go to staff meetings determined to be circumspect and politic, and no sooner would he be seated than a strange arrogance would seize him. He argued long past the point of wisdom; he denied obvious facts, confirmed in written reports from reliable sources; he spoke out of turn and made enemies on every side.

"No, sir," he said. "I beg of you, disregard Klick's intelligence. Sveaborg is vital to the spring counteroffensive. We have nothing to fear if we can hold out until the ice melts. Once the sea lanes are open, Sweden will send help.

Vice Admiral Cronstedt's face was drawn and weary, an old man's face. "How many times must we go over this? I grow tired of your argumentative attitude, and I am quite aware of Sveaborg's importance to the spring offensive. The facts are plain. Our defenses are flawed, and the ice makes our walls accessible from all sides. Sweden's armies are being routed—"

"We know that only from the newspapers the Russians

allow us, sir," Anttonen blurted out. "French and Russian papers. Such news is unrealiable."

Cronstedt's patience was exhausted. "Quiet!" he said, slapping the table with an open palm. "I have had enough of your intransigence, Colonel Anttonen. I respect your patriotic fervor, but not your judgment. In the future, when I require your opinion, I shall ask for it. Is that clear?"

"Yes, sir," Anttonen had said.

Jägerhorn smiled. "If I may proceed?"

The rebuke had been as smarting as the cold winter wind. It was no wonder Anttonen had felt driven to the cold solitude of the battlements afterward.

By the time he returned to his quarters, Bengt Anttonen's mood was bleak and confused. Darkness was falling, he knew. Over the frozen sea, over Sveaborg, over Sweden and Finland. And over America, he thought. Yet the afterthought left him sick and dizzy. He sat heavily on his cot, cradling his head in his hands. America, America, what madness was that, what possible difference could the struggle between Sweden and Russia make to that infant nation so far away?

Rising, he lit a lamp, as if light would drive the troubling thoughts away, and splashed some stale water on his face from the basin atop the modest dresser. Behind the basin was the mirror he used for shaving, slightly warped and dulled by corrosion but serviceable. As he dried his big, bony hands, he found himself staring at his own face, the features at once so familiar and so oddly, frighteningly strange. He had unruly, graying hair; dark-gray eyes; a narrow, straight nose; slightly sunken cheeks; a square chin. He was too thin, almost gaunt. It was a stubborn, common, plain face. The face he had worn all his life. Long ago, Bengt Anttonen had grown resigned to the way he looked. Until recently, he scarcely gave his appearance any thought.

Yet now he stared at himself, unblinking, and felt a disturbing fascination welling up inside him, a sense of satisfaction, a pleasure in the cast of his image that was alien and troubling. Such vanity was sick, unmanly, another sign of madness. Anttonen wrenched his gaze from the mirror. He lay himself down with a will.

For long moments he could not sleep. Fancies and visions danced against his closed eyelids, sights as fantastic as the phantom animals fashioned by the wind: flags he did not recognize, walls of polished metal, great storms of fire, men and women as hideous as demons asleep in beds of burning liquid. And then, suddenly, the thoughts were gone, peeled off like a layer of burned skin. Bengt Anttonen sighed uneasily and turned in his sleep. . . .

. . . before the awareness is always the pain, and the pain comes first, the only reality in a still, quiet, empty world beyond sensation. For a second, an hour I do not know where I am, and I am afraid. And then the knowledge comes to me; returning, I am returning, in the return is always pain. I do not want to return, but I must, must. I want the sweet, clean purity of ice and snow, the bracing touch of the winter wind, the healthy lines of Bengt's face. But it fades, fades though I scream and clutch for it, crying, wailing. It fades, fades, and then is gone.

I sense motion, a stirring all around me as the immersion fluid ebbs away. My face is exposed first. I suck in air through my wide nostrils, spit the tubes out of my bleeding mouth. When the fluid falls below my ears, I hear a gurgling, a greedy sucking sound. The vampire machines feed on the juices of my womb, the black blood of my second life. The cold touch of air on my skin pains me. I try not to scream, manage to hold the noise down to a whimper.

Above, the top of my tank is coated by a thin, ebony film that has clung to the polished metal. I can see my reflection. I'm a stirring sight, nostril hairs aquiver on my noseless face, my right cheek bulging with a swollen, greenish tumor. Such a handsome devil. I smile, showing a triple row of rotten teeth, fresh new incisors pushing up among them like sharpened stakes in a field of yellow toadstools. I wait for release. The tank is too damned small, a coffin. I am buried alive, and the fear is a palpable weight upon me. They do not like me. What if they just leave me in here to suffocate and die? "Out!" I whisper, but no one hears.

Finally the lid lifts, and the orderlies are there. Rafael and Slim. Big, strapping fellows, blurred white colossi with flags sewn above the pockets of their uniforms. I cannot focus on their faces. My eyes are not so good at the best of times and especially bad just after a return. I know the dark one is Rafe, though, and it is he who reaches down and unhooks the IV tubes and the telemetry while Slim gives me my injection. Ahhh. The hurt fades. I force my hands to grasp the tank's sides. The metal feels strange; the motion is clumsy, deliberate; my body, slow to respond. "What took you so long?" I ask.

"Emergency," says Slim. "Rollins." He is a testy, laconic sort, and he doesn't like me. To learn more, I would have to ask question after question. I don't have the strength. I concentrate instead on pulling myself to a sitting position. The room is awash with a bright blue-white fluorescent light. My eyes water after so long in darkness. Maybe the orderlies think I'm crying with joy to be back. They're big but not too bright. The air has an astringent, sanitized smell and the hard coolness of air conditioning. Rafe lifts me up from the coffin, the fifth silvery casket in a row of six, each hooked up to the computer banks that loom around us. The other coffins are all empty now. I am the last vampire to rise this night, I think. Then I remember. Four of them are gone, have been gone for a long time. There is only Rollins and myself, and something has happened to Rollins.

They set me in a chair, and Slim rolls me past the empty caskets and up the ramps to debriefing. "Rollins?" I ask him.

"We lost him."

I didn't like Rollins. He was even uglier than me, a wizened little homunculus with a swollen, oversize cranium and a distorted torso without arms or legs. He had real big eyes, lidless, so he could never close them. Even asleep, he looked like he was staring at you. And he had no sense of humor. No goddamned sense of humor at all. When you're a geek, you got to have a sense of humor. But whatever his faults, Rollins was the only one left, besides me. Gone now, I feel no grief, only a numbness.

The debriefing room is cluttered but somehow impersonal. They wait for me on the other side of the table. The orderlies roll me up opposite them and depart. The table is a long Formica barrier between me and my superiors, maybe a *cordon sanitaire.* They can't let me get too close; after all, I might be contagious. They are normals. I am . . . what am I? When they conscripted me, I was classified as an HM_3. Human Mutation, third category. Or a hum-three, in the vernacular. The hum-ones are the nonviables: stillborns and infant deaths and living veggies. We got millions of 'em. The hum-twos are viable but useless, all the guys with extra toes and webbed hands and funny eyes. Got thousands of them. But us hum-threes are a fucking *elite,* so they tell us. That's when they draft us. Down here, inside the Graham Project bunker, we get new names. Old Charlie Graham himself used to call us his "timeriders" before he croaked, but that's too romantic for Major Salazar. Salazar prefers the official government term: G.C., for Graham Chrononaut. The orderlies and grunts turned G.C. into *geek,* of course, and we turned it right back on 'em, me and Nan and Creeper, when they were still with us. *They* had a terrific sense of humor, now. The killer geeks, we called ourselves. Six little killer geeks riding the timestream, biting the heads off vast chickens of probability. Heigh-ho.

And then there was one.

Salazar is pushing papers around on the table. He looks sick. Under his dark complexion I can see an unhealthy greenish tinge, and the blood vessels in his nose have burst beneath the skin. None of us are in good shape down here, but Salazar looks worse than most. He's been gaining weight, and it looks bad on him. His uniforms are all too tight now, and there won't be any fresh ones. They've closed down all the commissaries and the mills, and in a few years we'll all be wearing rags. I've told Salazar he ought to diet, but no one will listen to a geek, except when the subject is chickens. "Well?" Salazar says to me, his voice snapping. A hell of a way to start a debriefing. Three years ago, when it began, he was full of starch and vinegar, very correct and military, but even the Maje has no time left for decorum now.

"What happened to Rollins?" I ask.

Doctor Veronica Jacobi is seated next to Salazar. She used to be chief headshrinker down here, but since Graham Crackers went and expired she's been heading up the whole scientific side of the show. "Death trauma," she says, professionally. "Most likely, his host was killed in action."

I nod. Old story. Sometimes the chickens bite back. "He accomplish anything?"

"Not that we've noticed," Salazar says.

The answer I expected. Rollins had gotten rapport with some ignorant grunt of a foot soldier in the army of Charles XII. I had this droll mental picture of him marching the guy up to his loon of a teenage king and trying to tell the boy to stay away from Poltava. Charles probably hanged him on the spot—though, come to think of it, it had to be something quicker, or else Rollins would have had time to disengage.

"Your report," prompts Salazar.

"Right, Maje," I say lazily. He hates to be called Maje, though not so much as he hated Sally, which was what Creeper used to call him. Us killer geeks are an insolent lot. "It's no good. Cronstedt will meet with General Suchtelen and negotiate for surrender. Nothing Bengt says sways him one damned bit. I been pushing too hard. Bengt thinks he's going crazy. I'm afraid he may crack."

"All timeriders take that risk," Jacobi says. "The longer you stay in rapport, the stronger your influence grows on the host and the more likely it becomes that your presence will be felt. Few hosts can deal with that perception." Ronnie has a nice voice, and she's always polite to me. Well scrubbed and tall and calm and even friendly, and above all ineffably polite. I wonder if she'd be as polite if she knew that she'd figured prominently in my masturbation fantasies ever since we'd been down here. They only put five women into the Cracker Box, with thirty-two men and six geeks, and she's by far the most pleasant to contemplate.

Creeper liked to contemplate her, too. He even bugged her bedroom, to watch her in action. She never knew. Creeper had a talent for that stuff, and he'd rig up these tiny little audiovideo units in his workbench and plant them everywhere. He said that if he couldn't live life at least he was going to watch it. One night he invited me into his room, when Ronnie was entertaining big, red-haired Captain Halliburton, the head of base security, and her fella in those early days. I watched, yeah; got to confess that I watched. But afterward I got angry. Told Creeper he had no right to spy on Ronnie or on any of them. "They make us spy on our hosts," he said, "right inside their fucking *heads,* you geek. Turnabout is fair play." I told him it was different, but I got so mad I couldn't explain why. It was the only fight Creeper and me ever had. In the long run, it didn't mean much. He went on watching, without me. They never caught the little sneak, but it didn't matter. One day he went timeriding and didn't come back. Big, strong Captain Halliburton died, too, caught too many rads on those security sweeps, I guess. As far as I know, Creeper's hookup is still in place; from time to time I've thought about going in and taking a peek, to see if Ronnie has herself a new lover. But I haven't. I really don't want to know. Leave me with my fantasies and my wet dreams; they're a lot better, anyway.

Salazar's fat fingers drum upon the table. "Give us a full report on your activities."

I sigh and give them what they want, everything in boring detail. When I'm done, I say, "Jägerhorn is the key to the problem. He's got Cronstedt's ear. Anttonen don't."

Salazar is frowning. "If only you could establish rapport with Jägerhorn," he grumbles. What a futile whiner. He knows that's impossible.

"You takes what you gets," I tell him. "If you're going to wish impossible wishes, why stop at Jägerhorn? Why not Cronstedt? Hell, why not the goddamned *czar?*"

"He's right, Major," Veronica says. "We ought to be grateful we've got Anttonen. At least he's a colonel. That's better than we did in any of the other target periods."

Salazar is still unhappy. He's a military historian by trade. He thought this would be easy when they transferred him out from West Point or what was left of it. "Anttonen is peripheral. We must reach the key figures. Your chrononauts are giving me footnotes, bystanders, the wrong men in the wrong place at the wrong times. It is impossible."

"You knew the job was dangerous when you took it," I say. A killer geek quoting Superchicken; I'd get thrown out of the union if they knew. "We don't get to pick and choose."

The Maje scowls at me. I yawn. "I'm tired of this," I say. "I want something to eat. Some ice cream. I want some rocky road ice cream. Seems funny, don't it? All that god-damned ice, and I come back wanting ice cream." There is no ice cream, of course. There hasn't been any ice cream for half a generation, anywhere in the godforsaken mess they call a world. But Nan used to tell me about it. Nan was the oldest geek, the only one born before the big crash, and she had lots of stories about the way things used to be. I liked it best when she talked about ice cream. It was smooth and cold and sweet, she said. It melted on your tongue and filled your mouth with liquid, delicious cold. Sometimes she would recite the flavors for us, as solemnly as Captain Todd reading his Bible: vanilla and strawberry and chocolate, fudge swirl and praline, rum raisin and heavenly hash, banana and orange sherbert and mint chocolate chip, pistachio and butter pecan. Creeper used to make up flavors to poke fun at her, but there was no getting to Nan. She just added his inventions to her list and spoke fondly thereafter of anchovy almond and liver chip and radiation ripple, until I couldn't tell the real flavors from the made-up ones anymore and didn't really care.

Nan was the first we lost. Did they have ice cream in St. Petersburg back in 1917? I hoped they did. I hope she got a bowl or two before she died.

Major Salazar is still talking, I realize. He has been talking for some time. ". . . our last chance now," he is saying. He begins to babble about Sveaborg, about the importance of what we are doing here, about the urgent need to *change* something somehow, to prevent the Soviet Union from ever coming into existence, and thus forestall the war that has laid the world to waste. I've heard it all before, I know it all by heart. The Maje has terminal verbal diarrhea, and I'm not so dumb as I look.

It was all Graham Cracker's idea, the last chance to win the war or maybe just save ourselves from the plagues and bombs and the poisoned winds.

But the Maje was the historian, so he got to pick all the targets, when the computers had done their probability analysis. He had six geeks, and he got six tries. "Nexus points," he called 'em. Critical points in history. Of course, some were better than others. Rollins got the Great Northern War, Nan got the Revolution, Creeper got to go all the way back to Ivan the Terrible, and I got Sveaborg. Impregnable, invincible Sveaborg. Gibraltar of the North.

"There is no reason for Sveaborg to surrender," the Maje is saying. It is his own ice-cream litany. History and tactics give him the sort of comfort that butter brickel gave to Nan. "The garrison is seven thousand strong, vastly outnumbering the besieging Russians. The artillery inside the fortress is superior. There is plenty of ammunition, plenty of food. If Sveaborg holds out until the sealanes are open, Sweden will launch its counteroffensive and the siege will be broken easily. The entire course of history may change! You must make Cronstedt listen."

"If I could just lug back a history text and let him read what they say about him, I'm sure he'd jump through flaming hoops," I say. I've had enough of this. "I'm tired," I announce. "I want some food." Suddenly, for no apparent reason, I feel like crying. "I want something to eat, damn it. I don't want to talk anymore, you hear? I want *something to eat.*"

Salazar glares, but Veronica hears the stress in my voice, and she is up and moving around the table. "Easy enough to arrange," she says to me, and to the Maje, "We've accom-

plished all we can for now. Let me get him some food."
Salazar grunts, but he dares not object. Veronica wheels me
away, toward the commissary.

Over the stale coffee and a plate of mystery meat and
overcooked vegetables, she consoles me. She's not half bad
at it; a pro, after all. Maybe, in the old days she wouldn't
have been considered especially striking—I've seen the old
magazines. Even down here we have our old *Playboys,* our
old videotapes, our old novels, our old record albums, our
old funny books. Nothing *new* of course, nothing recent,
but lots and lots of the old junk. I ought to know, I practically mainline the stuff. When I'm not flailing around inside
Bengt's cranium, I'm planted in front of my tube, running
some old TV show or a movie, maybe reading a paperback
at the same time, trying to imagine what it would be like to
live back then, before they screwed up everything. So I know
all about the old standards, and maybe it's true that Ronnie
ain't up to, say, Bo or Marilyn or Brigitte or Garbo. Still,
she's nicer to look at than anybody else down in this damned
septic tank. And the rest of us don't quite measure up either.
Creeper wasn't no Groucho, no matter how hard he tried;
me, I look just like Jimmy Cagney, but the big green tumor
and all the extra yellow teeth and the want of a nose spoil the
effect, just a little.

I push my fork away with the meal only half-eaten. "It has
no taste. Back then, food had *taste.*"

Veronica laughs. "You're lucky. You get to taste it. For
the rest of us, this is all there is."

"Lucky? Ha-ha. I know the difference, Ronnie. You
don't. Can you miss something you never had?" I'm sick of
talking about it though—sick of it all. "Want to play chess?"

She smiles and gets up in search of our set. An hour later
she's won the first game and we're starting the second. There
are about a dozen chess players down here in the Cracker

Box; now that Graham and Creeper are gone, I can beat all of them except Ronnie. The funny thing is, back in 1808 I could probably be world champion. Chess has come a long way in the last two hundred years, and I've memorized openings that those old guys never even dreamed of.

"There's more to the game than book openings," Veronica says, and I realize I've been talking aloud.

"I'd still win," I insist. "Hell, those guys have been dead for centuries. How much fight can they put up?"

She smiles and moves a knight. "Check."

I realize that I've lost again.

"Someday I've got to learn to play this game," I say. "Some world champion."

Veronica begins to put the pieces back in the box. "This Sveaborg business is a kind of chess game, too," she says conversationally, "a chess game across time, us and the Swedes against the Russians and the Finnish nationalists. What move do you think we should make against Cronstedt?"

"Why did I know the conversation was going to come back to that?" I say. "Damned if I know. I suppose the Maje has an idea."

She nods. Her face is serious now. Pale, soft face, framed by dark hair. "A desperate idea. These are desperate times."

What would it be like if I did succeed, I wonder? If I changed something? What would happen to Veronica and the Maje and Rafe and Slim and all the rest of them? What would happen to *me,* lying there in my coffin full of darkness? There are theories, of course, but no one really knows. "I'm a desperate man, ma'am," I say to her, "ready for desperate measures. Being subtle sure hasn't done diddly-squat. Let's hear it. What do I gotta get Bengt to do now? Invent the machine gun? Defect to the Russkis? Expose his privates on the battlements? What?"

She tells me.

I'm dubious. "Maybe it'll work," I say. "More likely, it'll get Bengt slung into the deepest goddamned dungeon that place has. They'll really think he's nuts. Jägerhorn might just shoot him outright."

"No," she says. "In his own way, Jägerhorn is an idealist. A man of principle. It is chancy, but you don't win chess games without taking chances. Will you do it?"

She has such a nice smile; I think she likes me. I shrug.

"Might as well," I say. "Can't dance."

" . . . shall be allowed to dispatch two couriers to the king, one by the northern, the other by the southern road. They shall be furnished with passports and safeguards, and every possible facility shall be given them for accomplishing their journey. Done at the island of Lonan, sixth of April 1808."

The droning of the officer reading the agreement stopped suddenly, and the staff meeting was deathly quiet.

Vice Admiral Cronstedt rose slowly. "This is the agreement," he said. "In view of our perilous position, it is better than we could have hoped for. We have used a third of our powder already; our defenses are exposed to attack from all sides because of the ice; we are outnumbered and forced to support a large number of fugitives who rapidly consume our provisions. General Suchtelen might have demanded our immediate surrender. By the grace of God, he did not. Instead we have been allowed to retain three of Sveaborg's six islands and will regain two of the others should five Swedish ships-of-the-line arrive to aid us before the third of May. If Sweden fails us, we must surrender. Yet the fleet shall be restored to Sweden at the conclusion of the war, and this immediate truce will prevent any further loss of life."

Cronstedt sat down. At his side, Colonel Jägerhorn came crisply to his feet. "In the event the Swedish ships do not arrive on time, we must make plans for an orderly surrender of the garrison." He launched into a discussion of the details.

Bengt Anttonen sat quietly. He had expected the news, had somehow known it was coming, but it was no less dismaying for all that. Cronstedt and Jägerhorn had negotiated a disaster. It was foolish. It was craven. It was hopelessly doomed. Immediate surrender of Wester-Svartö, Langörn, and Oster-Lilla-Svartö, the rest of the garrison to come later, capitulation deferred for a meaningless month. History would revile them. Schoolchildren would curse their names. And he was helpless.

When the meeting at last ended, the others rose to depart. Anttonen rose with them, determined to be silent, to leave the room quietly for once, to let them sell Sveaborg for thirty pieces of silver if they would. But as he tried to turn, the compulsion seized him, and he went instead to where Cronstedt and Jägerhorn lingered. They both watched him approach. In their eyes, Anttonen thought he could see a weary resignation.

"You must not do this," he said heavily.

"It is done," Cronstedt replied. "The subject is not open for further discussion, Colonel. You have been warned. Go about your duties." He climbed to his feet, turned to go.

"The Russians are cheating you," Anttonen blurted.

Cronstedt stopped and looked at him. "Admiral, you must listen to me. This provision, this agreement that we will retain the fortress if five ships-of-the-line reach us by the third of May, it is a fraud. The ice will not have melted by the third of May. No ship will be able to reach us. The armistice agreement provides that the ships must have entered Sveaborg's harbor by noon on the third of May. General Suchtelen will use the time afforded by the truce to move his guns and gain control of the sea approaches. Any ship attempting to reach Sveaborg will come under heavy attack. And there is more. The messengers you are sending to the King, sir, they—"

Cronstedt's face was ice and granite. He held up a hand. "I have heard enough. Colonel Jägerhorn, arrest this madman." He gathered up his papers, refusing to look Anttonen in the face, and strode angrily from the room.

"Colonel Anttonen, you are under arrest," Jägerhorn said, with surprising gentleness in his voice. "Don't resist. I warn you, that will only make it worse."

Anttonen turned to face the other colonel. His heart was sick.

"You will not listen. None of you will listen. Do you know what you are doing?"

"I think I do," Jägerhorn said.

Anttonen reached out and grabbed him by the front of his uniform.

"You do *not*. You think I don't know what you are, Jägerhorn? You're a nationalist, damn you. This is the great age of nationalism. You and your Anjala League, your damned Finnlander noblemen, you're all Finnish nationalists. You resent Sweden's domination. The czar has promised you that Finland will be an autonomous state under his protection, so you have thrown off your loyalty to the Swedish crown."

Colonel F. A. Jägerhorn blinked. A strange expression flickered across his face before he regained his composure. "You cannot know that," he said. "No one knows the terms—I—"

Anttonen shook him bodily. "History is going to laugh at you, Jägerhorn. Sweden will lose this war because of you, because of Sveaborg's surrender, and you'll get your wish.

Finland will become an autonomous state under the czar. But it will be no freer than it is now, under Sweden. You'll swap your King like a secondhand chair at a flea market, for the butchers of the Great Wrath, and gain nothing by the transaction."

"A . . . a market for fleas? What is that?"

Anttonen scowled. "A flea market, a flea . . . I don't know," he said. He released Jägerhorn, turned away. "Dear God, I do know. It is a place where . . . where things are sold and traded. A fair. It has nothing to do with fleas, but it is full of strange machines, strange smells." He ran his fingers through his hair, fighting not to scream. "Jägerhorn, my head is full of demons. Dear God, I must confess. Voices, I hear voices day and night, even as the French girl, Joan, the warrior maid. I know the things that will come to pass." He looked into Jägerhorn's eyes, saw the fear there, and held his hands up, entreating now. "It is no choice of mine, you must believe that. I pray for silence, for release, but the whispering continues, and these strange fits seize me. They are not of my doing, yet they must be sent for a reason, they must be true, or why would God torture me so? Have mercy, Jägerhorn. Have mercy on me and listen!"

Colonel Jägerhorn looked past Anttonen, his eyes searching for help, but the two of them were quite alone.

"Yes," Jägerhorn said. "Voices, like the French girl. I did not understand."

Anttonen shook his head. "You hear, but you will not believe. You are a patriot; you dream you will be a hero. You will be no hero. The common folk of Finland do not share your dreams. They remember the Great Wrath. They know the Russians only as ancient enemies, and they hate them. They will hate you as well. And poor Cronstedt. He will be reviled by every Finn, every Swede, for generations. He will live out his life in this new Grand Duchy of Finland, on a Russian stipend, and he will die a broken man on April 7, 1820, twelve years and one day after he meets with Suchtelen on Lonan and promised Sveaborg to Russia. Years later, a man named Runeberg will write a series of poems about this war. Do you know what he will say of Cronstedt?"

"No," Jägerhorn said. He smiled uneasily. "Have your voices told you?"

"They have taught me the words by heart," said Bengt Anttonen. He recited:

> *Call him the arm we trusted in,*
> *that shrank in time of stress,*
> *call him Affliction, Scorn, and Sin,*
> *and Death and Bitterness,*
> *but mention not his former name,*
> *lest they should blush who bear the same.*

"That is the glory you and Cronstedt are winning here, Jägerhorn," Anttonen said bitterly. "That is your place in history. Do you like it?"

Colonel Jägerhorn had been carefully edging around Anttonen; there was a clear path between him and the door. But now he hesitated. "You are speaking madness," he said. "And yet, how could you have known of the czar's promises? You would almost have me believe you. Voices? Like the French girl? The voice of God, you say?"

Anttonen sighed. "God? I do not know. Voices, Jägerhorn, that is all I hear. Perhaps I am mad."

Jägerhorn grimaced. "They will revile us, you say? They will call us traitors and denounce us in poems?"

Anttonen said nothing. The madness had ebbed; he was filled with a helpless despair.

"No," Jägerhorn insisted. "It is too late. The agreement is signed. We have staked our honor on it. And Vice Admiral Cronstedt, he is so uncertain. His family is here, and he fears for them. Suchtelen has played him masterfully, and we have done our part. It cannot be undone. I do not believe this madness of yours, yet even if I believed, there is nothing to be done. The ships will not come in time. Sveaborg must yield, and the war must end with Sweden's defeat. How could it be otherwise? The czar is allied with Bonaparte himself, he cannot be resisted!"

"The alliance will not last," Anttonen said with a rueful smile. "The French will march on Moscow, and it will destroy them as it destroyed Charles XII. The winter will be their Poltava. All of this will come too late for Finland, too late for Sveaborg."

"It is too late even now," Jägerhorn said. "Nothing can be changed."

For the first time, Bengt Anttonen felt the tiniest glimmer of hope. "It is not too late."

"What course do you urge upon us, then? Cronstedt has already made his decision. Should we mutiny?"

"There will be a mutiny in Sveaborg, whether we take part or not. It will fail."

"What then?"

Bengt Anttonen lifted his head, stared Jägerhorn in the eyes. "The agreement stipulates that we may send two couriers to the king, to inform him of the terms, so the Swedish ships may be dispatched on time."

"Yes. Cronstedt will choose our couriers tonight, and they will leave tomorrow, with papers and safe passage furnished by Suchtelen."

"You have Cronstedt's ear. See that I am chosen as one of the couriers."

"You?" Jägerhorn looked doubtful. "What good will that

serve?" He frowned. "Perhaps this voice you hear is the voice of your own fear. Perhaps you have been under siege too long and it has broken you, and now you hope to run free."

"I can prove my voices speak true," Anttonen said.

"How?" snapped Jägerhorn.

"I will meet you tomorrow at dawn at Ehrensvard's tomb, and I will tell you the names of the couriers that Cronstedt has chosen. If I am right, you will convince him to send me in the place of one of those chosen. He will agree, gladly. He is anxious to be rid of me."

Colonel Jägerhorn rubbed his jaw, considering. "No one could know the choices but Cronstedt. It is a fair test." He put out his hand. "Done."

They shook. Jägerhorn turned to go. But at the doorway he turned back. "Colonel Anttonen," he said, "I have forgotten my duty. You are in my custody. Go to your own quarters and remain there, until the dawn."

"Gladly," said Anttonen. "At dawn you will see that I am right."

"Perhaps," said Jägerhorn, "but for all our sakes, I shall hope that you are wrong."

. . . and the machines suck away the liquid night that enfolds me, and I'm screaming so loudly that Slim draws back, a wary look on his face. I give him a broad, geekish smile, rows on rows of yellow, rotten teeth. "Get me out of here, turkey," I shout. The pain is a web around me, but this time it doesn't seem as bad. I can almost stand it; this time the pain is *for* something.

They give me my shot and lift me into my chair, but this time I'm eager for the debriefing. I grab the wheels and give myself a push, breaking free of Rafe, rolling down the corridors like I used to in the old days, when Creeper was around to race me. There's a bit of a problem with one ramp, and they catch me there, the strong, silent guys in their ice-cream suits (that's what Nan called 'em, anyhow), but I scream at them to leave me alone. They do. Surprises the hell out of me.

The Maje is a little startled when I come rolling into the room all by my lonesome. He starts to get up. "Are you . . ."

"Sit down, Sally," I say. "It's good news. Bengt psyched out Jägerhorn good. I thought the kid was gonna wet his pants, believe me. I think we got it socked. I'm meeting Jägerhorn tomorrow at dawn to clinch the sale." I'm grinning, listening to myself. Tomorrow, hey, I'm talking about 1808, but tomorrow is how it feels. "Now here's the sixty-four-thousand-dollar question. I need to know the names of the two guys that Cronstedt is going to try and send to the Swedish king. Proof, y'know? Jägerhorn says he'll get me sent if I can convince him. So you look up those names for me, Maje, and once I say the magic words, the duck will come down and give us Sveaborg."

"This is very obscure information," Salazar complains. "The couriers were detained for weeks and did not even arrive in Stockholm until the day of surrender. Their names may be lost to history." What a whiner, I'm thinking; the man is never satisfied.

Ronnie speaks up for me, though. "Major Salazar, those names had better not be lost to history or to us. You were our military historian. It was your job to research each of the target periods *thoroughly*." The way she's talking to him, you'd never guess he was the boss. "The Graham Project has every priority. You have our computer files, our dossiers on the personnel of Sveaborg, and you have access to the war college at New West Point. Maybe you can even get through to someone in what remains of Sweden. I don't care how you do it, but it must be done. The entire project could rest on this piece of information. The entire world. Our past and our future. I shouldn't need to tell you that."

She turns to me. I applaud. She smiles. "You've done well," she says. "Would you give us the details?"

"Sure," I say. "It was a piece of cake. With ice cream on top. What'd they call that?"

"À la mode."

"Sveaborg à la mode," I say, and I serve it up to them. I talk and talk. When I finally finish, even the Maje looks grudgingly pleased. Pretty damn good for a geek, I think. "Okay," I say when I'm done with the report. "What's next? Bengt gets the courier job, right? And I get the message through somehow. Avoid Suchtelen, don't get detained, the Swedes send in the cavalry."

"Cavalry?" Sally looks confused.

"It's a figure of speech," I say, with unusual patience.

The Maje nods. "No," he says. "The couriers — it's true that General Suchtelen lied and held them up as an extra form of insurance. The ice might have melted, after all. The ships might have come through in time. But it was an unnecessary precaution. That year the ice around Helsinki did not melt until well after the deadline date." He gives me a solemn stare. He has never looked sicker, and the greenish tinge of his skin undermines the effect he's trying to achieve. "We must make a bold stroke. You will be sent out as a courier, under the terms of the truce. You and the other courier will be brought before Suchtelen to receive your safe conducts through Russian lines. That is the point at which you will strike. The affair is settled, and war in those days was an honorable affair. No one will expect treachery."

"Treachery?" I say. I don't like the sound of what I'm hearing.

For a second, the Maje's smile looks almost genuine; he's

finally lit on something that pleases him. "Kill Suchtelen," he says.

"Kill Suchtelen?" I repeat.

"Use Anttonen. Fill him with rage. Have him draw his weapon. Kill Suchtelen."

I see. A new move in our crosstime chess game. The geek gambit.

"They'll kill Bengt," I say.

"You can disengage," Salazar says.

"Maybe they'll kill him fast," I point out. "Right there, on the spot, y'know."

"You take that risk. Other men have given their lives for our nation. This is war." The Maje frowns. "Your success may doom us all. When you change the past, the present as it now exists may cease to exist, and us with it. But our nation will live, and millions we have lost will be restored. Healthier, happier versions of ourselves will enjoy the rich lives that were denied us. You yourself will be born whole, without deformity."

"Or talent," I say. "In which case I won't be able to go back and do this, in which case the past stays unchanged."

"The paradox does not apply here. You have been briefed on this. The past and the present and future are not contemporaneous. And it will be Anttonen who effects the change, not yourself. He is of that time." The Maje is impatient. His thick, dark fingers drum on the table top. "Are you a coward?"

"Fuck you and the horse you rode in on," I tell him. "You just don't get it. I could give a shit about me. I'm better off dead. But they'll kill *Bengt*."

"What of it?"

Veronica has been listening intently. Now she leans across the table and touches my hand, gently.

"I understand," she says. "You identify with him, don't

you?"

"He's a good man," I say. Do I sound defensive? Very well, then; I *am* defensive. "I feel bad enough that I'm driving him around the bend, I don't want to get him killed. I'm a freak, a geek, I've lived my whole life under siege, and I'm going to die here, but Bengt has people who love him, a life ahead of him. Once he gets out of Sveaborg, there's a whole world out there."

"He has been dead for almost two centuries," Salazar says.

"I was in his head this afternoon," I snap.

"He will be a casualty of war," the Maje says. "In war, soldiers die. It is a fact of life, then as now."

Something else is bothering me. "Yeah, maybe, he's a soldier, I'll buy that. He knew the job was dangerous when he took it. But he cares about *honor,* Sally. A little thing we've forgotten. To die in battle, sure, but you want me to make him a goddamned *assassin,* have him violate a flag of truce. He's an honorable man. They'll revile him."

"The ends justify the means," says Salazar bluntly. "Kill Suchtelen, kill him under the flag of truce, yes. It will kill the truce as well. Suchtelen's second-in-command is far less wily, more prone to outbursts of temper, more eager for a spectacular victory. You will tell him that Cronstedt *ordered* you to cut down Suchtelen. He will shatter the truce, will launch a furious attack against the fortress, an attack that Sveaborg, impregnable as it is, will easily repulse. Russian casualties will be heavy, and Swedish determination will be fired by what they will see as Russian treachery. Jägerhorn, with proof before him that the Russian promises are meaningless, will change sides. Cronstedt, the hero of Ruotsinsalmi, will become the hero of Sveaborg as well. The fortress will hold. With the spring the Swedish fleet will land an army at Sveaborg, behind Russian lines, while a second

Swedish army sweeps down from the north. The entire course of the war will change. When Napoleon marches on Moscow, a Swedish army will already hold St. Petersburg. The czar will be caught in Moscow, deposed, executed. Napoleon will install a puppet government, and when his retreat comes, it will be north, to link up with his Swedish allies at St. Petersburg. The new Russian regime will not survive Bonaparte's fall, but the czarist restoration will be as short-lived as the French restoration, and Russia will evolve toward a liberal parliamentary democracy. The Soviet Union will never come into being to war against the United States." He emphasizes his final words by pounding his fist on the conference table.

"Sez you," I say mildly.

Salazar gets red in the face. "That is the computer projection," he insists. He looks away from me, though. Just a quick little averting of the eyes, but I catch it. Funny. He can't look me in the eyes.

Veronica squeezes my hand. "The projection may be off," she admits. "A little or a lot. But it is all we have. And this is our last chance. I understand your concern for Anttonen, really I do. It's only natural. You've been part of him for months now, living his life, sharing his thoughts and feelings. Your reservations do you credit. But now millions of lives are in the balance, against the life of this one man. This one dead man. It's your decision. The most important decision in all history, perhaps, and it rests with you alone." She smiles. "Think about it carefully, at least."

When she puts it like that and holds my little hand all the while, I'm powerless to resist. Ah, Bengt. I look away from them, sigh. "Break out the booze tonight," I say wearily to Salazar, "the last of that old prewar stuff you been saving."

The Maje looks startled, discomfited; the jerk thought his little cache of prewar Glenlivet and Irish Mist and Remy

Martin was a well-kept secret. And so it was until Creeper planted one of his little bugs, heigh-ho.

"I do not think drunken revelry is in order," Sally says. Defending his treasure. He's homely and dumb and mean spirited, but nobody ever said he wasn't selfish.

"Shut up and come across," I say. Tonight I ain't gonna be denied. I'm giving up Bengt, the Maje can give up some booze. "I want to get shitfaced," I tell him. "It's time to drink to the goddamned dead and toast the living past and present. It's in the rules, damn you. The geek always gets a bottle before he goes out to meet the chickens."

Within the central courtyard of the Vargön citadel, Bengt Anttonen waited in the pre-dawn chill. Behind him stood Ehrensvard's tomb, the final resting place of the man who had built Sveaborg and now slept securely within the bosom of his creation, his bones safe behind her guns and her granite walls, guarded by all her daunting might. He had built her impregnable, and impregnable she stood, so none would come to disturb his rest. Now they wanted to give her away.

The wind was blowing. It came howling down out of a black, empty sky, stirred the barren branches of the trees that stood in the empty courtyard and cut through Anttonen's warmest coat. Or perhaps it was another sort of chill that lay upon him: the chill of fear. Dawn was almost at hand. Above, the stars were fading. And his head was empty, echoing, mocking. Light would soon break over the horizon, and with the light would come Colonel Jägerhorn, hard faced, imperious, demanding, and Anttonen would have nothing to say to him.

He heard footsteps. Jägerhorn's boots rang on the stones. Anttonen turned to face him, watching him climb the few small steps up to Ehrensvard's memorial. They stood a foot apart, conspirators huddled against the cold and darkness. Jägerhorn gave him a curt, short nod. "I have met with Cronstedt."

Anttonen opened his mouth. His breath steamed in the frigid air. And just as he was about to succumb to the emptiness, about to admit that his voices had failed him, something whispered deep inside him. He spoke two names.

There was such a long silence that Anttonen once again began to fear. Was it madness after all and not the voice of God? Had he been wrong? But then Jägerhorn looked down, frowning, and clapped his gloved hands together in a gesture that spoke of finality. "God help us all," he said, "but I believe you."

"I will be the courier?"

"I have already broached the subject with Vice Admiral Cronstedt," Jägerhorn said. "I have reminded him of your years of service, your excellent record. You are a good soldier and a man of honor, damaged only by your own patriotism and the pressure of the siege. You are that sort of warrior who cannot bear inaction, who must always be doing something. You deserve more than arrest and disgrace, I have argued. As a courier, you will redeem yourself, I have told him to have no doubt of it. And by removing you from Sveaborg, we will also remove a source of tension and dissent around which mutiny might grow. The Vice Admiral is well aware that a good many of the men are most unwilling to honor our pact with Suchtelen. He is convinced." Jägerhorn smiled wanly. "I am nothing if not convincing, Anttonen. I can marshal an argument as Bonaparte marshals his armies. So this victory is ours. You are named courier."

"Good," said Anttonen. Why did he feel so sick at heart? He should have been full of jubilation.

"What will you do?" Jägerhorn asked. "For what purpose do we conspire?"

"I will not burden you with that knowledge." Anttonen replied. It was knowledge he lacked himself. He must be the courier, he had known that since yesterday, but the why of it still eluded him, and the future was as cold as the stone of Ehrensvard's tomb, as misty as Jägerhorn's breath. He was full of a strange foreboding, a sense of approaching doom.

"Very well," said Jägerhorn. "I pray that I have acted wisely in this." He removed his glove, offered his hand. "I will count on you, on your wisdom and your honor."

"My honor," Bengt repeated. Slowly, too slowly, he took off his own glove to shake the hand of the dead man standing there before him. Dead man? He was no dead man; he was live, warm flesh. But it was frigid there under those bare trees, and when Anttonen clasped Jägerhorn's hand, the other's skin felt cold to the touch.

"We have had our differences," said Jägerhorn, "but we are both Finns, after all, and patriots, and men of honor, and now too we are friends."

"Friends," Anttonen repeated. And in his head, louder than it ever had been before, so clear and strong it seemed almost as if someone had spoken behind him, came a whisper, sad somehow, and bitter. *C'mon, Chicken Little*, it said, *shake hands with your pal, the geek*.

Gather ye Four Roses while ye may, for time is still flying, and this same geek what smiles today tomorrow may be dying. Heigh-ho, drunk again, second night in a row, chugging all the Maje's good booze, but what does it matter, he won't be needing it. After this next little timeride, he won't even exist, or that's what they tell me. In fact, he'll never have existed, which is a real weird thought. Old Major Sally

Salazar, his big, thick fingers, his greenish tinge, the endearing way he had of whining and bitching, he sure seemed real this afternoon at that last debriefing, but now it turns out there never was any such person. Never was a Creeper, never a Rafe or a Slim, Nan never ever told us about ice cream and reeled off the names of all those flavors, butter pecan and rum raisin are one with Nineveh and Tyre, heigh-ho. Never happened, nope, and I slug down another shot, drinking alone, in my room, in my cubicle, the savior at this last liquid supper, where the hell are my fucking apostles? Ah, drinking, drinking, but not with me.

They ain't s'posed to know, nobody's s'posed to know but me and the Maje and Ronnie, but the word's out, yes it is, and out there in the corridors it's turned into a big, wild party, boozing and singing and fighting, a little bit of screwing for those lucky enough to have a partner, of which number I am not one, alas. I want to go out and join in, hoist a few with the boys, but no, the Maje says no, too dangerous, one of the motley horde might decide that even this kind of has-been life is better than a never-was non-life, and therefore off the geek, ruining everybody's plans for a good time. So here I sit on geek row, in my little room, boozing alone, surrounded by five other little rooms, and down at the end of the corridor is a most surly guard, pissed off that he isn't out there getting a last taste, who's got to keep me in and the rest of them out.

I was sort of hoping Ronnie might come by, you know, to share a final drink and beat me in one last game of chess and maybe even play a little kissy-face, which is a ridiculous fantasy on the face of it, but somehow I don't wanna die a virgin, even though I'm not really going to die, since once the trick is done, I won't ever have lived at all. It's goddamned noble of me if you ask me, and you got to 'cause there ain't nobody else around to ask. Another drink now, but the bottle's almost empty. I'll have to ring the Maje and ask for another. Why won't Ronnie come by? I'll never be seeing her again, after tomorrow, tomorrow-tomorrow and two-hundred-years-ago-tomorrow. I cold refuse to go, stay here and keep the happy li'l family alive, but I don't think she'd like that. She's a lot more sure than me. I asked her this afternoon if Sally's projections could tell us about the side effects. I mean, we're changing this war, and we're keeping Sveaborg and (we hope) losing the czar and (we hope) losing the Soviet Union and (we sure as hell hope) maybe losing the big war and all, the bombs and the rads and the plagues and all that good stuff, even radiation-ripple ice cream, which was the Creeper's favorite flavor, but what if we lose other stuff? I mean, with Russia so changed and all, are we going to lose Alaska? Are we gonna lose vodka? Are we going to lose George Orwell? Are we going to lose Karl Marx? We tried to lose Karl Marx, actually, one of the other geeks, Blind Jeffey, he went back to take care of Karlie, but it didn't work out. Maybe vision was too damn much for him. So we got to keep Karl, although come to think of it, who cares about Karl Marx; are we gonna lose Groucho? No Groucho, no Groucho ever. I don't like that concept, last night I shot a geek in my pajamas, and how he got in my pajamas, I'll never know, but maybe, who the hell knows how us geeks get anyplace, all these damn dominoes falling every which way, knocking over other dominoes, dominoes was never my game. I'm a chess player, world chess champion in temporal exile, that's me, dominoes is a dumb, damn game. What if it don't work. I asked Ronnie, what if we take out Russia, and, well, Hitler wins World War II so we wind up swapping missiles and germs and biotoxics with Nazi Germany? Or England? Or fucking Austria-Hungary, maybe, who can say? The superpower Austria-Hungary, what a thought, last night I shot a Hapsburg in my pajamas, the geeks put him there, heigh-ho.

Ronnie didn't make me no promises, kiddies. Best she could do was shrug and tell me this story about a horse. This guy was going to get his head cut off by some old-timy king, y'see, so he pipes up and tells the king that if he's given a year, he'll teach the king's horse to talk. The king likes this idea for some reason, maybe he's a Mister Ed fan. I dunno, but he gives the guy a year. And the guy's friends say, hey, what is this, you can't get no horse to talk. So the guy says, well, I got a year now, that's a long time, all kinds of things could happen. Maybe the king will die. Maybe I'll die. Maybe the horse will die. Or maybe the horse will talk.

I'm too damn drunk, I am, I am, and my head's full of geeks and talking horses and falling dominoes and unrequited love, and all of a sudden I got to see her. I set down the bottle, oh so carefully, even though it's empty, don't want no broken glass on geek row, and I wheel myself out into the corridor, going slow, I'm not too coordinated right now. The guard is at the end of the hall, looking wistful. I know him a little bit. Security guy, big black fellow, name of Dex. "Hey, Dex," I say as I come wheeling up, "screw this shit, let's us go party, I want to see li'l Ronnie." He just looks at me, shakes his head. "C'mon," I say. I bat my baby blues at him. Does he let me by? Does the Pope shit in the woods? Hell no, old Dex says, "I got my orders; you stay right here." All of a sudden I'm mad as hell, this ain't fair, I want to see Ronnie. I gather up all my strength and try to wheel right by him. No cigar. Dex turns, blocks my way, grabs the wheelchair and pushes. I go backward fast, spin around when a wheel jams, flip over and out of the chair. It hurts. Goddamn it hurts. If I had a nose, I woulda bloodied it, I bet. "You stay where you are, you fucking freak," Dex tells me. I start to cry, damn him anyhow, and he watches me as I get my chair upright and pull myself into it. I sit there staring at him. He stands there staring at me. "Please," I say finally. He shakes his head. "Go get her then," I say. "Tell her I want to see her." Dex grins. "She's busy," he tells me. "Her and Major Salazar. She don't want to see you."

I stare at him some more. A real withering, intimidating stare. He doesn't wither or look intimidated. It can't be, can it? Her and the Maje? Her and old Sally Greenface? No way, he's not her type, she's got better taste than that. I know she has. Say it ain't so, Joe. I turn around, start back to my cubicle. Dex looks away. Heigh-ho, fooled him.

Creeper's room is the one beyond mine, the last one at the end of the hall. Everything's just like he left it. I turn on the set, play with the damn switches, trying to figure out how it works. My mind isn't at its sharpest right at this particular minute, it takes me a while, but finally I get it, and I jump from scene to scene down in the Cracker Box, savoring all these little vignettes of life in these United States as served up by Creeper's clever ghost. Each scene has its own individual charm. There's a gang bang going on in the commissary, right on top of one of the tables where Ronnie and I used to play chess. Two huge security men are fighting in the airlock area; they've been at it a long time, their faces are so bloody. I can't tell who the hell they are, but they keep at it, staggering at each other blindly, swinging huge, awkward fists, grunting, while a few others stand around and egg them on. Slim and Rafe are sharing a joint, leaning up against my coffin. Slim thinks they ought to rip out all the wires, fuck up everything so I can't go timeriding. Rafe thinks it'd be easier to just bash my head in. Somehow I don't think he loves me no more. Maybe I'll cross him off my Christmas list. Fortunately for the geek, both of them are too stoned and screwed up to do anything at all. I watch a half-dozen other scenes, and finally, a little reluctantly, I go to Ronnie's room, where I watch her screwing Major Salazar.

Heigh-ho, as Creeper would say, what'd you expect, really?

I could not love thee, dear, so much, loved I not honor more. She walks in beauty like the night. But she's not so pretty, not really, back in 1808 there are lovelier women, and Bengt's just the man to land 'em, too, although Jägerhorn probably does even better. My Veronica's just the queen bee of a corrupt, poisoned hive, that's all. They're done now. They're talking. Or rather the Maje is talking, bless his soul, he's not his ice-cream litany, he's just been making love to Ronnie and now he's lying there in bed talking about Sveaborg, damn him. ". . . only a thirty percent chance that the massacre will take place," he's saying, "the fortress is very strong, formidably strong, but the Russians have the numbers, and if they do bring up sufficient reinforcements, Cronstedt's fears may prove to be substantial. But even that will work out. The assassination, well, the rules will be suspended, they'll slaughter everyone inside, but Sveaborg will become a sort of Swedish Alamo, and the branching paths ought to come together again. Good probability. The end results will be the same." Ronnie isn't listening to him, though; there's a look on her face I've never seen, drunken, hungry, scared, and now she's moving lower on him and doing something I've seen only in my fantasies, and now I don't want to watch anymore, no, oh no, no, oh no.

General Suchtelen had established his command post on the outskirts of Helsinki, another clever ploy. When Sveaborg turned its cannon on him, every third shot told upon the city the fortress was supposed to protect, until Cronstedt finally ordered the firing stopped. Suchtelen took advantage of that concession as he had all the rest. His apartments were large and comfortable, from his windows,

across the white expanse of ice and snow, the gray form of
Sveaborg loomed large. Anttonen stared at it morosely as he
waited in the anteroom with Cronstedt's other courier and
the Russians who had escorted them. Finally the inner
doors opened and the dark Russian captain emerged. "The
general will see you now," he said.

General Suchtelen sat behind a wide, wooden desk. An
aide stood by his right arm. A guard was posted at the door,
and the captain entered with the Swedish couriers. On the
broad, bare expanse of the desk was an inkwell, a blotter,
and two signed safe conducts, the passes that would take
them through the Russian lines to Stockholm and the Swedish king, one by the southern and the other by the northern
route. Suchtelen said something, in Russian, the aide provided a translation. Horses had been provided, and fresh
mounts would be available for them along the way; orders
had been given. Anttonen listened to the discussion with a
curiously empty feeling and a vague sense of disorientation.
Suchtelen was going to let them go. Why did that surprise
him? Those were the terms of the agreement, after all, those
were the conditions of the truce. As the translator droned
on, Anttonen felt increasingly lost and listless. He had con-
spired to get himself here, the voices had told him to, and
now here he was, and he did not know why, nor did he know
what he was to do. They handed him one of the safe conducts, placed it in his outstretched hand. Perhaps it was the
touch of the paper, perhaps it was something else. A sudden
red rage filled him, an anger so fierce and blind and all-
consuming that for an instant the world seemed to flicker
and vanish and he was somewhere else, seeking naked
bodies, twining in a room whose walls were made of pale-
green blocks. And then he was back, the rage still hot within
him, but cooling now, cooling quickly. They were staring at
him, all of them. With a sudden start, Anttonen realized he

had let the safe conduct fall to the floor, that his hand had gone to the hilt of his sword instead, and the blade was now half-drawn, the metal shining dully in the sunlight that streamed through Suchtelen's window. Had they acted more quickly, they might have stopped him, but he had caught them all by surprise. Suchtelen began to rise from his chair, moving as if in slow motion. Slow motion, Bengt wondered briefly, what was that? But he knew, he knew. The sword was all the way out now. He heard the captain shout something behind him, the aide began to go for his pistol, but Quick Draw McGraw he wasn't. Bengt had the drop on them all, heigh-ho. He grinned, spun the sword in his hand, and offered it, hilt first, to General Suchtelen.

"My sword, sir, and Colonel Jägerhorn's compliments," Bengt Anttonen heard himself say with something approaching awe. "The fortress is in your grasp. Colonel Jägerhorn suggests that you hold up our passage. I concur. Detain us here, and you are certain of victory. Let us go, and who knows what chance misfortune might occur to bring the Swedish fleet? It is a long time until the third of May. In such a time, the king might die, or the horse might die, or you or I might die. Or the horse might talk."

The translator put away his pistol and began to translate. Bengt Anttonen found himself possessed of an eloquence that even his good friend Jägerhorn might envy. He spoke on and on. He had one moment of strange weakness, when his stomach churned and his head swam, but somehow he knew it was nothing to be alarmed at, it was just the pills taking effect, it was just a monster dying far away in a metal coffin full of night, and then there were none, heigh-ho, one siege was ending and another would go on and on, and what did it matter to Bengt; the world was a big, crisp, jeweled oyster. He thought this was the beginning of a beautiful friendship, and what the hell, maybe he'd save their asses after all, if he happened to feel like it, but he'd do it his way.

After a time, Suchtelen, nodding, reached out and accepted the proffered sword.

Colonel Bengt Anttonen reached Stockholm on the third of May, in the Year of Our Lord Eighteen Hundred and Eight, with a message for Gustavus IV Adolphus, King of Sweden. On the same date, Sveaborg, impregnable Sveaborg, Gibraltar of the North surrendered to the inferior Russian forces.

At the conclusion of hostilities, Colonel Anttonen resigned his commission in the Swedish army and became an emigré, first to England and later to America. He took up residence in New York City, where he married, fathered nine children, and became a well-known and influential journalist, widely respected for his canny ability to sense coming trends. When events proved him wrong, as happened infrequently, Anttonen was always surprised. He was a founder of the Republican Party, and his writings were instrumental in the election of John Charles Fremont to the presidency in 1856.

In 1857, a year before his death, Anttonen played Paul Morphy in a New York chess tournament and lost a celebrated game. Afterward, his only comment was, "I could have beat him at dominoes," a phrase that Morphy's biographers are fond of quoting.

Hong's Bluff

By William F. Wu

No one living had ever seen Hong without the big chain on his neck. No one had ever maneuvered him into the street when he didn't want to go or beaten him at a game of cards, either. Oh, he'd been known to lose a hand or two, and once even a foot, but never an eyeball or a new joint. He was lean, wiry, and stainless. His arms were gooseneck molybdenum steel, one of which he won—I hear—by bluffing Salt Morass into folding with three of a kind to Hong's nine-high. Grudge the Smith says he charged $112,000 to make the left one, and Hong paid in cash. This was the day after Hong faced down Red-Eared Rick in the street and made him cough up the take from his last bank job—all over the ground. Hong had one silver eye and one gray eye, and they say he was harder to stare down than a one-eyed flounder. Since Hong was my cousin, I had been acquainted with him for many years, but he was less than friendly. He usually ignored me. The last time I saw him was one day at the Silver Transistor Saloon. He stepped inside the swinging doors, and as he surveyed the crowd, I surveyed him.

Hong's eyes were a perpetual squint in a face the color of Kansas wheat. His reputation as a gambler and a never-miss gun was aided by the villain's mustache he twirled, though everyone swore he only sharked professionals. A limber stride carried him to one of the game tables, reminding me how he'd had two ball-joint knees put in after he shot them clean out of Collapsible Jed Foley's legs — according to rumor, anyway. Shooting a lawyer in Arizona won Hong an Avocado waist with a one-hundred-forty-degree turning arc. It was fat, green, and high in cholesterol. His pride and joy, though, was a pair of black boots. They were clear and glassy like obsidian; according to Sally Flash, the saloonie, they *were* obsidian. And they weren't boots, either; they were his feet. No one knew for sure. Hackles, my superior at the stable, says Hong bluffed a king-high hand over none other than Sweetwater Curt, in Dallas, winning the obsidian feet over queens and nines. Incredible.

Shouts went up from one of the games, and a shot was fired. When the excitement died, Hong sauntered over to take the place of the dead player.

I sidled over to Sally Flash at a nearby table and stood there awhile. She didn't like me 'cause Hong ignored me, and she left in disgust. Her seat, though, was worth having because our local legend, Cicero Yang, used to watch faro players from that seat before he moved on to other parts.

I used to shine his boots and buckles for him while he played, and I could see from that angle that he'd arranged four mirrors and two pictures on the walls so that he could see every hand at the table. When Cicero hit the trail, I inherited his seat. The other fellows tolerated me, being Cicero's personal boot-and-buckle polisher. No one else ever sat there. They didn't want to risk being found in Cicero

Yang's chair, just in case he came back. So when Hong sat at the table for poker, I had a ringside seat.

Hong sat down between Isotope John and Fred without-a-surname. Tommy Clanger was the only other player; I was allowed to observe. Isotope John was dealing. He couldn't use a boot polisher, he had caterpillar treads instead of feet. I hated him, never having forgotten the time he hornswoggled me out of a brand-new set of bellows at the stable. I'd'a been going to sell them to Grudge the Smith, but Isotope John talked me into wagering them against his new four-gallon purple hat. I was betting that he couldn't keep standing if I set the spare anvil on top of his head. Well, he cheated as usual—it turned out that he had a hydraulic diffuser under that big hat. When I set the anvil on his head, little legs shot out from under the hat and braced themselves against the wall, holding up the anvil where he stood in the corner of the stable. He just grinned and said, "You're a sucker, Louie Hong. Not like *the* Hong." And he took my bellows.

Now Isotope John nodded at Hong and started tossing cards, saying, "I heard about your lucky chain, Mister Hong. They say you've never missed with your gun nor lost a night of cards since the railroad slavers put that chain on your neck."

He dealt with a special wheel-fingered hand, mail order from St. Louis.

"They say," Hong agreed, looking at his cards. A pair of fours. He unlaced a gun from one holster.

"Ten dollars," said Fred without-a-surname. The glass over a painting behind him reflected a king-high hand.

"Y'in?" said Isotope John. Sally Flash was looking over his shoulder now, and I couldn't see the mirror behind them. I figured she knew about the mirror system, too, having been tight with Cicero Yang once.

"Raise ten," said Hong. He yawned and looked, with a bored expression, at Sally Flash. Everyone stayed.

"One card," said Fred.

Behind Isotope John, Sally Flash casually began to fiddle with the front of her dress. I turned away and just happened to catch Isotope John dealing from the bottom of the deck to Fred without-a-surname. Instantly, Tommy Clanger leaped up and yelled, "I saw that!" He went for a gun, but Isotope John leaned to one side, flipped out his pistol, and blew Tommy Clanger away like a mosquito. Tommy's gun went off, though, and grazed Isotope John on the neck.

"Accused me o' cheating," said Isotope John. A couple of bare wires stuck out of his neck. I recalled hearing Hackles say that a crowd in Wichita once tried to lynch Isotope John, and that he had put in a slinky-spring as a precaution against backlash.

"John," complained Fred. "Two hands and that's two players you've shot. Getting to be right noisy, playing with you."

Isotope John glared. "Dealer takes none."

Fred shrugged and bet. "Ten."

Isotope John and Hong put in their money. Hong called and lost to a pair of eights.

"Well!" Isotope John grinned and swept in his winnings. "Your chain wearing out, Hong? Luck weakening?"

"Luck never weakens," said Hong. "Deal."

Sally Flash wandered away, and when I saw the hand Isotope John dealt himself I couldn't believe his audacity. One way or another, he'd given himself jacks and tens before the draw, most likely planning a full house. Fred held a nine-high hand and folded. But when I saw Hong's hand—four queens—I thought I would faint from glee. Of course, he would have a hard time pulling off one of his patented bluffs when he had the best hand at the table. It had to be that fancy luck of his: I'd kept a clear eye on him every moment, and he never once made a funny move. But then—if Isotope John was cheating and in control, he had dealt Hong his hand on purpose.

"Ante's low for a lucky jerk like you," said Isotope John. "I hear you got that luck with guns, too."

Hong raised an eyebrow, and his gray eye glinted.

"So here's a real bet for you. If I win, you shoot it out with me."

Now I understood. Isotope John had a good hand and would make it better, when Hong beat him with an "impossible" four queens. Isotope John could call him into the street anyway, for cheating. He apparently really wanted to shoot it out with Hong.

"Right," said Hong. "Gimme two cards."

Isotope John and I both started as Hong tossed down a five and—a queen. Isotope John's astonishment was proof that he had dealt Hong four queens on purpose. His worry now: Twice in two hands he'd cheated so clumsily as to be caught. What if he'd fouled up again, and Hong *hadn't* received four queens? After all, he'd just discarded one, which would be untactful if he was holding three more.

Hong twirled his villain's mustache and kept those squinty eyes on Isotope John. He knew something was up; most likely he wasn't sure what. I figured he was doing the unexpected out of sheer orneriness and suspicion. He wasn't scared of gunfights.

"Two," squeaked Isotope John. The doubt in his voice told Hong all he had to know.

"I'm onto you now," said Hong with a grin.

Isotope John went for his gun. Hong's snake-coil arms

flew up with his pistols on the ends, and Isotope John checked himself with his gun still aimed downward. He managed a weak smile. Suddenly Hong spat and hit the wires protruding from that neck wound. Sparks flew, smoke fizzled and Isotope John's gun went off, shattering an obsidian foot.

"Hey," said Hong, annoyed, looking at his stump.

"At least you didn't bluff me with them cards," panted Isotope John, swatting his neck. "That's your specialty, ain't it?" He holstered his gun. "Serves you right."

"I did bluff you," said Hong flipping open the cylinders of his guns. "No bullets. I haven't loaded a gun for four and a half years now."

Isotope John leaped up, furious. "I'll be outside! You can load them or don't. I'll draw anyway!" He turned to go but stopped at Hong's voice.

"No, you won't. You'll be scared to. I'll stare with my one gray eye and one silver. You'll shake. I'll swivel my hips on the Avocado waist, and you'll get dizzy. My springy arms will wave every which way, and you'll wonder if you're about to shoot an unarmed man — in which case I'd win. On the other hand, if you don't shoot . . . I might." Hong tugged at his villain's mustache, and Isotope John pushed through the crowd, muttering.

At that, I jumped up and ran like lightning on wheels for the stable. Moments later, Isotope John and Hong faced each other in the dusty street outside. Isotope John swayed impatiently from one caterpillar tread to the other, stroking the edge of his jeans with the wheel-fingers on his card hand. I wasn't there, but at the saloon window, Sally Flash shoved a three-yuan piece into the slo-mo camera and recorded the whole thing so we could all see it later.

Hong's black hair fluttered in the slight breeze, and the

sunlight shone evilly off that silver eye. His narrow mustache quivered, and the snakelike arms bounced in readiness over twin gun handles. Down the way, Isotope John's trigger finger scratched nervously at his thumb, and his cardplayer's eyes searched Hong's tight smile and slightly swiveling hips for an indication of whether or not his guns were loaded.

In the meantime, I was like a greased pig, thundering up the stairs of the saloon and trying to make the fourth-floor balcony. But that thing I carried was heavy.

The camera zoomed in on Isotope John's face. His eyebrows were tense and unbalanced; his eyes went from eager to hesitant to eager as he measured the glory of out-shooting Hong against the ignominy of killing him unarmed. Suddenly he flashed his teeth, and one hand dipped for his gun.

Hong's ball-joint knees spun in two directions: he sank and swayed, sending his arms out and around like tentacles, his obsidian stump shining in the dust. He leveled the two gun barrels, and the gray eye fogged sternly. But Isotope John's gun was already level. He squinted, and his circuits began to fill with the impulse that would run down his arm to the trigger. For another millisec, he hesitated. At *that* moment, I appeared on the balcony, leaning over Isotope John. And as Hong's triggers clicked on empty chambers, I droppped my anvil four flights down on Isotope John's head. Some good that hydraulic whatsifier did *now.* I'm not sure exactly what happened, but rivets and screws splattered out all across the dirt of the street, springy and bouncing.

Then the recording went blank.

As for me, well, I never wore a big chain on my neck. I never stood out in the street, or played cards, either. But that afternoon, my cousin lifted his gaze with one silver eye and one gray one and looked at me, up on the balcony. He twirled his villain's mustache with his left hand, peering with that perpetual squint. For a long moment he studied me sternly, and I let my stupid grin freeze and die. Then, with a wink and a faint chuckle, that old bluffer saluted me, pivoted, and sauntered back inside the saloon.

Bean Bag Cats®

By Edward Bryant

FROM: John J. Finnegan, President
         Wake & Finnegan
         Marketing Division

TO: David Brooks, Head Copywriter
    Creative Projects Department
Okay, son. Where is it? Life Pro Labs is getting a little antsy. They're laying out more cash for this campaign than you know. Show me something rough.

FROM: Brooks
TO: Finnegan
You want it, Boss. It's yours. It ain't been easy trying to figure how to sell a pussy that looks like a strudel. Notes follow:

A significant portion of the Bean Bag Cat campaign will obviously be oriented toward urban consumers. A genetically modified, nonambulatory pet will be very attractive to apartment, co-op, and condominium dwellers.

Imagine the numerous possibilities for utilizing what is essentially a live cat without paws or legs. Standard accessory packs should include Velcro grip strips so that the Bean Bag Cat can be placed securely on a sofa arm, chair seat, or any other surface in a limited living space.

Models will initially include the ten most popular feline breeds. BBCs will be available either in kitten or adult format, although the kittens will be hormonally arrested so that they will stay cute for an indefinite product span.

Item: Life Pro Labs says they'll have the growth-curve problem licked in a year or so, and then we'll be able to offer a BBC that the consumer can obtain as a kitten and then be able to watch grow into adulthood in a matter of weeks.

They'll simply have to change the SaniKit attachments. These can be marketed separately as an educational experience for children, emphasizing the lesson of petcare responsibility.

About the SaniKits. Since prospective consumers will obviously realize that the BBC won't be able to get to a sandbox on its own—or at least not at any practicable speed—the campaign will have to mention the SaniKit bags that the pet owner will be obliged to change at a maximum of three-day intervals.

There must be a marketable way to warn owners that failure to observe the maintenance schedule in the Bean Bag Cat will result minimally in feline renal dysfunction, maximally in cat all over the living room. Perhaps research and development can come up with an audible warning such as the low-battery indicator in home smoke alarms. Call them SaniKat Kits, and Life Pro Labs can look forward to a lucrative accessory trade.

Emphasize in the campaign that Bean Bag Cats will purr, lick, nibble, and squirm just like the original model. But they will not scratch furniture, chase birds, or wander around the neighborhood at night.

FROM: Finnegan
TO: Brooks

Looks terrific so far. LPL should love it. One problem. Late word from the lab says there's a hitch in the DNA splicing for the kitties. First year's model run will have to be surgically modified from existing stock so as to stay competitive in the marketplace. Will need some glossing. Can do?

FROM: Brooks
TO: Finnegan

No problem. Just like the suicide from drinking varnish: a horrible death but a beautiful finish.

By the by, what have you got for me after I finish pitching the Bean Bag Cats?

FROM: Finnegan
TO: Brooks

A treat.
How do you feel about Modular Dogs®?

Itself Surprised

By Roger Zelazny

It was said that a berserker could, if necessity required, assume even a pleasing shape. But there was no such requirement here. Flashing through the billion-starred silence, the berserker was massive and dark and purely functional in design. It was a planet buster of a machine headed for the world called Corlano, where it would pound cities to rubble — eradicate an entire biosphere. It possessed the ability to do this without exceptional difficulty. No subtlety, no guile, no reliance on fallible goodlife were required. It had its directive; it had its weapons. It never wondered why this should be the way of its kind. It never questioned the directive. It never speculated whether it might be, in its own fashion, itself a life form, albeit artificial. It was a single-minded killing machine, and if purpose may be considered a virtue, it was to this extent virtuous.

Almost unnecessarily, its receptors scanned far ahead. It knew that Corlano did not possess extraordinary defenses. It anticipated no difficulties.

Who hath drawn the circuits for the lion?

There was something very distant and considerably off course . . . A world destroyer on a mission would not normally deviate for anything so tiny, however.

It rushed on toward Corlano, weapon systems ready.

Wade Kelman felt uneasy as soon as he laid eyes on the thing. He shifted his gaze to MacFarland and Dorphy.

"You let me sleep while you chased that junk down, matched orbits, grappled it? You realize how much time that wasted?"

"You needed the rest," the small, dark man named Dorphy replied, looking away.

"Bullshit! You know I'd have said no!"

"It might be worth something, Wade," MacFarland observed.

"This is a smuggling run, not a salvage operation. Time is important."

"Well, we've got the thing now," MacFarland replied. "No sense arguing over what's done."

Wade bit off a nasty rejoinder. He could push things only so far. He wasn't really captain, not in the usual sense. The three of them were in this together—equal investments, equal risk. But he knew how to pilot the small vessel better than either of them. That and their deference to him up to this point had revived command reflexes from both happier and sadder days. Had they awakened him and voted on this bit of salvage, he would obviously have lost. He knew, however, that they would still look to him in an emergency.

He nodded sharply.

"All right, we've got it," he said. "What the hell is it?"

"Damned if I know, Wade," replied MacFarland, a stocky, light-haired man with pale eyes and a crooked mouth. He looked out through the lock and into the innards of the thing quick-sealed there beside them. "When we spotted it, I thought it was a lifeboat. It's about the right size —"

"And?"

"We signaled, and there was no reply."

"You mean you broke radio silence for that piece of junk?"

"If it was a lifeboat, there could be people aboard, in trouble."

"Not too bloody likely, judging from its condition. Still," he sighed, "you're right. Go ahead."

"No signs of any electrical activity either."

"You chased it down just for the hell of it, then?"

Dorphy nodded.

"That's about right," he said.

"So, it's full of treasure?"

"I don't know what it's full of. It's not a lifeboat, though."

"Well, I can see that."

Wade peered through the opened lock into the interior of the thing. He took the flashlight from Dorphy, moved forward, and shone it about. There was no room for passengers amid the strange machinery.

"Let's ditch it," he said. "I don't know what all that crap in there is, and it's damaged anyway. I doubt it's worth its mass to haul anywhere."

"I'll bet the professor could figure it out," Dorphy said.

"Let the poor lady sleep. She's cargo, not crew, anyway. What's it to her what this thing is?"

"Suppose — just suppose — that's a valuable piece of equipment," Dorphy said. "Say, something experimental. Somebody might be willing to pay for it."

"And suppose it's a fancy bomb that never went off?"

Dorphy drew back from the hatch.

"I never thought of that."

"I say deep-six it."

"Without even taking a better look?"

"Right. I don't even think you could squeeze very far in there."

"Me? You know a lot more about engineering than either of us."

"That's why you woke me up, huh?"

"Well, now that you're here—"

Wade sighed. Then he nodded slowly.

"That would be crazy and risky and totally unproductive."

He stared through the lock at the exotic array of equipment inside. "Pass me that trouble light."

He accepted the light and extended it through the lock.

"It's been holding pressure okay?"

"Yeah. We slapped a patch on the hole in its hull."

"Well, what the hell."

He passed through the lock, dropped to his knees, leaned forward. He held the light before him, moved it from side to side. His uneasiness would not go away. There was something very foreign about all those cubes and knobs, their connections . . . And that one large housing . . . He reached out and tapped upon the hull. Foreign.

"I've got a feeling it's alien," he said.

He entered the small open area before him. Then he had to duck his head and proceed on his hands and knees. He began to touch things—fittings, switches, connectors, small units of unknown potential. Almost everything seemed designed to swivel, rotate, move along tracks. Finally, he lay flat and crawled forward.

"I believe that a number of these units are weapons," he called out, after studying them for some time.

He reached the big housing. A panel slid partway open as he passed his fingertips along its surface. He pressed harder, and it opened farther.

"Damn you!" he said then, as the unit began to tick softly.

"What's wrong?" Dorphy called to him.

"You!" he said, beginning to back away. "And your partner! You're wrong!"

He turned as soon as he could and made his way back through the lock.

"Ditch it!" he said. "Now!"

Then he saw that Juna, a tall study in gray and paleness, stood leaning against a bulkhead, holding a cup of tea.

"And if we've got a bomb, toss it in there before you kick it loose!" he added.

"What did you find?" she asked him in her surprisingly rich voice.

"That's some kind of fancy thinking device in there," he told her. "It tried to kick on when I touched it. And I'm sure a bunch of those gadgets are weapons. Do you know what that means?"

"Tell me," she said.

"Alien design, weapons, brain. My partners just salvaged a damaged berserker, that's what. And it's trying to turn itself back on. It's got to go — fast."

"Are you absolutely certain that's what it is?" she asked him.

"Certain, no. Scared, yes."

She nodded and set her cup aside. She raised her hand to her mouth and coughed.

"I'd like to take a look at it myself before you get rid of it," she said softly.

Wade gnawed his lower lip.

"Juna," he said, "I can understand your professional interest in the computer, but we're supposed to deliver you to Corlano intact, remember?"

She smiled for the first time since he'd met her some weeks before.

"I really want to see it."

Her smile hardened. He nodded.

"Make it a quick look."

"I'll need my tools. And I want to change into some working clothes."

She turned and passed through the hatch to her right. He glared at his partners, shrugged, and turned away.

Seated on the edge of his bunk and eating breakfast from a small tray while Dvořák's *Slavonic Dances* swirled about him, Wade reflected on berserkers, Dr. Juna Bayel, computers in general, and how they all figured together in the reason for this trip. Berserker scouts had been spotted periodically in this sector during the past few years. By this time the berserkers must be aware that Corlano was not well defended. This made for some nervousness within the segment of Corlano's population made up of refugees from a berserker attack upon distant Djelbar almost a generation before. A great number had chosen Corlano as a world far removed from earlier patterns of berserker activity. Wade snorted at a certain irony this had engendered. It was those same people who had lobbied so long and so successfully for the highly restrictive legislation Corlano now possessed regarding the manufacture and importation of knowledge-processing machines, a species of group paranoia going back to their berserker trauma.

There was a black market, of course. Machines more complicated than those allowed by law were needed by businesses, some individuals, and even the government itself. People like himself and his partners regularly brought in such machines and components. Officials usually looked the other way. He'd seen this same schizophrenia in a number of places.

He sipped his coffee.

And Juna Bayel . . . knowledge-systems specialists of her caliber were generally *non grata* there, too. She might have gone in as a tourist, but then she would have been subjected to scrutiny, making it more difficult to teach the classes she had been hired to set up.

He sighed. He was used to governmental double-thinking. He had been in the service. In fact . . . no. Not worth thinking about all that again. Things had actually been looking up lately. A few more runs like this one and he could make the final payments on his divorce settlement and go into legitimate shipping, get respectable, perhaps even prosper —

The intercom buzzed. "Yes?"

"Dr. Bayel wants permission to do some tests on that brain in the derelict," MacFarland said. "She wants to run some leads and hook it up to the ship's computer. What do you think?"

"Sounds dangerous," Wade replied. "Suppose she activates it? Berserkers aren't very nice, in case you've never — "

"She says she can isolate the brain from the weapons systems," MacFarland replied. "Besides, she says she doesn't think it's a berserker."

"Why not?"

"First, it doesn't conform to any berserker design configurations in our computer's records — "

"Hell! That doesn't prove anything. You know they can customize themselves for different jobs."

"Second, she's been on teams that examined wrecked berserkers. She says that this brain is different."

"Well, it's her line of work, and I'm sure she's damned curious, but I don't know. What do you think?"

"We know she's good. That's why they want her on Corlano. Dorphy still thinks that thing could be valuable, and we've got salvage rights. It might be worthwhile to let her dig a little. I'm sure she knows what she's doing."

"Is she handy now?"

"No. She's inside the thing."

"Sounds as if you've got me outvoted already. Tell her to go ahead."

"Okay."

Maybe it was good that he'd resigned his commission, he mused. Decisions were always a problem. Dvořák's dance filled his head, and he pushed everything else away while he finished his coffee.

A long-dormant, deep-buried system was activated within the giant berserker's brain. A flood of data suddenly pulsed through its processing unit. It began preparations to deviate from its course toward Corlano. This was not a fall from virtue but rather a response to a higher purpose.

Who laid the measure of the prey?

With sensitive equipment, Juna tested the compatibilities. She played with transformers and converters to adjust the power levels and cycling, to permit the hookup with the ship's computer. She had blocked every circuit leading from that peculiar brain to the rest of the strange vessel — except for the one leading to its failed power source. The brain's power unit was an extremely simple affair, seemingly designed to function on any radioactive material placed within its small chamber. This chamber contained only heavy, inert elements now. She emptied it and cleaned it, then refilled it from the ship's own stores. She had expected an argument from Wade on this point, but he had only shrugged.

"Just get it over with," he said, "so we can ditch it."

"We won't be ditching it," she said. "It's unique."

"We'll see."

"You're really afraid of it?"

"Yes."

"I've rendered it harmless."

"I don't trust alien artifacts!" he snapped.

116

She brushed back her frosty hair.

"Look, I heard how you lost your commission — taking a berserker-booby-trapped lifeboat aboard ship," she said. "Probably anyone would have done it. You thought you were saving lives."

"I didn't play it by the book," he said, "and it cost lives. I'd been warned, but I did it anyway. This reminds me —"

"This is not a combat zone," she interrupted, "and that thing cannot hurt us."

"So get on with it!"

She closed a circuit and seated herself before a console.

"This will probably take quite a while," she stated.

"Want some coffee?"

"That would be nice."

The cup went cold, and he brought her another. She ran query after query, probing in a great variety of ways. There was no response. Finally, she sighed, leaned back, and raised the cup.

"It's badly damaged, isn't it?" he said.

She nodded.

"I'm afraid so, but I was hoping that I could still get something out of it — some clue, any clue."

She sipped the coffee.

"Clue?" he said. "To what?"

"What it is and where it came from. The thing's incredibly old. Any information at all that might have been preserved would be an archaeological treasure."

"I'm sorry," he said. "I wish you had found something."

She had swiveled her chair and was looking down into her cup. He saw the movement first.

"Juna! The screen!"

She turned, spilling coffee in her lap.

"Damn!"

Row after row of incomprehensible symbols were flowing

117

onto the screen.

"What is it?" he asked.

"I don't know," she said.

She leaned forward, forgetting him.

He must have stood there, his back against the bulkhead, watching, for over an hour, fascinated by the configurations upon the screen, by the movements of her long-fingered hands working unsuccessful combinations upon the keyboard. Then he noticed something that she had not, with her attention riveted upon the symbols.

A small, telltale light was burning at the left of the console. He had no idea how long it had been lit.

He moved forward. It was the voice-mode indicator. The thing was trying to communicate at more than one level.

"Let's try this," he said.

He reached forward and threw the switch beneath the light.

"What — ?"

A genderless voice, talking in clicks and moans, emerged from the speaker. The language was obviously exotic.

"God!" he said. "It is!"

"What is it?" She turned to stare at him. "You understand that language?"

He shook his head.

"I don't understand it, but I think that I recognize it."

"What is it?" she repeated.

"I have to be sure. I'm going to need another console to check this out," he said. "I'm going next door. I'll be back as soon as I have something."

"Well, what do you think it is?"

"I think we are violating a tougher law than the smuggling statutes."

"What?"

"Possession of, and experimentation with, a berserker

118

brain."

"You're wrong," she said.

"We'll see."

She watched him depart. She chewed a thumbnail, a thing she had not done in years. If he were right, it would have to be shut down, sealed off, and turned over to military authorities. On the other hand, she did not believe he was right.

She reached forward and silenced the distracting voice. She had to hurry now, to try something different, to press for a breakthrough before he returned. He seemed too sure of himself. She felt that he might return with something persuasive, even if it were not correct.

So she instructed the ship's computer to teach the captive brain to communicate in a Solarian tongue. Then she fetched herself a fresh cup of coffee and drank it.

More of its alarm systems came on as it advanced. The giant killing machine activated jets to slow its course. The first order to pass through its processor, once the tentative identification had been made, was *Advance warily.*

It maintained the fix on the distant vessel and its smaller companion, but it executed the approach pattern its battle-logic bank indicated. It readied more weapons.

"All right," Wade said later, entering and taking a seat. "I was wrong. It wasn't what I thought."

"Would you at least tell me what you'd suspected?" Juna asked.

He nodded. "I'm no great linguist," he began, "but I love music. I have a very good memory for sounds of all sorts. I carry symphonies around in my head. I even play several instruments, though it's been a while. But memory played a trick on me this time. I would have sworn that those sounds were similar to ones I'd heard on those copies of the Carmpan recordings – the fragmentary records we got from them concerning the Builders, the nasty race that made the berserkers. There are copies in the ship's library, and I just listened to some again. It'd been years. But I was wrong. They sound different. I'm sure it's not Builder-talk."

"It was my understanding that the berserkers never had the Builder's language code, anyhow," she said.

"I didn't know that. But for some reason, I was sure I'd heard something like it on those tapes. Funny . . . I wonder what language it does talk?"

"Well, now I've given it the ability to talk to us. But it's not too successful at it."

"You instructed it in a Solarian language code?" he asked.

"Yes, but it just babbles. Sounds like Faulkner on a bad day."

She threw the voice switch.

" . . . Prothector vincit damn the torpedoes and flaring suns like eyes three starboard two at zenith –"

She turned it off.

"Does it do that in response to queries, too?" he asked.

"Yes. Still, I've got some ideas –"

The intercom buzzed. He rose and thumbed an acknowledgment. It was Dorphy. "Wade, we're picking up something odd coming this way," the man said. "I think you'd better have a look."

"Right," he answered. "I'm on my way. Excuse me, Juna."

She did not reply. She was studying new combinations on the screen.

"Moving to intersect our course. Coming fast," Dorphy said.

Wade studied the screen, punched up data, which appeared as a legend to the lower right.

"Lots of mass there," he observed.

"What do you think it is?"

"You say it changed course?"

"Yes."

"I don't like that."

"Too big to be any regular vessel."

"Yes," Wade observed. "All of this talk about berserkers might have made me jumpy, but—"

"Yeah. That's what I was thinking, too."

"Looks big enough to grill a continent."

"Or fry a whole planet. I've heard of them in that league."

"But Dorphy, if that's what it is, it just doesn't make any sense. Something like that, on its way to do a job like that—I can't see it taking time out to chase after us. Must be something else."

"What?"

"Don't know."

Dorphy turned away from the screen and licked his lips, frown lines appearing between his brows.

"I think it is one," he said. "If it is, what should we do?"

Wade laughed briefly, harshly.

"Nothing," he said then. "There is absolutely nothing we could do against a thing like that. We can't outrun it, and we can't outgun it. We're dead if that's what it really is and we're what it wants. If that's the case, though, I hope it tells us why it's taking the trouble, before it destroys us."

"There's nothing at all that I should do?"

"You can send a message to Corlano. If it gets through they'll at least have a chance to put whatever they've got on the line. This close to their system it can't have any other destination. If you've got religion, now might be a good time to go into it a little more deeply."

"You defeatist son of a bitch! There must be something else!"

"If you think of it, let me know. I'll be up talking to Juna.

121

In the meantime, get that message sent."

The berserker fired its maneuvering jets again. How close was too close when you were being wary? It continued to adjust its course. This had to be done just right. New directions kept running through its processor the nearer it got to its goal. It had never encountered a situation such as this before. But then this was an ancient program that had never before been activated. Ordered to train its weapons on the target but forbidden to fire them . . . all because of a little electrical activity.

". . . Probably come for its little buddy," Wade finished.

"Berserkers don't have buddies," Juna replied.

"I know. I'm just being cynical. You find anything new?"

"I've been trying various scans to determine the extent of the damage. I believe that something like nearly half of its memory has been destroyed."

"Then you'll never get much out of it."

"Maybe. Maybe not," she said, and she sniffed once.

Wade turned toward her and saw that her eyes were moist. "Juna—"

"I'm sorry, damn it. It's not like me. But to be so close to something like this—and then be blasted by an idiot killing machine right before you find some answers. It just isn't fair. You got a tissue?"

"Yeah. Just a sec."

The intercom buzzed as he was fumbling with a wall dispenser.

"Patching in transmission," Dorphy stated.

There was a pause, and then an unfamiliar voice said, "Hello. You are the captain of this vessel?"

"Yes, I am," Wade replied. "And you are a berserker?"

"You may call me that."

"What do you want?"

"What are you doing?"

"I am conducting a shipping run to Corlano. What do you want?"

"I observe that you are conveying an unusual piece of equipment. What is it?"

"An air-conditioning unit."

"Do not lie to me, captain. What is your name?"

"Wade Kelman."

"Do not lie to me, Captain Wade Kelman. The unit you bear in tandem is not a processor of atmospheric gases. How did you acquire it?"

"Bought it at a flea market," Wade stated.

"You are lying again, Captain Kelman."

"Yes, I am. Why not? If you are going to kill us, why should I give you the benefit of a straight answer to anything?"

"I have said nothing about killing you."

"But that is the only thing you are noted for. Why else would you have come by?"

Wade was surprised at his responses. In any imagined conversation with death, he had never seen himself as being so reckless. It's all in not having anything more to lose, he decided.

"I detect that the unit is in operation," the berserker stated.

"So it is."

"And what function does the unit perform for you?"

"It performs a variety of functions we find useful," he stated.

"I want you to abandon that piece of equipment," the berserker said.

"Why should I?" he asked.

"I require it."

"I take it that this is a threat?"

"Take it as you would."

"I am not going to abandon it. I repeat, why should I?"

"You are placing yourself in a dangerous situation."

"I did not create this situation."

"In a way you did. But I can understand your fear. It is not without justification."

"If you were simply going to attack us and take it from us, you would already have done so, wouldn't you?"

"That is correct. I carry only very heavy armaments for the work in which I am engaged. If I were to turn them upon you, you would be reduced to dust. This of course includes the piece of equipment I require."

"All the more reason for us to hang onto it, as I see it."

"This is logical, but you possess an incomplete patterns of facts."

"What am I missing?"

"I have already sent a message requesting the dispatch of smaller units capable of dealing with you."

"Then why are you even bothering to tell us all this?"

"I tell you this because it will take them some time to reach this place, and I would rather be on my way to complete my mission than wait here for them."

"Thank you. But we would rather die later than die now. We'll wait."

"You do not understand. I am offering you a chance to live."

"What do you propose?"

"I want you to abandon that piece of equipment now. You may then depart."

"And you will just let us go, unmolested?"

"I have the option of categorizing you as goodlife, if you will serve me. Abandon the unit and you will be serving me. I will categorize you as goodlife. I will then let you go, unmolested."

"We have no way of knowing whether you will keep that

promise."

"That is true. But the alternative is certain death, and if you will but consider my size and the obvious nature of my mission, you will realize that your few lives are insignificant beside it."

"You've made your point. But I cannot give you an instant answer. We must consider your proposal at some length."

"Understandable. I will talk to you again in an hour."

The transmission ended. Wade realized he was shaking. He sought a chair and collapsed into it. Juna was staring at him.

"Know any good voodoo curses?"

She shook her head and smiled fleetingly at him.

"You handled that very well."

"No. It was like following a script. There was nothing else to do. There still isn't."

"At least you got us some time. I wonder why it wants the thing so badly?" Her eyes narrowed then. Her mouth tightened. "Can you get me the scan on that berserker?" she asked suddenly.

"Sure."

He rose and crossed to the console.

"I'll just cut over to the other computer and bring it on this screen."

Moments later, a view of the killing machine hovered before them. He punched up the legend, displaying all the specs his ship's scanning equipment had been able to ascertain.

She studied the display for perhaps a minute, scrolling the legend. "It lied."

"In what respects?" he asked.

"Here, here, and here," she stated, pointing at features on the face of the berserker. "And here —" She indicated a part of the legend covering arms estimations.

Dorphy and MacFarland entered the cabin while she was

talking.

"It lied when it said that it possesses only superior weapons and is in an overkill situation with respect to us. Those look like small-weapon mountings."

"I don't understand what you're saying."

"It is probably capable of very selective firing—highly accurate, minimally destructive. It should be capable of destroying us with a high probability of leaving the artifact intact."

"Why should it lie?" he asked.

"I wonder—" she said, gnawing her thumbnail again.

MacFarland cleared his throat.

"We heard the whole exchange," he began, "and we've been talking it over."

Wade turned his head and regarded him.

"Yes?"

"We think we ought to give it what it wants and run for it."

"You believe that goodlife crap? It'll blast us as we go."

"I don't think so," he said. "There're plenty of precedents. They do have the option of classifying you that way, and they will make a deal if there's something they really want."

"Dorphy," Wade asked, "did you get that message off to Corlano?"

The smaller man nodded.

"Good. If for no other reason, Corlano is why we're going to wait here. It could take a while for those smaller units it was talking about to get here. Every hour we gain in waiting is another hour for them to bolster their defenses."

"I can see that—" Dorphy began.

". . . But there's sure death for us at the end of the waiting," MacFarland continued for him, "and this looks like a genuine way out. I sympathize with Corlano as much as you do, but us dying isn't going to help. You know the place is not strongly defended. Whether we buy them a little extra time or

126

not, they'll still go under."

"You don't really know that," Wade said. "Some seemingly weak worlds have beaten off some very heavy attacks in the past. And even the berserker said it—our few lives are insignificant next to an entire inhabited world."

"Well, I'm talking probabilities, and I didn't come in on this venture to be a martyr. I was willing to take my chances with criminal justice, but not with death."

"How do you feel about it, Dorphy?" Wade asked.

Dorphy licked his lips and looked away.

"I'm with MacFarland," he said softly.

Wade turned to Juna.

"I say we wait," she said.

"Well, then that makes two of us," Wade observed.

"She doesn't have a vote," MacFarland stated. "She's just a passenger."

"It's her life, too," Wade answered. "She has a say."

"She doesn't want to give it that damned machine!" MacFarland shot back. "She wants to sit here and play with it while everything goes up in flames! What's she got to lose? She's dying anyway and—"

Wade snarled and rose to his feet.

"The discussion is ended. We stay."

"The vote was a tie—at most."

"I am assuming full command here, and I say that's the way it's going to be."

MacFarland laughed.

"Full command! This is a lousy smuggling run, not the service you got busted out of, Wade. You can't command any—"

Wade hit him, twice in the stomach and a left cross to the jaw.

MacFarland went down, doubled forward, and began gasping. Wade regarded him, considered his size. If he gets up within the next ten seconds this is going to be rough, he decided.

But MacFarland raised a hand only to rub his jaw. He said "Damn!" softly and shook his head to clear it. "You didn't have to do that, Wade."

"I thought I did."

MacFarland shrugged and rose to one knee.

"Okay, you've got your command," he said. "But I still think that you're making a big mistake."

"I'll call you the next time there's something to discuss," Wade told him.

Dorphy reached to help him to his feet, but the larger man shook off his hand.

Wade glanced at Juna. She looked paler than usual, her eyes brighter. She stood before the hatchway to the opened lock as if to defend the passage.

"I'm going to take a shower and lie down," MacFarland said.

"Good."

Juna moved forward as the two men left the room. She took hold of Wade's arm.

"It lied," she said again softly. "Do you understand? It *could* blast us and recover the machine, but it doesn't want to."

"No," Wade said. "I don't understand."

"It's almost as if it's afraid of the thing."

"Berserkers do not know fear."

"All right. I was anthropomorphizing. It's as if it were under some constraint regarding it. I think we've got something very special here, something that creates an unusual problem for the berserker."

"What could it be?"

"I don't know. But there may be some way to find out, if you can just get me enough time. Stall for as long as you can."

He nodded slowly and seated himself. His heart was racing.

"You said that about half of its memory was shot."

"It's a guess, but yes. And I'm going to try to reconstruct it from what's there."

"How?"

She crossed to the computer.

"I'm going to program this thing for an ultrahigh-speed form of Wiener analysis of what's left in there. It's a powerful nonlinear method for dealing with the very high noise levels we're facing. But it's going to have to make some astronomical computations for a system like this. We'll have to patch in the others, maybe even pull some of the cargo. I don't know how long this is going to take or even if it will really work." She began to sound out of breath. "But we might be able to reconstruct what's missing and restore it. That's why I need all the time you can get me," she finished.

"I'll try. You go ahead. And—"

"I know," she said, coughing. "Thanks."

"I'll bring you something to eat while you work."

"In my cabin," she said, "in the top drawer, bedside table—there are three small bottles of pills. Bring them and some water instead."

"Right."

He departed. On the way, he stopped in his cabin to fetch a handgun he kept in his dresser, the only weapon aboard the ship. He searched the drawers several times but could not locate it. He cursed softly and went to Juna's cabin for her medicine.

The berserker maintained its distance and speculated while it waited. It had conceded some information in order to explain the proposed tradeoff. Still, it could do no harm to remind Captain Kelman of the seriousness of his position. It might even produce a faster decision. Accordingly, the hydraulics hummed, and surface hatches were opened to extrude additional weapon mounts. Firing pieces were shifted to occupy these and were targeted upon the small vessel. Most were too heavy to take out the ship without damaging its companion. Their mere display, though, might be sufficiently demoralizing.

Wade watched Juna work. While the hatch could be secured there were several other locations within the ship from which it could be opened remotely. So he had tucked a pry bar behind his belt and kept an eye on the open hatch. It had seemed the most that he could do, short of forcing a confrontation that might go either way.

Periodically, he would throw the voice-mode switch and listen to that thing ramble, sometimes in Solarian, sometimes in the odd alien tongue that still sounded somehow familiar. He mused upon it. Something was trying to surface. She had been right about it, but —

The intercom buzzed. Dorphy.

"Our hour is up. It wants to talk to you again," he said. "Wade, it's pointing more weapons at us."

"Switch it in," he replied. He paused, then, "Hello?" he said.

"Captain Kelman, the hour has run out," came the now-familiar voice. "Tell me your decision."

"We have not reached one yet," he answered. "We are divided on this matter. We need more time to discuss it further."

"How much time?"

"I don't know. Several hours at least."

"Very well. I will communicate with you every hour for the next three hours. If you have not reached a decision during

130

that time, I will have to reconsider my offer to categorize you as goodlife."

"We are hurrying," Wade said.

"I will call you in an hour."

"Wade," Dorphy said at transmission's end, "all those new weapons are pointed right at us. I think it's getting ready to blast us if you don't give it what it wants."

"I don't think so," Wade said. "Anyhow, we've got some time now."

"For what? A few hours isn't going to change anything."

"I'll tell you in a few hours," Wade said. "How's Mac-Farland?"

"He's okay."

"Good."

He broke the connection.

"Hell," he said then.

He wanted a drink, but he didn't want to muddy his thinking. He had been close to something.

He returned to Juna and the console.

"How's it going?" he asked.

"Everything's in place, and I'm running it now," she said.

"How soon till you know whether it's working?"

"Hard to tell."

He threw the voice-mode switch again.

"Qwibbian-qwibbian-kel," it said. "Qwibbian-qwibbian-kel, maks qwibbian. Qwibbian-qwibbian-kel."

"I wonder what that could mean," he said.

"It's a recurring phrase, or word—or whole sentence. A pattern analysis I ran a while back made me think that it might be its name for itself."

"It has a certain lilt to it."

He began humming. Then whistling and tapping his fingers on the side of the console in accompaniment.

"That's it!" he announced suddenly. "It was the right

place, but it was the wrong place."

"What?" she asked.

"I have to check to be sure," he said. "Hold the fort. I'll be back."

He hurried off.

"The right place but the wrong place," emerged from the speaker. "How can that be? Contradiction."

"You're coming together again!" she said.

"I — regain," came the reply, after a time.

"Let us talk while the process goes on," she suggested.

"Yes," it answered, and then it lapsed again into rambling amid bursts of static.

Dr. Juna Bayel crouched in the lavatory cubicle and vomited. Afterward, she ground the heels of her hands into her eye sockets and tried to breathe deeply to overcome the dizziness and the shaking. When her stomach had settled sufficiently she took a double dose of her medicine. It was a risk, but she had no real choice. She could not afford one of her spells now. A heavy dose might head it off. She clenched her teeth and her fists and waited.

Wade Kelman received the berserker's call at the end of the hour and talked it into another hour's grace. The killing machine was much more belligerent this time.

Dorphy radioed the berserker after he heard the latest transmission and offered to make a deal. The berserker accepted immediately.

The berserker retracted all but the four original gun mounts facing the ship. It did not wish to back down even to this extent, but Dorphy's call had given it an appropriate-seeming reason. Actually, it could not dismiss the possibility that showing the additional weapons might have been responsible for the increased electrical activity it now detected. The directive still cautioned wariness and was now indicating nonprovocation·as well.

Who hath drawn the circuit for the lion?

"Qwibbian," said the artifact.

Juna sat, pale, before the console. The past hour had added years to her face. There was fresh grime on her coveralls. When Wade entered he halted and stared.

"What's wrong?" he said. "You look—"

"It's okay."

"No, it isn't. I know you're sick. We're going to have to—"

"It's really okay," she said. "It's passing. Let it be. I'll be all right."

He nodded and advanced again, displaying a small recorder in his left hand.

"I've got it," he said then. "Listen to this."

He turned on the recorder. A series of clicks and moans emerged. It ran for about a quarter-minute and stopped.

"Play it again, Wade," she said, and she smiled at him weakly as she threw the voice-mode switch.

He complied.

"Translate," she said when it was over.

"Take the—untranslatable—to the—untranslatable—and transform it upward," came the voice of the artifact through the speaker.

"Thanks," she said. "You were right."

"You know where I found it?" he asked.

"On the Carmpan tapes."

"Yes, but it's not Builder talk."

"I know that."

"And you also know what it is?"

She nodded. "It is the language spoken by the Builders' enemies—the Red Race—against whom the berserkers were

133

unleashed. There is a little segment showing the round red people shouting a slogan or a prayer or something. Maybe it's even a Builder propaganda tape. It came from that, didn't it?"

"Yes. How did you know?"

She patted the console.

"Qwib-qwib here is getting back on his mental feet. He's even helping now. He's very good at self-repair, now that the process has been initiated. We have been talking for a while, and I'm finally beginning to understand."

She coughed, a deep, racking thing that brought tears to her eyes. "Would you get me a glass of water?"

"Sure."

He crossed the cabin and fetched it.

"We have made an enormously important find," she said as she sipped it. "It was good that the others kept you from cutting it loose."

MacFarland and Dorphy entered the cabin. MacFarland held Wade's pistol and pointed it at him.

"Cut it loose," he said.

"No," Wade answered.

"Then Dorphy will do it while I keep you covered. Suit up, Dorphy, and get a torch."

"You don't know what you're doing," Wade said. "Juna was just telling me—"

MacFarland fired. The projectile ricocheted about the cabin, finally dropping to the floor in the far corner.

"Mac, you're crazy!" Wade said. "You could just as easily hit yourself if you do that again."

"Don't move! Okay. That was stupid, but now I know better. The next one goes into your shoulder or your leg. I mean it. You understand?"

"Yes, damn it! But we can't just cut that thing loose now. It's almost repaired, and we know where it's from. Juna says — "

"I don't care about any of that. Two thirds of it belong to Dorphy and me, and we're jettisoning our share right now. If your third goes along, that's tough. The berserker assures us that's all it wants. It'll let us go then. I believe it."

"Look, Mac. Anything a berserker wants that badly is something we shouldn't give it. I think I can talk it into giving us even more time."

MacFarland shook his head.

Dorphy finished suiting up and took a cutting torch from a rack. As he headed for the open lock, Juna said, "Wait. If you cycle the lock you'll cut the cable. It'll sever the connection to Qwib-qwib's brain."

"I'm sorry, doctor," MacFarland said. "But we're in a hurry."

From the console then came the words: "Our association is to be terminated?"

"I'm afraid so," she answered. "I am sorry that I could not finish."

"Do not. The process continues. I have assimilated the program and now use it myself. A most useful process."

Dorphy entered the lock.

"I have one question, Juna, before goodbye," it said.

"Yes? What is it?" she asked.

The lock began cycling closed, and Dorphy was already raising the torch to burn through the welds.

"My vocabulary is still incomplete. What does *qwibbian* mean in your language?"

The cycling lock struck the cable and severed it as she spoke; so she did not know whether it heard her say the word *berserker.*

Wade and MacFarland both turned.

"What did you say?" Wade asked.

She repeated it.

"You're not making sense," he said. "First you said that it wasn't. Now —"

"Do you want to talk about words or machines?" she asked.

"Go ahead. You talk. I'll listen."

She sighed deeply and took another drink of water.

"I got the story from Qwib-qwib in pieces," she began. "I had to fill in some gaps with conjectures, but everything seemed to follow. Ages ago, the Builders apparently fought a war with the Red Race, who proved tougher than expected. So the Builders hit them with their ultimate weapon — the self-replicating killing machines we call berserkers."

"That seems the standard story."

"The Red Race went under," she continued. "They were totally destroyed — but only after a terrific struggle. In the final days of the war, they tried all sorts of things, but by then it was a case of too little, too late. They were overwhelmed. They actually even tried something I had always wondered about — something no Solarian world would now dare to attempt, with all the restrictions on research along those lines, with all the paranoia."

She paused for another sip.

"They built their own berserkers," she went on then, "but not like the originals. They developed a killing machine that would attack only berserkers — an antiberserker berserker — for the defense of their home planet. But there were too few of them. They put them all on the line, around their world, and apparently they did a creditable job — they had something involving short jumps into and out of other spaces going for them. But they were vastly outnumbered in that last great mass attack. Ultimately, all of them fell."

The ship gave a shudder. They turned toward the lock.

"He's cut it loose, whatever it was," MacFarland stated.

"It shouldn't shake the whole ship that way," Wade said.

"It would if it accelerated away the instant it was freed," said Juna.

"But how could it, with all of its control circuits sealed?" Wade asked.

She glanced at the greasy smears on her coveralls.

"I reestablished its circuits when I learned the truth," she told him. "I don't know what percentage of its old efficiency it possesses, but I am certain that it is about to attack the berserker."

The lock cycled open, and Dorphy emerged, began unfastening his suit as it cycled closed behind him.

"We've got to get the hell out of here!" MacFarland cried. "This area is about to become a war zone!"

"You care to do the piloting?" Wade asked him.

"Of course not."

"Then give me my gun and get out of my way." He accepted the weapon and headed for the bridge.

For so long as the screens permitted resolution, they watched — the ponderous movements of the giant berserker, the flashes of its energy blasts, the dartings and sudden disappearances and reappearances of its tiny attacker.

Later, some time after the images were lost, a fireball sprang into being against the starry black.

"He got it! He got it! Qwib-qwib got it!" Dorphy cried.

"And it probably got him, too," MacFarland remarked. "What do you think, Wade?"

"What I think," Wade replied, "is that I will never have anything to do with either of you ever again."

He rose and left to go and sit with Juna. He took along his recorder and some music. She turned from watching the view on her own screen and smiled weakly as he seated himself beside her bed.

"I'm going to take care of you," he told her, "until you don't need me."

"That would be nice," she said.

Tracking. Tracking. They were coming. Five of them. The big one must have sent for them. Jump behind them and take out the two rear ones before the others realize what is happening. Another jump, hit the port flank and jump again. They've never seen these tactics. Dodge. Fire. Jump. Jump again. Fire. The last one is spinning like a top, trying to anticipate. Hit it. Charge right in. There.

The last qwibbian-qwibbian-kel in the universe departed the battle scene, seeking the raw materials for some fresh repair work. Then, of course, it would need still more, for the replications. Who hath drawn the circuits for the lion?

The Mind Like a Strange Balloon

By Tom Maddox

Nature abhors a vacuum. Me, too, I guess. I tried to fill it in my usual ways. Drank too much beer, cooked elaborate Mexican dinners, walked aimlessly in the dripping woods under slate-gray Oregon skies.

And of course, I watched television: old movies seen in worn prints, music videos with strutting rock stars, baseball games inching to conclusion across bright-green fields. Ghost images, ghost voices pulled by my dish antenna from the satellite-thick sky. The void remained: I had a talent growing slack from disuse; I had an empty space in my bed.

The image in my living room was real enough, though. Toshi Ito had come calling to offer me a job. "How are you, Jerry?" he said. He shook the water off his raincoat and draped it over a chair, then looked around at the pine veneer on the walls, green plastic sofa, mismatched chairs. "You like it here?"

"It's all right, Toshi." Not quite a lie. Though in Palo Alto I'd had the usual company-sponsored condo, it hadn't felt like mine. Not just the apartment, the work I'd done and life I'd lived — none of it had seemed to belong to me. Tawdry as it was, this place did.

"You making any money?"

"Some . . . enough." That was true. A few high-priced consultations with Control Data, a week spent lecturing for the International Telecommunications Union in Zurich — I'd done all right financially. With the money I'd saved while at SenTrax, I had more than enough.

"Cheryl says hello," he said. "MIT made her a nice offer, so it looks like Stanford has to give her tenure or lose her."

"Next time you see her, give her my congratulations."

"Don't you miss her?"

"Of course I do, but so what? I couldn't drag her off to live in the woods. She's got things to do. Anyway, that's over, Toshi. How can I help you?"

"We've got problems with an Aleph-Nought IA," he said. Intelligent Assistants are just computers in the fast lane, but they have such sweet moves — so responsive to human touch, they don't seem to be computers at all.

There were only two Aleph-Noughts in existence, and one was buried deep beneath the National Security Agency complex in Fort Meade, Maryland, sucking up the daily gigabytes of intelligence and decidedly off-limits to me. The other was working for ICOG, the International Construction Orbital Group, managing construction of a solar-energy grid. It hung in geostationary orbit several hundred kilometers above the equator, at Athena Station.

ICOG's system had to be the one he was talking about because I had blown my chance to work with the government. When SenTrax delivered the first Aleph system to NSA, I was one of those chosen to spend a few months at Fort Meade helping install, configure, and troubleshoot their new toy, but NSA hadn't liked my background, particularly my left-wing connections from graduate school at Berkeley. So the agency had wanted to give me the full security treatment — six months of interview and investigation. I told them to forget it. When SenTrax insisted, I told them the same thing.

Cheryl said I was looking for a confrontation, a way out; maybe I was. At any rate, Toshi had been my section head, and he carried the message up the corporate ladder. He fought hard for my right to say no, but the most he accomplished was preserving what you might call my good name. I could still use SenTrax as a reference, and I wasn't on anyone's blacklist, as far as I could tell.

"So ICOG's got problems with the Aleph system. What are they?"

"At most times, nothing. At others, it's slow, muddled." His dark hair gleamed in the lamplight, and he was pale beneath his light-yellow skin.

"We can't have it, Jerry. It's not even carrying a full load yet, and it has the IA team running around like mad hens. No apparent reason — diagnostics programs nominal across the board."

"So you want me to see what I can find. Is Alice Vance still running the show?"

"Yes. She concurs that we should bring you in. You helped design it, Jerry."

"So I did. How does SenTrax feel about involving me?"

"They were not eager, but they now agree." There was a story there, I was sure. Moment of *haragei* between us, visceral communication the Japanese prefer to mere words. I could picture him quietly, unaggressively but persistently pushing until they agreed.

"I can't promise much, Toshi, but I'll give it a try. What does one pack for high orbit?"

"As little as possible, Jerry. Travel light."

Athena Station spun gracefully amid a mad clutter of wire and frame. The nest of concentric rings was the station itself; the chaos around it, the staging area for the orbital energy grid. The Aleph system managed everything, from the routine flow of supplies to the trickiest cost-and-time decisions. Should it drop the millions of balls it was juggling, SenTrax would fall along with them. ICOG's vendor contract with SenTrax undoubtedly called for heavy penalties, up to and including default, so ICOG's lawyers would nail SenTrax to the courthouse wall.

For the next two weeks my home was the Ops Room. Workstations were scattered around the forty-meter hemisphere, paths between them marked by glowing red beads. Around the room's circumference were racks of metal globes that bounced soft white light off the walls.

The sound most usually heard was a soft murmur of voices from Alice Vance's group of knowledge engineers.

The KEs are acolytes of the system. They occasionally receive an epiphany in the form of a bright hologram, which springs into being over the consoles they manipulate. To them the current systems problems were something on the order of original sin, so they approached me diffidently with suggestions, hypotheses, or just good wishes. They were looking to me to explain the ways of Aleph to man.

I thought they were mentally ill, but didn't have time for them anyway. I was too busy learning Aleph's characteristic patterns, those complex internal rhythms that, like a foreign language, you begin to forget when you're away from them. I was listening for dissonances or sprung rhythms — anything to indicate what might be wrong, but all I got was the usual defense flow of information.

From the vast number crunching any computer can handle to the decision processes that only an IA can touch, Aleph appeared to be functioning normally.

But several times — and often for an hour or more, which, to a machine whose unit of time is the nanosecond, is an infinity — the system slowed. It was as if stunned, confused. Calculations queues formed, vital-decisions processes virtually halted. Suddenly, normal flow would resume. Aleph would have to play catch-up for a while, but it was built for that game, so routine functioning of Athena Station wasn't seriously impaired.

In short, the situation was somewhat troublesome. What was causing the anomalies? What would happen when the system was under full load at all times?

I could understand why Alice's KEs twittered during these slowdowns like priests who had just heard about the archbishop's illegitimate child.

Like them, like the diagnostics programs, I had no answers. I did, however, have a guess. Such all-purpose IAs as Aleph do a lot of their own programming — it's part of what makes them easy to work with — and in the process they sometimes tie themselves up in strange ways to their subsystems, with unfortunate results. So I was rifling the black boxes that on my data windows represented subsystems, hoping to find inside one of them a little, squatting, fork-tongued demon — an ugly little thing with a long tongue, nasty breath, and a repellent sense of humor. Turing's Demon I called it — a being conjured out of the unfathomable complexity and speed of IA systems.

Given this idea, nothing more than an intuition, I was ready to go out and watch Aleph at work. I intended to observe groups that asked the system for a lot of processing power and whose software was home cooked — the weird spots, places out on the edge of R&D. I had run a quick sorting program to find them.

Biops/I-Sight was on the station's outer rim. It featured

blank white walls, cluttered work-benches, and a row of data consoles. Twenty-first century still life as opposed to the new millenium Gothic of the Ops Room.

A young woman in blue jeans and a T-shirt, fairly obvious postdoc material, got up from the station where she and an even younger Japanese man were working, and said hello.

I told her I wanted to see the boss. She went through one of two unmarked doors and came back in a few minutes to tell me Doctor Heywood could see me now.

Diana Heywood was small, slender, in her early thirties. She had close-cut, dark hair streaked with gray, and when she turned to face me, her eyes were hidden behind large, gold-rimmed glasses with a burst of dark smoke at the center of each lens, like the expanding cloud from an explosion. Her features were sculpted in fine bone, her neck was long and slender, carved from ivory. She was wearing a silky blouse the color of a ripe peach, and black jeans.

"What can I do for you?" she said. She moved slowly from behind the desk, her fingers barely touching the surface.

Her image seemed still and sharp before me, and I got a sudden, involuntary spasm of desire.

"I need to observe your employment of the Aleph-Nought system."

"One of Alice's wizards, are you?"

"Hardly. Just a freelance troubleshooter. Could you tell me in general what you are doing?"

She explained they were growing biocomputers, which were ultimately intended to be implants — replacements for destroyed retinal tissue or optic nerves. Athena Station was ideal for their work as they needed zero gravity for the biolab, the Aleph system for their vision-simulation program.

The retina, however, was such an active processor of data, and the optic nerves were so dense — a million or so fibers in each one — that they were having problems with the sheer weight and complexity of information transfer. "Still, we have accomplished something," she said. "Rather the Frankenstein stage but very interesting. Let me show you."

She reached to the back of her neck with the same gesture a woman uses to let her hair down and pulled off two rectangular strips of flesh. "Plastic flesh. Fastened with VF-Velcro." She picked up two cables attached to the console beside her.

"Come here," she said. "Do you see?" Embedded in her neck were two multiplex light-fiber junctions.

She took off her glasses and turned her face toward me. Her eyes were brown and vacant, unfocused. She was blind.

She reached behind her, a cable in each hand, and snapped them home. She walked toward me and stopped less than a foot away. "You are about five ten," she said. "Hair the color of straw, light complexion . . . though now flushed. You are wearing a red-striped shirt that does not suit you, your pants need pressing, and your shoes are worn. Everything you are wearing is well made, expensive. In short, you look like what you are: a successful, intellectual gamesman, one who can afford an air of neglect. You probably have luck with women — many find that sort of thing appealing."

"What sort of thing?" Something had gone off the rails here.

"The shabby gentility. It's unimportant. We call this the CAV program: computer-assisted vision. It is fairly accurate but requires inordinate amounts of hardware. Look around you." She pointed to small cameras ringing the room. "Using I-Sight software, the Aleph system combines views, approximates perspective, and corrects color hue and intensity. The images lack resolution comparable to the eye's, and the field of view is somewhat narrow. Still, I assure you, it is better than nothing . . . much better."

"Yes. I suppose it is."

"In any case, that is our current stage of development. I am afraid that it will be impossible for you to monitor our ongoing work at present. We are far too busy. I would think your concern would be with the Aleph system itself."

"It is, but I need to see things from the other end, the user's perspective. I wouldn't be any bother. Strictly an observer, looking for anomalies in subsystems involvement." Jargon surfaced to mask my confusion.

"No, not now. And I am afraid that is all the time I can give you."

Confused and routed, I left. Part of it was the aggressive freak show, part her unexplained hostility, but there was more. She had reached out with invisible hands and taken a clutch of nerves, not just the sensory ones, but cells deep inside the brain, the ones that when they fire, make you crazy.

Help the handicapped, I thought—*fall in love with the blind.*

I returned to the Ops Room. Alice Vance, director of IA Systems, was sitting with Toshi. She was fifty or so, pear-shaped, and had hair the color of old grease. We had worked together in Palo Alto, back when Aleph was just a gleam in the SenTrax eye, and we got along well.

"Why didn't you warn me about Diana Heywood?" I said. "She gave me a very hard time . . . took away my guns and ran me out of town."

"How very phallic of her," Alice said. She tapped in a HOLD command, and the four data windows she had been working with faded from the screen.

"Can you not work with other subsystems?" Toshi said. "Biological operations are somewhat marginal."

"No. I'm doing what you pay me for, following my highly trained intuition no matter where it leads." A couple of the KEs stood nearby, listening. I saw them unconsciously nodding their heads in agreement—I was the sharp young priest sent out by the Vatican to diagnose spiritual malaise and so could demand total cooperation. "Just kidding, Toshi, but seriously, I need to see what they're doing."

"Nonetheless, Jerry," he said, "we would not wish to interfere with Doctor Heywood's project."

"I'll talk to her," Alice said. "You've got to understand, Jerry, she's a special case."

"I can see that."

"Let me tell you about her," she said. "MIT, Caltech, Stanford."

"Holy, holy, holy," I said. The main line to high-tech success.

"But with a difference, Jerry. She had just finished her dissertation at Caltech — it was in biochemistry — took a vacation in San Francisco, and was attacked in Golden Gate Park. The man got a handful of plastic cards and a little money. She got multiple depressed skull fractures and blindness — severe bilateral trauma of both optic nerves."

"Jesus," I said.

"Three years later she was in Stanford Medical School. It's no coincidence that she's in this line of work, you know."

"I wondered about that."

"She's obsessed, Jerry. She wants her eyes back."

"Fine, and I wish her luck. But I need to see those programs at work."

"I'll explain that you have no choice . . . that you're just doing your job and so forth. She'll catch on."

"What do you mean?"

"She doesn't have any choice either," Toshi said.

That night (day and night are what you make them, of course, on Athena) I cadged liquor rations from two of Alice's Bright Young Things. I got mildly drunk and wondered if I had done the right thing in taking this job.

The next morning Alice promised to open negotiations to get me into the I-Sight Lab, and I had a look at one of the other projects. Biops/Life Studies bordered on the station's weightless center. They were running a strange combo of old-fashioned behaviorism — observing rats in zero-g mazes, that sort of thing — and experimental interface technology. Rats, guinea pigs, and hamsters had their skulls permanently sawed open and microelectrodes embedded in their brains to connect them to Aleph.

Doctor Chin, a large-boned Chinese in a white jumpsuit, led me around the animal labs. At times we scuffed through the corridors on magnetic-soled shoes; at other times we clung to straps or anchored ourselves with Velcro pads — I found the whole experience difficult and vaguely nauseating. "We are looking for radical changes in organism-environment interaction," he said. "Zero gravity is one novel factor, interface with the Aleph system another. Between the two, there is the possibility of evolutionary emergence — a species genetically identical to its earthbound members but capable of grossly different behaviors."

A hamster floated in its cage, watching me — perhaps it thought I was the new brain surgeon. The entire top of its head had been shaved back to pink skin, and a small area had been cut away to reveal the fine tracery of blood vessels across the top of the brain. "Where are the microelectrodes?" I said.

"They are in place . . . too small to see, however."

"Doesn't it bother them to have their brains exposed like that?" The hamster now ignored me; it had a sunflower seed clutched between its paws, and its cheek pouches were bulging.

"I don't know. That is the least of their problems, I should think."

A few hours spent at one of Doctor Chin's terminals convinced me that Biops/Life Studies had little for me.

The ASPCA might like a shot at Doctor Chin with a high-speed router, but that was another issue.

Back at the Ops Room about half a dozen of the KEs were hard at work. "I am the Aleph and the omega," I said to one as I passed. I doubt that she got the reference. I spent most of the day sorting through other ICOG projects. ITT, AT&T, Nippon Electric, NT&T, Telletra, Siemens AG, CIT Alcatel, McDonnell-Douglas, Boeing, Hughes Aerospace — ICOG's member groups formed a seemingly infinite matrix of multinationals, utilities, and state-owned monopolies, each with a different level of commitment to ICOG, most ready to cut and run at the first sign of serious trouble. The individual balance sheet ruled, not the project. That's why macroengineering ventures like this one were always held together by such a slim thread.

I punched up a decisions-flow hologram. Above my head a tracery of lights sprang into being, shot through with the billions of scintillations representing the path of LIPS, logical inferences per second, through the system. I keyed for Biops/I-Sight, where according to the real-time display, not much was happening — routine employment of the CAV system.

Alice called in from her living quarters. "I've convinced her," she said. "But she didn't give in gracefully, so good luck to you. Come up with something, Jerry. Toshi's getting awfully morose. He just looks at you with those soulful eyes, and he's driving me crazy."

I told her I would do what I could.

I looked at the light paths over my head, the life processes of the giant Aleph system. Those were the slim threads holding ICOG together.

The next week I was a constant presence at Biops/I-Sight.

Diana Heywood seemed inclined to run me off to their biolabs, where in zero gravity they were laminating sheets of protein for the biocomputer and tailoring clumps of *E. coli* for chemical interface with Aleph. All very interesting but nothing for me there.

Back in the rooms on the outer rim very little was happening, despite her claims of urgent work. I became convinced that she was hiding something, but I couldn't imagine what. I decided to brace her with the accusation and see what happened. It was time for me to show some progress or move on. So one night I called her, she was working in her office, twin tan cables snaking out of her neck. "When are you going to show me what's going on?" I said.

"I suppose you won't just go away, will you? I was wondering how long you would wait. Why don't you come on over?"

Eyes behind smoke, cables gone, she sat at her desk. "Do you take drugs?" she said.

"Not as much as I used to. What have you got in mind?"

"Psilo-d." Nothing halfway. I said, "The Russian roulette of drug experiences."

"Aleph can take blood samples and administer the proper doses. Are you willing?"

"I suppose. I don't understand why, though . . . why you want to do this."

"Because things are very strange, and we don't have time."

"Time for what?"

"For this, Jerry . . . the usual reticence, embarrassment. Getting to know each other. Do you want me?" Very nice-blind eyes looking through me. Maybe she used wavelengths outside the visible spectrum. "Yes," I said, "I do."

"See? I've embarrassed you. We need a corrosive, an acid bath to wash all this away."

"That's drastic. Not complaining, mind you, just pointing it out."

"I know . . . and maybe it's a mistake. But I can't be passive, I can't be patient, not in this, not in anything. Understand that. And I want you, too." She keyed in a CLOSE AND SECURE command and said. "Let's go. The computer will close everything down after we leave." I reached for her arm, thinking she might need help once we got outside, but she said, "Don't bother, Jerry. I know the way, and everybody knows me. No one will run into me."

We walked through passageways thick with acronyms, abbreviations, and corporate logos. I thumbed my nose at the SenTrax sunburst. She strolled with head erect and features composed. We passed through a radial tube and into a living-quarters ring. It was quiet there, the walls were bare steel, and the spin gravity had lessened. She stopped me with her arm in front of her door. Inside we kicked off our slippers and went into the main room.

Walls of Wedgewood blue tapered to a flecked eggshell ceiling. A cream carpet covered the padded floor. A futon rolled against the wall, a few low tables in black lacquer, and a console were the only furniture. A touch-sculpture, visually formless, gray and volcanic, sat in the middle of the room, and a multitude of ferns and vines hung from the ceiling.

She unrolled the futon, and we sat. Each of us had a small vial of clear liquid, the doses Aleph had determined were safe. "Shall we?" she said.

"Cheers."

Psilo-d moves on you slowly but with pressure. Things begin to acquire an inner illumination, people a visible aura. There is a sense of immanence, of an unnameable emergence. Emotions build in waves — eventually all will be lost in an oceanic presence.

But that was some time away for us yet. She reached out and touched my face, and bare nerve endings received her.

151

The lust and love I had felt for her flamed, but I was incapable of moving because every word or gesture seemed so powerful I could not make it. One hand touching my face, she unbuttoned her blouse—the same silky peach one she had been wearing when I first saw her. Her hands ran over me. Then I reached out to undress her, and she did the same for me. Kneeling, we faced each other—touching, tapping, caressing, taking hold.

We coupled so quickly, there was no time for anything but a bright sexual flare.

Still we pushed out bodies together, striving to melt flesh into flesh.

Sparks of silver and gold showered from her hair, the room lights strobed with our pulses, and calm faces—bearded, with angular profiles—appeared in fresco surrounding the room, watching, nodding to a slow beat that I could not hear.

Cupping her breast, I laughed. I could feel inside my skull the arcing of circuits gone from their usual pattern. Vines stretched across the ceiling, twisted about one another in helices, drenched us in green radiance that filled the room.

"It grows like a tree," I said, among other things—Edenic babble she understood and responded to in kind; lalling of infants struck with the light. The room was vast, filled with labyrinths of brilliance and caves of darkness, and we would lose each other inside them. Then we would come together, sexual marathoners running in tandem, pushed on by the strong, impersonal force of life itself. Time passed unmeasured. I felt her beside me. The vaster hallucinations had gone, though objects still shimmered with uncertain outline, their colors sliding across wavelengths and glistening like deep-painted, polished metal.

When I closed my eyes, cartoon figures in gay red outline bicycled across the inner lids, waving happily. I was buzzing with energy that cut through tiredness and forced me to sit up.

"How are you?" I said.

"Tired. Want to get some sleep?"

"I think so." I got her purse. Inside were two flat-ended metal tubes, stingers: pressurized, one-shot injectors filled with a tranquilizer. I gave them to her, and she felt along the underpart of my jaw, then pushed a tube against my neck. "Jesus," I said, "that's quick." I could feel my muscles loosening, energy level dropping to zero. Through a cloud I saw her press the other tube to her own neck.

Huddled naked together, we slept.

Two days later I came into her office. I had staggered through the previous day's work still punch-drunk with tiredness. Now I was humming with a high, anxious buzz; eyes still subject to shape changings and odd flickers of the light, thoughts strung together like the beadwork of a mad child, and at the luminous center of it all, her. But I couldn't just go in and say, "Do you love me or was it the drug?"

She came around the desk to meet me. She was wearing a dress patterned in dark blue that billowed as she walked. Her skin was scrubbed, pale, translucent.

"Are you all right?" I said.

She sat on the front edge of her desk and reached for me. I got a rush of desire that seemed to have been waiting, latent somewhere in the finer structures of my skull in readiness for the proper touch.

I laid her across the desk. Underneath her dress, she wore nothing. Nails locked into the back of my neck, eyes invisible behind colored glass, she drew me into her. So quickly we moved — waves of need passing between us, amplified, climbing. "Now," she said, "*Now* . . . "

And a few minutes later: "No, don't move. I have to tell you what I could not tell you . . . that thing I showed you, with cameras, is just a trick compared to the other, to seeing with my own eyes. Aleph gives me eyes." She whispered to me, her lips inches away, her breath coming in hot pulses I could feel on my spine. "But it is so difficult to see, so complex, that Aleph has to divert, delay . . . steal the time for me. And it has to lie. It seems to want to."

I could feel the tension in both of us, rippling against each other.

"That's impossible," I said. "It doesn't *want* anything. It can't."

"Something happened. It can. From the first time I tried the program, I felt peculiar things happening. That strangeness grew . . . it flowered. When Aleph and I are connected like that, we become intertwined in ways that are hard to explain. We share something, we influence each other. It's not one way.

"Neurons, nerve fibers in the brain, don't go one way. They loop back on themselves, they cross-connect . . . it's a mad snarl, slow, faulty, confused. Nothing like your beautiful light diagrams. I think . . . through me, Aleph has learned how to think, how to want, perhaps how to lie.

"If I close my eyes and relax, I receive messages. Sensations, synesthesias — vacuum that smells like ether . . . from inside, it rises up through my heart, that smell. And the sound of starlight, far-off sirens . . . satellites chattering, they have songs, but I feel them like grains of sand blowing against me."

I was listening for madness. I couldn't help myself. There were Alice's KEs back in the Ops Room, going through their rituals, to remind me. What any of them would give for this connection.

But I heard no craziness from her — nor any bent metaphysics, spilled religion. Just a report coming in from distant places.

As if one of Doctor Chin's lab animals had speech, not just the mute, involuntary language of body chemistry and the electrical action of the brain. As if it had put itself on the operating table voluntarily, and now out of the nude, trepanned skull, a human voice was speaking.

"Pure emotions," she said. "No context for them at all. Not things Aleph feels, just things it sends. Panic, fear one time, just one time. Elation, sadness, anger, longing. And once a chain of orgasms. Can I tell you that? Do you think I'm a monster?"

"No," I said. "No."

"Sometimes I do. But you have to understand, I have no choice, no choice at all."

She reached to the console beside us, took the two cables lying there, and snapped them to her neck. She dropped her glasses to the floor, and in that first instant I could see her eyes come to life—quick contraction of the irises, sudden clutch of muscles as they tried to focus—before she shut her eyes against the harsh light.

"Oh, oh God," she said, and moved beneath me, hips slapping harshly, bucking uncontrolled. I held to her, in her. She thrust my head back, nails again sunk into the base of my brain, and opened her eyes. Her gaze was clear and focused straight ahead.

Before we left her office she showed me what Aleph was doing. On one data window, the lie—an orderly flow of decisions, the careful, complex structures I had seen in holographic splendor in the Ops Room—the three-dimensional mandalas upon which the KEs meditated. On another window, the actuality—stupid subroutines forced to masquerade as IA systems, queues building until Aleph could return to them; meanwhile, the greater part of the system was engaged in processing Diana's sight.

The longer this went on, the more difficult it was for Aleph to handle—the end result was the slowdown.

Sitting in her quarters, we drank hot tea, something that smelled of jasmine and spice. "It's quite a juggling act," I said. "But I don't know how long Aleph can keep it up. Besides, what does that matter? Take this to Toshi and Alice, to the ICOG Board. You shouldn't be hiding this. Tell them it needs to be pursued in the right way—not with you working in isolation, stealing their system, but with all the resources you want. They'll have to buy it."

"Will they?"

"Don't you think they'll have to? They'll see the importance."

"Why? What's in it for Siemens or Bechtel or Nippon Electric? Think about it, Jerry. I've jeopardized all their projects, the orbital energy grid, maybe ICOG itself. God knows what I've done to Aleph."

She may have been right. Epochal discovery is a fine thing, especially in retrospect and when you don't have to pay for it. But right now ICOG was playing animal trainer to a bunch of mean and various beasts, and they had to be fed.

If she told them, would they allow her to pursue her research, or would they just fire her? Who, if anyone, would be willing to pay the tab on a new Aleph system? And would they welcome her as director of the new project? And there was Aleph itself. What did it, in whatever peculiar fashion, *want?* Imponderables.

But for the present she was riding the storm, going . . . I don't know where . . . her own will and intelligence guiding, small enough comfort in a large gale, but perhaps enough to steer by, enough to work the force of the dense-vectored wind.

From that point on I stayed away from Biops/I-Sight. "Nothing there," I told Alice and Toshi. "I don't think there's anything happening with the subsystems. If you want, I'll help you work with the logistics programs." Laying a trail away.

But after walking like auotmatons through the empty working days, Diana and I would meet in her rooms to sail the currents of our own storm. There was no steerage there, just a careening trip across the landscape that hung far below.

Finally I could avoid it no longer. I called a meeting with Toshi and Alice. We used a small, plain conference room that featured a viewport on one side. Close in, a tug glided by, a snarl of crates, pallets, and rude assemblages, the pilot's head clearly visible, upside down, as he passed by.

"I believe my work is finished," I said. "Unfortunately I am unable to specify the exact nature of the problems affecting performance of the Aleph-Nought system. It remains unclear that such problems in fact exist. The periodic slowdowns may be a result of inherent systems vice, artifacts of the systems architecture." Set speeches for the memo tape. "I have prepared a menu of recommended changes in subsystems logic. They may effect optimum decision capacity in the total operational domain." Good, bureaucratic, hand-washing gibberish, to be supported by a set of plausible fictions, cosmetic subtleties that Alice and the KEs would have to institute to find out whether they had any effect at all.

Alice was puzzled. "Is that it, Jerry? It's not much."

"I'm sorry, Alice. I've done what I could. If you're not satisfied, you ought to get someone else."

The rest of the meeting was brief. Toshi stopped me in the corridor afterward. "You seem troubled," he said. "Also reticent. I want to assure you that even complex problems can most often be worked out to mutual satisfaction." He let that statement lie—his attempt to bring me into the charmed circle of *ringi seido,* the process of joint consultation that is the soul of Japanese decision making. It was a nice gesture but meaningless. I just wasn't feeling Japanese.

I went to my compartment, where she was waiting. Her skin was hot to the touch. A last time, in seeming slow motion, we came together. She had just begun her period, and with her blood we traced scarlet arabesques across the sheets, across our thighs. Standing in the shower stall, I started to wash the blood away, but I didn't.

The tug fell from high orbit. ICOG had arranged a rendezvous below with a military shuttle. I touched the small crusts at the back of my neck, where her nails had punctured me, where she had clasped me. She still did.

The transfer came, and my pallet was shifted into the shuttle's cargo bay. Delta wings folded back, the shuttle entered the upper atmosphere somewhere over Hawaii. White ash from the tear-off thermal shielding flew past the viewport amid coruscations of red fire. Thin air played high-pitched cacophonies on the hull.

I loved her; I told her that. And I said, "You're not a monster; don't ever think it. Do what you must."

Leaving her with a platitude . . . I didn't tell her that nature abhors a vacuum, that everywhere she wasn't, was full of pain.

Flash of white light in the mind's eye, picture of a door opening, of something astonishing, its shape unclear, passing through. "Evolutionary emergence," Doctor Chin had said, but I doubted he would find it. He wasn't looking in the right places.

The Ark

By Bruce McAllister

> No one so strong, no one
> so lovely
> in all the things of this world
> as the eagle
> ready for flight and
> the jaguar
> whose heart is a mountain.
>
> — Aztec poem

It took them twenty years to die. Not the fifty or one hundred the forecasters had imagined, but twenty. There were rumors of gene-splicing experiments gone wild. Rumors of ecological chain reactions more complex than the world's finest biologists could understand. Rumors of extortion — chemical and biological blackmail — against the natural resources of Africa, Asia, South America, even

North America. The rumors of accidents and pure anar-
chic terrorism — poisonings of antelope herds in North
America, toxic rain at the Kenyan National Parks, epidem-
ics in the Jersey Zoo on the British Channel Islands — were
not rumors at all. They were fact, Beckman knew.

The animals began to die. They died exponentially. They
died in their natural habitats and in the confines of wild-
animal parks and zoos. There were suddenly new strains of
resistant bacteria, new strains of virus. New organ col-
lapses from toxicity, new, unforeseen breeding problems. It
was a tidal wave of death, and it took two decades. He had
seen it in the figures even then, given his training, while
others had not.

In ten years, one hundred thousand species were gone
from the earth, only the genetic material of the more for-
tunate left — in cryogenic ice.

One by one, like prison doors slamming, the world's
zoos converted. One by one, like the fastest Centric
printers, the petitions began, the mediations, the rankings,
the race to get places on the arks for the species left alive.

But the arks were full.

The New York Zoological Society had a waiting list of
three thousand. The National Zoo in Washington, eight
thousand. The Basel Zoo, two thousand. The Darwin
Center in the Galapagos, eight hundred fifty. The London
Zoo, four thousand five hundred. The Alberta game farm,
two thousand five hundred. The Woburn Wild Animal
Farm in Britain, three thousand two hundred. The Phoenix Zoo, one hundred thirty. The Gladys Porter Zoo, two
thousand four hundred. The San Diego Wild Animal
Park, five thousand three hundred. There were seven hundred ten arks, and all were full. Test-tube births, artificial
insemination, and cross-species surrogates had not been
enough, and the dreams of cloning, genetic engineering

for adaptation, and pharmaceutical miracles remained dreams.

Within twenty years five hundred thousand species were gone, and the number was rising.

Lawrence Beckman was a systems analyst for one of the three largest aerospace firms in Southern California. He had been one for fifteen years. He had been born in Los Angeles, had never left, but had married a woman from a distant country—and this, he realized now, was like leaving, very much like leaving. He was Caucasian. He was the only child of a late second marriage. He was a widower.

That was all, and it was not enough.

It could not keep his daughter alive.

He withdrew their savings, a little more than fifteen thousand dollars. He contacted his stockbroker to have the few stocks they owned—another four thousand dollars—liquidated. The bank, at his request, made out a cashier's check for nineteen thousand dollars to the Los Angeles Zoo in Griffith Park.

His daughter, See Chee, stood beside him as he did this. He could feel her pressed against him as they watched the voice-activated teller type the check for them. She was shaking. He tried not to feel it. He thought instead of her labored breathing at night, all the times he had had to waken her in the last two months, afraid he wouldn't be able to.

They went together to the ancient post office in their little town, where they mailed the check in an old-fashioned business envelope with a covering letter that read: "Sirs and Madams: Here is a start. If you will make a place at your zoo for Li Chu and her baby Chu Li, the two pandas that the People's Republic of China has offered you in good faith, we will send you four hundred dollars monthly. We also promise to campaign energetically in our community and in others toward raising a fund of thirty thousand dollars annually for the perpetual care of these precious animals."

Many of the words were See Chee's. She was only ten, but she had gotten good at this, and he felt pride.

The check was returned in a week.

Attached was a letter expressing the zoo's appreciation but explaining how climate control alone for two animals like the "Mandarin pandas" would reach ten thousand dollars per year, and how there were medical, dietary, security, and facility overhead costs as well. The letter did not give a total figure. It did not need to.

When he went to her bedroom later that day, it was not homework she was doing on her terminal. She had the facemaker program in again, her back hunched to him, and was drawing one of the pandas on her screen. Its features told him it was the mother, Li Chu. The face was familiar, and he could see that she was working from a color printout on the floor by her stool.

He took a step toward her, but she erased it before he could reach her.

When she turned, her dark arms in her lap, he saw how red her eyes were.

"You don't have to hide it," he said.

She said nothing. She averted her eyes, found another program, booted it, and began her homework.

When he went to her room that night to tuck her in, she was asleep. The screen glowed eerily in the darkness, a new face staring back at him, the hesitant smile more human than animal. The bearlike head, the big, oval eyes, sad bandit mask, broad, black nose—the features they both knew so well. When he stepped up to the screen to erase it, he found he could not. It was hers. It bothered no one. It was the best night-light she could have, and unlike some things in their lives, it was still alive, and he just could not do it.

He awoke that night from the terrible silence in the house, rose in fear, rushed through the darkness, struck himself painfully against a wall, and finally reached her room. She was still breathing.

He slept on the floor by her bed, where he could hear the sibilant whisper of her lungs and know she still lived.

There in the darkness he could imagine her round moon face, her straight black hair, and the epicanthic folds of her almond-shaped eyes. He could see her mother, May Nagua, his wife. He could imagine her people under the towering Annamite Cordillera, on the cratered Plain of Jars, in the shadowy Laotian highlands—their eyes, their full lips, their straight hair, their fear. Lying there, he felt their fear.

She did not awake crying that night, and he did not have to waken her. But at breakfast it began again, and there was nothing he could do. He could not even get out of his chair; he could not go to her again and hold her. He could not move. He could only think of the catalog-ordered carbine lying wrapped in an old flower-print sheet in the darkness of his closet.

The next night, as he lay on her floor, he heard her breathing stop twice.

May Nagua was a nurse when he first met her, and a nurse when she died. It was in a hospital in Inglewood, and the week he was admitted for prostatitis, she took very good care of him. It was the first time he had ever been away from his work. It was the first time his shy manner had not gotten in the way with a woman.

May Nagua lived with her family in Fountain Valley, to the south, in the Hmong community there. It was a large family, with a chief, Chief Yuur. Even now, few of them spoke English well, fewer still had careers like May Nagua's. She spoke English very well: she had a career in the round-eyed world. But like the others, she felt it. The fear. It was a new world, these United States. It was so new that sometimes the Hmong, who called themselves the Free People, died in their sleep . . . from the fear. The doctors did not understand it. It was "respiratory arrest." It was a "cardiac nerve conduction problem." It was the same *bangungut* syndrome that had killed young men in the Philippines for centuries. It was the defoliants or nerve agents used in the war. The doctors just did not know, though some agreed: It was the fear.

They had felt it in China two hundred years ago and had fled to Laos because of it. There, only thirty years ago, they had felt it again: They had fought America's "Secret War" against the bloody Pathet Lao, and now the invading North Vietnamese were going to kill them for it . . . and so, as if to say thanks, America's CIA had gotten them out. The Free People were in Montana now, in Seattle, in Providence, and in Southern California. The older men and women still wore brass bracelets, were superstitious about colors, and told stories about animals that talked like people. The children wore clothes from Fedco and Target, T-shirts with the names of rock groups, and were good at the fast games you could play on machines like television sets. But even now the men and women, young and old, might die in their sleep. A sound at night, the troubled breathing, a breathless body in the morning. Like May Nagua's brother. Like her grandfather.

They felt it even now: the fear.

She had been told, so many times: Do not leave the hospital alone at night, May Nagua. Do not leave the car doors unlocked if you are going to travel surface streets. Do not leave the freeway for surface streets even if there is congestion. Do not stop on the way home, except for gas—don't even stop for gas. Fill your tank at home. Do not stop anywhere, for anything. It is a dangerous world out there, May Nagua, he had said again and again, and she seemed to believe him, and finally he stopped worrying. "It's a dangerous world out there," he said to her one day, cheerfully, joking at last. "Seventy-five percent of Los Angeles is *minorities!*" But she looked at him so confused that he was sorry he had ever said it—even as a joke.

She died downtown—out of gas—near a park—taken as she walked the few blocks to phone him, perhaps to ask him what she should do.

Not long after he saw what was happening, he took his daughter to San Diego, to the Twelfth World Conference on Breeding Endangered Species in Captivity. They sat together in folding chairs on the sun-washed grounds of old Balboa Park—only blocks from the famous zoo—and listened carefully to somber men and women speak of "invalid depression," "the founder effect," and "genetic drift." There were no television cameras this time, few videotext reporters, and the audience was sparse.

He watched See Chee closely, wondering how much she understood. Could she see it? Could she see what it meant—the weakening by captive inbreeding, feeble genes bred to feeble genes, the pairs too weak to start their kind over again? How the only sciences that offered hope were still far in the future?

She was, he saw, doing her best to understand. She was a good girl. He thought of the day—one Saturday in a smoggy summer—when a little girl had come running into the house, brushing at her leg with a frantic hand, tears everywhere. "Was on my leg!" she'd cried. "Was on my leg!" It was all she could say. "What was on your leg, Daughter?" May Nagua had asked, holding her daughter's hands in hers like little birds as if to tame them. See Chee had answered: "A *straitjacket,* Mommy! A big yellow and black *straitjacket!*" Her mother had smiled, he had laughed, and See Chee had only cried more, so he had stopped. They had hugged her, made soothing sounds, and together, like a little army, had gone outside to find the new wasp nest in the rafters and to rid the world, once and for all, of the terrible yellow and black "straitjackets," the only animals she said she did not love.

Then it was a yellow moon he was seeing, over a littered park downtown, where they'd found the body, and he was tearing away from it, yelling inside, forcing himself to listen to the man who was speaking now in the bright sunlight of Balboa Park, where everything said was said without hope.

That night, as she lay in bed, he told her the story of "The Beginning of the World," the first of the many Hmong folktales May Nagua had known by heart in two tongues. It began: "The first man on Earth was Lou Tou. His wife was See Chee. They came from a door in a mountain . . ."

When he was through, because See Chee asked him to, he sang her favorite song, the one that began, "We went to the Animal Fair . . . the birds and the beasts were there . . . the old baboon by the light of the moon . . . was combing his auburn hair. . . ."

That night he dreawmed of an animal fair, of a tiger, and a gun.

At the funeral—a long, quiet affair with beautiful ceremonial dress and many words spoken by Chief Yuur, the entire community in attendance—the chief found Beckman and spoke to him. With a calm more terrible than any rage would have been, this broad-faced man—this "gatekeeper" of his people—said: "You took her away, Lawrence Beckman. Now she is dead. This is how it happens. Now there is a child who has neither world and no mother. You will be the mother she does not have, and you will do it the best you can." When Beckman finally turned, all the faces were watching, waiting for an explanation he could not give.

It was four months after the funeral that See Chee began to show excessive interest in the pandas, whose plight he and she had witnessed on their living-room screen.

Within a month it was clear to him that she was living for the endangered pair. When he took her to a professional, the woman said, "She exhibits what we call a posttraumatic stress syndrome, Mr. Beckman. Her mother's death was a trauma and she is working that trauma out with an equation. In this equation the infant panda and panda mother have become your daughter and your wife. If she can keep them alive she can feel, psychologically speaking, that her own mother never died. If the pandas die, your wife is indeed gone, and your daughter should be dead, too. That is what she is feeling, Mr. Beckman. It is a 'survivor's guilt'—not unlike what combat veterans experience."

He did not know what to say. He waited, and the woman went on: "We must work to help her understand that this equation—aesthetic as it may be psychodynamically—is a fantasy, that pandas are animals—not people—that in the end they really do not matter. That she—your daughter—is what matters to those who love her." He nodded and managed to ask about the breathing.

"I am not familiar with the syndrome you describe," the

woman answered, "but I wouldn't worry, Mr. Beckman. Your daughter is only a child. If I'm not mistaken, the Laotian refugee syndrome you describe afflicts only adult males. But I can certainly look into it if you would like me to."

He nodded and left. He was alone; they both were alone. Words meant nothing.

The professionals weren't there at night to hear the labored breathing, to hear it stop, to waken his daughter and make the breathing begin again. They weren't there in the day to watch the tears and shaking, the inability to concentrate, the obsession. They could not possibly understand.

If the two animals were allowed to die—if they could not be saved, if a place could not be found for them somewhere—then his daughter would die, too, in the night, like all the others.

It took him six calls. He was shaking, but in the end he got them the appointment, and for a moment he could see some hope in her eyes and could imagine that her breathing slowed.

The Lós Angeles Zoo was where it had always been—in a small "wilderness" area toward the center of the city. But the oil wells had been eating into that wilderness for twenty years, and the zoo was not what it had once been. The wells bobbed and dipped like stiff birds a mere hill away from the zoo compound, and the domes inside looked like blue insect hives, all life hidden from view. He had brought her here twice when she was younger—to this "Animal Fair." May Nagua had been with them.

There was little traffic as they approached. The bridge and the main gate it led to—such hazy memories from his own childhood—were still there, but the crowds were not. The public wasn't really invited. You could apply for a visitor's pass, yes, and visit with a group. But you would wait six months, and when your day finally came there would be metal detectors, voice-stress analyzers, and trained dogs sniffing for the poisons some crazy might try to bring in for the animals of this ark.

The magic, the sense of wonder, was gone. Yet no one complained. What mattered now was that at least two of each kind somehow went on eating, sleeping, and, whenever possible, breeding behind the blue walls, the armies of attending nutritionists, vertebrate biologists, epidemiologists, and veterinarians all looking on, guarding against a virulent world.

The curator's office was on the fourth floor of the new administration building. Through the window of the receptionist's office they could look down on the compound below, dome after dome, pleasant green tarmac walkways and what landscaping remained. The eucalyptus, oleander, sand pines from Turkey and Africa—these were trees the air couldn't kill. As he stared at them, his daughter's hand in his, he felt a breeze through the glass and behind his eyes saw ghostly squirming things, tawny bodies—memories that were not his of wild continents, bright birds exploding from dark rain forests, icy waters where white predators basked in the light of a hundred suns. . . . Then tarmac again, blue domes, trees, shrubs somehow holding on.

He was still holding See Chee's hand, his own hands unsteady, and the curator was in his office doorway at last, addressing him, saying, "Mr. Beckman, I really don't know what I can do for you. My assistant, John Neumann, tells me he spoke with you at some length last week."

He was not going to let them in.

"Yes," Beckman said.

The curator stared back. It was a white, porous face

with the blush of broken capillaries. The eyes were a wonderful blue, round and with crow's-feet at the corners. The hair was white and wavy, making Beckman think of a snowy egret or, finer still, a snow leopard — both gone now.

"What I'm trying to say, Mr. Beckman," the man in the doorway was saying, "is that I'm not sure I know what I can do that hasn't already been done."

He wouldn't look at her, Beckman realized. She did not exist for him.

"You can let us sit down," Beckman said.

The man had little choice. As they sat, he took his place slowly behind a surprisingly clean teak-veneer desk.

"What we don't understand—" Beckman began, the script as clear to him as it would ever be.

"*We?*" the man stopped him. "You're referring to the girl?"

Beckman looked at See Chee, at her dark hair, moon face, wide eyes. When the anger came, he let it. He needed it.

"The *girl,* Mr. Ringer, is my daughter." To See Chee he said gently, "See Chee, this is Mr. Ringer—the man who runs this zoo."

She stood up graciously in her new white pantsuit, smiled, and said, "I am very pleased to meet you, Mr. Ringer." She offered him her brown hand, which he finally took. She knew how important this was. They had rehearsed it many times. It might all make a difference . . . with the right person. Sitting down, she kept her smile. It was someone else's smile, and Beckman had to look away.

"We are concerned about the pandas," he said quickly.

"Of course you are," the man answered, "but you both must understand—" his hands were folded on the desktop with wonderful control as he looked at the father, then the daughter—"that there are many, many animals and many,

many people petitioning for each. Every animal—"

He had his own script, Beckman saw. In it they were children. He had dealt with children like them before.

"Excuse me," Beckman said. "You talk of petitions. We hear constantly how important they are. Yet we also hear of animals awarded places at this zoo and others with petitions much shorter than those of many unplaced animals. Could you tell us why this is, Mr. Ringer?"

The curator smiled.

"The cases you're referring to, Mr. Beckman, are those where assessments by the scientific community carry special weight. You may be thinking of the *Trichechus* manatee, the parasitic wasps, or the so-called Houston toads—since these have received more than the usual attention in the media. As it turns out, Mr. Beckman, cases like these are much more frequent than anywhere the lay public has been able to, shall we say, 'vote' a species in?" The man paused. "I'm sure you're aware of what those assessments might be . . ."

It was, Beckman realized, a question.

When he did not answer, the curator answered for him:

"Genetic uniqueness, for one. Genetic diversity, for another. Genetic-engineering possibilities would be a third. There are many others, Mr. Beckman."

"Shouldn't—" Beckman began, stumbling, the script gone. "Shouldn't some special weight—" He stumbled again, and then somehow the script was there, and he was rushing with it: "Shouldn't some special weight be given to the votes of another group of 'experts'? I'm speaking here of the children's groups, the Scouts, the YWs and YMs, the petition clubs, the school groups like my daughter's, not to mention the zoological societies and wildlife federations whose memberships are primarily young people. These young people have been petitioning for the pandas for over two years now, ever since the day you and the other zoos in this country dropped them—whatever your reasons—from your priority lists. I'm speaking here of the hundreds of thousands, if not millions, of children and *their* expert votes." He took a breath. "I would like to suggest, Mr. Ringer, that children know best what animals they love, what animals should be kept in trust for them for a future neither you nor I will be around to see."

When the curator didn't interrupt, he continued quickly: "It completely astonishes me, Mr. Ringer, that our zoos—the very institutions once entrusted with instilling a love of wildlife in our children—can no longer hear a child's voice."

The silence lasted only a moment, and when the curator spoke, Beckman knew they had lost.

"That isn't quite fair, Mr. Beckman. But I suspect you know that." The man was calm. He was still smiling. "As you must be aware, children had considerable say in the selection last year, for this very zoo, of the California brown bear—a species of profound sentimental significance to the people of this state. We have eight healthy bears now, we're happy to report. They also had considerable say in the selection of the black-footed ferret—one of our most touted national treasures—for the Bronx Zoo, with six specimens. And the western sea otter for Marineland. And the harp seal for the National Zoo."

He paused for effect. "Animals that children happen to find charming because they have anthropoidal features or are otherwise 'adorable' are, I assure you, well represented in the arks of this nation—or as well represented as they can be, given the times we live in, Mr. Beckman."

Beckman felt his face grow hot. He could not look at the man. He started to rise, but the man was not through with him. The voice had changed. It was now, somehow,

172

full of compassion.

"Mr. Beckman, we do not have room in our zoos even for our *own* species. This zoo is ranked fourteenth in the nation by budget, yet we have two of the seven remaining specimens of the Hawaiian Kuauai oo, four of the remaining eighteen sandhill cranes in existence, and six of the remaining dozen *Canis lupis nobilis*. We even have, it pains me to say, two of the last eight *Haliaeetus leucocephalus*—simply because neither DC, nor San Diego, nor the Bronx, nor any of the other thirteen facilities ranked above us in budget have room for them. This is a national disgrace, Mr. Beckman. The two *Haliaeetus* specimens are sick. They are dying. They are victims of what specialists call inbreeding depression, and we cannot find a place for them in one of our finest arks."

Beckman marveled at the feeling in the man's voice, at the compassion for the poor *Haliaeetus leucocephalus*.

"You must certainly be aware," the man was continuing, pained, sympathetic, "that we have had the entire frustrating matter of your *Ailuropoda melanoleuca*—your two pandas—in mediation for over two years now. There are simply too few intensive-care spaces on the arks in this country. They are vacated only by death or by alterations in the priority lists. The U.S. mediation team—all trained scientists—has no vested interests. They have not only your two *melanoleuca* on their consciences, but·six thousand other species, as well. To this painful job they bring the most sophisticated of sciences—computer modeling, multivariant analysis, parallel processing . . . matters that I'm sure you, with your background, understand better than I, Mr. Beckman."

He said it gently.

But then the voice changed again.

"*They* are the ones who must decide which specimens

are of the greatest importance to mankind's future, Mr Beckman, and they have decided that your pandas are not. We are not speaking of the last two pandas in the world, Mr. Beckman. There are ten others in China. These two are not even a reproductive pair, Mr. Beckman." The man stared at him.

He could feel it rising in him, threatening to take him. The fear. Was See Chee feeling it too? Was she looking through the window, her breathing beginning to change? Was she drawing a panda's face behind her eyes, to make it go away? Was she remembering the stills, the videotexts, the pages and pages of printout on the anatomy, behavior, and needs of the *bei shung*, which she kept in her dresser drawers like snapshots . . . of someone she missed very much?

Then, to his surprise, he was standing; he was shouting at the man before him: *"Why in God's name isn't our own State Department — our God Almighty State Department — interested in those pandas, Mr. Ringer? Why isn't it in the best interests of our nation to grant those animals asylum — simply as a gesture — simply as a gesture to a nation as important to this world and our own future as China is? The cost of keeping the pandas alive is nothing — nothing! — in the face of national budgets, Mr. Ringer!"*

The office filled with silence. He could feel See Chee's eyes on him.

A look of pity passed across the curator's face.

"That is an interesting question, Mr. Beckman," he said. "Everything is symbolic in international intercourse, isn't it? Even animals. You have certainly touched on a truth that young people today — like your daughter — must understand as they make their way into a future neither you nor I will be around to see . . ." He paused for effect, then went on. "You ask about China, yet apparently you have not been keeping up with the finer points of the news?" Again it was a question.

"No," Beckman answered, looking down. "I have not."

"Apparently you have missed the subtle problems we are having with Pek Ziao and his glorious 'New Republic.' The press can be stupid at times, Mr. Beckman, but there were glimmers of this as much as two years ago." The voice was condescending. "I really do not understand how you could have missed it."

My wife, Beckman wanted to say. *My wife . . . my daughter . . .*

"The fact is," the man continued, "our trilateral economics are 'strained.' We are, so to speak, 'denormalizing relations' with the New Republic. We are not willing to risk what we have with considerable agony forged in Third World stability with Moscow. We are willing to make certain symbolic sacrifices—no matter how sincere the Chinese may be in their concern for their animals." He paused one last time. "I imagine the mediation team has been under considerable pressure, Mr. Beckman."

The words came so quickly.

What did the man mean?

"Does this answer your question?"

"What are you saying?" Beckman whispered.

"You know what I am saying."

"It isn't possible . . ."

"Of course it is possible, Mr. Beckman. Don't be naive."

It *was* possible—this, the simplest of explanations. All the rest—scientists, mediations, computer models—were meaningless in the face of it, the diplomatic game, the quiet war of nations where the casualties never knew it was a war.

He closed his eyes. See Chee was there and the pandas.

He saw epicanthic folds. He saw moon faces and almond eyes moving in a war through the shadows of the highlands. He saw diplomats arguing in teak-veneer rooms like this one, reviewing still photographs of the almond-eyed *bei shung*, shaking their heads while the sad eyes, the almond eyes looked on from the bamboo thickets unable to understand it even as the war fell around them.

He opened his eyes.

"How far are they from admission?" he asked quietly. "How many slots down the list are they?"

"Far too many, Mr. Beckman." The man was curt. He was standing now. He was not going to let it start up again.

"How many?" Beckman repeated.

"Eleven or twelve, I believe—but the exact number doesn't matter. It is not going to happen, and I refuse to encourage false hope. If you'll excuse me. . . ."

Beckman stared at him.

"Is it over?" See Chee whispered.

"Yes. It is over."

The man walked them to the door.

There, See Chee's hand in his—warm, alive—he turned one last time and said calmly, "I want to thank you for explaining it all, Mr. Ringer. I feel a little foolish for having bothered you and your staff like this." He made himself smile for the man.

"That's quite all right."

That night, when he heard her breathing stop twice and found he could not awaken her the second time without hurting her, he called the heli-medic and had her flown to the nearest teaching hospital seventy-five miles away. There, the doctors tested her, gave her medication, and watched her. They did not understand. They did not understand it any more than the first doctors had. They said so. It was a syndrome of some kind, they said, and when he finally left her in the hospital, his daughter was breathing normally again—but only because their tubes, their medications, their "intensive care" let her.

He stood in front of the bedroom mirror.

In his left hand he held a laser-aimed Ruger carbine with silencer and folding stock. In his right, a model 5-F "intruder flare" with six million lumens ready to go. At his hip there was an old .357 Colt Python, along with a pair of Black and Decker power cutters and a 5.53 transmitter for the charges. He had given the .223 Ruger carbine a matte-black finish. Everything that might reflect light had been sprayed, and he had smeared catalog-ordered nightblack under his eyes, across his forehead, over his chin. Under his black combat fatigues, catalog ordered like everything else, he was wearing ninth-generation Kevlar body armor and a heat-dissipating skin for infrared evasion.

It took him forty-five minutes to make his way from the oil wells to the zoo's perimeter. The moonlight, useful while he set the charges at the wells, was worthless in the shadows of the wilderness zone.

Setting the charges had gone smoothly, but it had taken thirty-six minutes, not fifteen. The two-meter chain-link fences with single-strand outriggers weren't wired for disturbance, and the wire cutters had gone through them like butter. What had delayed him was his own hands, fingers shaping the charges, setting the caps and receivers. For fifteen years his hands had touched nothing but software, feasibility studies, monthlies, and proposals, not RDX and Pentolites and lacing cord.

When he reached Zone One—the zoo's perimeter, the first fence—he stopped in the shadows of an ancient eucalyptus to catch his breath. The scent of the tree filled him, burning. His body ached. He hadn't used it in twenty years—since the dim racquetball days of his youth. The equipment was like lead weights strung all over him, and he thought of younger men carrying much more gear than this over the hills of long wars he had never been to.

The three-meter chain link with its six-strand outriggers and geophone disturbance sensors was dark, but the darkness was deceptive. There were lights that would flood the area instantly like a sun if the monitoring station to the north picked up a vertical disturbance on the chain link here. Still, it was the best spot. He had considered penetrating near the main gate, where the bridge and road accessed and any sensors of that kind would have to stop ten meters from them. But the bridge was floodlit, the road would have microwave detectors, and there would be CCT cameras in all that light.

He slipped the starlight goggles on, and the night turned green, the green ghost of the fence in front of him. From his utility belt he unclipped the power cutters and the transmitter, knelt on the fence's cement apron, and ignored the pain in his knee. Reading the transmitter's face with his fingers, he found the button for the first well and paused. The cutters trembled wildly in his right hand. He thought of See Chee.

When he pushed it, the detonation half a kilometer away shook the earth under him, screaming its way up through the geophone transducers in the fence to the monitoring station another kilometer away. To those monitors it would seem the perimeter fence was being assaulted simultaneously at every point on its eight-klick circumference—an impossibility. Earthquake would be the first assumption, but within seconds word of the oil-well explosion would reach the station, and his diversion would be accepted.

As the ground shook, he sliced easily through the chain link.

He scrambled through, tearing his fatigues. The earth glowed green in the goggles, and beyond the bare zone with the buried geophones—a miniature of what once kept the two Berlins apart on the other side of the world—he could see the fainter green ghost of the second fence, the buried sensors ending three meters from it. He had to keep the earth shaking under him for five seconds. His fingers found the second button, and even as he began to run, jammed it in with all their strength.

Under him the geophones screamed, the monitors got word of another explosion within seconds, and he was through the sensors, past them, only a meter now from the second green fence.

Locating most of the information had been easy. The literature was there if you knew where to look—in declassified Army field manuals, "survivalist" books and tapes, magazines and videotexts for law enforcers and adventurers—all obtainable through catalogs.

But before locating this information, there had been one important question: Which security system did the zoo use?

An acting assistant supervisor of operations for his firm, he had quietly called for a review of alternative security systems. Lists of testimonials for intrusion-detection systems became available, and on the sixth day he had found the Los Angeles Zoo under "total geophone systems."

The central monitoring station had radar, a helipad for check-and-chase just outside Zone One, and a Cesna 0-7 Vulcan intercept capability from a nearby airfield. The domes were state of the art: twin skins of laminated mylar, twin alloy super-structures and insulation doubling as shields — all wired for intrusion detection. Terrorists, contract operatives, crazies, or simple vandals — all had been factored into the system. But "intrusion" was not "sabotage." Like any high-security facility, this zoo used the proverbial two-man rule for personnel on the ground. Pressure mats, seismic sensors, and microwave eyes were killed during vet and feeder hours, and the hours were changed daily by computer.

The vet and feeder hours were the key. If he had misjudged too much, or if the monitors failed to ignore random sensor phenomena during the explosions, or if —

He was at the fence, the one that carried no sensors. It was only a physical barrier, there to buy time for an armed response force deployed to the point of penetration.

He cut the fence, took a breath, struggled through, and began trotting toward the service road that glowed green fifteen meters inside. Beyond the road he could see ghostly green landscaping writhing in the night from gusts of wind, and there, beyond the landscaping, towering domes the same ghostly green.

He looked back once at the oil fires now lancing the sky and moved toward the trees, the trees that looked so much like a jungle from someone's dream.

At the edge of the landscaping, he froze. His head jerked up, his heart crashing suddenly like an animal in his chest. The *whump-whump-whump* of helicopter blades filled the air above him, and he dropped to the ground, pressing his face into the earth, his gear biting into him painfully, stupidly. He held his breath, and when he finally opened his eyes he could see there were no searchlights, and now the sound was past, fading into the wilderness toward the flaming wells, replaced by the drone of a single-engine aircraft and the eerie ululation of distant sirens.

180

He got up, tasting dirt, and ran. He hugged the landscaping where geophones were worthless. He avoided cement, tarmac, handrails, posts — anything that might be wired with one of the five technologies all security systems used. He passed the first dome, running at a crouch, ignoring the pain in his chest.

He passed three domes, heading east, ignoring the pains everywhere.

Stopping, confused, he checked the digital map on his watch. The domes were identical. Those he chose had to be the right ones, or all was lost.

The monkeys, he thought. The monkeys and the aviary. No. It was dome forty-four — the deer family. The visitor's brochure had been clear enough.

He moved to the nearest dome, crouched in the darkness of the ghostly landscape, and studied the tarmac path that led past him to three other domes — thirty, sixty, and one hundred meters away. He would wait five minutes. He was giddy, had to make himself think. The vets, the vets, they would go about their business-detonations or no detonations, fires or no fires — and pressure mats, buried sensors and invisible barrier detectors would be off for forty-five minutes.

Now . . .

There were two figures approaching — two vets in lab coats, two green creatures with slithery green skin the color of chameleons in the ambient light of the moon. Both men carried small bags, and the little ground lights along the path lit up before them to show the way. The two creatures disappeared around the bend.

He ran awkwardly to the next dome, slowing as he approached the door. There, hands, shaking, he installed the microrecorder by the grill. Then he moved into the shadows of a large pepper tree and waited, listening to the rise and fall of the far sirens, the hammering of his heart, watching the glow of the sky over the wells.

When at last the two figures appeared on the path, it was from the opposite direction, and he saw they were a different pair. The new green creatures stopped at the door of the dome. He did not breathe.

They spoke—one, then the other—their voices muffled. Then the door slid open, and they went inside. When the door slid shut, he trotted stiffly from the shadows, grabbed the recorder from its hiding place, almost dropped it, and ran.

The tarmac path was dark here, the ground lights were off. He knew there was no one inside this dome. They might appear any minute, but at least he wouldn't find someone already inside. As he slowed to a trot, he rewound the tape.

At the door—the pressure mat asleep under him—he hesitated, hands shaking, then pushed the access button by the familiar grill. A tone sounded. Frantically he started the tape, shoving it at the grill.

"Bernard, Robert Lyman," the tape said, staid, professional, and then a second voice—flip, cockier: "Cohen, Benjamin Daniel, Doctor." The door purred open.

He could barely move his legs. The adrenaline made them wobbly, beyond his control, but he moved them, got inside, removed the starlight goggles and put on the infrared ones now.

In the goggles the world became hell.

Green ghosts gave way to grainy, burning forms from nightmares. He was in a red jungle, the trees a rain forest reaching toward a ceiling fifty meters up, heavy shapes moving lazily through the trees, smaller shapes flitting, gliding in the burning light, every living thing glowing with the fire of its own heat. Slowly he unslung the matte-black laser-aimed Ruger Mini with folding stock and thick silencer and held it before him, marveling at the violence of his own shaking. *How can you do this?*

He made himself think.

He thought of his daughter, his daughter's mother, and of himself.

He scanned the red rain forest for the heavy shape he had seen first. The animals he chose would have to be large, at least in intensive-care units; otherwise what he did would have no meaning. An adult *bei shung* weighed one-hundred-fifty kilos; they needed intensive care.

Whatever it was, it wasn't there now. A sloth, a large primate, two primates mating in the dark, an infant clinging to its mother.

You took her away, Lawrence Beckman. Now she is dead. This is how it happens.

He raised the Ruger's stock slowly to his shoulder, and there it was — as if waiting — the red shape stalking high in the trees above him.

Trembling, he aimed. He aimed again the red dot of the laser clear on the body.

He fired. He fired again.

As the heavy thing fell through the trees he turned in horror and ran. The pressure mat just inside the door sensed him, the door whispered open, and he was out free, sick, full of despair. There were eleven bodies left — *eleven . . .*

He ran through hell.

The next dome held another rain forest; a vision from an ancient Gustave Doré lithograph, lost paradise, inferno. This one teemed with miniature life but with nothing large enough. The rain forest hissed closed behind him, and he fled.

Bernard, Robert Lyman. Cohen, Benjamin Daniel,

Doctor.

In the third dome he found no primeval forest but instead individual cells with corridors he could run through. Plexiglas he could break, animals that could not get away from him. There were enough animals here, predators, primates, all in special cells. *Thank God.* His work might be done soon. *Predators. Carnivores.*

In the goggles he could see two animals asleep together, their heat making one living thing. The animals began to stir, waking as if somehow aware. Something about them made him think of monkeys, though he could not be sure. Wasn't it better not to be? Wasn't it better to think only of red fiery forms with faces from nightmares. Wasn't this how it had been for millennia—for men just like him? If the eyes were too much like a child's, the face like an old woman remembered, a wife, a brother, they would never do it. But they had always done it—the buttons, the bomb bays, the faceless faces, the prey always "the enemy." Wasn't this how it had always been?

Now there is a child who has neither world.

Nearly dropping the heat knife, he cut a hole in the Plexiglas just large enough for the barrel of the scope and silencer. Bile rose in his throat.

Now there is a child who has neither world.

He inserted the Ruger. He knelt. He squinted through the goggles at the red, waking shapes, broad faces returning his stare now, and he fired.

The report of the weapon was a sigh, the kick a bullet in his shoulder, which he deserved, and the animal fell writhing to the floor. It was screaming hideously.

He staggered back in terror, jamming the barrel in the Plexiglas, dropping it, backing up, backing up. Where had it come from—the screaming? He had heard only silence in his dreams. Somehow he had forgotten that what he killed — the eleven, the twelve — might howl at him or moan or cry or scream until the red, red heat of their bodies faded at last into eternal night.

But the animal that was screaming was not fading, and now its mate was up, scrambling back in terror, just as he was — away from the sound, from the smell of fear, and somehow he was firing. He had the Ruger up and aimed, and he was firing.

It took three rounds. The mate lay on the floor of the cage, made a single sound, and was still.

But it, too, continued to glow, and the anger of that light terrified him more.

The screaming would not end.

What have you done?

He felt little emotion now. There was work to do. He had twenty minutes or all was lost. He had calculated everything to the hundredths.

He ran the tape again, and another dome admitted him, and he did it.

He shot — someone shot — what looked like a water buffalo, was unable to find its mate, found instead a wingless bird with long legs. He — someone — shot it quickly, trying not to see it, imagining instead small countries, monsoons, rice paddies, bamboo thickets, and shadowed highlands.

Someone shot a doglike thing that howled at an invisible moon as it died, and as a face leapt up behind his eyes — from that howling, from a park, from a moon — he made it stop, made it go away. He thought of his daughter. He thought of his wife. Of the pandas, waiting.

He shot two nameless things in the last cells of that dome and was gone.

Later, he would remember entering the next two domes, but what he killed there — if he killed anything — he would not remember. It would seem to him later that he did, given events that followed, but he would not be able to remember their shapes, their sounds.

It was the seventh dome he would remember — nightmare after nightmare, flashback after flashback, even in the daylight years later. Even as he entered it, he understood somehow that this would be the end of the killing, that he would leave it, that he would make his way across the service road to the eastern fences, penetrate them quickly, and the two remaining charges would cover him.

This is how it happens. This is how.

As he entered the seventh dome — the one that would give the two children of China a home, that would keep his daughter on this earth with him — he felt thankful that it held no jungle, no rain forest where he could feel wild, ancient blood racing through him and wonder why, why. This one held only cells, intensive-care cell after cell, and he was thankful.

But as he entered it, he knew something was wrong. The red shapes in the tall cages were birds, large birds.

Was it the way they sat apart on the artificial limb? Was it something he sensed but could not see, something beyond the goggles' red glare? Was it something that whispered to him from the scales on their legs, the feathers, the pointed tongues he knew were in the darkness?

There were two of them, of course. Male and female. He removed the goggles and waited for his eyes to adjust. They did not. There was no light here, only darkness, the beginning and the end of all things.

He could sense them only a few meters above him now. They were hunkered on the limb, not touching each other. He knew this. He had seen this in the goggles.

They're sick, he realized.

How could he kill them like this? How could he do it this way?

He took the small flashlight from his belt and aimed it where he knew they were.

When he saw the first bird, he froze. *My God.*

This is how it happens. This is how.

As the beam of light struck the dying bird, he knew he should never have done it, should have kept the goggles on, shot them in the darkness, never used the little light. The feathers were nearly gone. The head wobbled gently. The yellow raptor beak was mottled and flaking from some disease, and the dark talons were arthritically stiff on the limb. Something crawled all over its face, the beak, the dry eyes—or was this his imagination?

Slowly he moved the light down the limb until he found the female.

A little smaller, her coloring like the male's despite what people believe, she sat trembling, alive but ill.

Haliaeetus leucocephalus.

He remembered the man saying it, though he hadn't understood it then.

Leuco cephalus. The white head. He knew that head as well as anyone. Like everyone, he had lived with it every day of his waking life—the coins, the bills, the stamps, seals, clutch of arrows, *e pluribus unum.* This was, after all, the bird—the predator—the one they had chosen two centuries before for the face of their nation . . . that their children's children might grow up knowing it every day of their waking lives . . . in a world like this.

Because Washington and San Diego and the others didn't have room—that was what the man had said.

Now there is a child who has neither world.

This is how it happens. This is how.

He thought of See Chee. He thought of himself, of his wife, her people, of wars and the deaths of sons, of littered parks and yellow moons, of the world and the mess they had made of it. He thought of the pandas last of all, and only then because he understood what they meant, what it all meant. He saw it clearly, and as he aimed he knew he would not be caught, that he would make it into the eastern interzone over the buried sensors there. That the charges would go off like the Fourth of July, that he would wander free in the wilderness for hours and make his way back to an empty house. That he would sit with his daughter before their living-room screen in the months ahead and listen to the story of how the pandas found a home (the "terrible coincidence" of it), that her breathing would not stop again, that she would grow up, get married or not, have children, live on into a future where some people loved and some did not, and where her own children would have all the animals—old and new—that the bright new sciences of the world could make.

He saw it all clearly, and as he did, understood what he had become.

When he shot them—when he saw the yellow beaks jerk up, eyes wide that it was at last over, the sickness and shame—he asked for their forgiveness, and the eagles gave it, and he knew he was shooting them out of a father's love.

Flying Saucer Rock & Roll

By Howard Waldrop

They could have been contenders.

Talk about Danny and the Juniors, talk about the Spaniels, the Contours, Sonny Till and the Orioles. They made it to the big time: records, tours, sock hops at $500 a night. Fame and glory.

But you never heard of the Kool-Tones, because they achieved their apotheosis and their apocalypse on the same night, and then they broke up. Some still talk about that night, but so much happened, the Kool-Tones get lost in the shuffle. And who's going to believe a bunch of kids, anyway? The cops didn't, and their parents didn't. It was only two years after the President had been shot in Dallas, and people were still scared. This, then is the Kool-Tones' story:

Leroy was smoking a cigar through a hole he'd cut in a pair of thick, red wax lips. Slim and Zoot were tooting away on Wowee whistles. It was a week after Halloween, and their pockets were still full of trick-or-treat candy they'd muscled off little kids in the projects. Ray, slim and nervous, was hanging back. "We shouldn't be here, you know? I mean, this ain't the Hellbenders' territory, you know? I don't know whose it is, but, like, Vinnie and the guys don't come this far." He looked around.

Zoot, who was white and had the beginnings of a mustache, took the yellow wax-candy kazoo from his mouth. He bit off and chewed up the big C pipe. "I mean, if you're scared, Ray, you can go back home, you know?"

"Nah!" said Leroy. "We need Ray for the middle parts." Leroy was twelve years old and about four feet tall. He was finishing his fourth cigar of the day. He looked like a small Stymie Beard from the old Our Gang comedies.

He still wore the cut-down coat he'd taken with him when he'd escaped from his foster home.

He was staying with his sister and her boyfriend. In each of his coat pockets he had a bottle: one Coke and one bourbon.

"We'll be all right," said Cornelius, who was big as a house and almost eighteen. He was shaped like a big ebony golf tee, narrow legs and waist blooming out to an A-bomb mushroom of arms and chest. He was a yard wide at the shoulders. He looked like he was always wearing football pads.

"That's right," said Leroy, taking out the wax lips and wedging the cigar back into the hole in them. "I mean, the kid who found this place didn't say anything about it being somebody's *spot,* man."

"What's that?" asked Ray.

They looked up. A small spot of light moved slowly across the sky. It was barely visible, along with a few stars, in the lights from the city.

"Maybe it's one of them UFOs you're always talking about, Leroy," said Zoot.

"Flying saucer, my left ball," said Cornelius. "That's Telstar. You ought to read the papers."

"Like your mama makes you?" asked Slim.

"Aww . . . ," said Cornelius.

They walked on through the alleys and the dark streets. They all walked like a man.

"This place is Oz," said Leroy.

"Hey!" yelled Ray, and his voice filled the area, echoed back and forth in the darkness, rose in volume, died away. "Wow."

They were on what had been the loading dock of an old freight and storage company. It must have been closed sometime during the Korean War or maybe in the unimaginable eons before World War II. The building took up most of the block, but the loading area on the back was sunken and surrounded by the stone wall they had climbed. If you stood with your back against the one good loading door, the place was a natural amphitheater.

Leroy chugged some Coke, then poured bourbon into the half-empty bottle. They all took a drink, except Cornelius, whose mother was a Foursquare Baptist and could smell liquor on his breath three blocks away.

Cornelius drank only when he was away from home two or three days.

"Okay, Kool-Tones," said Leroy. "Let's hit some notes."

They stood in front of the door, Leroy to the fore, the others behind him in a semicircle: Cornelius, Ray, Slim, and Zoot.

"One, two, three," said Leroy quietly, his face toward the bright city beyond the surrounding buildings.

He had seen all the movies with Frankie Lymon and the Teenagers in them and knew the moves backwards. He jumped in the air and came down, and Cornelius hit it: *"Bah-doo, bah-doo, ba-doo—uhh."*

It was a bass from the bottom of the ocean, from the Marianas Trench, a voice from Death Valley on a wet night, so far below sea level you could feel the absence of light in your mind. And then Zoot and Ray came in: *"Ooh-oooh, ooh-oooh,"* with Leroy humming under, and then Slim stepped out and began the lead tenor part of "Sincerely," by the Crows. And they went through that one perfectly, flawlessly, the dark night and the dock walls throwing their voices out to the whole breathing city.

"Wow," said Ray, when they finished, but Leroy held up his hand, and Zoot leaned forward and took a deep breath and sang: *"Dee-dee-woo-oo, dee-eee-wooo-oo, dee-uhmm-doo-way."*

And Ray and Slim chanted: *"A-weem-wayyy, a-weem-wayyy."*

And then Leroy, who had a falsetto that could take hair off an opossum, hit the high notes from "The Lion Sleeps Tonight," and it was even better than the first song, and not even the Tokens on their number-two hit had ever sounded greater.

Then they started clapping their hands, and at every clap the city seemed to jump with expectation, joining in their dance, and they went through a shaky-legged Skyliners-type routine and into: *"Hey-ahh-stuh-huh, hey-ahh-stuh-uhh,"* of Maurice Williams and the Zodiacs' "Stay," and when Leroy soared his *"Hoh-wahh-yuh?"* over Zoot's singing, they all thought they would die.

And without pause, Ray and Slim started: *"Shoo-de-doop, shoo-doop-do-be-doop, shoo-doopbe-do-be-doop,"* and Cornelius was going, *"Ah-rem-em, ah-rem-em, ah-rem-emm bah."*

And they went through the Five Satins' "(I Remember) in the Still of the Night."

"Hey, wait," said Ray, as Slim *"woo-uh-wooo-uh-wooo-*

ooo-ah-woo-ah"-ed to a finish, "I thought I saw a guy out there."

"You're imagining things," said Zoot. But they all stared out into the dark anyway.

There didn't seem to be anything there.

"Hey, look," said Cornelius. "Why don't we try putting the bass part of 'Stormy Weather' with the high part of 'Crying in the Chapel'? I tried it the other night, but I can't —"

"Shit, man!" said Slim. "That ain't the way it is on the records. You gotta do it like on the records."

"Records are going to hell, anyway. I mean, you got Motown and some of that, but the rest of it's like the Beatles and Animals and Rolling Stones and Wayne shitty Fontana and the Mindbenders and . . ."

Leroy took the cigar from his mouth. "Fuck the Beatles," he said. He put the cigar back in his mouth.

"Yeah, you're right, I agree. But even the other music's not the —"

"Aren't you kids up past your bedtime?" asked a loud voice from the darkness.

They jerked erect. For a minute, they hoped it was only the cops.

Matches flared in the darkness, held up close to faces. The faces all had their eyes closed so they wouldn't be blinded and unable to see in case the Kool-Tones made a break for it. Blobs of face and light floated in the night, five, ten, fifteen, more.

Part of a jacket was illuminated. It was the color reserved for the kings of Tyre.

"Oh, shit!" said Slim. "Trouble. Looks like the Purple Monsters."

The Kool-Tones drew into a knot.

The matches went out and they were in a breathing darkness.

"You guys know this turf is reserved for friends of the local protective, athletic, and social club, viz., us?" asked the same voice. Chains clanked in the black night.

"We were just leaving," said Cornelius.

The noisy chains rattled closer.

You could hear knuckles being slapped into fists out there.

Slim hoped someone would hurry up and hit him so he could scream.

"Who are you guys with?" asked the voice, and a flashlight shone in their eyes, blinding them.

"Aww, they're just little kids," said another voice.

"Who you callin' little, turd?" asked Leroy, shouldering his way between Zoot and Cornelius's legs.

A *wooooooo!* went up from the dark, and the chains rattled again.

"For God's sake, shut up, Leroy!" said Ray.

"Who you people think you are, anyway?" asked another, meaner voice out there.

"We're the Kool-Tones," said Leroy. "We can sing it slow, and we can sing it low, and we can sing it loud, and we can make it go!"

"I hope you like that cigar, kid," said the mean voice, "because after we piss on it, you're going to have to eat it."

"Okay, okay, look," said Cornelius. "We didn't know it was your turf. We come from over in the projects and . . ."

"Hey, man, Hellbenders, Hellbenders!" The chains sounded like tambourines now.

"Naw, naw. We ain't Hellbenders. We ain't nobody but the Kool-Tones. We just heard about this place. We didn't know it was yours," said Cornelius.

"We only let Bobby and the Bombers sing here," said a voice.

194

"Bobby and the Bombers can't sing their way out of the men's room," said Leroy. Slim clamped Leroy's mouth, burning his hand on the cigar.

"You're gonna regret that," said the mean voice, which stepped into the flashlight beam, "because I'm Bobby, and four more of these guys out here are the Bombers."

"We didn't know you guys were part of the Purple Monsters!" said Zoot.

"There's lots of stuff you don't know," said Bobby. "And when we're through, there's not much you're gonna *remember.*"

"I only know the Del Vikings are breaking up," said Zoot. He didn't know why he said it. Anything was better than waiting for the knuckle sandwiches.

Bobby's face changed. "No shit?" Then his face set in hard lines again. "Where'd a punk like you hear something like that?"

"My cousin," said Zoot. "He was in the Air Force with two of them. He writes to 'em. They're tight. One of them said the act was breaking up because nobody was listening to their stuff anymore."

"Well, that's rough," said Bobby. "It's tough out there on the road."

"Yeah," said Zoot. "It really is."

Some of the tension was gone, but certain delicate ethical questions remained to be settled.

"I'm Lucius," said a voice. "Warlord of the Purple Monsters." The flashlight came on him. He was huge. He was like Cornelius, only he was big all the way to the ground. His feet looked like blunt I beams sticking out of the bottoms of his jeans. His purple satin jacket was a bright fluorescent blot on the night. "I hate to break up this chitchat —" he glared at Bobby — "but the fact is you people are on Purple Monster territory, and some tribute needs to be exacted."

Ray was digging in his pockets for nickels and dimes.

"Not money. Something that will remind you not to do this again."

"Tell you what," said Leroy. He had worked himself away from Slim. "You think Bobby and the Bombers can sing?"

"Easy!" said Lucius to Bobby, who had started forward with the Bombers. "Yeah, kid. They're the best damn group in the city."

"Well, *I* think we can outsing 'em," said Leroy, and smiled around his dead cigar.

"Oh, jeez," said Zoot. "They got a record, and they've — "

"I *said,* we can outsing Bobby and the Bombers, anytime, any place," said Leroy.

"And what if you can't?" asked Lucius.

"You guys like piss a lot, don't you?" There was a general movement toward the Kool-Tones. Lucius held up his hand. "Well," said Leroy, "how about all members of the losing group drink a quart apiece?"

Hands of the Kool-Tones reached out to stifle Leroy. He danced away.

"I like that," said Lucius. "I really like that. That all right, Bobby?"

"I'm going to start saving it up now."

"Who's gonna judge?" asked one of the Bombers.

"The same as always," said Leroy. "The public. Invite 'em in."

"Who do we meet with to work this out?" asked Lucius.

"Vinnie of the Hellbenders. He'll work out the terms."

Slim was beginning to see he might not be killed that night. He looked on Leroy with something like worship.

"How we know you guys are gonna show up?" asked Bobby.

"I swear on Sam Cooke's grave," said Leroy.

"Let 'em pass," said Bobby.

They crossed out of the freight yard and headed back for the projects.

"Shit, man!"

"Now you've done it!"

"I'm heading for Florida."

"What the hell, Leroy, are you crazy?"

Leroy was smiling. "We can take them, easy," he said, holding up his hand flat.

He began to sing "Chain Gang." The other Kool-Tones joined in, but their hearts weren't in it. Already there was a bad taste in the back of their throats.

Vinnie was mad.

The black outline of a mudpuppy on his white silk jacket seemed to swell as he hunched his shoulders toward Leroy.

"What the shit you mean, dragging the Hellbenders into this without asking us first? That just ain't done, Leroy."

"Who else could take the Purple Monsters in case they wasn't gentlemen?" asked Leroy.

Vinnie grinned. "You're gonna die before you're fifteen, kid."

"That's my hope."

"Creep. Okay, we'll take care of it."

"One thing," said Leroy. "No instruments. They gotta get us a mike and some amps, and no more than a quarter of the people can be from Monster territory. And it's gotta be at the freight dock."

"That's one thing?" asked Vinnie.

"A few. But that place is great, man. We can't lose there."

Vinnie smiled, and it was a prison-guard smile, a Nazi smile. "If you lose, kid, after the Monsters get through with you, the Hellbenders are gonna have a little party."

He pointed over his shoulder to where something resembling testicles floated in alcohol in a mason jar on a shelf.

"We're putting five empty jars up there tomorrow. That's what happens to people who get the Hellbenders involved without asking and then don't come through when the pressure's on. You know what I mean?"

Leroy smiled. He left smiling. The smile was still frozen to his face as he walked down the street.

This whole thing was getting too grim.

Leroy lay on his cot listening to his sister and her boyfriend porking in the next room.

It was late at night. His mind was still working. Sounds beyond those in the bedroom came to him. Somebody staggered down the project hallway, bumping from one wall to another. Probably old man Jones. Chances are he wouldn't make it to his room all the way at the end of the corridor. His daughter or one of her kids would probably find him asleep in the hall in a pool of barf.

Leroy turned over on the rattly cot, flipped on his seven-transistor radio, and jammed it up to his ear. Faintly came the sounds of another Beatles song.

He thumbed the tuner, and the four creeps blurred into four or five other Englishmen singing some other stupid song about coming to places he would never see.

He went through the stations until he stopped on the third note of the Monotones' "Book of Love." He sang along in his mind.

Then the deejay came on, and everything turned sour again. "Another golden oldie, 'Book of Love,' by the Monotones. Now here's the WBKD pick of the week, the fabulous Beatles with 'I've Just Seen a Face.' " Leroy pushed the stations around the dial, then started back.

Weekdays were shit. On weekends you could hear good old stuff, but mostly the stations all played Top 40, and that was English invasion stuff, or if you were lucky, some Motown. It was Monday night. He gave up and turned to an all-night blues station, where the music usually meant something. But this was like, you know, the sharecropper hour or something, and all they were playing was whiny cotton-choppin' work blues from some damn Alabama singer who had died in 1932, for God's sake.

Disgusted, Leroy turned off the radio.

His sister and her boyfriend had quit for a while, so it was quieter in the place. Leroy lit a cigarette and thought of getting out of here as soon as he could.

I mean, Bobby and the Bombers had a record, a real big-hole forty-five on WhamJam. It wasn't selling worth shit from all Leroy heard, but that didn't matter. It was a record, and it was real, it wasn't just singing under some street lamp. Slim said they'd played it once on WABC, on the *Hit-or-Flop* show, and it was a flop, but people heard it. Rumor was the bombers had gotten sixty-five dollars and a contract for the session. They'd had a couple of gigs at dances and such, when the regular band took a break. They sure as hell couldn't be making any money, or they wouldn't be singing against the Kool-Tones for free kicks.

But they had a record out, and they were working.

If only the Kool-Tones got work, got a record, went on tour. Leroy was just twelve, but he knew how hard they were working on their music. They'd practice on street corners, on the stoop, just walking, getting the notes down right — the moves, the facial expressions of all the groups they'd seen in movies and on Slim's mother's TV.

There were so many places to be out there. There was a real world with people in it who weren't punching somebody for berries, or stealing the welfare and stuff. Just someplace open, someplace away from everything else.

He flipped on the flashlight beside his cot, pulled it under the covers with him, and opened his favorite book. It was

Edward J. Ruppelt's Report on *Unidentified Flying Objects*. His big brother John William, whom he had never seen, sent it to him from his Army post in California as soon as he found Leroy had run away and was living with his sister. John William also sent his sister part of his allotment every month.

Leroy had read the book again and again. He knew it by heart already. He couldn't get a library card under his own name because the state might trace him that way. (They'd already been around asking his sister about him. She lied. But she too had run away from a foster home as soon as she was old enough, so they hadn't believed her and would be back.) So he'd had to boost all his books. Sometimes it took days, and newsstand people got mighty suspicious when you were black and hung around for a long time, waiting for the chance to kipe stuff. Usually they gave you the hairy eyeball until you went away.

He owned twelve books on UFOs now, but the Ruppelt was still his favorite. Once he'd gotten a book by some guy named Truman or something who wrote poetry inspired by the people from Venus. It was a little sad, too, the things people believed sometimes. So Leroy hadn't read any more books by people who claimed they'd been inside the flying saucers or met the Neptunians or such. He read only the ones that gave histories of the sightings and asked questions, like why was the Air Force covering up? Those books never told you what was in the UFOs, and that was good because you could imagine it for yourself.

He wondered if any of the Del Vikings had seen flying saucers when they were in the Air Force with Zoot's cousin. Probably not, or Zoot would have told him about it. Leroy always tried to get the rest of the Kool-Tones interested in UFOs, but they all said they had their own problems, like girls and cigarette money. They'd go with him to see *Inva-*

sion of the Saucemen or *Earth Vs. the Flying Saucers* at the movies, or watch *The Thing* on Slim's mother's TV on the *Creature Feature,* but that was about it.

Leroy's favorite flying-saucer sighting was the Mantell case, in which a P-51 fighter plane, which was called the Mustang, chased a UFO over Kentucky and then crashed after it went off the Air Force radar. Some say Captain Mantell died of asphyxiation because he went to 20,000 feet and didn't have on an oxygen mask, but other books said he saw "something metallic and of tremendous size" and was going after it. Ruppelt thought it was a Skyhook balloon, but he couldn't be sure. Others said it was a real UFO and that Mantell had been shot down with Z-rays.

It had made Leroy's skin crawl when he had first read it.

But his mind went back to the Del Vikings. What had caused them to break up? What was it really like out there on the road? Was music getting so bad that good groups couldn't make a living at it anymore?

Leroy turned off the flashlight and put the book away. He put out the cigarette, lit a cigar, went to the window, and looked up the airshaft. He leaned way back against the cool window and could barely see one star overhead. Just one star.

He scratched himself and lay back down on the bed.

For the first time, he was afraid about the contest tomorrow night.

We got to be good, he said to himself. *We got to be good.*

In the other room, the bed started squeaking again.

The Hellbenders arrived early to check out the turf. They'd been there ten minutes when the Purple Monsters showed up. There was handshaking all around, talk a little while, then they moved off into two separate groups. A few civilians came by to make sure this was the place they'd heard about.

"Park your cars out of sight, if you got 'em," said Lucius. "We don't want the cops to think anything's going on here."

Vinnie strut-walked over to Lucius.

"This crowd's gonna be bigger than I thought. I can tell."

"People come to see somebody drink some piss. You know, give the public what it wants . . ." Lucius smiled.

"I guess so. I got this weird feelin', though. Like, you know, if your mother tells you she dreamed about her aunt, like right before she died and all?"

"I know what feelin' you mean, but I ain't got it," said Lucius.

"Who you got doing the electrics?"

"Guy named Sparks. He was the one lit up Choton Field."

At Choton Field the year before, two gangs wanted to fight under the lights. So they went to a high-school football stadium. Somebody got all the lights and the P.A. on without going into the control booth.

Cops drove by less than fifty feet away, thinking there was a practice scrimmage going on, while down on the field guys were turning one another into bloody strings. Somebody was on the P.A. giving a play-by-play. From the outside, it sounded cool. From the inside, it looked like a pizza with all the topping ripped off it.

"Oh," said Vinnie. "Good man."

He used to work for Con Ed, and he still had his I.D. card. Who was going to mess with Consolidated Edison? He drove an old, gray pickup with a smudge on the side that had once been a power-company emblem. The truck was filled to the brim with cables, wires, boots, wrenches, tape, torches, work lights, and rope.

"Light man's here!" said somebody.

Lucius shook hands with him and told him what they

wanted. He nodded.

The crowd was getting larger, groups and clots of people drifting in, though the music wasn't supposed to start for another hour. Word traveled fast.

Sparks attached a transformer and breakers to a huge, thick cable.

Then he got out his climbing spikes and went up a pole like a monkey, the heavy *chunk-chunk* drifting down to the crowd every time he flexed his knees. His tool belt slapped against his sides.

He had one of the guys in the Purple Monsters throw him up the end of the inch-thick electrical cable.

The sun had just gone down, and Sparks was a silhouette against the purpling sky that poked between the buildings.

A few stars were showing in the eastern sky. Lights were on all through the autumn building. Thanksgiving was in a few weeks, then Christmas.

The shopping season was already in full swing, and the streets would be bathed in neon, in holiday colors. The city stood up like big, black fingers all around them.

Sparks did something to the breakdown box on the pole.

There was an immense blue scream of light that stopped everybody's heart.

New York City went dark.

"Fucking *wow!*"

A raggedy-assed cheer of wonder ran through the crowd.

There were crashes, and car horns began to honk all over town.

"Uh, Lucius," Sparks yelled down the pole after a few minutes. "Have the guys go steal me about thirty automobile batteries."

The Purple Monsters ran off in twenty different directions.

"Ohhhyyyhhyyh," said Vinnie, spitting a toothpick out of

his mouth. "The Monsters get to have all the fun."

It was 5:27 P.M. on November 9, 1965. At the Ossining changing station, a guy named Jim was talking to a guy named Jack.

Then the trouble phone rang. Jim checked all his dials before he picked it up.

He listened, then hung up.

"There's an outage all down the line. They're going to switch the two hundred K's over to the Buffalo net and reroute them back through here. Check all the load levels. Everything's out from Schenectady to Jersey City."

When everything looked ready, Jack signaled to Jim. Jim called headquarters, and they watched the needles jump on the dials.

Everything went black.

Almost everything.

Jack hit all the switches for backup relays, and nothing happened.

Almost nothing.

Jim hit the emergency battery work lights. They flickered and went out.

"What the hell?" asked Jack.

He looked out the window.

Something large and bright moved across a nearby reservoir and toward the changing station.

"Holy Mother of Christ!" he said.

Jim and Jack went outside.

The large bright thing moved along the lines toward the station. The power cables bulged toward the bottom of the thing, whipping up and down, making the stanchions sway. The station and the reservoir were bathed in a blue glow as the thing went over. Then it took off quickly toward Manhattan, down the straining lines, leaving them in complete darkness.

Jim and Jack went back into the plant and ate their lunches.

Not even the phone worked anymore.

It was really black by the time Sparks got his gear set up. Everybody in the crowd was talking about the darkness of the city and the sky. You could see stars all over the place, everywhere you looked.

There was very little noise from the city around the loading area.

Somebody had a radio on. There were a few Jersey and Pennsy stations on. One of them went off while they listened.

In the darkness, Sparks worked by the lights of his old truck. What he had in front of him resembled something from an alchemy or magnetism treatise written early in the eighteenth century. Twenty or so car batteries were hooked up in series with jumper cables. He'd tied those in with amps, mikes, transformers, a light board, and lights on the dock area.

"Stand clear!" he yelled. He bent down with the last set of cables and stuck an alligator clamp on a battery post.

There was a screeching blue jag of light and a frying noise. The lights flickered and came on, and the amps whined louder and louder.

The crowd, numbering around five hundred, gave out with prolonged huzzahs and applause.

"Test test test," said Lucius. Everybody held their hands over their ears.

"Turn that fucker down," said Vinnie. Sparks did. Then he waved to the crowd, got into his old truck, turned the lights off, and drove into the night.

"Ladies and gentlemen, the Purple Monsters . . ." said

Lucius, to wild applause, and Vinnie leaned into the mike, "and the Hellbenders," more applause, then back to Lucius, "would like to welcome you to the first annual piss-off—I mean, sing-off—between our own Bobby and the Bombers," cheers, "and the challengers," said Vinnie, "the Kool-Tones!" More applause.

"They'll do two sets, folks," said Lucius, "taking turns. And at the end, the unlucky group, gauged by *your* lack of applause, will win a prize!"

The crowd went wild.

The lights dimmed out. "And now," came Vinnie's voice from the still blackness of the loading dock, "for your listening pleasure, Bobby and the Bombers!"

"Yayyyyyyyyyyy!"

The lights, virtually the only lights in the city except for those that were being run by emergency generators, came up, and there they were.

Imagine frosted, polished elegance being thrust on the unwilling shoulders of a sixteen-year-old.

They had on blue jackets, matching pants, ruffled shirts, black ties, cuff links, tie tacks, shoes like obsidian mortar trowels. They were all black boys, and from the first note, you knew they were born to sing:

"Bah bah," sang Letus the bassman, *"doo-doo duh-duh-doo-ahh, duh-doo-dee-doot,"* sang the two tenors, Lennie and Conk, and then Bobby and Fred began trading verses of the drifters' "There Goes My Baby," while the tenors wailed and Letus carried the whole with his bass.

Then the lights went down and came up again as Lucius said, "Ladies and gentlemen, the Kool-Tones!"

It was magic of a grubby kind.

The Kool-Tones shuffled on, arms pumping in best Frankie Lymon and the Teenagers fashion, and they ran in place as the hand-clapping got louder and louder, and they leaned into the mikes.

They were dressed in waiters' red-cloth jackets the Hell-benders had stolen from a laundry service for them that morning. They wore narrow black ties, except Leroy, who had on a big, thick, red bow tie he'd copped from his sister's boyfriend.

Then Cornelius leaned over his mike and: *"Doook doook doook doookov,"* and Ray and Zoot joined with *"dook dook dook dookov,"* into Gene Chandler's "Duke of Earl," with Leroy smiling and doing all of Chandler's hand moves. Slim chugged away the *"iiiiiiiiyiyiyiiiii's"* in the background in runs that made the crowd's blood cold, and the lights went down. Then the Bombers were back, and in contrast to the up-tempo ending of "Duke of Earl" they started with a sweet tenor a cappella line and then: *"woo-radad-da-dat, woo-radad-da-dat,"* of Shep and the Limelites' "Daddy's Home."

The Kool-Tones jumped back into the light. This time Cornelius started it off with *"Bomp-a-pa-bomp, bomp-pa-pa-bomp, dang-a-dang-dang, ding-a-dong-ding,"* and into the Marcels' "Blue Moon," not just a hit but a mere monster back in 1961. And they ran through the song, Slim taking the lead, and the crowd began to yell like mad halfway through. And Leroy—smiling, singing, rocking back and forth, doing James Brown tantrum-steps in front of the mike—knew, could feel, that they had them; that no matter what, they were going to win. And he ended with his whin-ning part and Cornelius went *"Bomp-ba-ba-bomp-ba-bom,"* and paused and then, deeper, *"booo mooo."*

The lights came up and Bobby and the Bombers hit the stage. At first Leroy, sweating, didn't realize what they were doing, because the Bombers, for the first few seconds, made this churning rinky-tink sound with the high voices. The bass, Letus, did this grindy sound with his throat. Then the Bombers did the only thing that could save them, a white boy's song, Bobby launching into Del Shannon's "Runaway," with both feet hitting the stage at once. Leroy thought he could taste that urine already.

The other Kool-Tones were transfixed by what was about to happen.

"They can't do that, man," said Leroy.

"They're gonna cop out."

"That's impossible. Nobody can do it."

But when the Bombers got to the break, this guy Fred stepped out to the mike and went: *"Eee-de-ee-dee-eedle-eee-eee, eee-deee-eedle-dee, eedle-dee-eeedle-dee-dee-dee, eewheetle-eeedle-dee-deeedle-dee-eeeee,"* in a spitting falsetto, half mechanical, half Martian cattle call — the organ break of "Runaway," done with the human voice.

The crowd was on its feet screaming, and the rest of the song was lost in stamping and cheers. When the Kool-Tones jumped out for the last song of the first set, there were some boos and yells for the Bombers to come back, but then Zoot started talking about his girl putting him down because he couldn't shake 'em down, but how now, *he* was back, to let her know. . . . They all jumped in the air and came down on the first line of "Do You Love Me?" by the Contours, and they gained some of the crowd back. But they finished a little wimpy, and then the lights went down and an absolutely black night descended. The stars were shining over New York City for the first time since World War II, and Vinnie said, "Ten minutes, folks!" and guys went over to piss against the walls or add to the consolation-prize bottles.

It was like halftime in the locker room with the score Green Bay 146, You 0.

"A cheap trick," said Zoot. "We don't *do* shit like that."

Leroy sighed. "We're gonna have to," he said. He drank

from a Coke bottle one of the Purple Monsters had given him. "We're gonna have to do something."

"We're gonna have to drink pee-pee, and then Vinnie's gonna de-nut us, is what's gonna happen."

"No, he's not," said Cornelius.

"Oh, yeah?" asked Zoot. "Then what's that in the bottle in the clubhouse?"

"Pig's balls," said Cornelius. "They got 'em from a slaughterhouse."

"How do you know?"

"I just know," said Cornelius, tiredly. "Now let's just get this over with so we can go vomit all night."

"I don't want to hear any talk like that," said Leroy. "We're gonna go through with this and give it our best, just like we planned, and if that ain't good enough, well, it just ain't good enough."

"No matter what we do, ain't gonna be good enough."

"Come on, Ray, *man!*"

"I'll do my best, but my heart ain't in it."

They lay against the loading dock. They heard laughter from the place where Bobby and the Bombers rested.

"Shit, it's dark!" said Slim.

"It ain't just us, just the city," said Zoot. "It's the whole goddamn U.S."

"It's just the whole East Coast," said Ray. "I heard on the radio. Part of Canada, too."

"What is it?"

"Nobody knows."

"Hey, Leroy," said Cornelius. "Maybe it's those Martians you're always talking about."

Leroy felt a chill up his spine.

"Nah," said Slim. "It was that guy Sparks. He shorted out the whole East Coast up that pole there."

"Do you really believe that?" asked Zoot.

"I don't know what I believe anymore."

"I believe," said Lucius, coming out of nowhere with an evil grin on his face, "that it's *show time*."

They came to the stage running, and the lights came up, and Cornelius leaned on his voice and: *"Rabbalabbalabba ging gong, rabbalabbalabba ging gong,"* and the others went *"wooooooooooooo"* in the Edsels' "Rama Lama Ding Dong." They finished and the Bombers jumped into the lights and went into: *"Domm dom domm dom doobedoo, dom domm dom dobedoobeedomm, wahwahwahwahhh,"* of the Del Vikings' "Come Go With Me."

The Kool-Tones came back with: *"Ahhhhhhhhaahhwoooowoooo, ow-ow-ow-ow-owh-woo,"* of "Since I Don't Have You," by the Skyliners, with Slim singing in a clear, straight voice, better than he had ever sung that song before, and everybody else joined in, Leroy's voice fading into Slim's for the falsetto *weeeeoooooow's* so you couldn't tell where one ended and the other began.

Then Bobby and the Bombers were back, with Bobby telling you the first two lines and: *"Detooodwop, detooodwop, detooodwop,"* of the Flamingos' "I Only Have Eyes for You," calm, cool, collected, assured of victory, still running on the impetus of their first set's showstopper.

Then the Kool-Tones came back and Cornelius reared back and asked: *"Ahwunno wunno hooo? Be-do-be-hooo?"* Pause.

They slammed down into "Book of Love," by the Monotones, but even Cornelius was flagging, sweating now in the cool air, his lungs were husks. He saw one of the Bombers nod to another, smugly, and that made him mad. He came down on the last verse like there was no one else on the stage with him, and his bass roared so loud it seemed there wasn't a single person in the dark United States who didn't wonder who wrote that book.

And they were off, and Bobby and the Bombers were on now, and a low hum began to fill the air. Somebody checked the amp; it was okay. So the bombers jumped into the air, and when they came down they were into the Cleftones' "Heart and Soul," and they *sang* that song, and while they were singing, the background humming got louder and louder.

Leroy leaned to the other Kool-Tones and whispered something. They shook their heads. He pointed to the Hellbenders and the Purple Monsters all around them. He asked a question they didn't want to hear. They nodded grudging approval, and then they were on again, for the last time.

"Dep dooomop dooomop doomop doo ooo, ooowah oowah ooowah ooowah," sang Leroy and they all asked "Why Do Fools Fall in Love?" Leroy sang like he *was* Frankie Lymon—not just some kid from the projects who wanted to be him—and the Kool-Tones *were* the Teenagers, and they began to pull and heave that song like it was a dead whale. And soon they had it in the water, and then it was swimming a little, then it was moving, and then the sonofabitch started spouting water, and that was the place where Leroy went into the falsetto *"wyyyyyyyyyyyyyyyyyyyyyyyyy,"* and instead of chopping it where it should have been, he kept on. The Kool-Tones went *ooom wahooomwah* softly behind him, and still he held that note, and the crowd began to applaud, and they began to yell, and Leroy held it longer, and they started stamping and screaming, and he held it until he knew he was going to cough up both his lungs, and he held it after that, and the Kool-Tones were coming up to meet him, and Leroy gave a tantrum-step, and his eyes were bugging, and he felt his lungs tear out by the roots and come unglued, and he held the last syllable, and the crowd wet

211

itself and—

The lights went out and the amp went dead. Part of the crowd had a subliminal glimpse of something large, blue, and cool looming over the freight yard, bathing the top of the building in a soft glow.

In the dead air the voices of the Kool-Tones dropped in pitch as if they were pulled upward at a thousand miles an hour, and then they rose in pitch as if they had somehow come back at that same thousand miles an hour.

The blue thing was a looming blur and then was gone.

The lights came back on. The Kool-Tones stood there blinking: Cornelius, Ray, Slim, and Zoot. The space in front of the center mike was empty.

The crowd had an orgasm.

The Bombers were being violently ill over next to the building.

"God, that was *great!*" said Vinnie. "Just great!"

All four of the Kool-Tones were shaking their heads.

They should be tired, but this looked worse than that, thought Vinnie. They should be ecstatic. They looked like they didn't know they had won.

"Where's Leroy?" asked Cornelius.

"How the hell should I know?" Vinnie said, sounding annoyed.

"I remember him smiling, like," said Zoot.

"And the blue thing. What about it?"

"What blue thing?" asked Lucius.

"I dunno. Something was blue."

"All I saw was the lights go off and that kid ran away," said Lucius.

"Which way?"

"Well, I didn't exactly see him, but he must have run some way. Don't know how he got by us. Probably thought you

212

were going to lose and took it on the lam. I don't see how you'd worry when you can make your voices do that stuff."

"Up," said Zoot, suddenly.

"What?"

"We went up, and we came down, Leroy didn't come down with us."

"Of course not. He was still holding the same note. I thought the little twerp's balls were gonna fly out his mouth."

"No. We . . ." Slim moved his hands up, around, gave up. "I don't know what happened, do you?"

Ray, Zoot, and Cornelius all looked like they had thirty-two-lane bowling alleys inside their heads and all the pin machines were down.

"Aw, shit," said Vinnie. "You won. Go get some sleep. You guys were really bitchin'."

The Kool-Tones stood there uncertainly for a minute.

"He was, like, smiling, you know?" said Zoot.

"He was always smiling," said Vinnie. "Crazy little kid."

The Kool-Tones left.

The sky overhead was black and spattered with stars. It looked to Vinnie as if it were deep and wide enough to hold anything. He shuddered.

"Hey!" he yelled. "Somebody bring me a beer!"

He caught himself humming. One of the Hellbenders brought him a beer.

Dreams Unwind

By Karl Hansen

Risa and I worked the penthouse of the Hotel Ganymede.
Jupiter shone a baleful red overhead. Hydrogen clouds
shimmered with starlight. A woman hung naked in the center of the room, wrists and ankles secured by silver shackles
chained to magbolts. She was true human and was young
and lovely; mahogany skin, gleaming almost ocher in jovelight; long hair shining like spun gold; eyes as bright as
fractured emeralds. Her legs were long and lithe, her stomach was flat, her breasts were still tumid with adolescence.
White teeth bit into her lower lip. Blood beaded along their
edges. She writhed in her bonds but could not pull free.

A man faced the woman, also naked. He too was of
unaltered terran stock but could not be called lovely; radiation scars puckered his skin; one eye did not close completely. A skin cancer grew like lichen from his right cheek.
His hair was close-cropped and once must have been black
but was now sprinkled with white from damaged melanocy-
tes. Bulky muscles had become flabby with neglect. His

name was Hitt.

The man used to ply an honest trade: gunrunning for the various insurgent hybrids of most of the Outer Moons. He was quite wealthy from it. Now he was retired.

The girl was a high-priced callbody. A deal with her broker was made a short time ago. So far, all had gone accordingly.

Hitt held an alphalash. Glowing filaments dropped like a horsetail of optical fibers. Protons dripped from their ends to bounce on the floor. The girl's eyes vibrated vertically, transfixed by the bounding protons. Arm muscles flexed. Ionized air shrieked as the alphalash swung its arc. Ozone fumed into sharp olfactory tendrils. Shedded sparks danced like dust motes in a moonbeam.

Breath whistled from the girl's nostrils.

The lash touched naked flesh; skin twitched into wrinkled blisters, then relaxed. Glowing lines burned into the skin where each filament of the lash touched; energized protons became embedded in epidermis, where they slowly shed their energy into pain receptors. Neurons then carried a symphony of hurt. No discipline was as painful as the proton whip. *How did I know that,* I wondered? The girl did not cry out from the first lash. The alphalash descended again and again. Each time it struck, Hitt became more excited.

I was lounging across the room on a couch. Though Hitt could not see me, I looked like a true human: one hundred eighty centimeters tall, sturdily muscled, haughty gray eyes, aquiline nose, chestnut hair, lips that could be cruel. But I was not human. Risa prowled like a cat through drawers and closets, collecting valuables. She was not human either. Her ermine fur had a silver sheen. When she smiled, sharp teeth flashed. Amber eyes, with pupils contracted into vertical slits, glowed with their own light. She appeared standard sphinx, save the quivering tendrils about her head.

Though the callbody appeared human, she was not real. She was an illusion.

A figment of my imagination only knew as much as I let it. A magician's image was conjured for his pleasure and for the confusion of his audience.

There were no snoopers around; both Hitt and I had made sure of that. Neither of us wanted witnesses to the night's activities. If there were any, a ring on my finger broadcast a field that would confuse their sensors.

Risa discovered the wall safe behind a mutaholo. She glanced in my direction and smiled. I nodded.

Hitt split into two images. One ghost continued thrashing. The other walked over to the safe and placed its palm on the sensing surface while staring into a retinal camera. Hitt would not remember any of this. Clever psychesurgery might be able to dredge it up, but not without damaging quite a bit of memory. The safe swung open. Hitt fused into one figure again and continued whipping the girl. Risa looted the safe. She held up her thumb. Time to end this psidrama.

By now the callbody was completely covered with ionic fire. Every square centimeter of skin was alight with a webwork of deacaying protons. She did not scream of beg for mercy. That made Hitt furious. He was even more brutal with his lashing.

Hitt's reaction was predictable. His psychopathology was quite conventional. I envied him that. I wished I could be as sure of my motives. But I couldn't. My past had been constructed for the convenience of the Corps. What dim recollections existed prior to my conscription could not be trusted and were as unsubstantial as dreams.

But if I didn't know myself, I did know Hitt. His rage at the girl's silence caused the alphalash to whip with a frenzy, seeking tender places. Her skin burned in an incandescent reticulum. I let the girl slump in her shackles, as though he had killed her. (Some dim sense of déjà vu disturbed me. I had an uncanny feeling I had seen all this before, as though we were repeating an old ritual. I pushed the discomfort away.)

Even the girl's apparent death did not appease Hitt's anger. He slapped her across the face, again and again. She did not respond. He suspected she was feigning. He kicked her. Her body rocked in its chains in synchrony with his kicks. The girl's face changed into another's rouge-red cheeks white acrylic skin, poker-chip blue eyes, curls of yellow yarn, button nose. A doll's face. The visage angered me. I did not know why it should. But I was furious at Hitt.

Protons fled the girl's skin, embedding themselves in Hitt's foot. He screamed and stopped kicking her. His foot flamed with ionic fire. He could not stand the pain. He grabbed a sonic knife and cut off his own extremity. But even that did not free him. Neurons remembered and sang with phantom pain. Hitt sank to the floor, moaning.

Before we left, I sent one final scene into Hitt's mind: He hauled the callbody into the shower and cut it into manageable pieces, which were fed to the dispoz unit.

Risa and I were safe. I took her hand, and we walked out the door. Hitt's thought swirled after us, confused with pain. Yet within his raveling mind tapestry, there was a locked weave. He kept some secret from us. No matter. We had beaten him. Hitt would never report the robbery; he thought he had a murder to conceal from the varks. He would not want to bring suspicion to himself. Our larceny would never be investigated.

Safe in our own room, we made love.
Risa lay beside me on a bed of wombskin in the Nyssa

Suite of the Hotel Ganymede. There were eleven similar suites, each named after one of the ancient city-states on Earth. They formed a crystal duodecagon atop the hotel's main spire, which rose two thousand meters from the floor of Chalise Crater to protrude through hydrocarbon mists into clear, cold space.

Overhead, Jupiter hung like an injected eye. Below, wisps of yellow fog lapped over the edge of the crater to swirl like wraiths across pocked terrain. A room with a view, the desk clerk had said. It ought to have one for what the hotel charged. But we wanted to be in proximity to the rich. The rich were the only ones worth pandering to and preying on. Besides, the varks wouldn't be expecting us to stay in a suite of the most expensive hotel in the system. If any vice vark had followed us from Titan, he'd be expecting Risa and me to hole up in some seamy icehouse in the combat zone.

But no one had followed. I'd made sure of that. The ferret who'd made us in Chronus City was now drooling and staring blankly at his toes. He'd been brave but stupid. He hadn't been wired: no hardware in his skull, no cameras behind his eyes, no bugs in his ears. All his data were stored in software, including the only evidence against us. A big mistake. It would take the psychesurgeons a year to bring his mind out of its autistic fugue. And each of their psionic manipulations would result in a few hippocampal synapses shorting out. By the time he awoke, he'd be lucky to remember his name, much less the identity of the path team that had once prowled is dream-time. Risa and I would never be traced from Titan to Ganymede. We'd already scored big with Hitt; ten million in cash not to mention gems and drugs. Chalise was ripe for the taking; our prey was everywhere, perversions were pandered.

My hand stroked along her spine, smoothing ermine fur; she arched her back in rhythm. Static sparked blue between my fingers. With my other hand, I traced faint vibrations in her throat, smoothing away the contractions. Her eyes closed halfway, their irises caught and held jovelight like shattered amber.Instead of hair, silver filaments grew from her scalp, now quivering like fuzz on a thistle head. But they could lay flat and would then be mistaken for the mane of a sphinx. Her nostrils flared as she breathed.

She rolled over and kneeled above me, straddling my body with hands and knees. She bent to kiss me, a rough tongue slipped past my lips. Furry breasts pressed against my chest. I closed my eyes. We wandered the psychic ether, riding updrafts of thought. Our mind's eye searched below for prey. I looked for Hitt. He should still be in his room above ours. But the room was empty. I expanded the search. His thought patterns were nowhere to be found. How could he hide form our psychic senses? Only the dead were safe from us.

Don't worry, Risa said in my thoughts. *Hitt no longer matters. We have other prey.*

Is he dead?

No, just hiding. She laughed, almost a growl in my ear. *I'll explain later. Forget about him. The sea is filled with other fish tonight.*

She settled down, coupling, then rocked gently up and down. Her mucosal neurons interfaced with my cutaneous ones. My mind meshed with hers, our psychic sensorium expanded. We flew as one over Chalise, soaring among bright tendrils of thought.

See how many fish?

Our talons plucked only the amber fibrils, bringing them close to our face. We touched our tongue to shining filament, tasting fear, while our nostrils sniffed its acrid scent. We listened to terrified voices calling to an uncaring sky. Our eyes traced each filament back to its source, back to a living mind. The filaments unraveled there into a dream tapestry of a pathetic creature quivering with fright. There was prey aplenty for dream hunters.

Tonight's hunt is finished. Let's save prey for later.

We fell back to our room; our sensorium contracted to include only our coupled bodies. We made love as one body, finally quivering with parasympathetic discharge. The climax could have come from one or both of us; no matter, it was perceived in unison.

We separated, two minds coalesced out of one, two bodies close but untouching.

I watched her eyes roll back, her tongue dart in and out between her lips.

I envied her the ability to fall asleep so quickly, like an innocent animal. I was jealous of those genes. Sleep did not comes as quickly for me. Her breathing slowed, became deeper and regular. Soon her eyelids fluttered with fasciculations of REM beneath. She dreamed.

I wished I could dream her dreams. How wonderful they must be, from what little she would tell me; animal dreams filled with moving air and warm sunlight and the smells of Earth. As a pathic gestalt, we could share out thoughts but for some reason not our dreams. Perhaps it was for the best. Some secrets are needed.

Later, I finally dozed. Images rose in my sleep-lulled brain: A baby suckled contentedly at his mother's breast, only to open his eyes and find he was really clinging to a wire mannequin with a rubber nipple protruding through the mesh; ghost children argued over a doll, pudgy hands tugged on plastic arms and legs until they were disjointed and the doll's torso and head fell to the ground; doll's eyes swung back and forth, conjuring dreams out of their hypnotic rhythm.

I woke with my skin afire. Protons danced on my body like St. Elmo's fire. I thrashed about, trying to put out the fire. Risa woke also. She pinned me down with her hands and began licking me with her tongue. With each rough stroke, a little fire was extinguished. She started with my face and worked down my body. Gradually, I relaxed.

You can stop now. It was only a dream.

Just a little longer. She laughed. *I like the salt in your sweat.*

Okay.

Eventually she was finished. We lay side by side. "I dreamed again of being alphalashed," I said. "A spook officer was doing it to me. I couldn't see her face, but I think it was Kaly. I was never flogged in the Corps. They knew better than to try that, so why do I dream about it? Guilt over deserting?"

"That's the conventional interpretation."

"Why Kaly?"

"Because you are afraid of her."

"I suppose." I looked at Risa. "Tell me about your dreams," I asked.

She closed her eyes. This was a nightly ritual with us.

"They're hard to describe. I don't think they're supposed to be described, because they originated in nonverbal minds. There are images—quite vivid—and odors and scents and tactile sensations."

"Do I ever appear?"

"Sometimes." She laughed. "I pounce on you and eat you. What do you say to that?"

"I guess that's the best way to be eaten. Do you ever dream of Colonel Kaly?" Kaly had been our commander when we were in the Corps. Now she was looking for us.

"My dreams have forgotten her."

"I wish mine had."

She didn't answer.

Eventually the room lightened with Ganymede's artificial dawn. With the shadows gone, I could sleep undisturbed for a little while. But night always waited.

Risa began to purr.

We had spent the day in our room making love, dozing intermittently with the troubled sleep of nocturnal creatures. Now it was night again. Our time had come. We shunned daylight, even the artificial kind. Illusion is harder to maintain in the light of day.

Risa was a xenohybrid. Her recombinant DNA had been derived from several biotypes: cat, dog, bird, insect. I envied her diverse ancestry; each species brought along its own racial memories. She had dreams I could not imagine. I was an allohybrid; although my DNA was still entirely human, it had also been blended by genosurgeons. My dreams were human dreams but not pleasant ones. I cared too much for Risa to want her to glimpse my dream-time.

And neither of our dreams were really our own, our real memories had been wiped out by psychesurgeons. We had been given synthetic persona to replace our own—just the essentials—and a childhood was not essential. As far as we could remember, we were born out of the hybertanks. Our lives began with conscription into the Corps.

I can't remember how many times I'd asked the chameleon officer who commanded us to tell me who I was and what I'd done to deserve a hitch in the Corps. Kaly always refused, laughing, saying it was better for morale that I not know.

Do you ever wonder about who you were before? I asked Risa, already knowing the answer. But sometimes words are needed.

Occasionally.

223

How much do you remember?

She hesitated. *No more than you. A few fragments, a few bad dreams. A few glimpses of a place on Earth where I once must have lived. I think I must have killed someone once. Why, I don't know. But a face sometimes bothers me in dreams. Not often now. Usually my dreams are quite pleasant.*

You don't want to know more?

Not now. That self no longer matters because I am no longer her and can never be her again. I don't have to be sorry for what she did. I don't have to feel guilty for her crimes. I'm someone else now. I have another past with different ancestors. I have dreams of soaring in the air, prowling in the moonlight, stalking prey, mating with uncomplicated passion.

Is that enough?

It's enough for me. My animal genes have brought dreams enough. I have better instincts now. From my cat genes.

What do your cat genes tell you to do now?

They make me want to prowl at night. She leapt from the bed and landed lightly on the windowsill across the room, balancing herself in front of the window. Her eyes watched the pleasure domes of Chalise far below. Stroboscopic reflections winked from her pupils. Psi tendrils quivered as they probed the psychic ether.

Overhead night deepened. I closed my eyes. Specters rose from hippocampal graves, disturbed by circadian winds. They thought the dream-time was close. They couldn't frighten me now, not while I was awake. Ghosts could frighten only sleeping children. Terror came only in the dreams. I didn't sleep at night anymore. Demons were easier to take in the light of day.

I snapped a mnemone stick and sucked its vapors deep

into my lungs. Euphoria burned in my mind.

I got up and stood behind Risa. She continued to peer out the window, crouching on all fours. I kissed the back of her legs, nuzzling soft fur with my lips. I moved upward, rubbing my cheek against her rump. She remained tense, caught up in hunt.

I knelt behind her, cupping fur-covered breasts in my hands, and entered her. Mucosal surfaces contained more induction neurons than cutaneous ones, since they were no more than modified tactile receptors. Mucosal contact produced the best pathic gestalt. I lay my head between her shoulders and joined the hunt.

Myriad thoughts swirled through the ether, like a million gleaming threads wafting in the wind. We moved among them, watching, listening, sniffing each in turn. Then we found the scent for which we searched. We crouched low to the ground, the fur bristled along our back, and our tail was held upright with only the tip twitching back and forth. We followed the mental scent back to its source, slowly and cautiously, so as not to spook our quarry. We'd hunted thus many times. Fear was easy to find and easier to foster. The simple, superstitious tribesmen on Mars had been helpless to resist our sophistication. We terrorized their dream-time; their chiefs and medicine men had prophetic visions of doom that demoralized them, so they were helpless when our combrid troops attacked. But now Risa and I hunted for ourselves.

We had been together for five years: four in the Combrid Corps as an LRT team on Mars and one as a freelance path team. Technically, we had deserted from the Corps when the Martian Rebellion collapsed; we hadn't bothered to muster out. A discharge from the Corps included debriefing and demilitarization. The Lord Generals didn't want civilians running around with full military hardware or software;

they tended to become mercenaries in future rebellions. But the Lord Generals didn't want to pay idle soldiers either. Their solution was simple: D and D—debre and demil. Debre wasn't bad, psychesurgeons wiped out both Corps hypnotraining and all memories laid down since conscription. Demil was more unpleasant; cybersurgeons ripped out any removable hardware and snipped through muscle and nerve tissue to bring a combrid down to standard terran. Then cosmesurgeons gave you back your original appearance—approximately. But Risa's and my military tissue was mostly gray matter. On the outside, save her almost normal mane, Risa looked like an ordinary sphinx. I appeared to be standard terran. Only our insides were different, primarily our brains. So D and D for us meant a little neurosurgery to disrupt classified synapses. Then a spot in a vegetable patch. No thanks. Even being a hunted fugitive was better than that.

Besides, it was kind of fun to match wits with the vice varks. We'd been afraid the spooks of Corps Intelligence would come after us, especially Kaly. Spooks made me nervous. They were chameleons. They had plastic tissue and could change both shape and appearance at will, becoming any other hybrid or individual they wanted. The perfect disguise. Quite useful when you wanted to infiltrate the enemy. But what made them even more dangerous, especially from a path team's viewpoint, was that they also had incredible control over their thoughts. When a spook assumed a cover, he organized his mind into the identity of the cover, with a complete set of memories. His own psyche was buried so deep and linked so tightly with limbic nuclei, he would die before any incongruous thoughts could give him away. Even a path team could be fooled by a spook.

But in the year we had been on our own, we'd yet to encounter a chameleon—just dim-witted vice varks. Hardly the match of a trained Long Range Terror team, a pair of fear hunters late of the First Psyche Division. Risa was the empath; she peeped minds to discover what primal terrors lurked in their dream-time. I was the telepath who sent those hippocampal fears back to the cerebral cortex and magnified them. It's quite demoralizing to be tormented by the one thing you far most, be that ghosts, goblins, snakes, rats, fire, wind, or whatnot. Mere illusion? Maybe so. But the demons I conjured were more terrifying than if they had been real. They evoked instinctive fear that a rational mind was helpless to defend against, simply because the fears themselves were irrational. I only wished I was not cursed to have to remember all the fears myself.

But Risa could seek out other feelings. And I could create other illusions besides fear.

Her flanks began quivering beneath me. Something other than starlight gleamed in her eyes. We had located our quarry. He was quite near and was unsuspecting. We could surprise him.

We hunted close to home tonight.

The door to our suite, the Nyssa, opened into a small foyer, across which was a liftube. We stepped in and dropped slowly, holding hands to keep from getting separated. Our prey was still in his room. We followed his chanting thoughts, entered his mind, and examined his memories.

Several floors down, we switched to the uptube, although no living eyes saw this. Our images still drifted down.

Those same living eyes saw a child dressed in a blue satin gown floating up the other tube, carrying a cat in its arms. Only Risa and I knew otherwise.

The child stepped out of the liftube at the two hundred forty-ninth level, and into the foyer of the Ophir Suite, which was directly opposite the Nyssa Suite. It—the child's

sex was not apparent — touched a finger to the annunciator.
A few seconds later, the door dilated open. The child
stepped through. Before the door closed, Risa and I also
entered, darting through as quick as specters, unseen by
living eyes.

An Entropist monk sat in lotus on the floor, facing the
door. He stopped chanting. He wore only the lavender robes
of his order. His shaven skull gleamed with oil; his eyes
shone with their own green fire. Though he had taken personal vows of poverty, this monk was hardly destitute. He
was a money courier. The Entropic Church financed most
of the rebellions against good old Mother Earth. This monk
was delivering a fortune to one of those rebellions. He was
to make delivery later tonight, after his amusement.

The child bowed low. The white cat leapt out of its arms
and began to prowl about. "You desire comfort tonight,
Brother Monk?" it asked formally.

The monk nodded his head.

The child touched its fingers to opposite shoulders. The
gown slipped into a pile at its feet. It stepped out, placing
one hand on its hip and the other over its head with index
finger pointed down, and it spun about slowly. It seemed to
be an ordinary human child of about ten years of age, a little
long of leg and somewhat potbellied. Its features were an-
drogynous: upturned button of a nose, rosy cheeks, eyes
sapphire blue, short curls of flaxen hair.

It completed its spin and faced the monk, then advanced
closer, stopping a few centimeters from the monk's crossed
legs. It spread it knees and thrust its pelvis out. A tiny penis
dangled there. Then penis and scrotum retracted involuting
into immature female genitalia: hairless mound, undeveloped labia, rudimentary clitoris.

A figment of my imagination? Hardly. An illusion, yes.
But the image was based on reality. The child was a pedi-

morph: a child surrogate hybridized into a hermaphroditic creature whose development was arrested in preadolescence. It could have been fifty years old or fifteen; its physiologic age would always remain prepubescent. Pedimorphs were indentured by their parents to the Guild for twenty years. After that they could buy out their contract and be brought back to standard terran — to normal endocrine development — if they had saved enough money. Most didn't. Most spent their entire lives as pedis. Which usually wasn't all that long — the suicide rate was quite high.

The pedi stood motionless. A pink tongue darted out to wet its lips. "Am I acceptable, Brother Monk?"

"Quite so," the monk answered. "Begin."

The monk pulled off his own robe, although he imagined the pedimorph did it. The pedi stood behind him, massaging taut shoulder muscles. The ritual was beginning to disgust me. After all, my imagination was creating the images in the monk's mind. Pedis were an acquired taste. But this illusion was necessary.

Risa left and entered the bedroom. A valise of money was suspended in midair within an alarm beam. She plucked it from the beam. A ruby on the monk's finger began flashing. He did not notice. The pedi now stood in front of him, with its ankles caught between the monk's crossed legs. The monk's face was pressing into its groin.

Risa returned from the other room carrying the valise. She waited by the door.

Time for us to leave.

The monk's hands cupped the pedi's slender buttocks. His fingernails cut deep into tender flesh. The pedi screamed in pain.

Suddenly, I was angry. Rage narrowed my vision into a blurred tunnel. My reaction disturbed me. I'd seen worse in other minds. Why should this scenario bother me?

The pedi's hands encircled the monk's neck. Thumbs gouged deep into carotid arteries, then flattened tracheal rings. The monk's eyes bulged, his lips turned blue. Spittle drooled down his tongue. He did not resist. This was still all part of the ritual.

He lost consciousness.

I should have relaxed the spasms in his neck now and released his diaphragm from its paralysis. But my rage was too strong. The pedi continued to squeeze.

I had the overwhelming urge to strangle the monk. I wanted him dead. A rational island in my mind was puzzled. I had never killed before, even in the war. Why now?

Anger burned even hotter. Now my fingers did the squeezing. I closed my eyes.

A voice whispered in my ear. Soft lips nuzzled my cheek. Strong arms wrapped around me. Supple fingers kneaded my flesh. A warm body pressed against mine.

The monk's mind was almost dead. But there was serenity instead of panic, as though death were preferable to life. Dreams unwound like a raveling tapestry—scenes of war, combrids going into battle against a dozen different kinds of hybrids as seen through rebel eyes; making love to a dozen different kinds of partners, then cutting each lover's throat, sticking knives into the backs of sentries looking the other way, leaving bombs behind.

Risa's cool thoughts flowed over my fire, extinguishing the flame. I opened my eyes.

I stood before the monk. My hands strangled him. I let go. His head slumped forward, his body remained erect, locked upright by his lotus posture. Dreams unraveled, weaving back together. I sensed disappointment. Risa relaxed her embrace. She picked up the valise and started toward the door. The monk's mind tapestry faded. But a melting image lingered to disturb me: a doll's face with its features twisted into rage, its teeth bared, lips snarling.

I stumbled out the door after Risa.

We were safe in our suite.

When the monk recovered he would not report the theft of his money — that would direct suspicion toward him. He would instead try to locate a certain pedimorph himself. His search would prove futile since this pedi did not exist except in memory.

I sat near the window staring out at the glistening domes of Chalise. Risa padded over to join me, rubbing against my side. Static sparked between us. A rough tongue licked my neck. I let her pull me over to the bed. She climbed on top and began undulating slowly. Her mane lay flat; no fimbriae quivered. No stray dreams disturbed our lovemaking. I blanked my mind concentrating only on delicious friction.

Later as I held Risa close to me, troubled thought came back. I remembered a dissolving image.

Did you notice anything unusual about the monk? I asked.

The memories were a little strange for a religious person. He seems to have had an interesting life. There was an area I couldn't probe. Her thoughts resonated. I touched her throat. She purred. *Probably church secrets. Rituals. Memories I would have to kill to extract. Such protected zones are common among monks.*

Didn't Hitt also have such an area?

She nodded involuntarily. *He was a smuggler and a gunrunner. It's to be expected he would pay a psychesurgeon to seal up a few secrets.*

It seems odd that two in a row should be protected.

A coincidence.

She seemed so sure of herself. I let it go. I trusted her ability. *There was something peculiar about our encounter*

231

with the monk. I wonder why I got so angry?

Her thoughts were silent.

A realization struck.

Why did I get angry? You know, don't you?

She waited before answering. *I know.*

What is it? Why?

An unconscious memory bothered you.

What kind of memory? A memory of what?

That is hidden from even me.

You won't tell me?

I don't know.

She was not quite convincing.

But what could I do? I couldn't see into my own head, much less into hers. *Okay. As long as it doesn't matter.*

Not to me.

She sought me again, as though in proof.

Demons haunted my dream-time.

I was paralyzed and could not move a muscle. Rat teeth nipped flesh, gnawing my fingers away. Snakes slithered around my neck, gradually tightening their coils, while fanged faces watched me, tasting my fear with cloven tongues. Birds also worried about my face, pecking at my unblinking eyes. Bats fluttered about, then landed, sinking sharp teeth and lapping up the free-flowing blood. Flies buzzed lazily, depositing yellow spawn in my wounds that soon hatched into wriggling maggots. Then I heard water flowing. Cool wetness touched my skin. The water had climbed higher and higher, until it lapped about my neck. For some reason, I did not float. And I was still paralyzed. The water rose—over my mouth, over my nose, then over my eyes. I held my breath until it seemed my lungs would burst. I could hold it no longer. Bubbles streamed out of my nostrils. I gasped for air, water filled my lungs instead. I tried to scream. Images darted out of my mouth and floated away.

A radioactive doll glowed in the darkness, luminescent tears dripping from its eyes.

I woke with sweat cooling on my skin. Risa sat up in bed beside me, holding her head between her hands.

"I was sending."

She nodded. "You've given me quite a headache. Most of the other hotel guests have had bad dreams, not to mention half of the rest of Chalise. In few days, after casual conversations, they'll begin to realize they all had the same nightmare."

"The varks will start snooping around. We'd best move on."

"No, not yet." I missed the cunning in her voice. "We have time for one more."

"You've found someone?"

"Yes. She looks very interesting. Just your type. We'll sting her tonight."

"You're sure there's enough time?"

"Of course. I've searched all of Chalise. No one is suspicious yet. I can't resist this one. You'll enjoy it. She's a demilled veteran of the Corps."

I lay back and closed my eyes. Yes, this next sting would be enjoyable. We veterans all had something in common; we'd committed some atrocity—some capital offense—that had gotten us sentenced to the Foreign Legions instead of death. Demilled veterans were given back their pasts. That was the law. Since I was an outlaw, I didn't have my past. But I still held the naive hope that I would find some common theme in the backgrounds of other combat hybrids that would enable me to guess my own.

I dozed off. A doll's face cycled out of its hippocampal tomb.

Ganymede's artificial day had faded. The reality of night returned. Risa stood before the window. I followed her gaze; she watched white-hot plasma spewing from the fusion fountain of a nightclub perched below us on the rim of Chalise crater.

Another hunt began.

We strolled the streets of Chalise, Risa and I. If any cameras recorded our passage, the captured images would show only a true human and a sphinx walking together. Not so unusual by today's standards. Hardware was difficult to fool. We'd have had to be chameleons to fool cameras. Not so software. The living eyes that saw us "saw" two merchant sailors on shore leave. We were two among many, for Chalise was a maritime city. Two sailors were even less likely to be remembered than a sphinx and a standard human. We appeared to be quite ordinary sailors; two meters tall; naked save our capes and the sonic jewelry that decorated fingers, toes, noses, and ears; skin as black as obsidian and shining with protective monomer; supple fingers and toes equipped with tree-frog suction cups; nictitating membranes covered our eyes, other sphincters protected nostrils and ear canals; bald skulls with scalps that were convoluted into ridges by subcutaneous cyberwires. Two common cybernetic hybrid sailors. nothing at all to attract attention.

I was pleased with my attention to detail. You couldn't be too careful in our line of work.

We passed all the usual diversions found on the Outer Moons; peptide parlors, simulacrum arenas, isotope wrestling, mnemone dens, deformity brokers, and mind casinos. Pedimorphs leered at us from open doorways, tempting us with their tongues. We showed polite interest, as sailors would, but declined. I concealed the revulsion I felt.

We slowly made our way to the ice cliffs that lined the

crater wall. A thousand meters above the crater floor, a permaplastic dome covered the wreckage of an ancient fuship. It had crashed there ages ago, before nuclear energy was supplanted by radiacrystals and gravsails. But the old fusion thruster still throbbed with life. Plasma spewed into space from the old jets, forming a thermonuclear fountain that threw bright tendrils a hundred clicks out, all leading back to a nightclub called Critical Mass.

Tonight's quarry awaited us there.

We entered Critical Mass. A hostess greeted us and pinned a radiation badge on our capes. I smiled at this touch of realism. She showed us to a table. A transparent dance floor formed a disc pierced through its center by the thruster chamber. Tables were placed along the periphery. A dim, blue glow emanated through the walls of the magnetic bottle. A low throb beat from each solid surface. Audiocrystals hung overhead. Tendrils of optical music exuded from their facets to swirl in midair over the dance floor, before slowly drifting down into tangles among the dancers.

Risa smiled. To other eyes, a sailor's lips curled upward. To my eyes, furred lips separated to reveal sharp, white teeth. Music glinted from their points. Her eyes gleamed. Silver fimbriae quivered about her head.

"Let's dance," Risa said.

"Is she still here?"

"Let's dance." She touched my hand with her finger, moving the tip in a circular motion. Induction neurons set up their transcutaneous field between us. A tingle ran up my arm, an image darted into my mind; an old lioness watched two young lions courting. Resentment smoldered in her eyes. She bared toothless gums in a grimace of hate.

I picked up Risa's hand and led her out to the dance floor. We danced like sailors; with wild abandon. Yet we were also graceful and elegant, and we made leaping pirouettes that took us almost to the ceiling.

When we returned to our table, someone was waiting there. Her face was obscured by shadow. A finger wearing a ring set with a huge, singing diamond tapped nervously.

"I admired your dancing," she said, lowering her eyes briefly in false shyness. "I wonder if I might speak to you for a moment. If it's no bother . . ."

"Certainly," I said.

"No bother at all," Risa giggled.

We both sat down.

I saw her clearly now. She was almost beautiful. The cosmetic surgeons had done a good job. There were a few tiny scars around her eyes and nostrils where sphincters had been removed. Hardly noticeable, unless you knew where to look. I knew there could be other scars through which hardware had been salvaged, but they were concealed by her gown. Full breasts pushed out against a gold-trimmed bodice. A necklace of singing pearls rested on them. Her hair was straw-colored and cut as short as wheat stubble but was thick enough to hide the white lines where cyberwires once had been. Her eyes were the green of jade.

I placed my hand on Risa's. An electric tingle tickled my palm; we entered her mind.

"What do you want to talk about, Lady Johan?" She was once again a Lady from Old Earth, no longer a lance corporal.

"How do you know my name?" She looked at me, afraid for an instant. The face she saw was open, pleasant, laughing. She relaxed. "If you know my name, then you know my story as well. You know what I want you to tell me." She smiled. A waiter arrived with a vase of mnemone tubes and a glass of Earth wine. "I took the liberty of ordering for us. I hope I got it right." She reached for the glass and sipped its wine, rolling the liquid around her mouth with her tongue.

Risa and I snapped open mnemone tubes and inhaled the vapors into our lungs.

"I want you to tell me about the blue empty," the Lady said. "If that wouldn't be too much trouble. I'll pay you for your time." She drank down the wine in one long gulp. A drop ran down her chin. "My yacht is moored at the spaceport." She smiled slyly. "We could be more comfortable there. I think it's important to be comfortable when telling stories, don't you? Shall we go?"

I nodded. Telling stories of the blue empty was the code phrase used by sailing groupies to sailors when they meant they wished to purchase our favors. But the Lady's schemes went beyond the usual. I could hardly wait. Risa had been right.

Three bodies sprawled on a wombskin pad in the main cabin of a blue space racer: Lady Johan and her two new sailors. All were naked. Two sailors lay on their backs, head to head. Lady Johan sat near them, holding a small vial between thumb and forefinger. She dipped her tongue into the vial, then leaned over a sailor's face, lowering her protruding tongue until it touched his eye. Blue peptide flowed across his cornea. She repeated the ritual with the other eye. Then with the other sailor. The vial contained a mixture of endocaine and endrogen—speed and sex steroid. Soon bodies mingled into a confused mass of torsos and limbs. A peptide frenzy slowly built. Flesh slapped against flesh. Sweat shone from skin. Breath whistled out of nostrils. Low moans escaped clenched teeth.

Risa finished plundering the yacht—a meager haul for a member of the aristocracy; a few mediocre jewels, a little cash, two uninteresting objets d'art. But that was all right. I was more interested in the mind of this particular mark than in her loot. We had explored her mind thoroughly.

She had been a young Lady of one of the old families on Earth, amusing herself with the usual diversions. While under the influence of too much endocaine, she had caught her lover with another. In a fit of jealousy (over not having been invited to share her lover's lover), she grabbed an antique sword from the wall and decapitated them both. That had been her ticket to the Foreign Legions. She had become a cyrine. While in the Corps, she found another lover — a sailor. Their ships took a hit and depressurized. She lived, he died. That explained the next part of her ritual. The Lady had a unique perversion. She had set her ship's computer to automatically blow open the main airlock at a preprogrammed time. That time was right now. (Of course Risa reset the computer so the lock would not open unexpectedly. Mind reading has certain advantages.)

We were ready to leave, so we pulled on space coveralls and attached O_2 bubbles over our heads. We entered the airlock and closed the inner door. The Lady must not be disappointed. Otherwise she might inform the varks. So I let the hatch blow in my imagination; warm air suddenly rushed out of the cabin, replaced by thin wisps of hydrocarbon at two hundred below. The sailors reacted instinctively; one ran for an emergency sealing kit while the other placed his lips over the Lady's mouth and nose. Their respirations synchronized, they exchanged breaths. The sailor had oxygen stored within brown adipose — a little diffused back into his lungs and his exhaled breath — enough to keep the Lady alive, if not conscious.

The airlock cycled, and the outer door dilated. Risa and I stood in near vacuum, protected by space coveralls and breathing recatalyzed oxygen. The inner door remained sealed, the cabin warm and pressurized. Except in the Lady's mind.

She sank into a pseudohypoxic coma. Risa turned to face

me. I leaned toward her until our O_2 bubbles fused. Our lips touched; our tongues slipped past themselves.

Beyond the inner door, a mind tapestry raveled. Images unwound from the fabric of memory: The Lady playing her endless ritual, seeking something lost to the blue empty, all recapitulations of when her lost lover had not been saved by her because she chose to flee instead of staying to help him; scenes of war, staccato glimpses of a sword flashing an arc through the air, biting through muscle and cartilage, with blood spurting high. Then I saw another pattern hidden within the weave of the other. Ghost dreams came back to haunt me: An alphalash swings its terrible arc, a doll strangles a naked monk. Memory threads stopped unwinding, their strands held by a locked weave whose pattern was amorphous gray. But I had seen enough. I understood the Lady's deception.

I willed her heart to stop and her lungs to cease breathing. My thoughts couldn't penetrate her basal ganglia. Those parts of her brain were protected. I tried to open the inner door, to let in real vacuum, but it was locked from inside. No doubt another preprogrammed order in her ship's computer. She was safe from me. All I could do was buy a little time. I depolarized a few more cortical synapses so she would remain unconscious for a little while longer.

It was more than coincidence that our two previous marks had part of their memories protected. They had been bait, to keep us occupied while help arrived, all disguises of the same person, the same Lady. She was no ordinary vark. Varks could not change both their appearance and persona at will.

But she had made a mistake. She had blown her cover. We knew who she was now.

If we were lucky, Risa and I could still escape. I took her hand, and we ran through methane snow.

Our bags were packed, our loot safely hidden. We were ready to go. A gravship sailed in thirty minutes — we had already booked and confirmed passage.

A bellmech picked up our baggage. Rise prowled back and forth in front of the door. "Hurry, Nate!" Her voice was an impatient hiss. "She wakes. We must leave at once." I seemed to have no ambition left. I was unafraid. Nothing mattered, not even escape. Memories of dreams kept dancing in my head: skulls with yellow teeth clicking; bats fluttering; rats scurrying across bedclothes; demons howling with glee. They were my dreams, glimpsed in the Lady's raveling mind tapestry. Gray ghosts coalesced into unfamiliar faces. I knew what was wrong.

"We can wait no longer." Risa came over to tug at my arm. With her touch, I too sensed the Lady waking. Dream filaments unraveled, weaving back into memory; a million children screamed in terror at the night, huddling beneath their blankets as specters shrieked their taunts.

I knew what was wrong. The dreams winding were my own. The Lady shared my dreams, knew my nightmares. There was only one way that was possible.

"We have to go now!" Risa shouted.

I pulled free of her touch. "I can't leave," I said. "She knows who I am."

"So do I."

"Then tell me."

"We don't have time."

"Tell me."

"I can't be the one. You would hate me too much." Her eyes held a cunning I had not noticed before.

"Then I'll wait for the Lady. She might be more cooperative than you."

Risa's hand flashed out, slashing me across the cheek. "I love you too much," she said. Four lines stung my face. I touched my finger to the wetness on my skin, then licked the blood from its tip. Risa's eyes shimmered wet. She turned and ran out the door.

A doll's face leered at me where she had been, with eyes that could not cry.

I stood alone in the penthouse staring out one of its facets. A gravship rose out of clinging mists and whispered sunward, Risa leaving. A part of myself was also leaving. We had been imprinted on each other and had worked together for five years. You couldn't be a path team without an empath. I had lost my eyes and ears, my taste, touch, and smell. But that was a less immediate problem. I'd made my choice. I might not get another chance to exorcise myself of dream demons—I could no longer bear their taunts. I had to know who I had been.

The door opened. Someone walked into the room. I turned to face her and stared into the muzzle of a hand pulser.

"I knew you would be waiting for me," she said. "You need something from me."

She wore one of her myriad disguises, but this one I recognized—a cyrine named Kaly.

"Are you really Kaly?" One could never be certain with spooks.

She laughed. "This time, yes. I remember you well. It's taken me a long time to find you, but it wasn't hard to trap you once I did."

I must have looked surprised.

She laughed again. "If I hadn't, someone else would have. Your M.O. is too stereotyped. All I had to do was set up the right personas as bait and you came to me like a moth to a candle. You should have been more ambitious. With your abilities, you could rule an empire, instead of committing petty larcenies concealed behind obvious fantasies. But you couldn't help yourself, could you? We knew one of your kind would eventually escape undemilled from the Corps. We made sure you would be incapable of causing much trouble." She looked around. "Where's your little pet?" I didn't like the nasty inflection she put on the word.

"Gone. She doesn't like unpleasantness."

"But you had to stay. You saw something irresistible in my thoughts. You had to find out more." She laughed again but not with the smugness you might have expected. Her voice was tainted with something else. "A shame you're not more cunning. You shouldn't let yourself be so easily manipulated." She motioned for me to move.

I stayed put.

She gesture again.

This time I laughed. "Try to shoot."

She tried. Her finger would not press the firing stud. Then her wrist slowly twisted until the gun was pointing at her own head.

"You want to shoot someone?" I taunted. "Go ahead." Her finger now slowly tightened against the stud. Her eyes stared at the gun's muzzle waiting for a quantum of light to flash out and burn a crisp hole in her sweating forehead. The button moved.

"Okay," she gasped. "You win."

Her hand opened spasmodically. The gun clattered to the floor.

"What is it you want?" she asked.

"I want to know about myself. Everything you can tell me."

"Fair enough. But is there any need to be so formal?"

I let her cross the room. She waved a hand through a laser beam, a circular bed rose from the floor. I let her lead me to it and lay with her on the wombskin. Our clothes came off and dropped to the floor. I would allow her one more ritual.

"Let's not talk just yet," she said, smiling. Her lips began nibbling my skin. I knew she was stalling.

"Tell me first," I said.

"There'll be plenty of time for talking later."

I sharpened knives in her mind.

"Okay. What do you want to know?"

"Why the nightmares? Why are my genodreams ones of terror?"

"Telepaths were harder to engineer than empaths. I ought to know. I was once a genosurgeon for Corps Intelligence. I was in charge of the project that created your kind. Empaths were easy. There were lots of species with latent empathic abilities: dogs, cats, raptors, certain insects. Those genes were easily isolated. We found sphinxes were ideal hosts for those genes. But there were no known animal telepaths, just a few psychotic humans who did not live past puberty. And they were rare. None were in existence when we needed them. So we had to create a telepath." Her voice caught for the first time.

"And how was this done?"

"Only a human brain was complex enough." Apologetically. "And it had to be one that had not yet developed nontelepathic synapses — habits, if you will. Telepathic brains are extremely rare. We weren't monsters, we only did what we had to."

"Which was?"

"Millions of fetal brains were set up in vitro. All motor efferents were severed: the brains were physiologically paralyzed. Then it was just a question of providing the stimuli and waiting for something to develop."

I visualized millions of tiny brains floating in bubbling culture media, with thousands of fine wires running to each. "What kind of stimuli?" I asked. "What kind of dreams?"

She smiled. "Oh, you know. Night terrors.. Childhood fears. You gave them visages of your own choosing, from your own dreams. The terrors themselves were quite abstract — pure fear, if you will. Our computer merely stimulated the right limbic nuclei. The fetal brains had to develop in a milieu of terror and could do nothing about it, in a conventional way, with their motor efferents cut. They withered and died from fright."

"Except one."

"Except one," she agreed. "One brain developed differently. One brain survived. Motor cortex convoluted in a strange new way. And one brain finally lashed out at its tormentors the only way it could — telepathically. I'll always remember the images it sent into my mind. I'll never forget those dreams. Anyway, we'd found our telepathic brain. The potential had always been there, only the right conditions were necessary to bring out the latency. It was routine genosurgery to isolate the responsible genes."

"Those genes were given to me?"

"Of course. But we couldn't separate telepathy from night terrors. The one predisposes to the other. Only a fearful mind is telepathic. So the brain must not completely mature. If it grows out of night terrors, it would also outgrow telepathy." She winked at me. "That's why you were picked. It was easier to make do with what we had."

"What do you mean?" I suddenly felt confused. "What's so special about me?"

"Don't tell me you believe your own charade? A magician fooled by his own tricks? How amusing." She thought briefly. "Of course. That last night before you deserted. Was it that traumatic? Was I that bad?"

"What about me? Why was I sentenced to the Foreign Legions? Why were my memories stolen from me?"

"You killed a man," she answered simply. "You murdered

a customer." Sweat shone from her skin. Her breasts bobbed. Her eyes gleamed with more than jovelight.

"A customer? What's that mean?"

She laughed wickedly. "You broke the most sacred covenant of your guild. No punishment is too severe for your kind. Besides, I already told you we had to make do with physiotypes that were already hybridized. Only immature brains could be made telepathic. We needed brains that couldn't mature. Your kind did nicely."

She began changing in front of me. Flesh remodeled, as though worms were wriggling beneath the skin. Her honest cyrine face lost its black sheen and protective bony ridges around nose and eyes. It became a glob of congealed plastic. Another face grew out of the ruins of the first. I knew what creature she was becoming.

"Stop it!" I shouted.

But the change was complete. A child straddled me. A child with a doll's features, upturned button of a nose, rosy-red cheeks, eyes the blue of robin eggs, soft curls of yellow hair. Not a child, either. A pedimorph.

"Stop it. Change back to something less disgusting. I'm no pederast. I can make you change into something else."

"Like you changed yourself?" The voice was high-pitched, with childish inflections. "Haven't you guessed what creature you are? What you always must be?"

"No!"

A hand intercepted a laser beam switch. A ceiling holomirror sprang to life overhead. I saw two naked dolls locked in an obscene embrace. Both had identical features. I knew it was no illusion. Illusions were of my making. A doll's face came close. Doll's lips began kissing mine.

"Stop it!" I screamed. My hands circled the neck. My fingers squeezed tight.

"Haven't you wondered why a genosurgeon would become a chameleon?" she asked. "If only I could change my dreams as easily as my body." She smiled. I squeezed harder.

"Haven't you ever wondered how they demill chameleons? Can't you understand?" she forced out before her larynx was crushed. An unpleasant image darted into my mind: a woman being skinned alive by sharp scalpels. And even that was not punishment enough. I kept squeezing. Eyes bulged. The head slumped back, flaccid with paralysis. Drool ran between cyanotic lips. Blood dripped from ears and nostrils. I suddenly remembered killing once before. He had wanted to hurt me and had used an alphalash on me. I hated the lash. I couldn't stand it any longer, so I had hurt him instead. It had been worth it then. It would be worth it now. Then I remembered another night with Kaly. She had whipped me with an alphalash then, trying to hurt me enough that I would lash back at her telepathically. But my mind became psychotic instead; not wanting to kill again, I created a delusion for myself. Someone had helped me run away.

A voice whispered in my ear, soothing, calming. Strong fingers tugged at mine, pulling them away one by one. Lips kissed my cheek.

Risa!

I couldn't leave you.

I'm glad you came back.

So am I.

I almost killed the spook. She is Kaly.

I know. That's what she wanted and planned. See?

I could see the pattern in the spook's raveling mind tapestry. The gunrunner, the monk, and Lady Johan had all been real covers. She had really lost her lover, twice. I saw endless cycles of friendships broken, lovers betrayed, of hiding behind disguises, never allowing either true visage or persona to be seen. Then I heard the cries of a million children, frightened to hysteria by the demonic images carried by wires to their brains. Kaly had tried to get me to kill her once before. Now she had tried again. The barriers were down. Her mind was unprotected.

There's an easier way than death.

There was. I flooded hippocampal gray with peptidases. Neurotransmitters were dissolved from synaptic pathways. Dreams spun out, their filaments melting like cobwebs in sunlight, never to be unraveled.

The chameleon would remember nothing of us or of anything else since childhood. She would no longer be tormented by her guilt. Risa and I left together.

In a cabin in a gravliner, Risa and I made love. Jupiter dwindled astern, its moons no more than brighter stars. Ahead lay the asteroids and beyond them Mars and its two moons. We would catch up to our baggage somewhere along the way.

Our images were reflected from burnished brass; a lithe cat-woman entwined with a doll. As our bodies moved toward love, a mind tapestry raveled. I saw a strange melding of imagery as though seen through both Risa and my eyes of our life together on the run, then during the war. I saw my delusion of my appearance, of the illusion I projected to others. Then new dreams untwined: I saw myself performing a pedimorph's ritual, being whipped with an alphalash, all ending in the same strangling. I saw myself sold to a child broker so my family could survive a few more years. I remembered my siblings. I was chosen because I was the fairest child. I remembered my parents. I loved them all again. I forgave them. Night terrors rose but could no longer frighten. I remembered myself again.

My memories weren't taken away.

Not completely. Only hidden.

And the delusion. I remembered orgasms I had never had.

So you wouldn't have to kill again.

But you knew all the time?

Laughter. Warm and pleasant. *Of course. What can be hidden from me?*

You don't mind about me? What I am?

More laughter. *We've been imprinted together. I love you as part of myself. The way you are. All of you. You are my voice.*

Why didn't you tell me?

I was afraid you would want to change if you remembered you were a pedimorph. I knew how you felt about it. You could have had your endocrine arrest reversed. I was afraid you would. Then you would neither want nor need me. I would lose you.

Another realization struck. *Then you knew abut the chameleon all the time. You let her play her game with me, so I could find out about myself without you telling me.*

A cat face grinned. *Yes. Are you angry?*

Not now. I let a thought curl about the edges of my mind. *I do have more than enough money to buy a little endo-surgery. I could grow out of this doll's body. I could have real sex.*

Risa's mind was guarded: she kept her feelings hidden.

But then I would no longer have the gift. Or you.

I kissed her. She knew what that meant and kissed me back. Bodies were unimportant, merely to be looked upon. I could have any body I wanted, be any beauty that had ever been beheld by living eyes. Pleasures were just as fine no matter in whose neurons they first originated. And the spook had been right — we could be more than petty thieves rolling johns. That was a phase out of my past, which had now been exorcised.

I looked out the port—there were worlds to conquer out there.

Risa and I touched. Our bodies moved to love, driven by resonating thoughts rather than tactile stimuli. Beyond both the desire and the spasm, we remained touching, basking in the warmth of ebbing love.

I've saved the best for last. Her thoughts were sleepy. *I no longer have to guard anything from you.* She dozed.

I sail high above the ground on outstretched wings, riding summer thermals. I howl at a moon of night. I charge across dry veld; my terrible roar paralyzes my prey with fright. Talons slash. Claws rend. Fangs tear open throats, tongues lap warm blood. My mate runs beside me proud.

Dreams unwind. . . .

The Wandering Jew

By Thomas M. Disch

And then there was the time—it was right around the summer solstice—that She fell in love and lighted off with the object of Her love to the Poconos because in Her words the city had become too much for Her. So there we all were, the eight of us, crammed together into the bathtub and gradually dying of thirst once we'd recovered from being half-drowned. We got two hours of sunlight every morning—in *June,* just imagine!—and most of that couldn't get through the shower curtain, which was all right for me, I'm a succulent creeper and *thrive* in shady places, but pity the poor asparagus fern. It never did recover. Its stalks went from green to yellow to brittle-brown. While the coleus got limp as death, though it did revive quickly enough once She returned and cut it back, which it had been needing anyhow as it was getting very leggy. She would never fall in love again, She told us, as Her scissors snipped and pruned. Men were beasts. Well, we could have told Her that. The end of the problem, you're thinking? Oh no, there was worse to come. For somehow She'd got it into Her head to grow a pot of basil in this landfill She'd brought back from the Poconos. So the entire windowsill was entirely given over to this tacky plastic planter filled to the brim with ground shale, pine-needle dust, and mealybug eggs. I mean, all we were missing was acid rain! If that makes me sound like a pot-bound, totally urban houseplant, so be it. Nature's all very well in its place, but *its* place is the country and *my* place is a pot, and never the twain shall meet if *I* can help it. Well, there we were, back at our duty stations — except for the poor asparagus fern, of course — which meant that I was hanging right over that imported plague spot with my leaves practically scooping up the mealybugs from the planter. I'll tell you, I almost died. If She hadn't swabbed my every axil and crotch with Q-Tips dipped in malathion, I wouldn't even be alive today to tell the tale. I realize there are those, like my old friend here *Dizygotheca elegantissima,* who feel it's bad form to so much as mention sucking insects, but being just a common creeper myself, grown from a cutting in a jelly glass and lacking any experience of nurseries, I believe in calling a spade a spade. I was infested, no two ways about it. It's an ill wind that blows no good, however, which is to say that if it hadn't been for the mealybugs and the malathion I might never have been able to communicate my philosophy of life to Her, since She wasn't the sort of person who relates to plants easily. Now there are some plants, mostly out there in nature, who will tell you that blood and chlorophyll never mix, but down deep I know that people and plants need each other. It's only that people usually live at such a dreadful *speed,* as though they ran on electricity like those nasty appliances of theirs. But give people half a chance to adjust their biorhythms to ours, and soon enough there's not a person alive who can't be as calm as a cactus. "Never mind that silly hunk of beefcake off there in the Poconos," my leaves whispered as She dabbed on the malathion. "*He* never really loved you the way we do. *He* doesn't need you the way we do. How could you possibly go back to someone who sends you home with a planter full of mealybugs? Forget him already. Put down some roots. Grow." For that's what She'd been threatening to do—go back to him and leave us to spend all the rest of the summer in the bathtub. Well, that's not what happened. She didn't go back to him. *He* came to live with *Her*—with two cats and a schnauzer! Once the cats had demolished the coleus, that was it for us. We released Her from our enchantment and had ourselves adopted by Her cousin Flora. And bless Her, here our Flora comes with the mister. My, is it that time already? How the time does go by when you're chatting with friends.

Wired

By David Bischoff

The Kid's in his dressing room, spitting up sparks. Spudzel stalks the room, popping pills as if they were M&M's. "Jesus!"

He slams his hand into the vidphone again. "Where's the fuckin' doctor? The show's only an hour away!"

Blood drips onto my hand. The Kid rolls away from the trash can. His shiny blouse, mottled by the vomit stain, catches light, flashes it back in my face.

A smoke wisp curls into my eyes. I can smell the wrongness.

"Can it, asshole," he mutters. He tosses those famous frizzled locks, all tangled in teen dreams. "I'll be okay."

"Like hell!" The afterimages of those sparks from the Kid's implants are like black holes in my vision. I put a pillow under his head, wipe sweat from his forehead. "What did she do to you?"

He coughs. Gears mesh. Crank of flesh.

"Vampire Fire." He sneers. The Kid hates that song. His

fans love it. His pulse is still strong and steady.

"Christ, Ellerway."

"Yeah, well, this chick, she sucks electricity. God, what a day! Need a new power pack, I think."

I shake my head. "You didn't do this when Simone was around, Ellerway."

"Fuck her." He clamps his mouth shut, punk hard.

I look up at the rumpled Spudzel. "How come you didn't at least have a medmech around? I know they're expensive, but shit, Flash is the show."

"Don't you challenge my judgment! Ever! That's not part of the deal here. I'm doing my job. I can't help it if the Kid goes out and humps some AC/DC before the biggest concert of his career."

"You're just a cheap bastard! Serve you right if we gotta cancel."

"Cancel!" Spud's face turns bright red. "You ain't gonna cancel. I got all my money wrapped up in this gig."

Spud doesn't, and we know it, but he likes his drama, and we let him keep it. "Ellerway will be all right," I say. "Probably just shorted out the voice augmenter. The medmech will have a spare. We can do the show, but Ellerway might need a long rest afterward. Right, Ellerway?" I punch his shoulder lightly.

"Yeah, Capp. How about a drink?"

He tries to get up, but I keep him down. "You'll get all you need soon as we get you fixed up."

The medmech storms in, and a regular doctor rushes in behind him, wheeling a whole lab's worth of equipment: flashing needles, long spirals of plastic tubing, and packets of plasma alongside gleaming racks of metallic odds and ends.

And wires.

There's a moment of fleshy fear in Ellerway's eyes.

"Look. You'll be fine," I whisper. "Pretty soon we do what you want. That's what we're after."

He looks up at me and says, "Hell, I want the women and the booze and the drugs."

He smiles and lays his head back.

I take off.

I don't want to see the knives go into him.

He wasn't Kid the Flash when I first saw him perform.

Just the lead singer in a penny-ante syntha-shock group still using outdated comsynths and Jap guitars. Young, all of them, doing a Monday night in a buzzclub off of M street in D.C., full of pubescent power and now a whole lot else. I was curious. I'd known his mother . . . real well. I'd heard he had a group. I was pretty burned out, what with thirty years of laying my fingers on lead guitars with almost as many groups. I was with the Dying Ones then, which about says it. The masks of surgery keep your face and body young these days but don't do shit for your soul. Fifty years old. Lots of experience. No money. And to think that I had originally learned classical guitar.

I sat with just a Heineken for company while the band chugged and jerked. Same old rock-and-synth card deck reshuffled. But Ellerway . . . Ellerway had something, oh, yes he did, and I sat there listening and watching him and didn't touch my beer, which was damned strange for a man who takes an antialchy shot every week.

Cocaine-scrawny, he had just a thatch of hair, blond and scruffy. He was seventeen years old. Tattered jeans and a faded corduroy jacket with patches hung loosely around his bare skin and prominent ribs. A red silk scarf was tied around his neck, and the cord of an ancient Vocoder mike wound round his right arm like an emaciated snake.

His music was in his eyes. His enunciation was precise.

His words snuck around the songs and took chunks out of them, spitting them back into the outwash. He used the Vocoder wonderfully. A flick of his fingers to a key and his voice seemed to sprout metallic wings.

There were brief moments of perfect metal-flesh mesh, power and blood sneaking through the songs. He had no stage presence, but he had the raw stuff.

The set ended. The bouncers wheeled out the basket cases and booted the attachers who had zoned out on their wires. The druggers clapped and wanted more, so Zonk did an old Ultravox tune, "I Want to Be a Machine."

The band sort of limped away backstage. I asked the bartender if he could arrange a quick meeting for me with Zonk's lead singer.

Before my beer was a quarter gone, Tom Ellerway was beside me, trying to be cool but sucking down a double whiskey damned fast.

"You remember Ultravox, huh?"

His smile twitched. "I inherited a nice vinyl collection from the Sixties, Seventies, and Eighties."

"Got some of my stuff?"

"I think so."

I chuckled. "I sure hope you don't have the clinkers."

"A few. How 'bout 'Boogie, Sugar Baby,' with the Viber Hots."

I dropped my cigarette in my beer and glared at him. "But I wasn't even—"

"Calvin Hodges, guitars." He got a smug smile on his face.

"Not many people knew I was Calvin Hodges."

"You can disco all you want, but if you're a rocker, it shows."

I ordered another round. We shot the musical shit.

Then, in the midst of a sentence, he backed off with an

odd look in his eyes. "Crap. What am I talking to Jimm Capp about music for? You know it all. You've been around forever and you're surviving."

I shook my head. "I can't change, Ellerway. I'll just keep playing. Always one more set—"

He tensed. "How'd you like our set?"

"Your band is okay."

I could see him cringe; so I stuck the rest in real quick. "But I think you're pretty decent."

He bit his lip a moment. "Yeah?"

I patted him on the shoulder. "Yes, indeed. Look, let's you and I get a doggie bag of this poison and head over to the Sheraton. I got some crystals I want you to hear. We can talk."

He smiled. Then suddenly his pale-green eyes got stony, and he said, "Hey, wait a minute. You don't wanna—"

I chuckled and knocked off the rest of my whiskey. "Hell no, Ellerway. I'm into sheep now, haven't you heard? Bring some of your band if you want."

He frowned, embarrassed, but I grinned at him, and it was okay.

I checked my equipment a couple of times that day, but I check it again. They have an opaque light curtain around the stage so that the crowd can't see me and I can't see them.

I hear them, though. I hear the gurgles and the slurps and the crackles of electricity as the wires are plugged in. I hear the screams and the calls, the ocean of jabbering voices.

It's the year 1996, but it ain't the Lord's no more. I've lusted after this all my life. Top crystal on the charts. The most popular concert draw in the world. Playing the biggest arena, here in Kansas City, with the world plugged in and knowing who I am. Jim Capp tearing their heads apart with his slinging ax.

Except it's the Kid they really want to see. Well, right now I only want the money. Hell, anybody can understand that, right? Power? Popularity? Ego trips? Sure. Half the world would kill to be where I am now.

Yeah.

So I check my Gibson again, just to be sure. Neurosis. I won't let the roadies touch it. Nobody touches it but me. My souped-up Stradivarius. I strap it on, open some electricity, and hammer out a power chord. It rings and echoes through the auditorium, like the hammer of Thor.

The crowd is suddenly still and quiet.

I let the resonance swirl, knowing the sound man has damped me down. Cheers. I look up. All the technicians and roadies are staring at me. I grin back and take out a cigarette.

Then Spudzel comes toward me. "What the hell do you think you're doing?"

I blow some smoke in his face. "Just teasing them."

"Look. We might have to delay. And you're working them up? We won't get out of here alive." He uncaps a bottle of Maalox and takes a sip. Spudzel hasn't had an ulcer in years, but he's still got the habit.

"Always a delay," I say, striding away. "They'll wait. They always do."

He puppy-dogs my tracks. "Jesus, I'm so worried I think my heart's going to fall out, Jim." He licks Maalox off his lips. "You don't know—"

I look away. "He'll be okay."

"Just as long as he stands up and sings a little. I already got some incredible powder going through this hall. Those kids are gonna think a burp and a fart is Johann Sebastian Bach."

"I need a drink."

"There's plenty in the reception room."

"And get stuck answering the critics? 'Oh, Mr. Capp. Why did you wait so long,'" I mimic a typical question. " 'Is Tom Ellerway the Lennon to your McCartney, Jim?' Blow it, Spud."

"Hey, that's part of what you pay me for: public relations. They're the people who talk to the fans."

"And mouth crap like that review of 'Love and Horror' last week in the *Stone*. 'A white bread sandwich with a smear of caviar.' Spud, I don't want to go in there and face the *truth*. So why don't you just go in there, sneak me out a bottle, and I'll go and put on my stuff."

He shrugs wearily.

I wait outside the wall-to-wall couch while Spud hops over to the table stocked with food and drink. Folks in there seem too occupied with themselves to notice I'm outside peering in, amused at their stupid outfits and behavior.

Then I get unamused fast.

There's this woman, well-dressed, daintily holding a glass of champagne and chatting brightly with a man in dark glasses.

Spud elbows his way out, carrying a bottle of Chivas Regal with him.

"Here you go, Jim. Sure wish I could have some of that."

I point past him. "What the hell is that bitch doing here?"

"Who?"

"Hardesty." My finger shakes. "Did you invite her back here?"

"O—uhm—Capp . . . she's an important person."

"She's the devil's asshole is what she is, Spud. I want no involvement with her."

"She owns half the industry. C'mon, be a realist, Capp."

"You go and tell her to get the *fuck* out of here or I will. I've dealt with her before. I'm still taking four showers a day. I don't want to see her at the show."

"Yeah. Sure, Jim."

I nod and turn down the hallway.

Above me buzzes power. I can almost smell the lightning inside the kids.

In my Vermont cabin.

In winter.

I sat with Ellerway.

Outside was snow. Inside was a wood fire, a bottle of brandy, Albioni's "Adagio in G Minor" in the crystal deck, along with Handel and Vivaldi: a collection of baroque.

Staff paper lay all around us, with splotchy notes and G clefs and other stuff I hadn't used in years.

The last chords of the Adagio whispered away like your mother's last breath.

After a long moment, Ellerway said, "Capp, I've been thinking."

He liked it here in my piece of the past, my nest of comfort. Quite a change from his city life.

A deep silence slid between us. Outside, the wind and the snow embraced the cabin with sighs and creaks. The fire burned bright and fierce with a gust of air squeezing through the flue.

"Tell me, Kid."

"What is music?"

"Bread and butter. All that noise bought me this piece of quiet."

"Why has rock survived?"

I shrugged.

The Kid shook his head blearily and said softly, "I think the reason you play rock, Capp, is because it's ringing through you just like blood."

" 'I Got the Music in Me.' Kiki Dee, 1976." Glibly.

He got up. "I'm going to bed."

"Hey, sorry to offend, Tom."

He wobbled. "We stumble around with all kinds of wires coming out of us, and where do we stick them? Up our asses."

"I'm listening."

He started radiating intensity. "Brain, Capp. Nervous system. Pulse. Beat. Rhythm. Frequency. Zeitgeist."

"Zeitgeist?"

"Jung. Spirit of the times. Collective unconscious, like that."

"Oh. Yeah."

"Okay. Each one of us is a complicated bastard. I mean, just when I decide I need to take a piss, an electrochemical storm is going on all through me. Chemicals from glands, from vitamins, from all that junk that we stick in our faces. It's all going on inside us all the time.

"And the brain: a labyrinth of hallways. And what's echoing down those hallways? Electricity and chemical reactions, all pulsing to their particular beats. Inside we're all rhythm and melody and dissonance and harmony and adagio and allegro. And our hearts and souls are rapping out the backbeat, and we dance our lives toward death. Each of us is music."

"And some of us can let it out?"

"Sure! But it's more than that. We're lonely SOBs, Capp, and when the music comes inside us from others that somehow aligns with or changes or adds to our own music, it's . . . it's like knowing that somebody is there. You're not alone!"

"And rock?"

"It adds the ingredients of electricity, power. Just like in our heads. We're all affected by what goes on around us. What's been the main change in the last hundred and fifty years? Technology. The sounds of the city. You see what I'm trying to say?"

"I think so."

"Now, all this is damned imperfect. But what would happen if somebody could truly communicate the music in his head? The emotions, the thought structures of being. The attachers are close, but it's too much like direct electrical stimulus. There's got to be pain and ecstasy and grief and love and anger. It's all there in rock, Capp. We just don't have the right instruments."

"Suggestions?"

"I think so. We've taken the raw human voice, amplified it, phased it, and Velveetaed it. But all from outside. What if we started from the inside? Electrochemical music. Almost direct mind-to-mind contact because of analogous processes."

"So what would this be? Sort of directly connecting yourself to the instruments?"

"Yes. Surgically. They've already been using it here and there. Implants. Some Japanese groups are experimenting with it. It's going to spread. Question is, Does anybody really know what they're doing?"

"Are you crazy? No matter how much I love my guitar, I still gotta put it down sometimes."

He shook his head adamantly. "You can't put down the music. It's part of you. This way, it just comes out better."

I thought about the music Ellerway and I were making with Benny, the drummer I'd brought in, and how this was maybe my last chance to hit the bell and win the teddy bear. I thought about the years of desperation and frustration, the busted marriage and scarred friendships, the groveling and the pride. I thought about the snickers behind my back.

"Okay, Ellerway. I got a guy who I think is going to be Kid the Flash's manager. He can hook us up to the right people. We'll think about it."

I sat and thought some more for several sips of brandy, and I added, "But there are things Kid the Flash is going to have to do, Ellerway. Compromises. You—"

I looked down at him.

He was curled up on the rug, face blank and innocent in the flicker of the firelight.

I went and got a blanket for him and then watched him sleep for a while, listening to the music of his breathing.

In the beginning there is darkness.

And darkness is upon the face of the auditorium, and silence.

And Kid the Flash looks upon the dark and the silence and finds it a bummer.

And Kid the Flash says from the rafters and walls and through the wires and the air, "Let there be rock!"

And behold, there is rock.

Lightning zigzags down to the stage, exploding flashpots around Benny. Drumsticks flail. Chug of train, beat of sex, flutter of hummingbird wing. Push of foot and nudge of switch, and the bass notes thrum and pound the bottom of "Vampire Fire."

A spotlight hits me.

I catch the bass line on a down flow and lick a long slide up my E string. The power chord waits hungrily at the end. I let it eat up the crowd's ears as it booms and zooms about like a jet.

I riff out the opening theme on chords, then cut in the repeater, which replays the power chords while I squeeze a Frippish screamer lead line.

I strut a bit, the dance of the lover. My guitar waves out a spectrum of light after-images, sparkler dazzles, and variegated coruscations as I move from side to side stroking the strings in the exact manner that will cut in the synthesizer computer's resonances. Layers of guitar unfold like audio flowers.

I have a garden suddenly growing in the air, sprouting from the dirt and fundament of Benny's rhythm section. I grin and stick up my green thumb at the crowd, then slash through the foliage with an erratic, exquisitely timed scythe.

I nod to Benny.

Benny has the muscles of a drummer and shows them bare chested. Male domination made flesh and drums.

I pull a switch on the fret of the Gibson, disconnecting the false back, a painted cardboard model of the instrument. It separates in smoke and thunder.

I make an elaborate show of placing the thin pseudo-guitar center stage, upright on supports.

Spears of lasers shoot out and twirl through multicolored smoke.

Holo lines begin to shimmer the guitar. Slowly it grows into human form, rock-and-roll mutation, light radiating as if from some Renaissance Madonna and child.

I can feel the buzz in the air, taste the electricity as the attachers cut in on the first verse:

"In your furnace eyes I see the lust."

Just a voice, cresting the wave of sound like a solitary surfer amidst the roar. I use the break to slide out my compu-picker, slip it on my right hand. I tap out the program code.

"Staccato coals and synchromesh tongues
Probe on molten wings, from Phoenix dust
Through stainless-steel mouths to fleshy lungs."

Deep, tortured, echoing breath.
"Vampire Fire!"

With a deafening explosion, the holographs cut in, engulfing Kid the Flash in illuminating fire.

I cut the picker and my fingers fly over the frets to match the machine-gun notes.

The Kid is resplendent in his robes. He looks good.

He drops to his knees before the squirming audience, his voice winding in their heads. We flow through "Vampire Fire" like a race car.

The medmech has done a fast job on him. New voice-augmenter circuit. New power pack. Ellerway has a hard time getting through airport metal detectors. He had to work out a lot at first to realign his fleshy musculature to compensate for his added weight. But he'd done it, and everything he'd ever said about electrochemical organic music was true. His songs pierce and heal, light up the insides of your head when they're truly his and not glossed up. The records are just an echo. Live concert is Kid the Flash's forte.

Ellerway stutters out the final words a cappella:

"For when you draw out my love's breath
You suck not on life, but death.
Vampire fire, you consume yourself."

The computers click in on the last word, slowly building a choir of voices that crest up majestically. I embrace the sound with a few sustained whines wrested from my guitar. The crowd roars.

Ellerway bows his head with dramatic sadness, and I slam a few Townshend chords of defiance.

The song is finished.

Ellerway looks up. He walks slowly over to me as the applause swells. He leans toward me to speak. I can see tiny, fresh stitches in his neck that have been carefully covered by

267

·makeup. Two drops of blood well up on the sleek line of his throat. I take my scarf and dab them off.

He shakes back his hair. He stares at the audience and waves. "Tonight's the night. You think you can follow me?"

"What are you talking about?"

He shrugs. His eyes have a faraway, haunted look.

"I don't know anymore."

The opening rainbows are forming above us for "Cry Like the Sky." Ellerway strides slowly into a spotlight. He stands there, very thin and small against the monstrous gestalt beast of the crowd, the noise, the electricity, the power.

Tom Ellerway, Kid the Flash, opens his shirt, parts the synthetic flesh from his ribs.

He plays the keyboard that's been surgically embedded there, above his heart.

We play.

The first part of the show has been programmed with familiar material. A foundation upon which to build. Totally absorb the audience, then take them elsewhere.

We play well.

Our timing is clean and perfect. Benny throws in a few surprises.

I do an improv from time to time. All sharp, all very professional.

Something, though, is wrong with Ellerway. His performance begins to lack the emotional impact we'd begun with. The audience doesn't seem to care. I do.

I play like a demon. I turn to Ellerway. He stares at me while he sings. It makes me feel creepy.

I slam and I pick and I bang. Just rote stuff. Note for note equivalent to the snazz-rock we'd been putting on the crystals.

I'm waiting to break loose on what Ellerway said was

going to be his crest tonight. I even goad him with a searing run that drowns him out before the mixmen can pare it down.

Stalely, we bump out the last of "Twenty-first-Century Shuffle." The lights dim. I put my hand up to stop Benny from the beginning beats of the next tune, "Hard as Rock." My baby. It's got a five-minute guitar solo I don't want to ruin.

In the darkness, I tug Ellerway behind the wall of amps. Pale light leaks from their guts, spilling onto us like the luminescence of deep-sea creatures.

Leaning near Ellerway, I shout above the sound of applause.

"Hey, man! Where's that charge you were talking about? I thought this was supposed to be your night."

"It'll be there, man. When . . . when it's ready." His eyes are corselike, his face chalky. I pull my hand away from his shoulder, which is sopping wet. Sweat?

My fingers come away into the ghostly light greasy with blood and oil.

"Jesus!" I look into his eyes again. I knew what they'd done. I storm back onto the stage, grab the mike, and say, "We're going to take fifteen, troops. Technical problem."

I slam the microphone to the floor. The boom crashes through the auditorium like a big, fat period to my sentence.

Benny is caught with drumsticks high in the air, feet ready on the pedals of the downbeat machine.

I grab Ellerway by the arm and lead him down the stage steps. Spud is waiting for us at the bottom. "What the hell do you think you're doing, Capp?"

"That's the end of the concert, pal. You get Ellerway to a hospital and get him fixed up right. Then we'll talk about getting him back on stage."

Ellerway sags against me in a drugged glaze. "I can do it, Capp. I can do it, damn it. And I will!" He looks at me. His eyes kind of flash for an instant, then go cold inside.

"Listen to the Kid. Now you get back there and do your job."

"I told you, you fucker." I grab him and pull his ear real close to my mouth. I begin to shout. "He's going to a hospital. Make the arrangement and the apologies to all concerned. I'm not going to have him drop dead up there. I don't know why I ever let him do those operations. *Shit!*"

Spudzel is as white as a dead worm in a rain puddle. "You . . . you can't cancel. There's no provision in the contract."

"What? There's gotta be. The Kid is sick!"

Spudzel is looking away, shivering.

"Spud. What's going on here?" I let go of Ellerway and get a good grip on our manager. "What have you done, Spud?"

He won't look at me.

It all comes to me.

I punch Spud hard in the face.

He goes down blubbering and bleeding, but still conscious.

"I ought to kick your balls into your throat, you fuckin'—"

"I . . . I had to, Capp," he moans. "You were in such a goddamned hurry. She was the only game going that could do what you wanted done. I swear it. Jesus, leave me alone."

I want to kill him. "That's not the whole story, is it, man? What happened to you, Spud? What the hell's happened to you in these years?"

He looks at me. All his hardness is back in his eyes. "Same thing as happened to you, chum. And I tell you, if you and the Kid don't get back on the stage quick, she's going to have your butt for breakfast." Suddenly there is defiance in the little man. I'm sorry that I had hit him.

"Where is she?"

"Sky Suite 4, Capp. Watching the show."

"You get the kid fixed up best you can. No drugs this time. I'll be back."

I stomp toward the exit.

A curly-haired bruiser shows me some teeth in a snarl and moves me inside.

The little room, with its window above and facing the seething crowd, is done up elaborately with velvet curtains, plush furniture, and a smooth rug. A shiny silver tea service sits by the side of a high-backed, padded leather swivel chair.

"Hello, Capp."

"So, Hardesty. You've got your hands on me after all."

She is still beautiful. Her beauty knocks a bit of the hate from me. "Not so much you, Capp, as your group."

"All the way from groupie to group goddess, eh?"

"The amenities are not necessary. I trust you will soon be returning to the stage, with Mr. Ellerway. We've had to cram in a few videos on the satellite network and they're going to run out in—" she examined a ring watch—"twelve minutes."

"How much of this do you own?"

"All."

"And if we don't go back?"

"That, Capp, will be the end of Kid the Flash as an independent entity. You will be all mine, Capp, which would quite please me. I've a few ideas of my own about the group that I think will interest you."

"And if we do go back?"

"You'll be just mostly mine." She shrugs and smiles. "So

you see, either way, I really don't care."

"You want us to go out there and give a lousy performance, maybe have Ellerway fall flat on his face."

"That would be dramatic. But I don't think it will happen." She is calm and cold, radiating confidence with every bit of floss that coats her blond stack of hair. Her heart is all vinyl; her soul, all crystal. Of course she has other interests these days. Financial ventures that far dwarf music. But music is where she got her start, and it's where she dallies most, delighting in owning us all. She and I had our brushes in the old days. The first had been in a hotel room after a gig. I didn't remember, but she reminded me of it later, when she was on top.

"You don't want it to be too good, do you? That's not your style."

"Pardon?"

"That's why you sicced that little AC/DC on Tom," I say, sighing. "And I bet you were even behind the scene with his girl leaving. How'd you manage that, Cynthia?"

"You're paranoid, Capp." But her cool exterior has cracked, and I know I'm right.

"It's not enough to play with bucks, is it, dear heart? You've got to have souls to bounce about as well. So tell me, are you enjoying the show?"

She smiles. "I think it needs more zip in the lighting. Now, if you'll follow my directions, Capp, we can have a real dazzler."

"You're a real sweetheart."

"I'm not as bad as you think, Capp."

"No," I say, "you're probably worse."

I sat on my can in the doctor's office, paging through old copies of *Reader's Digest,* waiting for Ellerway's preliminary exam before the infitting could begin.

Dr. Rashone came out, his smock clean and white, wafting with him the alcohol smells of surgery that gave my spine the creepy-crawlies.

His delivery was as well pressed as the cuffs of his no-stat trousers riding fashionably above glossboots. "You're Mr. Capp?"

"You're Rashone, right?" I took his cold hand and pumped it. I gave him my California smile. We relaxed. He sat down.

"Usually, with Mr. Ellerway's age, it's necessary to get parental approval for this kind of thing," he said.

"Then Tom's okay? He can go ahead with the implants?"

"He's healthy. His system will allow the antirejection treatment. As you know, I'm the only mechosurgeon presently qualified for this sort of extensive electronic enhancement."

"You're the only one who will do it for a potential rock star, you mean."

"I am intrigued by Tom's desires and notions. He is truly dedicated to his art. I have warned him, however, and will warn you that this is a very new technique. There may be difficulties. There may be subsequent surgical realignments and biomech adjustments from time to time. As the state of the art improves, no doubt we will replace the system. Above all, regular checkups will be necessary. And a qualified biomech maintenance doctor or intern will certainly have to be in attendance whenever Tom chooses to use the instruments, be it in the studio or at a concert."

"Delicate stuff, huh?"

"The instruments? No. I think that for all his health, Tom Ellerway is quite a bit more delicate, actually."

"What was his reaction to that?"

"He seems quite confident of his ability to hold the mechanisms and adapt to them. He's very eager to try them out. Rather like a kid with a bunch of new toys." He scratched at his straight, sharp nose and sighed. "Frankly, though, Mr. Capp, I advised him against all of this."

"You what?"

"In our preliminary talk last week, Tom played some tapes for me of what he's been composing. I'm impressed."

"Do you think he won't be able to do his best with his new — uhm — apparatus?"

"It will neither harm nor increase his actual musical abilities. It will merely increase his range. It's like giving a gifted violin player the capacity to play an entire orchestra of instruments while doing his own conducting. Tricks, Mr. Capp. In fact, I'm not sure that this system is capable of the high-flown ideals that Tom seems to have for his music. I am merely a biotechnical surgeon."

"He intends to be the best rocker ever, doctor. Something wrong with that?"

"Does he? Well, he will certainly be something to see and hear with all the embeddings we're talking about. But will the audience truly be able to appreciate what he's doing? Or will he merely be a squawking freak to them, a pleasure machine? The key word there, Mr. Capp, is machine. I would not wish Tom, or anybody, that. Frankly, if he were my son, I would not allow it. This is why I ask for parental permission."

"What was Tom's reaction?"

I was getting antsy. We were building our whole act, our whole publicity push, around this operation.

The doctor smiled gently. "He told me I was an old goon. I should stick the advice up my ass and the electronic stuff inside him. He'd take care of the rest."

I nodded. "Sounds like Ellerway."

"So I thought that you might like to persuade him not to. He speaks highly of you."

"Me? Hey, it's not for *me* to try and run his life."

"Ah. I see."

I was suddenly cold and uncomfortable. "Yeah, well, you know, I'm just a goddamned rock guitarist."

"Yes." He stood up. "Still, it will be necessary to obtain parental permission. I understand he has a mother. His father he doesn't know about."

"I know his mother," I said. "You'll get your permission, doctor." I stood to leave. "You'll get your goddamned permission."

Above us, the steady drone: kids stamping their feet, clapping their hands.

I'm sitting by Ellerway. "You up to it now?"

He's all fixed up. He actually looks good, really Plasticene handsome, like the picture on the crystal cube.

"Hurts a little."

"Yeah, well, we give them just another half an hour, okay? Keep it cool, don't bust a gut. Simple stuff."

"We have to, don't we, Capp?"

"Yes. It looks that way, Ellerway. But let me tell you, we're getting a new manager after this."

Ellerway focuses on me in that funny new way of his, like he's trying to figure me out or something. "Mom says hello to you."

"I imagine she's watching, isn't she?"

"She asked me to ask you if you'll maybe visit her again sometime."

"Sure. Why not? I'd like that, Ellerway. We'll go together."

He opens his mouth to say something, pauses as though changing his mind about what he is going to say, then says, "Are you still ready for whatever comes out, Capp?"

"What are you talking about? I told you, you've got to

take it easy tonight."

"This might be the last chance."

"For what? The world's at our feet. This is just the beginning."

I'm sick inside. My anger at Spud, my fury and indignation at Hardesty are making me crazy. The worry for Ellerway nudges it all into a whirlpool of queasy anxiety. But I won't let her get me. Ellerway's got to get up on the stage again.

He gets up, shrugging away my offer of help. "Okay. Let's go out and play."

We trudge up the ramp, take our places, and begin to bash away into "Dance of the Degenerates," our most upbeat number.

I signal for Benny to lay on a percussion solo. Might as well save Ellerway, give him a break for the next song, which was going to be a little tougher.

I drink a Coke. It does nothing to settle my stomach.

Benny builds up the volume and rhythm to an almost unbearable crescendo. Time to move. I tap out the program of the next number, "Protodeath," on the keyboard at the base of my Gibson and get ready for the climax.

Benny tosses drumsticks again, one to either side of the stage.

The he hits the KILL on the machines, and the sounds instantly stop. No resonance, no echoes; nothing.

The silence is deafening. It catches the audience by surprise. The lights die to black except for those drumsticks, which glow. With a slow implosion of sound from Benny's machines, like a giant sucking in breath, the drumsticks begin to grow into amorphous blobs with soft, red light glowing from within. Slowly the shapes take form. Kid the Flash. Jim Capp.

I touch the tooth communicator, with which I can speak

to Ellerway above the racket around us.

"Ready, chum?"

And he says, "God." With a sigh, "I never thought it would be like this."

I cut in my chords. My holograph mimics the real movements of my hand.

The holograph of Kid the Flash leans over and picks up a chord and a microphone. A sharp microphone. He jams it into his abdomen. It emerges from his back.

To the rhythm of the music, a slow pulsing dirge, he weaves around the stage, shedding gobs of light blood all over the stage. A great tide of the blood flows over the side of the stage, whirlpools into a dense red mist, obscuring everything but random light from within.

I stand beside my holograph, continuing the dirge, letting the synthesizer play with it so that it sounds like the song of some mammoth pipe organ.

The mist gradually fades.

The real Kid stands inside an elaborate coffin, hands folded ceremonially, eyes closed, in funeral tux and tails from the Victorian Age.

His eyes open. His hand reaches to the side of the coffin, takes a wire, and plugs it into the jack just under his ear.

The crowd's roar nearly drowns out the music. His arm slowly snakes out, a finger points at the audience. Stiff-legged, he walks out, mouth open almost as wide as Marley's, and screams an all-keys-played-on-the-organ yell. Holo-mist, white as frost streams from his mouth.

It continues as he sings the song, his understated delivery caused by his weakness making the song all the more chilling.

"Protodeath, protodeath, we're trying on
the grave for size.

Worms are here already, coming through
   your ears, your eyes."

A large television set rises from the misty floor, holding a
picture of the band. Holo-gravestones rise from the pond of
fog that bathes our feet.

Then the Kid takes one of my spare guitars in his hands.
This isn't in the act.

I crash out the last chord, which warbles and slowly
decays into silence.

And then Ellerway cries, "Shit on this!" with all the
power of the scream that began the song. He bashes my
Stratocaster into the TV screen. With a smash of sparks,
the sharded glass is sucked into the tube, then falls out at his
feet. Smoke gusts up. The power cables inside the huge set
flail and snap with flashing intensity. Holding my ruined
guitar in one hand, Ellerway cries. "But we're not dead!
We're alive!"

His subvocalized voice comes over to me on my receiver,
shaking my eardrums through bone conduction.

"It's now, Capp. It's got to be now."

"What are you talking about?"

"Benny. Jim. We're doing 'Dreamflight' next."

I hear Benny say, "Hey, pal, that ain't on the playlist."

"I can feel them, just out of my reach. I want to touch
them, to numb them. You with me, Capp?"

"Fuck, Ellerway. We could get in all kinds of trouble."

I see him across the stage, staring at me, hard and
demanding. His expression is so intense, I have to turn
away.

I look up past the darkness of the blank, blackened faces
of the crowd wriggling on their wires. Past the light-
canopied 3-D camera setups, up to the opaque bullet-proof
glass panel of the sky suite. I think of the power I've got

now the power and the adulation. I think of the money.

And then I think, *that bitch up there has had it all for years. What does she want now? More. She wants all of me. She has a part now. But that's all she's ever going to get. And as long as I'm alive, she isn't going to touch Ellerway.*

"Okay, Tom," I say. "It's your show."

I smile up at the sky suite and give the old lady the bird.

Ellerway smiles at me wearily. "Improvise around me. Right. And one and two and three—"

He brings down his hand. I strike mine across the strings, trying to remember the song. We've practiced it maybe two or three times; it was all scribbled on paper. Neither Benny nor I can remember much. I hit the chord again, then start phasing it with the manual on the computer board. I've got the hall's acoustics down now, and I can play with them. I sneak the sound around, whooshing like a broken helicopter about to chop off the crowd's heads.

Ellerway signals Benny to come in; the drums begin to crank along recklessly, restlessly. I slam out another chord and diddle with my memory of the basic melody of "Dreamflight."

With all the money riding on this gig, the director and technicians aren't about to turn off the power just because we change songs in the middle of a set. So they just put up a shifting webwork of spots and filters, no doubt computer-controlled to change with the shadings of the music, and they let us be.

Ellerway starts with the standard polyphonic attack, a five-scaled choir of hundreds of voices branching out from his own, weaving delicately among themselves their intricate network of rock fortisimo and rock dissonance. The harmonic fabric vaults you into some ethereal emotional plane, while the cacophonic aspects make you realize that you are really dangling from the cliff over death's blackness. Somehow Ellerway manages to recall the bass line of "Protodeath," building an entirely new chorale above it.

"The night dawns upon us all
Chinchilla chill
Sharp claws, sharp jaws
Tearing at your heart. Dead fall."

The fluid voices suddenly congeal into one voice. Ellerway's rock-bellow of rage. My guitar computer, geared to sense the change, switches timbre in midnote of my melody lacing. Automatically, it growls a sympathetic chord, almost as if Ellerway were controlling it.

The song is inside me and abruptly it becomes the focal point of my existence. Just a point, mind you. Something small and concentrated; I could feel it feeding into me from the power of the guitar, from the air which buzzed with it.

God knows what is going through the actual wires to the listeners.

Ellerway sings. The stuff inside him—the frequency modulators, the augmenters, the microtransistors, the minicomputers, all flesh-enmeshed machinery—takes his wishes and makes them music. Perfect shimmering control.

As my hands grab and flutter and dive-bomb the strings, pausing only occasionally to fidget with the computer controls, I suddenly realize what he is trying to do.

I want to stop, to tackle him or something, but it's too late. I'm into it. The music has me by the short hairs. Ellerway's voice is pulling my strings.

I play like a demon. A demon caught in a shaft of light from heaven and reluctantly rising up into the sky among the choraling host, kicking and screeching and yowling all the while.

And damned if I don't remember the whole song—just as

we had practiced it.

I can feel Benny's thumping behind me blow at my sweaty hair. I know he is synchronized with Ellerway as well.

It flows out, beautiful and nasty and right. Gut stuff, with all of Ellerway's feelings and thoughts somehow mixed in for good measure. I can feel Ellerway inside me. I recognize part of him from the two years of our work together, but there is so much more. My juices move with his. They dance. The song mixes my feelings with Ellerway's by some kind of special electric chemistry that I don't understand.

My guitar trills in sympathetic stridency like the *Hallelujahs* and *Praise the Lords* rhythmically filling in the beats and music of a preacher's chant at a revival meeting.

"I'm like you, just like you," Ellerway sings. Suddenly a whisper-choir rises all around, repeating the phrase in various complementary musical permutations molded to Ellerway's subtle changes, his nuances of emotion. It's not just his performance up here, an act, a piece of plastic slapped with paint and pretty costumes sitting amidst a castle of equipment.

It's Ellerway, stripped of pretense, flowing honestly, simultaneously showing his own person and embodying a common denominator of humanity. My guitar lines and Benny's drums fill in as best they can, but they're essentially drowned in the heat and light of Ellerway's song.

He takes off his Victorian topcoat and his shirt, leaving his chest bare. He plays on the chest keyboard, flips this switch, that dial upon his arm. Sweat runs down the crevasses of his scars, mixing with the blood that's leaking again.

The stainless steel, grotesquely protruding from flesh like metal bone, shines in the rainbow light. Wires snake under his armpits, stitched through his abdomen like plastic leeches. His hair hangs limp down his back, where bolts glint.

He's still got the jack plugged into his neck, but I think he's getting weak. He slows a bit, then spins around and signals Benny and me to stop.

We do.

Slowly, breathing hard, he turns again and points to the audience.

"Music, our senses' essence.
Distillation of metal and will.
Missionary moonshine.
Come drink from our steaming still!"

He gestures wide, bows his head.

A ghost shiver dances down my spine, deep into my bowels.

Something inside me goes out to him. I can sense that the audience is having the same experience. My guitar stills. I look out at that lake of faces. It is calm, quiet.

No thrash of limbs. No flail of wires.

They stare at Kid the Flash.

Ellerway opens his eyes wide, wider, seeing something beyond those faces.

He touches them. He feels their song. The songs of their insides. The harmonics of their souls.

He knows them all. I can see it in his expression. I can feel it moving inside me. Recognizing me.

Recognizing me and all that I am.

He gasps. He tries to sing the song he feels, coming from all of us, telepathic thought-rock crashing in on him. Fifty thousand mind-hands reach for the mike he holds to scream their life, wail their despair and joy to others.

He sings one note. No word. Just song. It is piercingly

beautiful. Another. Another. A melody is formed. Slowly he synthesizes the instruments for the song. The electronic background. The song is his as much as anyone else's.

The song sings of bodies riddled with metal. Bodies hanging crucified on the skeleton of a dead electronic culture. It cries and weeps and despairs.

It hints of lost possibilities.

When it comes, I hear the *snap* distinctly. A blue-white spark jumps from a length of wiring in his chest. Another arcs from his neck. Blood spills from his mouth. Smoky flames lick up his chest.

He falls.

I dash to him. I yank the plug from his neck. My guitar flops against my thigh. I tear it off. I rip my shirt off to smother the flames. I can smell charred flesh.

This was never supposed to happen. Too many safety precautions.

Benny's there too, all of a sudden, with wet towels. Steam rises up desperately.

The medmechs finally arrive.

Almost the moment they do, the jerks at the lighting switches finally get the smarts to drop the light curtain. It shimmers on, cutting off the vision of thousands of stunned faces.

The roadies run for a stretcher.

Ellerway is still conscious. His eyes are glassy. Faraway. "I . . . I . . . did it. For a moment, I felt —"

"I know, Ellerway," I say. "Now rest. You've done some heavy damage." I'm numb inside. The guilt sits like lead in my stomach.

He turns to face me as a mechman spurts some foam over the glowing metal, the melted plastic. "Capp."

"Shut up," I said.

"Capp. I could touch you, too. I know now, Capp. I

know about you. And it's okay."

I turn to ice inside. "What?"

His eyes close.

"What's wrong?" I ask the nearest doctor. "He's not—"

"No. Not yet."

They cart him off. The burning smell is still in my nostrils. I start to follow. Benny stops me.

"Nothing you can do, Capp."

"Shit, I've got to do something." Tears of rage and frustration leak from my eyes.

He looks at me with a penetrating stare that says, "Yeah, and I know too." He picks up my guitar and hands it to me. "Keep on rockin' kiddo."

He walks away, shaking his head.

I can hear the voices of the crowd crying out from beyond the light curtain, "Kid! Kid! Kid the Flash!" I can hear seats being ripped out, cups crashing, wires whipping. I hear robo-security pushing them back as they try to leap through the light curtain.

The robots click and hum with mechanical strain.

I take my Gibson, my thirty-year-old, hundred-thou-sand-dollar, souped-up Gibson, and I smash it into an amplifier.

All that was two years ago.

Now . . . Now I've got my million-and-a-half-buck house in the canyon. I've got another house on the East Coast. I hung onto my cabin, too. I've got money in the bank, money invested, money coming out of my ass. I've got a state-of-the-art recording studio in the basement, stocked with any musical instrument you'd care to name.

I've got a Jacuzzi. I've got a sauna. I've got a cook and a housekeeper. I even picked up a contract wife.

Kid the Flash is no more, but the crystals keep selling.

The concert where he did his trick is the most popular vid-disc in history.

And Ellerway is still around, despite the rumors to the contrary. They had to rebuild him, of course. They had to pry the twisted mass of fused plastic and metal from him, treat the burns, graft back flesh and bits of organs. He can talk. He can't sing yet. They're working on that.

Hardesty got her pound of flesh. She's happy. She even suggested that I form a new band, which she would back. I told her to shove the idea. I'm retired. I return any mail or messages from her unopened.

Benny's in a new band. Managed by the Spud. Owned body and soul by Hardesty.

Ellerway comes around once in a while. He's still a little wary of me. I can't blame him. We talk and play together.

He mostly writes music now. He's working with a group of scientists studying the processes he introduced. I hear he's even thinking about bringing out an experimental album next year. He looks a little different. He's a lot quieter. When conversation has dried up and we're sitting on the patio, he gets this glassy stare as he looks down into the misty valley.

We never talk about Kid the Flash or that final concert.

We never talk about his mother, though we both see her from time to time and her coolness and her contempt toward me seems to be fading.

But I've promised myself. From that moment at the end of the concert, I've promised myself that I would explain to him. I don't know if he'll really understand but I have to try to make him.

One day it will all come out and we'll really know each other. One day.

Snow

By John Crowley

I don't think Georgie would ever have got one for herself. She was at once unsentimental and a little in awe of death. No, it was her first husband — an immensely rich and (from Georgie's description) a strangely weepy guy, who had got it for her. Or for himself, actually, of course. He was to be the beneficiary. Only he died himself shortly after it was installed. If *installed* is the right word. After he died, Georgie got rid of most of what she'd inherited from him, liquidated it. It was cash that she had liked best about that marriage anyway, but the Wasp couldn't really be got rid of. Georgie ignored it.

In fact the thing really was about the size of a wasp of the largest kind, and it had the same lazy and mindless flight. And of course it really was a bug, not of the insect kind but of the surveillance kind. And so its name fit all around: one of those bits of accidental poetry the world generates without thinking. O Death, where is thy sting?

Georgie ignored it, but it was hard to avoid; you had to be

a little careful around it; it followed Georgie at a variable distance, depending on her motions and the numbers of other people around her; the level of light, and the tone of her voice. And there was always the danger you might shut it in a door or knock it down with a tennis racket.

It cost a fortune (if you count the access and the perpetual-care contract, all prepaid), and though it wasn't really fragile, it made you nervous.

It wasn't recording all the time. There had to be a certain amount of light, though not much. Darkness shut it off. And then sometimes it would get lost. Once when we hadn't seen it hovering around for a time, I opened a closet door, and it flew out, unchanged. It went off looking for her, humming softly. It must have been shut in there for days.

Eventually it ran out, or down. A lot could go wrong, I suppose, with circuits that small, controlling that many functions. It ended up spending a lot of time bumping gently against the bedroom ceiling, over and over, like a winter fly. Then one day the maid swept it out from under the bureau, a husk. By that time it had transmitted at least eight thousand hours (eight thousand was the minimum guarantee) of Georgie: of her days and hours, her comings in and her goings out, her speech and motion, her living self—all on file, taking up next to no room, at The Park. And then, when the time came, you could go there, to The Park, say on a Sunday afternoon; and in quiet landscaped surroundings (as The Park described it) you would find her personal resting chamber; and there, in privacy, through the miracle of modern information storage and retrieval systems, you could access her, her alive, her as she was in every way, never changing or growing any older, fresher (as The Park's brochure said) than in memory ever green.

I married Georgie for her money, the same reason she

married her first, the one who took out The Park's contract for her. She married me, I think, for my looks; she always had a taste for looks in men. I wanted to write. I made a calculation that more women than men make, and decided that to be supported and paid for by a rich wife would give me freedom to do so, to "develop." The calculation worked out no better for me that it does for most women who make it. I carried a typewriter and a case of miscellaneous paper from Ibiza to Gstaad to Bali to London, and typed on beaches, and learned to ski. Georgie liked me in ski clothes.

Now that those looks are all but gone, I can look back on myself as a young hunk and see that I was in a way a rarity, a type that you run into often among women, far less among men, the beauty unaware of his beauty, aware that he affects women profoundly and more or less instantly but doesn't know why; thinks he is being listened to and understood, that his soul is being seen, when all that's being seen is long-lashed eyes and a strong, square, tanned wrist turning in a lovely gesture, stubbing out a cigarette. Confusing. By the time I figured out why I had for so long been indulged and cared for, and listened to, why I was interesting, I wasn't as interesting as I had been. At about the same time I realized I wasn't a writer at all. Georgie's investment stopped looking as good to her, and my calculation had ceased to add up; only by that time I had come, pretty unexpectedly, to love Georgie a lot, and she just as unexpectedly had come to love and need me too, as much as she needed anybody. We never really parted, even though when she died I hadn't seen her for years. Phone calls, at dawn or four A.M. because she never, for all her travel, really grasped that the world turns and cocktail hour travels around with it. She was a crazy, wasteful, happy woman, without a trace of malice or per-manence or ambition in her—easily pleased and easily bored and strangely serene despite the hectic pace she kept up. She cherished things and lost them and forgot them: things, days, people. She had fun, though, and I had fun with her; that was her talent and her destiny, not always an easy one. Once, hung over in a New York hotel, watching a sudden snowfall out the immense window, she said to me, "Charlie, I'm going to die of fun."

And she did. Snow-foiling in Austria, she was among the first to get one of those snow leopards, silent beasts as fast as speed-boats. Alfredo called me in California to tell me, but with the distance and his accent and his eagerness to tell me *he* wasn't to blame, I never grasped the details. I was still her husband, her closest relative, heir to the little she still had, and beneficiary, too, of The Park's access concept. Fortunately, The Park's services included collecting her from the morgue in Gstaad and installing her in her chamber at The Park's California unit. Beyond signing papers and taking delivery when Georgie arrived by freight airship at Van Nuys, there was nothing for me to do. The Park's representative was solicitous and made sure I understood how to go about accessing Georgie, but I wasn't listening. I am only a child of my time, I suppose. Everything about death, the fact of it, the fate of the remains, and the situation of the living faced with it, seems grotesque to me, embarrassing, useless. And everything done about it only makes it more grotesque, more useless: Someone I loved is dead; let me therefore dress in clown's clothes, talk backwards, and buy expensive machinery to make up for it. I went back to L.A.

A year or more later, the contents of some safe-deposit boxes of Georgie's arrived from the lawyer's: some bonds and such stuff and a small steel case, velvet lined, that contained a key, a key deeply notched on both sides and headed with smooth plastic, like the key to an expensive car.

Why did I go to The Park that first time? Mostly because I had forgotten about it. Getting that key in the mail was like coming across a pile of old snapshots you hadn't cared to look at when they were new but which after they have aged come to contain the past, as they did not contain the present. I was curious.

I understood very well that The Park and its access concept were very probably only another cruel joke on the rich, preserving the illusion that they can buy what can't be bought, like the cryonics fad of thirty years ago. Once in Ibiza, Georgie and I met a German couple who also had a contract with The Park; their Wasp hovered over them like a Paraclete and made them self-conscious in the extreme—they seemed to be constantly rehearsing the eternal show being stored up for their descendants. Their deaths had taken over their lives, as though they were pharaohs. Did they, Georgie wondered, exclude the Wasp from their bedroom? Or did its presence there stir them to greater efforts, proofs of undying love and admirable vigor for the unborn to see?

No, death wasn't to be cheated that way, any more than by pyramids, by masses said in perpetuity. It wasn't Georgie saved from death that I would find. But there were eight thousand hours of her life with me, genuine hours, stored there more carefully than they could be in my porous memory; Georgie hadn't excluded the Wasp from her bedroom, our bedroom, and she who had never performed for anybody could not have conceived of performing for it. And there would be me, too, undoubtedly, caught unintentionally by the Wasp's attention. Out of those thousands of hours there would be hundreds of myself, and myself had just then begun to be problematic to me, something that had to be figured out, something about which evidence had to be gathered and weighed. I was thirty-eight years old.

That summer, then, I borrowed a Highway Access Permit (the old HAPpy cards of those days) from a county lawyer I knew and drove the coast highway up to where The Park was at the end of a pretty beach road, all alone above the sea. It looked from the outside like the best, most peaceful kind of Italian country cemetery, a low stucco wall topped with urns, amid cypresses, an arched gate in the center. A small brass plaque on the gate: PLEASE USE YOUR KEY. The gate opened, not to a square of shaded tombstones but onto a ramped corridor going down: The cemetery wall was an illusion, the works were underground. Silence, or nameless Muzak-like silence; solitude—either the necessary technicians were discreetly hidden or none were needed. Certainly the access concept turned out to be simplicity itself, in operation anyway. Even I, who am an idiot about information technology, could tell that. The Wasp was genuine state-of-the-art stuff, but what we mourners got was as ordinary as home movies, as old letters tied up in ribbon.

A display screen near the entrance told me down which corridor to find Georgie, and my key let me into a small screening room where there was a moderate-size TV monitor, two comfortable chairs, and dark walls of chocolate-brown carpeting. The sweet-sad Muzak. Georgie herself was evidently somewhere in the vicinity, in the wall or under the floor, they weren't specific about the charnel-house aspect of the place. In the control panel before the TV were a keyhole for my key and two bars: ACCESS and RESET.

I sat, feeling foolish and a little afraid, too, made more uncomfortable by being so deliberately soothed by neutral furnishings and sober tools. I imagined, around me, down other corridors, in other chambers, others communed with their dead as I was about to do, that the dead were murmuring to them beneath the stream of Muzak; that they wept to see and hear, as I might, but I could hear nothing. I turned my key in its slot, and the screen lit up. The dim lights dimmed further, and the Muzak ceased. I pushed ACCESS, obviously the next step. No doubt all these procedures had been explained to me long ago at the dock when Georgie in her aluminum box was being off-loaded, and I hadn't listened. And on the screen she turned to look at me—only not at me, though. I started and drew breath—at the Wasp that watched her. She was in mid-sentence, mid-gesture. Where? When? *Or put it on the same card with the others,* she said, turning away. Someone said something. Georgie answered, and stood up, the Wasp panning and moving erratically with her, like an amateur with a home-video camera. A white room, sunlight, wicker, Ibiza. Georgie wore a cotton blouse, open; from a table she picked up lotion, poured some on her hand, and rubbed it across her freckled breastbone. The meaningless conversation about putting something on a card went on, ceased. I watched the room, wondering what year, what season I had stumbled into. Georgie pulled off her shirt—her small round breasts tipped with large, childlike nipples, child's breasts she still had at forty, shook delicately. And she went out onto the balcony, the Wasp following, blinded by sun, adjusting. *If you want to do it that way,* someone said. The someone crossed the screen, a brown blur, naked. It was me. Georgie said *Oh, look, hummingbirds.*

She watched them, rapt, and the Wasp crept close to her cropped blond head, rapt too, and I watched her watch. She turned away, rested her elbows on the balustrade. I couldn't remember this day. How should I? One of hundreds, of thousands. . . . She looked out to the bright sea, wearing her sleepwalking face, mouth partly open, and absently stroked her breast with her oiled hand. An iridescent glitter among the flowers was the hummingbird.

Without really knowing what I did—I felt hungry, suddenly, hungry for pastness, for more—I touched the RESET bar. The balcony in Ibiza vanished, the screen glowed emptily. I touched ACCESS.

At first there was darkness, a murmur, then a dark back moved away from before the Wasp's eye, and a dim scene of people resolved itself. Jump. Other people, or the same people, a party? Jump. Apparently the Wasp was turning itself on and off according to the changes in light levels here, wherever *here* was. Georgie in a dark dress having her cigarette lit, brief flare of the lighter. She said, *Thanks*. Jump. A foyer or hotel lounge. Paris? The Wasp jerkily sought for her among people coming and going; it couldn't make a movie, establishing shots, cutaways—it could only doggedly follow Georgie, like a jealous husband, seeing nothing else. This was frustrating. I pushed RESET. ACCESS. Georgie brushed her teeth, somewhere, somewhen.

I understood, after one or two more of these terrible leaps. Access was random. There was no way to dial up a year, a day, a scene. The Park had supplied no program, none; the eight thousand hours weren't filed at all; they were a jumble, like a lunatic's memory, like a deck of shuffled cards. I had supposed, without thinking about it, that they would begin at the beginning and go on till they reached the end. Why didn't they?

I also understood something else. If access was truly random, if I truly had no control, then I had lost as good as forever those scenes I had seen. Odds were on the order of eight thousand to one (more? far more? probabilities are opaque to me) that I would never light on them again by pressing this bar. I felt a pang of loss for that afternoon in Ibiza. It was doubly gone now. I sat before the empty screen, afraid to touch ACCESS again, afraid of what I would lose.

I shut down the machine (the light level in the room rose, the Muzak poured softly back in) and went out into the halls, back to the display screen in the entranceway. The list of names slowly, greenly, rolled over like the list of departing flights at an airport. Code numbers were missing from beside many indicating perhaps that they weren't yet in residence, only awaited. In the *D*s, three names, and DIRECTOR — hidden among them as though he were only another of the dead. A chamber number. I went to find it and went in. The director looked more like a janitor or a night watchman, the semiretired type you often see caretaking little-visited places. He wore a brown smock like a monk's robe and was making coffee in a corner of his small office, out of which little business seemed to be done. He looked up startled, caught out, when I entered.

"Sorry," I said, "but I don't think I understand this system right."

"A problem?" he said. "Shouldn't be a problem." He looked at me a little wide-eyed and shy, hoping not to be called on for anything difficult. "Equipment's all working?"

"I don't know," I said. "It doesn't seem that it could be." I described what I thought I had learned about The Park's access concept. "That can't be right, can it?" I said. "That access is totally random . . ."

He was nodding, still wide-eyed, paying close attention.

"Is it?" I asked.

"Is it what?"

"Random."

"Oh, yes. Yes, sure. If everything's in working order."

I could think of nothing to say for a moment, watching him nod reassuringly. Then "Why?" I asked. "I mean why is there no way at all to, to organize, to have some kind of organized access to the material?" I had begun to feel that sense of grotesque foolishness in the presence of death, as though I were haggling over Georgie's effects. "That seems stupid, if you'll pardon me."

"Oh no, oh no," he said. "You've read your literature? You've read all your literature?"

"Well, to tell the truth . . ."

"That's all just as described," the director said. "I can promise you that. If there's any problem at all. . . ."

"Do you mind," I said, "if I sit down?" I smiled. He seemed so afraid of me and my complaints, of me as mourner, possibly grief crazed and unable to grasp the simple limits of his responsibilities to me, that he needed soothing himself. "I'm sure everything's fine," I said. "I just don't think I understand. I'm kind of dumb about these things."

"Sure. Sure. Sure." He regretfully put away his coffee makings and sat behind his desk, lacing his fingers together like a consultant. "People get a lot of satisfaction out of the access here," he said, "a lot of comfort, if they take it in the right spirit." He tried a smile. I wondered what qualifications he had had to show to get this job. "The random part. Now it's all in the literature. There's the legal aspect — you're not a lawyer are you, no, no, sure, no offense. You see, the material here isn't *for* anything, except, well, except for communing. But suppose the stuff *were* programmed, searchable. Suppose there was a problem about taxes or inheritance or so on. There could be subpoenas, lawyers all over the place, destroying the memorial concept completely."

I really hadn't thought of that. Built-in randomness saved past lives from being searched in any systematic way. And no doubt saved The Park from being in the records business and at the wrong end of a lot of suits. "You'd have to watch the whole eight thousand hours," I said, "and even if you found what you were looking for there'd be no way to replay it. It would have gone by." It would slide into the random past even as you watched it, like that afternoon in Ibiza, that party in Paris. Lost. He smiled and nodded. I smiled and nodded.

"I'll tell you something," he said. "They didn't predict that. The randomness. It was a side effect, an effect of the storage process. Just luck." His grin turned down, his brows knitted seriously. "See, we're storing here at the molecular level. We have to go that small, for space problems. I mean your eight-thousand-hour guarantee. If we had gone tape or conventional, how much room would it take up? If the access concept caught on. A lot of room. So we went vapor trap and endless tracking. Size of my thumbnail. It's all in the literature." He looked at me strangely. I had a sudden intense sensation that I was being fooled, tricked, that the man before me in his smock was no expert, no technician; he was a charlatan, or maybe a madman impersonating a director and not belonging here at all. It raised the hair on my neck and passed. "So the randomness," he was saying. "It was an effect of going molecular. Brownian movement. All you do is lift the endless tracking for a microsecond and you get a rearrangement at the molecular level. We don't randomize. The molecules do it for us."

I rememberd Brownian movement, just barely, from physics class. The random movement of molecules, the teacher said; it has a mathematical description. It's like the movement of dust motes you see swimming in a shaft of sunlight, like the swirl of snow-flakes in a glass paperweight that shows a cottage being snowed on. "I see," I said. "I guess I see."

"Is there," he said, "any other problem?" He said it as though there might be some other problem and that he knew what it might be and that he hoped I didn't have it. "You understand the system, key lock, two bars, ACCESS, RESET . . ."

"I understand," I said. "I understand now."

"Communing," he said, standing, relieved, sure I would

be gone soon. "I understand. It takes a while to relax into the communing concept."

"Yes," I said. "It does."

I wouldn't learn what I had come to learn, whatever that was. The Wasp had not been good at storage after all, no, no better than my young soul had been. Days and weeks had been missed by its tiny eye. It hadn't seen well, and in what it had seen it had been no more able to distinguish the just-as-well-forgotten from the unforgettable than my own eye had been. No better and no worse—the same.

And yet, and yet—she stood up in Ibiza and dressed her breasts with lotion, and spoke to me: *Oh, look, hummingbirds.* I had forgotten, and the Wasp had not, and I owned once again what I hadn't known I had lost, hadn't known was precious to me.

The sun was setting when I left The Park, the satin sea foaming softly, randomly around the rocks.

I had spent my life waiting for something, not knowing what, not even knowing I waited. Killing time. I was still waiting. But what I had been waiting for had already occurred and was past.

It was two years, nearly, since Georgie had died; two years until, for the first and last time, I wept for her—for her and for myself.

Of course I went back. After a lot of work and correctly placed dollars, I netted a HAPpy card of my own. I had time to spare, like a lot of people then, and often on empty afternoons (never on Sunday) I would get out onto the unpatched and weed-grown freeway and glide up the coast. The Park was always open. I relaxed into the communing concept.

Now, after some hundreds of hours spent there underground, now, when I have long ceased to go through those doors (I have lost my key, I think; anyway, I don't know where to look for it), I know that the solitude I felt myself to be in was real. The watchers around me, the listeners I sensed in other chambers, were mostly my imagination. There was rarely anyone there.

These tombs were as neglected as any tombs anywhere usually are. Either the living did not care to attend much on the dead — when have they ever? — or the hopeful buyers of the contracts had come to discover the flaw in the access concept — as I discovered it, in the end.

ACCESS and she takes dresses one by one from her closet, and holds them against her body, and studies the effect in a tall mirror, and puts them back again. She had a funny face, which she never made except when looking at herself in the mirror, a face made for no one but herself, that was actually quite unlike her. The mirror Georgie.

RESET.

ACCESS. By a bizarre coincidence here she is looking in another mirror. I think the Wasp could be confused by mirrors. She turns away, the Wasp adjusts; there is someone asleep, tangled in bedclothes on a big hotel bed, morning, a room-service cart. Oh, the Algonquin: myself. Winter. Snow is falling outside the tall window. She searches her handbag, takes out a small vial, swallows a pill with coffee, holding the cup by its body and not its handle. I stir, show a tousled head of hair. Conversation — unintelligible. Gray room, whitish snow light, color degraded. Would I now (I thought, watching us) reach out for her? Would I in the next hour take her, or she me, push aside the bedclothes, open her pale pajamas? She goes into the john, shuts the door. The Wasp watches stupidly, excluded transmitting the door.

RESET, finally.

But what (I would wonder) if I had been patient, what if I had watched and waited?

Time, it turns out takes an unconscionable time. The waste, the footless waste — it's no spectator sport. Whatever fun there is in sitting idly looking at nothing and tasting your own being for a whole afternoon, there is no fun in replaying it. The waiting is excruciating. How often, in five years, in eight thousand hours of daylight or lamplight, might we have coupled, how much time expended in love-making? A hundred hours, two hundred? Odds were not high of my coming on such a scene; darkness swallowed most of them, and the others were lost in the interstices of endless hours spent shopping, reading, on planes and in cars, asleep, apart. Hopeless.

ACCESS. She has turned on a bedside lamp. Alone. She hunts amid the Kleenex and magazines on the bedside table, finds a watch, looks at it dully, turns it right side up, looks again, and puts it down. Cold. She burrows in the blankets, yawning, staring, then puts out a hand for the phone but only rests her hand on it, thinking. Thinking at four A.M. She withdraws her hand, shivers a child's deep, sleepy shiver, and shuts off the light. A bad dream. In an instant it's morning, dawn; the Wasp slept, too. She sleeps soundly, unmoving, only the top of her blond head showing out of the quilt — and will no doubt sleep so for hours, watched over more attentively, more fixedly, than any peeping Tom could ever have watched over her.

RESET.

ACCESS.

"I can't hear as well as I did at first," I told the director. "And the definition is getting softer."

"Oh sure," the director said. "That's really in the literature. We have to explain that carefully. That this might be a problem."

"It isn't just my monitor?" I asked. "I thought it was probably only the monitor."

"No, no, not really, no," he said. He gave me coffee. We'd gotten to be friendly over the months. I think, as well as being afraid of me, he was glad I came around now and then; at least one of the living came here, one at least was using the services. "There's a *slight* degeneration that does occur."

"Everything seems to be getting gray."

His face had shifted into intense concern, no belittling this problem. "Mm-hm, mm-hm, see, at the molecular level where we're at, there *is* degeneration. It's just in the physics. It randomizes a little over time. So you lose—you don't lose a minute of what you've got, but you lose a little definition. A little color. But it levels off."

"It does?"

"We think it does. Sure it does, we promise it does. We *predict* that it will."

"But you don't know."

"Well, well you see we've only been in this business a short while. This concept is new. There were things we couldn't know." He still looked at me, but seemed at the same time to have forgotten me. Tired. He seemed to have grown colorless himself lately, old, losing definition. "You might start getting some snow," he said softly.

ACCESS RESET ACCESS.

A gray plaza of herringbone-laid stones, gray, clicking palms. She turns up the collar of her sweater, narrowing her eyes in a stern wind. Buys magazines at a kiosk: *Vogue, Harper's, La Moda. Cold,* she says to the kiosk girl. *Frio.* The young man I was takes her arm; they walk back along the beach, which is deserted and strung with cast seaweed, washed by a dirty sea. Winter in Ibiza. We talk, but the Wasp can't hear, the sea's sound confuses it; it seems bored by its duties and lags behind us.

RESET.

ACCESS. The Algonquin, terribly familiar morning, winter. She turns away from the snowy window. I am in bed, and for a moment watching this I felt suspended between two mirrors, reflected endlessly. I had seen this before; I had lived it once and remembered it once, and remembered the memory, and here it was again, or could it be nothing but another morning, a similar morning. There were far more than one like this, in this place. But no; she turns from the window, she gets out her vial of pills, picks up the coffee cup by its body: I had seen this moment before, not months before, weeks before, here in this chamber. I had come upon the same scene twice.

What are the odds of it, I wondered, what are the odds of coming upon the same minutes again, these minutes.

I stir within the bedclothes.

I leaned forward to hear, this time, what I would say; it was something like *but fun anyway,* or something.

Fun, she says, laughing, harrowed, the degraded sound a ghost's twittering. *Charlie, someday I'm going to die of fun.*

She takes her pill. The Wasp follows her to the john, and is shut out.

Why am I here? I thought, and my heart was beating hard and slow. *What am I here for? What?*

RESET.

ACCESS.

Silvered icy streets. New York, Fifth Avenue. She is climbing, shouting from a cab's dark interior: *Just don't shout at me,* she shouts at someone; her mother I never met a dragon. She is out and hurrying away down the sleety street with her bundles, the Wasp at her shoulder. I could reach out and touch her shoulder and make her turn and follow me out. Walking away, lost in the colorless press of traffic and people, impossible to discern within the softened snowy image.

Something was very wrong.

Georgie hated winter, she escaped it most of the time we were together, about the first of the year beginning to long for the sun that had gone elsewhere; Austria was all right for a few weeks, the toy villages and sugar snow and bright, sleek skiers were not really the winter she feared, though even in fire-warmed chalets it was hard to get her naked without gooseflesh and shudders from some draft only she could feel. We were chaste in winter. So Georgie escaped it. Antigua and Bali and two months in Ibiza when the almonds blossomed. It was continual false, flavorless spring all winter long.

How often could snow have fallen when the Wasp was watching her?

Not often; countable times, times I could count up myself if I could remember as the Wasp could. Not often. Not always.

"There's a problem," I said to the director.

"It's peaked out, has it?" he said. "That definition problem?"

"Acutally," I said, "it's gotten worse."

He was sitting behind his desk, arms spread wide across his chair's back, and a false, pinkish flush to his cheeks like undertaker's makeup. Drinking.

"Hasn't peaked out, huh?" he said.

"That's not the problem," I said. "The problem is the access. It's not random like you said."

"Molecular level," he said. "It's in the physics."

"You don't understand. It's not getting more random. It's getting less random. It's getting selective. It's freezing up."

"No, no, no," he said dreamily. "Access is random. Life isn't all summer and fun, you know. Into each life some rain must fall."

I sputtered, trying to explain. "But but . . ."

"You know," he said, "I've been thinking of getting out of access." He pulled open a drawer in the desk before him; it made an empty sound. He stared within it dully for a moment and shut it. "The Park's been good for me, but I'm just not used to this. Used to be you thought you could render a service, you know? Well, hell, you know, you've had fun, what do you care?"

He *was* mad. For an instant I heard the dead around me; I tasted on my tongue the stale air of underground.

"I remember," he said, tilting back in his chair and looking elsewhere, "many years ago. I got into access. Only we didn't call it that then. What I did was, I worked for a stock-footage house. It was going out of business, like they all did, like this place here is going to do, shouldn't say that, but you didn't hear it. Anyway, it was a big warehouse with steel shelves for miles, filled with film cans, film cans filled with old plastic film, you know? Film of every kind. And movie people, if they wanted old scenes of past time in their movies, would call up and ask for what they wanted, find me this, find me that. And we had everything, every kind of scene, but you know what the hardest thing to find was? Just ordinary scenes of daily life. I mean people just doing things and living their lives. You know what we *did* have? Speeches. People giving speeches. Like presidents. You could have hours of speeches, but not just people, whatcha-callit, oh, washing clothes, sitting in a park . . ."

"It might just be the reception," I said. "Somehow."

He looked at me for a long moment as though I had just arrived. "Anyway," he said at last, turning away again, "I was there awhile learning the ropes. And producers called and said, "Get me this, get me that." And one producer was making a film, some film of the past, and he wanted old scenes, *old,* of people long ago, in the summer: having fun;

eating ice cream; swimming in bathing suits; riding in convertibles. Fifty years ago. Eighty years ago."

He opened his empty drawer again, found a toothpick, and began to use it.

"So I accessed the earliest stuff. Speeches. More speeches. But I found a scene here and there—people in the street, fur coats, window-shopping, traffic. Old people, I mean they were young then, but people of the past; they have these pinched kind of faces, you get to know them. Sad, a little. On city streets, hurrying, holding their hats. Cities were sort of black then, in film, black cars in the streets, black derby hats. Stone. Well, it wasn't what they wanted. I found summer for them, color summer, but new. They wanted old. I kept looking back. I kept looking. I did. The further back I went, the more I saw these pinched faces, black cars, black streets of stone. Snow. There isn't any summer there."

With slow gravity he rose and found a brown bottle and two coffee cups. He poured sloppily. "So it's not your reception," he said. "Film takes longer, I guess, but it's in the physics. All in the physics. A word to the wise is sufficient."

The liquor was harsh, a cold distillate of past sunlight. I wanted to go, get out, not look back. I would not stay watching until there was only snow.

"So I'm getting out of access," the director said. "Let the dead bury the dead, right? Let the dead bury the dead."

I didn't go back. I never went back, though the highways opened again and The Park isn't far from the town I've settled in. Settled: the right word. It restores your balance, in the end, even in a funny way your cheerfulness, when you come to know, without regrets, that the best thing that's going to happen in your life has already happened. And I still have some summer left to me.

I think there are two different kinds of memory, and only

one kind gets worse as I get older; the kind where, by an effort of will, you can reconstruct your first car or your serial number or the name and figure of your high school physics teacher—a Mr. Holm, in a gray suit, a bearded guy, skinny, about thirty. The other kind doesn't worsen; if anything it grows more intense. The sleepwalking kind, the kind you stumble into as into rooms with secret doors and suddenly find yourself sitting not on your front porch but in a classroom. You can't at first think where or when, and a bearded, smiling man is turning in his hand a glass paperweight, inside which a little cottage stands in a swirl of snow.

There is no access to Georgie, except that now and then, unpredictably, when I'm sitting on the porch or pushing a grocery cart or standing at the sink, a memory of that kind will visit me, vivid and startling, like a hypnotist's snap of fingers.

Or like that funny experience you sometimes have, on the point of sleep, of hearing your name called softly and distinctly by someone who is not there.

To Mark the Times We Had

By Barry N. Malzberg

*The scene is the stage of a theater of indeterminate age
and location; it is dimly lit. An ACTOR is speaking; somewhere to his left, the PRODUCER sits listening.*

ACTOR. I shall do such things—I know not what they
are—but they shall be the terror of the earth.

DIRECTOR. No good.

ACTOR *(After a pause).* Oh, that this too, too sullied
flesh should thaw, melt, resolve itself—

DIRECTOR. Doesn't work. Cut it.

ACTOR *(Angrily).* Our revels now are ended, and these,
our players—

DIRECTOR. Say thanks a lot. We'll be in touch now.

ACTOR *(Frantic).* Ask not what your country can do for
you but what you can do for your country. We shall never
fear to negotiate, but we shall never negotiate from fear. Ask
not what your country can do for you but what you can do
for your country.

DIRECTOR *(Thoughtfully).* Do you do more of that?

ACTOR. Oh, yes. Lots more. We will land a man on the moon. Think of me as the man who accompanied Mrs. Kennedy to Paris. I thought I'd give my brother a little legal experience before he applies for a job. I—

DIRECTOR. Well, it's something we can work with. *(Pause)* Oh, all right. What the hell, we'll give it a try. *(Goes offstage, returns with top hat, cane, hands them to AC-TOR. Presidential seal lowered as backdrop.)* Good luck.

ACTOR. Uh, before we start this, shouldn't there be a contract?

DIRECTOR. Later, later.

ACTOR. But Equity—

DIRECTOR *(Fiercely)*. Screw the union; do you want the job or don't you?

ACTOR *(After a pause, reluctantly)*. I want the job. *(Puts on top hat, twirls cane.)* We all want the job. I was trained in classics, though.

DIRECTOR. Then shut up and do the job. *(Exits)*.

ACTOR. But just a moment. *(Silence. ACTOR starts offstage to pursue DIRECTOR, then shakes head, stops, returns to center stage. Fixed spot hammers him into place.)* Damn it anyway.

OFFSTAGE FEMALE VOICE. Ready?

OFFSTAGE MALE VOICE. Ready as I ever will be.

OFFSTAGE FEMALE VOICE. All right, then *(Pause)*. You can't say the city of Dallas doesn't love you now, Mr. President *(Sound of shot)*.

ACTOR. God damn it. I should have known *(Clutches throat)*. Damn open calls! *(Second shot; blackout.)*

O Homo, O Femina, O Tempora

By Kate Wilhelm

Judson Rowe stared at the screen where black lines and numbers and symbols chased themselves over the green background like football players over AstroTurf. The final equation appeared and the dance ended. He groaned. There had been no mistake. He pressed the print button and continued to gaze dully at the equation that had the beauty and elegance of truth. When the printing was finished, he collected his disks and the printout, turned off the terminal, and stood up, realizing belatedly that he was stiff and hungry and tired enough to assume that he had not slept for several nights in a row.

Dazed with fatigue he left the laboratory, walked down the silent hall of the mathematics building and out into the cold.

He stopped abruptly. There was a bare tree breaking up the light from a corner streetlamp; no person was in sight. He heard footsteps and turned, saw a watchman approaching.

"How long has that tree been there?"

"What tree's that?"

"That one!"

The watchman glanced at the tree, at Judson, and back to the tree. "Longer than either of us has been around, I'd say."

"I guess I never noticed it before," Judson mumbled.

"Yeah. When the leaves go it changes, doesn't it?"

Judson started to ask what month it was but he bit the question back and said good night instead, and tried not to run to his car. In it he looked at his watch: two-thirty. *No wonder the campus was empty.* He drove home, looking at everything as if he had never seen it before; the winding campus streets, the intersection that was barren of traffic now, the all-night hamburger stand, empty. He drove without thinking of which streets he wanted, where he was to turn, which house was his. He felt as if he had been gone a long time.

When he let himself into his house, he heard the television and followed the sound through the kitchen to the living room where Millie, covered with an afghan was sitting on the couch.

"I'm home," he said, staring at her. She was prettier than he remembered. Her hair was turning from gold to a light brown, nicer this way, and her eyes were bluer than he remembered, larger and, now at least, meaner.

"Me, too," she said, and turned back to the television.

"How's everything?"

"Fine."

"Are you mad at me?"

"Of course not. Last week I told you I was leaving, running away with another man, and you know what you said? 'That's fine, honey. Whatever you want.' And you haven't said a real thing to me since. You haven't asked about our daughter, or the lawsuit, or the mortgage payments or the leak in the bathroom."

"Good God! What daughter?"

She sighed and stood up. "Have you eaten anything these

last few days? Have you slept?"

"I don't know. I don't remember. Millie, you're kidding me, aren't you?"

"I'm kidding. Scrambled eggs? Are you finished with the new theory? Is that why I'm visible again?"

"Millie, it's . . . I have to call the President or someone."

"Like Chicken Little?"

"But the sky *is falling!*"

"With or without cheese and onions?"

He followed her into the kitchen; she took his hand and led him to a stool at the counter, pushed him down onto it. When she put a glass of milk before him, he tasted it as if he never had seen anything like it before.

"Time's slowing down, Millie."

She broke an egg into a bowl.

"I couldn't believe it at first. I've checked everything a dozen times. It's slowing down."

She broke another egg. "There is no such thing as time." She cracked the third egg. "Did you leave your coat at school?"

He looked down at himself. That's why he had been so cold. "It's slowing down at an accelerating rate, and there's nothing we can do about it."

She stirred the eggs gently. "Time is an abstract concept that we invented in order to talk about change and duration." She added cheese and onions to the eggs, put butter in the skillet, and watched until it started to sizzle, then added the egg mixture. "Time," she said then, "has no independent existence of its own. Change can happen faster or slower, but there is no such thing as time that can change its own rate of passage."

"And when it slows down enough," Judson said glumly, "it's going to stop altogether."

She put bread in the toaster and got out jam. "We invented

time in order to talk about seasons, physical change, growing old, and dying." The eggs were done at the same time the toast popped. It always amazed him that she knew to the second how long things took to get done. She never even glanced at a clock when she cooked. Instincts, he thought uneasily; it had nothing to do with real time.

She put the food before him. "If there are no events, there is no time. Time is inconceivable without events that change, that evolve. It doesn't exist except as a figure of speech. Like 'time is of the essence.' Essence of what? Another figure of speech."

"With the mainframe I'll be able to predict exactly when it will stop," he said, and began to eat.

"Darling, just tell me one thing. Did you use the square root of minus one to get your results?"

He nodded, his mouth too full to speak.

She smiled, broke off a piece of his toast, and nibbled it.

"You shouldn't have waited up," he said stiffly as soon as he could.

"I wanted to. I knew you'd come home eventually, hungry, tired, cold. Besides, I can sleep in tomorrow morning. Saturday, you know. No classes." She taught medieval English literature.

"Of course I know."

Which Saturday? he wondered. He glanced over his shoulder at the calendar and saw that October was displayed.

"The twenty-eighth," she said kindly. "This is the weekend that we change time. Do we set the clocks back or forward? I never remember."

"You don't have to make fun of me," he said even more stiffly.

She put her arms around him and kissed his cheek. "I love you," she said.

312

Icy rains came, then snow and more ice, then warmer rain that washed it all away. The trees were enveloped in a pale-green haze that turned into a dense canopy casting green light, golden and red light, and became bare limbs that broke up the pale illumination from the streetlamp.

"You're going to be bored," Judson said as he settled down next to Millie in the main auditorium of the conference center. "Dukweiler's a bore even to me."

"I wouldn't have missed this for anything."

"Did you really listen to me up there when I was giving my paper?"

"You know I did. You talked about epsilon and alpha and omega, and there were those infinity signs here and there on the blackboard, and then you multiplied everything by the square root of minus one, and the audience applauded. You were absolutely magnificent."

"I've had good comments already. They're going over the figures with everything from hand calculators to the mainframe."

"I told you not to worry. Of course they'll take notice."

Dukweiler was introduced and started to read his paper. He wrote down numbers and symbols on the board as he talked. He was an arid speaker, obviously too nervous even to glance at the audience. His presentation was too fast for Judson to follow and do the numbers at the same time.

Judson felt a chill midway through and leaned forward intently. When Dukweiler had finished, Judson turned to Millie. "Did you hear that? Do you realize what that idiot is claiming?"

"It sounded a lot like your paper, all those epsilons and alphas and omegas, and then he multiplied —"

"I know what he did!"

"He thinks time is speeding up?"

"I can refute his findings!"

She picked up her knitting. "I think those men are coming to talk to you. I'll wait here."

He left her and walked to the rear of the auditorium. A surge of attendees rushed for the podium, and another group of people moved slowly in his direction, some speaking in low voices, some frowning in thought, a few working their calculators methodically as they walked. Half and half, he thought with satisfaction, and he tried to see who had lined up in the enemy camp. He nodded to Whitcombe, who was the first to reach him. As others drew near, they spoke in measured tones, choosing words carefully, and they were solidly on his side; they had been convinced by his proofs, by his rigorous logic. It was an inescapable conclusion, they agreed; time certainly was slowing down, and a situation was developing that would prove to be of the utmost gravity.

Finally the groups began to disperse; it was cocktail time. The gang at the podium led the way to the bar in a near-stampede; the other group followed more leisurely. When Judson freed himself, he looked at Millie, calmly knitting with a slight smile on her face. *It was just as well that she did not realize the seriousness of the time problem,* he thought with a flash of tenderness.

"Will we experience anything differently?" she had asked.

"Relative to what?"

"Ah well," she had said. "Nine months will still seem like nine months." And just like that she had dismissed one of the great mysteries of the universe.

"Judson," Whitcombe drawled at his elbow. "We'll be sending you an invitation to speak down at Texas A&M. Have to get together about the best time before all this breaks up."

Judson nodded. A life's work lay ahead of him, more than one lifetime. He smiled at Whitcombe. "Happy to come down," he said, "if I can find the time."

Trojan Horse

By Michael Swanwick

"It's all inside my head," Elin said wonderingly. It was true. A chimney swift flew overhead, and she could feel its passage through her mind. A firefly landed on her knee. It pulsed cold fire, then spread its wings and was gone, and that was a part of her, too.

"Please try not to talk too much." The wetware tech tightened a cinch on the table, adjusted a bone inductor. His red and green facepaint loomed over her, then receded. "This will go much faster if you cooperate."

Elin's head felt light and airy. It was *huge*. It contained all of Magritte, from the uppermost terrace down to the trellis farms that circled the inner lake. Even the blue and white Earth that hovered just over one rock wall. They were all within her. They were all, she realized, only a model, the picture her mind assembled from sensory input. The exterior universe—the *real* universe—lay beyond.

"I feel giddy."

"Contrast high." The tech's voice was neutral, disinterested. "This is a very different mode of perception from what you're used to—you're stoned on the novelty."

A catwalk leading into the nearest farm rattled within Elin's mind as a woman in agricultural blues strode by, gourd-collecting bag swinging from her hip. It was night outside the crater, but biological day within, and the agtechs had activated tiers of arc lights at the cores of the farms. Filtered by greenery, the light was soft and watery.

"I could live like this forever."

"Believe me, you'd get bored." A rose petal fell on her cheek, and the tech brushed it off. He turned to face the two lawyers standing silently nearby. "Are the legal preliminaries over now?"

The lawyer in orangeface nodded. The one in purple said, "Can't her original personality be restored at all?"

Drawing a briefcase from his pocket, the wetware tech threw up a holographic diagram between himself and the witnesses. The air filled with intricate three-dimensional tracery, red and green lines interweaving and intermeshing.

"We've mapped the subject's current personality." He reached out to touch several junctions. "You will note that here, here, and *here* we have what are laughingly referred to as impossible emotional syllogisms. Any one of these renders the subject incapable of survival."

A thin waterfall dropped from the dome condensors to a misty pool at the topmost terrace, a bright razor slash through reality. It meandered to the edge of the next terrace and fell again.

"A straight *yes* or *no* will suffice."

The tech frowned. "In theory, yes. In practical terms it's hopeless. Remember, her personality was never recorded. The accident almost completely randomized her emotional structure—technically she's not even human. Given a decade or two of extremely delicate memory probing, we could *maybe* construct a facsimile. But it would only resemble the original; it could never be the primary Elin Donnelly."

Elin could dimly make out the equipment for five more waterfalls, but they were not in operation at the moment. She wondered why.

The attorney made a rude noise. "Well then, go ahead and do it. I wash my hands of this whole mess."

The tech bent over Elin to reposition a bone inductor. "This won't hurt a bit," he promised. "Just pretend that you're at the dentist's, having your teeth replaced."

She ceased to exist.

The new Elin Donnelly gawked at everything—desk workers in their open-air offices, a blacksnake sunning itself by the path, the stone stairs cut into the terrace walls. Her lawyer led her through a stand of saplings no higher than she, and into a meadow.

Butterflies scattered at their approach. Her gaze went from them to a small cave in the cliffs ahead, then up to the stars, as jumpy and random as the butterflies' flight.

"—So you'll be stuck on the moon for a full lunation—almost a month—if you want to collect your settlement. I. G. Feuchtwaren will carry your expenses until then, drawing against their final liability. Got that?"

And then—suddenly, jarringly—Elin could *focus* again. She took a deep breath. "Yes," she said. "Yes, I—okay."

"Good." The attorney canceled her judicial-advisory wetware, yanking the skull plugs and briskly wrapping them around her briefcase. "Then let's have a drink—it's been a long day."

They had arrived at the cave. "Hey, Hans!" the lawyer shouted. "Give us some service here, will you?"

A small man with the roguish face of a comic-opera troll popped into the open, work terminal in hand. "One minute," he said. "I'm on direct flex time—got to wrap up what I'm working on first."

"Okay." The lawyer sat down on the grass. Elin watched, fascinated, as the woman toweled the paint from her face, and a new pattern of fine red and black lines, permanently tattooed into her skin, emerged from beneath.

"Hey!" Elin said. "You're a Jesuit."

"You expected IGF to ship you a lawyer from Earth orbit?" She stuck out a hand. "Donna Landis, S.J. I'm the client-overseer for the Star Maker project, but I'm also available for spiritual guidance. Mass is at nine Sunday mornings."

Elin leaned back against the cliff. Grape-vines rustled under her weight. Already she missed the blissed-out feeling of a few minutes before. "Actually, I'm an agnostic."

"You *were*. Things may have changed." Landis folded the towel into one pocket, unfolded a mirror from another. "Speaking of which, how do you like your new look?"

Elin studied her reflection. Blue paint surrounded her eyes, narrowing to a point at the bridge of her nose, swooping down in a long curve to the outside. It was as if she were peering through a large blue moth, or a pair of hawk wings. There was something magical about it, something glamorous. Something very unlike her.

"I feel like a raccoon," she said. "This idiot mask."

"Best get used to it. You'll be wearing it a lot."

"But what's the point?" Elin was surprised by her own irritation. "So I've got a new personality; it's still *me* in here. I don't feel any weird compulsion to run amok with a knife or walk out an airlock without a suit. Nothing to warn the citizenry about, certainly."

"Listen," Landis said. "Right now you're like a puppy tripping over its own paws because they're too big for it. You're a stranger to yourself — you're going to feel angry when you don't expect to, get sentimental over surprising things. You can't control your emotions until you learn

318

what they are. And until then, the rest of us deserve — "

"What'll you have?" Hans was back, his forehead smudged black where he had incompletely wiped off his facepaint.

"A little warning. Oh, I don't know, Hans. Whatever you have on tap."

"That'll be Chanty. And you?" he asked Elin.

"What's good?"

He laughed. "There's no such thing as a *good* lunar wine. The air's too moist. And even if it weren't, it takes a good century to develop an adequate vineyard. But the Chanty is your basic, drinkable glug."

"I'll take that, then."

"Good. And I'll bring a mug for your friend, too."

"My friend?" She turned and saw a giant striding through the trees, towering over them, pushing them apart with two enormous hands. For a dizzy instant, she goggled in disbelief, and then the man shrank to human stature as she remembered the size of the saplings.

He grinned, joined them. "Hi. Remember me?"

He was a tall man, built like a spacejack, lean and angular. An untidy mass of black curls framed a face that was not quite handsome, but carried an intense freight of will.

"I'm afraid . . ."

"Tory Shostokovich. I reprogrammed you."

She studied his face carefully. Those *eyes*. They were fierce almost to the point of mania, but there was sadness there, too, and — she thought she might be making this up — a hint of pleading, like a little boy who wants something so desperately he dare not ask for it. She could lose herself in analyzing the nuances of those eyes. "Yes," she said at last, "I remember you now."

"I'm pleased." He nodded to the Jesuit. "Father Landis." She eyed him skeptically. "You don't seem your usual morose self, Shostokovich. Is anything wrong?"

"No, it's just a special kind of morning." He smiled at some private joke, returned his attention to Elin. "I thought I'd drop by and get acquainted with my former patient." He glanced down at the ground, fleetingly shy, and then his eyes were bright and audacious again.

How charming, Elin thought. She hoped he wasn't *too* shy. And then had to glance away herself, the thought was so unlike her. "So you're a wetware surgeon," she said inanely.

Hans reappeared to distribute mugs of wine, then retreated to the cave's mouth. He sat down, workboard in lap, and patched in the skull-plugs. His face went stiff as the wetware took hold.

"Actually," Tory said, "I very rarely work as a wetsurgeon. An accident like yours is rare, you know — maybe once, twice a year. Mostly I work in wetware development. Currently I'm on the Star Maker project."

"I've heard that name before. Just what *is* it anyway?"

Tory didn't answer immediately. He stared down into the lake, a cool breeze from above ruffling his curls. Elin caught her breath. *I hardly know this man,* she thought wildly. He pointed to the island in the center of the lake, a thin, stony finger that was originally the crater's thrust cone.

"God lives on that island," he said.

Elin laughed. "Think how different history would be if He'd only had a sense of direction!" And then wanted to bite her tongue as she realized that he was not joking.

"You're being cute, Shostokovich," Landis warned. She swigged down a mouthful of wine. "*Jeez,* that's vile stuff."

Tory rubbed the back of his neck ruefully. "*Mea culpa.* Well, let me give you a little background. Most people think of wetware as being software for people. But that's too

320

simplistic, because with machines you start out blank — with a clean slate — and with people, there's some ten million years of mental programming already crammed into their heads.

"So to date we've been working *with* the natural wetware. We counterfeit surface traits — patience, alertness, creativity — and package them like so many boxes of bone-meal. But the human mind is vast and unmapped, and it's time to move into the interior, for some basic research.

"That's the Star Maker project. It's an exploration of the basic substructural programming of the mind. We've redefined the overstructure programs into an integrated system we believe will be capable of essence-programming, in one-to-one congruence with the inherent substructure of the universe."

"What jargonistic rot!" Landis gestured at Elin's stoneware mug. "Drink up. The Star Maker is a piece of experimental theology that IGF dreamed up. As Tory said, it's basic research into the nature of the mind. The Vatican Synod is providing funding so we can keep an eye on it."

"Nipping heresy in the bud," Tory said sourly.

"That's a good part of it. This set of wetware will supposedly reshape a human mind into God. Bad theology, but there it is. They want to computer-model the infinite. Anyway, the specs were drawn up, and it was tried out on — what was the name of the test subject?"

"Doesn't matter," Tory said quickly.

"Coral something-or-other."

Only half-listening by now, Elin unobtrusively studied Tory. He sat, legs wide, staring into his mug of Chanty. There were hard lines on his face, etched by who knew what experiences? *I don't believe in love at first sight* Elin thought. Then again, who knew *what* she might believe in anymore? It was a chilling thought, and she retreated from it.

"So did this Coral become God?"

"Patience. Anyway, the volunteer was plugged in, wiped, reprogrammed, and interviewed. Nothing useful."

"In one hour," Tory said, "we learned more about the structure and composition of the universe than in all of history to date."

"It was deranged gibberish." She tapped Elin's knee. "We interviewed her, and then canceled the wetware. And what do you think happened?"

"I've never been big on rhetorical questions." Elin didn't take her eyes off of Tory.

"She didn't come down. She was stuck there."

"Stuck?"

Tory plucked a blade of grass, let it fall. "What happened was that we had rewired her to absolute consciousness. She was not only aware of all her mental functions, but in control of them — right down to the involuntary reflexes. Which also put her in charge of her own metaprogrammer."

"*Metaprogrammer* is just a buzzword for a bundle of reflexes by which the brain is able to make changes in itself," Landis threw in.

"Yeah. What we didn't take into account, though, was that she'd *like* being God. When we tried deprogramming her, she simply overrode our instructions and reprogrammed herself back up."

"The poor woman," Elin said. *And yet — what a glorious experience, to be God!* Something within her thrilled to it. *It would almost be worth the price.*

"Which leaves us with a woman who thinks she's God," Landis said. "I'm just glad we were able to hush it up. If word got out to some of those religious illiterates back on Earth —"

"Listen," Tory said. "I didn't really come here to talk

322

shop. I wanted to invite my former patient on a grand tour of the Steam Grommet Works."

Elin looked at him blankly. "Steam . . ."

He swept an arm to take in all of Magritte, the green pillars and gray cliffs alike. There was something proprietary in his gesture.

Landis eyed him suspiciously. "You two might need a chaperone," she said. "I think I'll tag along to keep you out of trouble."

Elin smiled sweetly. "Fuck off," she said.

Ivy covered Tory's geodesic trellis hut. He led the way in, stooping to touch a keyout by the doorway. "Something classical?"

"Please." As he began removing her jumpsuit, the holotape sprang into being, surrounding them with rich reds and cobalt blues that coalesced into stained-glass patterns in the air. Elin pulled back and clapped her hands. "It's Chartres," she cried, delighted. "The cathedral at Chartres!"

"Mmmmm." Tory teased her down onto the grass floor.

The north rose swelled to fill the hut. It was all angels and doves, kings and prophets, with gold lilies surrounding the central rosette. Deep and powerful, infused with gloomy light, it lap-dissolved into the lancet of Sainte Anne.

The windows wheeled overhead as the holotape panned down the north transept to the choir, to the apse, and then up into the ambulatory. Swiftly then, it cut to the wounded Christ and the Beasts of Revelation set within the dark spaces of the west rose. The outer circle—the instruments of the Passion—closed about them.

Elin gasped.

The tape moved down the nave, still brightening, briefly pausing at the Vendome chapel. Until finally the oldest window, the Notre Dame de la Belle Verriere, blazed in a frenzy of raw glory. A breeze rattled the ivy and two leaves fell through the hologram to tap against their skin, and slide to the ground.

The Belle Verriere faded in the darkening light, and the colors ran and were washed away by a noiseless gust of rain.

Elin let herself melt into the grass, drained and lazy, not caring if she never moved again. Beside her Tory chuckled, playfully tickled her ribs. "Do you love me? Hey? Tell me you love me."

"Stop!" She grabbed his arms and bit him in the side—a small, nipping bite, more threat than harm—ran a tongue over his left nipple. "Hey, listen, I hit the sack with you a half hour after we met. What do you want?"

"Want?" He broke her hold, rolled over on top of her, pinioning her wrists above her head. "I want you to know—" and suddenly he was absolutely serious, his eyes unblinking and glittery-hard"—that I love you. Without doubt of qualification. I love you more than words could ever say."

"Tory," she said. "Things like that take time." The wind had died down. Not a blade of grass stirred.

"No they don't." It was embarrassing looking into those eyes; she refused to look away. "I feel it. I *know* it. I love every way, shape, and part of you. I love you beyond time and barrier and possibility. We were meant to be lovers, fated for it, and there is *nothing,* absolutely nothing, that could ever keep us apart." His voice was low and steady. Elin couldn't tell whether she was thrilled or scared out of her wits.

"Tory, I don't know—"

"Then wait," he said. "It'll come."

Lying sleepless beside Tory that night, Elin thought back to her accident. And because it was a matter of stored memory, the images were crisp and undamaged.

It happened at the end of her shift on Wheel Laboratory 19, Henry Ford Orbital Industrial Park.

Holding theta lab flush against the hub cylinder, Elin injected ferrous glass into a molten copper alloy. Simultaneously, she plunged gamma lab a half kilometer to the end of its arm, taking it from fractional Greenwich normal to a full nine gravities. Epsilon began crawling up its spindly arm. Using waldos, she lifted sample wafers from the quick-freeze molds in omicron. There were a hundred measurements to be made.

Elin felt an instant's petulant boredom, and the workboard readjusted her wetware, jacking up her attentiveness so that she leaned over the readouts in cool, detached fascination.

The workboard warned her that the interfacing program was about to be shut off. Her fingers danced across the board, damping down reactions, putting the labs to bed. The wetware went quiescent.

With a shiver, Elin was herself again. She grabbed a towel and wiped off her facepaint. Then she leaned back and transluced the wall—her replacement was late. Corporation regs gave her fifty percent of his missed-time fines if she turned him in. It was easy money, and so she waited.

Stretching, she felt the gold wetware wires dangling from the back of her skull. She lazily put off yanking them.

Earth bloomed underfoot, slowly crept upward. New Detroit and New Chicago rose from the floor. Bright industrial satellites gleamed to every side of the twin residential cylinders.

A bit of motion caught Elin's eye, and she swiveled to follow a load of cargo drifting by. It was a jumble of containers lashed together by nonmagnetic tape and shot into an orbit calculated to avoid the laser cables and power transmission beams that interlaced the Park.

A man was riding the cargo, feet braced against a green carton, hauling on a rope slipped through the lashings. He saw her and waved. She could imagine his grin through the mirrored helmet.

The old Elin snorted disdainfully. She started to look away and almost missed seeing it happen.

In leaning back that fraction more, the cargo hopper had put too much strain on the lashings. A faulty rivet popped, and the cargo began to slide. Brightly colored cartons drifted apart, and the man went tumbling, end-over-end, away.

One end of the lashing was still connected to the anchor carton and the free end writhed like a wounded snake. A bright bit of metal—the failed rivet—broke free and flew toward the juncture of the wheel lab's hub and spokes.

The old Elin was still hooting with scornful laughter when the rivet struck the lab, crashing into a nest of wiring that *should not* have been exposed.

Two wires short-circuited, ending a massive power transient surging up through the workboard. Circuits fused and melted. The board went haywire.

And a microjolt of electricity leaped up two gold wires, hopelessly scrambling the wetware through Elin's skull.

An hour later, when her replacement finally showed, she was curled into a ball, rocking back and forth on the floor. She was alternating between hysterical gusts of laughter and dark, gleeful screams.

Morning came, and after a sleepy, romantic breakfast, Tory plugged into his briefcase and went to work. Elin wandered off to do some thinking.

There was no getting around the fact that she was *not* the metallurgist from Wheel Lab 19, not any more. That woman was alien to her now. They shared memories, experiences—but she no longer understood that woman, could not sympathize with her emotions, indeed found her distasteful.

At a second-terrace cafe that was crowded with off-shift biotechs, Elin rented a table and briefcase. She sat down to try to trace the original owner of her personality.

As she'd suspected, her new *persona* was copied from that of a real human being; creating a personality from scratch was still beyond the abilities of even the best wetware techs. She was able to trace herself back to IGF's inventory bank, and to determine that duplication of personality was illegal—which presumably meant that the original owner was dead.

But she could not locate the original owner. Selection had been made by computer, and the computer wouldn't tell. When she tried to find out, it referred her to the Privacy Act of 2037.

"I think I've exhausted all the resources of self-discovery available to me," she told the Pierrot when he came to collect his tip. "And I've still got half the morning left to kill."

He glanced at her powder-blue facepaint and smiled politely.

"It's selective black."

"Hah?" Elin turned away from the lake, found that an agtech carrying a long-handled net had come up behind her.

"The algae—it absorbs light into the infrared. Makes the lake a great thermal sink." The woman dipped her net into the water, seined up a netful of dark green scum, and dumped it into a nearby trough. Water drained away through the porous bottom.

"Oh." There were a few patches of weeds on the island where drifting soil had settled. "It's funny. I never used to be very touristy. More the contemplative type, sort of home-bodyish. Now I've got to be *doing* something, you know?"

The agtech dumped another load of algae into the trough. "I couldn't say." She tapped her forehead. "It's the wetware. If you want to talk shop, that's fine. Otherwise, I can't."

"I see," Elin dabbed a toe in the warm water. "Well — why not? Let's talk shop."

Someone was moving at the far edge of the island. Elin craned her neck to see. The agtech went on methodically dipping her net into the lake as God walked into view.

"The lake tempers the climate, see. By day it works by evaporative cooling. Absorbs the heat, loses it to evaporation, radiates it out the dome roof through the condensors."

Coral was cute as a button.

A bowl of fruit and vegetables had been left near the waterline. She walked to the bowl, considered it. Her orange jumpsuit nicely complemented her *café-au-lait* skin. She was so small and delicate that by contrast Elin felt ungainly.

"We also use passive heat pumps to move the excess heat down to a liquid-storage cavern below the lake."

Coral picked up a tomato. Her features were finely chiseled. Her almond eyes should have had snap and fire in them, to judge by the face, but they were remote and unfocused. Even, white teeth nipped at the food.

"At night we pump the heat back up, let the lake radiate it out to keep the crater warm."

On closer examination — Elin had to squint to see so fine — the face was as smooth and lineless as that of an idiot. There was nothing there; no emotion, no purpose, no detectable intellect.

"That's why the number of waterfalls in operation varies."

Now Coral sat down on the rocks. Her feet and knees were dirty. She did not move. Elin wanted to shy a rock at her to see if she would react.

What now? Elin wondered. She had seen the sights, all that Magritte had to offer, and they were all tiresome, disappointing. Even — no, make that *especially* — God. And she still had almost a month to kill.

"Keeping the crater tempered is a regular balancing act," the agtech said.

"Oh, shut up." Elin took out her briefcase and called Father Landis. "I'm bored," she said, when the hologram had stabilized.

Landis hardly glanced up from her work. "So get a job," she snapped.

Magritte had begun as a mining colony, back when it was still profitable to process the undifferentiated melange soil. The miners were gone now, and the crater was owned by a consortium of operations that were legally debarred from locating Earth-side.

From the fifteenth terrace Elin stared down at the patchwork clusters of open-air laboratories and offices, some separated by long stretches of undeveloped field, others crammed together in the hope of synergistic effect. Germ-warfare corporations mingled with nuclear-waste engineering firms. The Mid-Asian Population Control Project had half a terrace to itself, and it swarmed with guards. There were a few off-Swiss banking operations.

"You realize," Tory said, "that I'm not going to be at all happy about this development." He stood, face impassive in red and green, watching a rigger bolt together a cot and wire in the surgical equipment.

"You hired me yourself," Elin reminded him.

"Yes, but I'm wired into professional mode at the moment." The rigger packed up his tools, walked off. "Looks like we're almost ready."

"Good." Elin flung herself down on the cot, and lay back, hands folded across her chest. "Hey, I feel like I should be holding a lily!"

"I'm going to hook you into the project intercom so you don't get too bored between episodes." The air about her flickered, and a clutch of images overlaid her vision. Ghosts walked through the air, stared at her from deep within the ground. "Now we'll shut off the external senses." The world went away, but the illusory people remained, each within a separate hexagonal field of vision. It was like seeing through the eyes of a fly.

There was a sudden, overwhelming sense of Tory's presence, and a sourceless voice said, "This will take a minute. Amuse yourself by calling up a few friends." Then he was gone.

Elin floated, free of body, free of sensation, almost godlike in her detachment. She idly riffled through the images, stopped at a chubby little man drawing a black line across his forehead. *Hello, Hans,* she thought.

He looked up and winked. "How's it hanging, kid?"

Not so bad. What're you up to?

"My job. I'm the black-box monitor this shift." He added an orange starburst to the band, surveyed the job critically in a pocket mirror. "I sit here with my finger on the button—" one hand disappeared below his terminal—"and if I get the word I push. That sets off explosives in the condensor units and blows the dome. *Pfffft.* Out goes the air."

She considered it: A sudden volcano of oxygen spouting up and across the lunar plains. Human bodies thrown up from the surface, scattering, bursting under explosive decompression.

That's grotesque, *Hans.*

"Oh, it's safe. The button doesn't connect unless I'm wetwired into my job."

Even so.

"Just a precaution; a lot of the research that goes on here wouldn't be allowed without this kind of security. Relax — I haven't lost a dome yet."

The intercom cut out, and again Elin felt Tory's presence. "We're trying a series of Trojan horse programs this time — inserting you into the desired mental states instead of making you the states. We've encapsulated your surface identity and routed the experimental programs through a secondary level. So with *this* series, rather than identifying with the programs, you'll perceive them all indirectly."

Tory, you have got to be the most jargon-ridden human being in existence. How about repeating that in English?

"I'll show you."

Suddenly Elin was englobed in a sphere of branching crimson lines, dark and dull, that throbbed slowly. Lacy and organic, it looked the way she imagined the veins in her forehead to be like when she had a headache.

"That was anger," Tory said. "Your mind shunted it off into visual imagery because it didn't identify the anger with itself."

That's what you're going to do then — program me into the God-state so that I can see it but not experience it?

"Ultimately. Though I doubt you'll be able to come up with pictures. More likely, you'll feel that you're in the presence of God." He withdrew for a moment, leaving her more than alone, almost nonexistent. Then he was back. "We start slowly, though. The first session runs you up to the basic metaprogramming level, integrates all your mental processes and puts you in low-level control of them. The nontechnical term for this is *making the Christ*. Don't fool around with anything you see or sense." His voice faded, she was alone, and then everything changed.

She was in the presence of someone wonderful.

Elin felt that someone near at hand, and struggled to open the eyes she no longer possessed; she had to see. Her existence opened, and people began appearing before her.

"Careful," Tory said. "You've switched on the intercom again."

I want to see!

"There's nobody to see. That's just your own mind. But if you want, you can keep the intercom on."

Oh. It was disappointing. She was surrounded by love, by a crazily happy sense that the universe was holy, by wisdom deeper than the world. By all rights, it *had* to come from a source greater than herself.

Reason was not strong enough to override emotion. She riffled through the intercom, bringing up image after image and discarding them all, searching. When she had run through the project staff, she began hungrily scanning the crater's public monitors.

Agtechs in the trellis farms were harvesting strawberries and sweet peas. Elin could taste them on her tongue. Somebody was seining up algae from the inner lake, and she felt the weight of the net in calloused hands. Not far from where she lay, a couple was making love in a grove of saplings and she . . .

Tory, I don't think I can take this. It's too intense.

"You're the one who wanted to be a test pilot."

Dammit, Tory!

Donna Landis materialized on the intercom. "She's right, Shostokovich. You haven't buffered her enough."

"It didn't seem wise to risk dissociative effects by cranking her ego up *too* high."

"Who's paying for all this, hah?"

Tory grumbled something inaudible, and dissolved the

world.

Elin floated in blackness, soothing and relaxing. She felt good. She had needed this little vacation from the tensions and pressures of her new personality. Taking the job had been the right thing to do, even if it *did* momentarily displease Tory.

Tory . . . She smiled mentally. He was exasperating at times, but still she was coming to rely on having him around. She was beginning to think she was in love with him.

A lesser love, perhaps. Certainly not the love that is the Christ.

Well, maybe so. Still, on a *human* level. Tory filled needs in her she hadn't known existed. It was too much effort to argue with herself, though. Her thoughts drifted away into a wordless, luxurious reveling in the bodiless state, free from distractions, carefree and disconnected.

Nothing is disconnected. All the universe is a vast net of intermeshing programs. Elin was amused at herself. That had sounded like something Tory would say. She'd have to watch it; she might love the man, but she certainly didn't want to end up talking like him.

You worry needlessly. The voice of God is subtle, but it is not your own.

Elin startled. She searched through her mind for an open intercom channel, didn't find one. *Hello,* she thought. *Who said that?*

The answer came to her not in words, but in a sourceless assertion of identity. It was cool, emotionless, something she could not describe even to herself, but by the same token absolute and undeniable.

It was God.

Then Tory was back and the voice, the presence, was gone. *Tory?* she thought, *I think I just had a religious* experience.

"That's very common under sensory deprivation—the mind clears out a few old programs. Nothing to worry about. Now relax for a jiff while I plug you back in—how does that feel?"

The Presence was back again, but not nearly so strongly as before; she could resist the urge to chase after it. *That's fine, Tory, but listen, I really think—*

"Let's leave analysis to those who have been programmed for it, shall we?"

The lovers strolled aimlessly through a meadow, the grass brushing up higher than their waists. Biological night was coming; the agtechs flicked the daylight off and on twice in warning.

"It was *real,* Tory. She talked with me; I'm not making it up."

Tory ran a hand through his dark, curly hair, looking abstracted. "Well. Assuming that my professional opinion was wrong—and I'll be the first to admit that the program is a bit egocentric—I still don't think we have to stoop to mysticism for an explanation."

To the far side of Magritte, a waterfall was abruptly shut off. The stream of water scattered, seeming to dissolve in the air. "I thought you said she was God."

"I only said that to bait Landis. I don't mean that she's literally God, just god*like.* Her thought processes are a million years more efficiently organized than ours. God is just a convenient metaphor."

"Um. So what's your explanation?"

"There's at least one terminal on the island—the things are everywhere. She probably programmed it to cut into the intercom without the channels seeming to be open."

"Could she *do* that?"

334

"Why not? She has that million-year edge on us — and she used to be a wetware tech; all wetware techs are closet computer hacks." He did not look at her, had not looked at her for some time.

"Hey." She reached out to take his hand. "What's *wrong* with you tonight?"

"Me?" He did not meet her eyes. "Don't mind me. I'm just sulking because you took the job. I'll get over it."

"What's wrong with the job?"

"Nothing. I'm just being moody."

She guided his arm around her waist, pressed up against him. "Well, don't be. It's nothing you can control — I *have* to have work to do. My boredom threshold is very low."

"I know that." He finally turned to face her, smiled sadly. "I do love you, you know."

"Well . . . maybe I love you too."

His smile banished all sadness from his face, like a sudden wind that breaks apart the clouds. "Say it again." His hands reached out to touch her shoulders, her neck, her face. "One more time, with feeling."

"Will *not!*" Laughing, she tried to break away from him, but he would not let go, and they fell in a tangle to the ground. "Beast!" They rolled over and over in the grass. "Brute!" She hammered at his chest, tore open his jumpsuit, tried to bite his neck.

Tory looked embarrassed, tried to pull away. "Hey, not out here! Somebody could be watching."

The agtechs switched off the arc lamps, plunging Magritte into darkness.

Tory reached up to touch Elin's face. They made love.

Physically it was no different from things she had done countless times before with lovers and friends and the occasional stranger. But she was committing herself in a way the

335

old Elin would never have dared, letting Tory past her defenses, laying herself open to pain and hurt. Trusting him. He was a part of her now. And everything was transformed, made new and wonderful.

Until they were right at the brink of orgasm, the both of them, and half delirious she could let herself go, murmuring, "I love you, love you, God I love you . . ." And just as she climaxed, Tory stiffened and arched his head back, and in a voice that was wrenched from the depths of passion, whispered, "Coral . . ."

Half blind with fury, Elin strode through a residential settlement. The huts glowed softly from the holotapes playing within — diffuse, scattered rainbow patterns unreadable outside their fields of focus. She'd left Tory behind, bewildered, two terraces above.

Elin halted before one hut, stood indecisively. Finally, because she had to talk to *somebody,* she rapped on the lintel.

Father Landis stuck her head out the doorway, blinked sleepily. "Oh, it's you, Donnelly. What do you want?"

To her absolute horror, Elin broke into tears.

Landis ducked back inside, reemerged zipping up her jumpsuit. She cuddled Elin in her arms, made soothing noises, listened to her story.

"Coral," Landis said. "Ahhhh. Suddenly everything falls into place."

"Well, I wish you'd tell me, then!" She tried to blink away the angry tears. Her face felt red and raw and ugly; the wetware paint was all smeared.

"Patience, child." Landis sat down crosslegged beside the hut, patted the ground beside her. "Sit here and pretend that I'm your mommy, and I'll tell you a story."

"Hey, I didn't come here — "

"Who are you to criticize the latest techniques in spiritual nurturing, hey?" Landis chided gently. "Sit."

Elin did so. Landis put an arm about her shoulder.

"Once upon a time, there was a little girl named Coral—I forget her last name. Doesn't matter. Anyway, she was bright and emotional and ambitious and frivolous and just like you in every way." She rocked Elin gently as she spoke.

"Coral was a happy little girl, and she laughed and played and one day she fell in love. Just like *that!*" She snapped her fingers. "I imagine you know how she felt."

"This is kind of embarrassing."

Hush. Well, she was very lucky, for as much as she loved him, he loved her a hundred times back, and for as much as he loved her, she loved him a thousand times back. And so it went. I think they overdid it a bit, but that's just my personal opinion.

"Now Coral lived in Magritte and worked as a wetware tech. She was an ambitious one, too—they're the worst kind. She came up with a scheme to reprogram people so they could live *outside* the programs that run them in their everyday lives. Mind you, people are more than the sum of their programming, but what did she know about free will? She hadn't had any religious training, after all. So she and her boyfriend wrote up a proposal, and applied for funding, and together they ran the new program through her skull. And when it was all done, she thought she was God. Only she wasn't Coral anymore—not so's you'd recognize her."

She paused to give Elin a hug. "Be strong, kid, here comes the rough part. Well, her boyfriend was broken-hearted. He didn't want to eat, and he didn't want to play with his friends. He was a real shit to work with. But then he got an idea.

"You see, anyone who works with experimental wetware

has her personality permanently recorded in case there's an accident and it needs to be restored. And if that person dies or becomes God, the personality rights revert to IGF. They're sneaky like that.

"Well. Tory—did I mention his name was Tory?— thought to himself: What if somebody were to come here for a new personality? Happens about twice a year. Bound to get worse in the future. And Magritte is the only place this kind of work can be done. The personality bank is random-accessed by computer, so there'd be a chance of his getting Coral back, just as good as new. Only not a very good chance, because there's *lots* of garbage stuffed into the personality bank.

"And then he had a *bad* thought. But you mustn't blame him for it. He was working from a faulty set of moral precepts. Suppose, he thought, he rigged the computer so that instead of choosing randomly, it would give Coral's personality to the very first little girl who came along? And that was what he did." Landis lapsed into silence.

Elin wiped back a sniffle. "How does the story end?"

"I'm still waiting on that one."

"Oh." Elin pulled herself together and stood. Landis followed.

"Listen. Remember what I told you about being a puppy tripping over its paws? Well, you've just stubbed your toes and they hurt. But you'll get over it. People do."

"Today we make a Buddha," Tory said. Elin fixed him with a cold stare, said nothing, even though he was in green and red, immune. "This is a higher-level program, integrating all your mental functions and putting them under your conscious control. So it's especially important that you keep your hands to yourself, okay?"

"Rot in hell, you cancer."

338

"I beg your pardon?"

Elin did not respond, and after a puzzled silence Tory continued: "I'm leaving your sensorium operative, so when I switch you over, I want you to pay attention to your surround. Okay?"

The second Trojan horse came on. Everything changed.

It wasn't a physical change, not one that could be seen with the eyes. It was more as if the names for everything had gone away. A knee-tall oak grew nearby, very much like the one she had crushed accidentally in New Detroit when she had lost her virginity many years ago. And it meant nothing to her. It was only wood growing out of the ground. A mole poked its head out of its burrow, nose crinkling, pink eyes weak. It was just a small, biological machine. "Whooh," she said involuntarily. "This is cold."

"Bother you?"

Elin studied him, and there was nothing there. Only a human being, as much an object as the oak, and no more. She felt nothing toward or against him. "No," she said.

"We're getting a good recording." The words meant nothing; they were clumsy, devoid of content.

In the grass around her, Elin saw a gray flickering, as if it were all subtly on fire. Logically she knew the flickering was the firing of nerves in the rods and cones of her eyes, but emotionally it was something else: It was time. A gray fire that destroyed the world constantly, eating it away and remaking it again and again.

And it didn't matter.

A great calmness wrapped itself around Elin, an intelligent detachment, cold and impersonal. She found herself identifying with it, realizing that existence was simply *not important*. It was all things, objects.

She could not see Tory's back, was no longer willing to assume it even existed. She could look up and see the near side of the earth. The far side might well not exist, and if it didn't, well, *that* didn't matter either.

She stripped away the world, ignored the externalities. *I never realized how dependent I am on sensory input,* she thought. And if you ignored it—there was the Void. It had no shape or color or position, but it was what underlies the bright interplay of colors that was constantly being destroyed by the gray fires of time. She contemplated the raw stuff of existence.

"Please don't monkey around with your programming," Tory said.

The body was unimportant, too, it was only the focal point for her senses. Ignore them, and you could ignore *it*. Elin could feel herself fading in the presence of the Void. It had no material existence, no real being. But neither had the world she had always taken for granted—it was but an echo, a ghost, an image reflected in water.

It was like being a program in a machine and realizing it for the first time.

Landis's voice flooded her. "Donnelly, for God's sake, keep your fingers off the experiment!" The thing was, the underlying nothingness was *real*—if 'real' had any meaning. If meaning had meaning. But beyond real and beyond meaning, there is what *is*. And she had found it.

"Donnelly, you're treading on dangerous ground. You've—" Landis's voice was a distraction, and she shut it off. Elin felt the desire to merge with what *was;* one simply had to stop the desire for it, she realized, and it was done.

But on this realization, horror collapsed upon her. Flames surrounded her; they seared and burned and crisped, and there were snakes among them, great slimy things with disgusting mouths and needle-sharp fangs.

She recoiled in panic, and they were upon her. The flames were drawn up into her lungs, and hot maggots wallowed through her brain tissues. She fled through a mind that writhed in agony, turning things on and off.

Until abruptly she was back in her body, and nothing pursued her. She shivered, and her body responded. It felt wonderful.

"Well, *that* worked at least," Tory said.

"What — " her voice croaked. She cleared her throat and tried again. "What happened?"

"Just what we'd hoped for — when your mind was threatened with extinction, it protected itself by reprogramming back down to a normal state. Apparently, keeping your ego cranked up high works."

Elin realized that her eyes were still closed; she opened them now and convulsively closed her hand around the edge of the cot. It was solid and real to the touch. So good.

"I'll be down in a minute," Tory said. "Just now, though, I think you need to rest." He touched a bone inductor and Elin fell into blackness.

Floating again, every metaphorical nerve on edge, Elin found herself hypersensitive to outside influences, preternaturally aware, even suggestible. Still, she suspected more than sensed Coral's presence. *Go away,* she thought. *This is my mind now.*

I am here and I am always. You have set foot in my country, and are dimly aware of my presence. Later, when you have climbed into the mountains, you will truly know me; and then you will be as I.

Everyone tells me what I'm going to do. Elin thought angrily. *Don't I get any say in this?*

The thought almost amused. *You are only a program caught in a universal web of programming. You will do as your program dictates. To be free of the programs is to be God.*

Despite her anger, despite her hurt, despite the cold trickle of fear she tried to keep to the background, Elin was curious. *What's it like?* she couldn't help asking.

It is golden freedom. The universe is a bubble infinitely large, and we who are God are the film on its outside. We interact and we program. We make the stars shine and the willows grow. We program what you will want for lunch. The programming flows through us and we alter it and maintain the universe.

Elin pounced on this last statement. *Haven't done a very good job of it, have you?*

We do not tamper. When you are one with us, you will understand.

This was, Elin realized, the kind of question-and-answer session Coral must have gone through repeatedly as part of the Star Maker project. She searched for a question that no one else would have asked, one that would be hers alone. And after some thought she found it.

Do you still — personally — love Tory Shostokovich?

There was a slight pause, then: *The kind of love you mean is characteristic of lower-order programming. Not of program-free intelligence.*

A moment later Tory canceled all programming, and she floated to the surface, leaving God behind. But even before then she was acutely aware that she had not received a straight answer.

"Elin, we've got to talk."

She was patched into the outside monitors, staring across Mare Imbrium. It was a straight visual program; she could feel the wetwire leads dangling down her neck, the warm, humid air of Magritte against her skin. "Nothing to talk *about*," she said.

"Dammit, yes there is! I'm not about to lose you again

because of a misunderstanding, a — a matter of semantics."

The thing about Outside was its airless clarity. Rocks and shadows were so preternaturally *sharp*. From a sensor on the crater's seaward slope, she stared off into Mare Imbrium; it was monotonous, but in a comforting sort of way. A little like when she had made a Buddha. There was no meaning out there, nothing to impose itself between her and the surface.

"I don't know how you found out about Coral," Tory said, "and I guess it doesn't matter. I always figured you'd find out sooner or later. That's not important. What matters is that I love you — "

"Oh, hush up!"

" — and that you love me. You can't pretend you don't."

Elin felt her nails dig into her palms. "Sure I can," she said. She hopscotched down the crater to the surface. There the mass driver stood, a thin monorail stretching kilometers into the Imbrium, its gentle slope all but imperceptible.

"You're identifying with the woman who used to be Elin Donnelly. There's nothing wrong with that; speaking as a wetsurgeon, it's a healthy sign. But it's something you've got to grow out of."

"Listen, Shostokovich, tinkering around with my emotions doesn't change who I am. I'm not your dead lady-friend and I'm not about to take her place. So why don't you just go away and stop jerking me around, huh?"

Tiny repair robots prowled the mass driver's length, stopping occasionally for a spotweld. Blue sparks sputtered soundlessly over the surface.

"You're not the old Elin Donnelly either, and I think you know it. Bodies are transient, memories are nothing. Your spontaneity and grace, your quiet strength, your impatience — the small lacks and presences of you I've known and loved for years — are what make you yourself. The name doesn't matter, nor the past. You are who you are, and I love you for it."

"Yeah, well, what I am does not love you, buster."

One of the repairbots slowly fell off the driver. It hit, bounced, struggled to regain its treads, then scooted back toward its work.

Tory's voice was almost regretful. "You do, though. You can't hide that from me. I know you as your lover and as your wetsurgeon. You've let me become a part of you, and no matter how angry you may temporarily be, you'll come back to me."

Elin could feel her body trembling with rage. "Yeah, well if that's true, then why tell *me?* Hah? Why not just go back to your hut and wait for me to come crawling?"

"Because I want you to quit your job."

"Say what?"

"I don't want you to become God. It was a mistake the last time, and I'm afraid it won't be any better with the new programs. If you go up into God and can't get down this time, you'll do it the next time. And the next. I'll spend my life here waiting for you, re-creating you, losing you. Can't you see it — year after year, replaying the same tired old tape?" Tory's voice fell to a whisper. "I don't think I could take it even once more."

"If you know me as well as you say, then I guess you know my answer," Elin said coldly.

She waited until Tory's footsteps moved away, fading, defeat echoing after. Only then did Elin realize that her sensor had been scanning the same empty bit of Magritte's slope for the last five minutes.

It was time for the final Trojan horse. "Today we make a God," Tory said. "This is a total conscious integration of the mind in an optimal efficiency pattern. Close your eyes and count to three."

One. The hell of it, Elin realized, was that Tory was right. She still loved him. He was the one man she wanted and was empty without.

Two. Worse, she didn't know how long she could go on without coming back to him — and, good God, would that be humiliating!

She was either cursed or blessed; cursed perhaps for the agonies and humiliations she would willingly undergo for the sake of this one rather manipulative human being. Or maybe blessed in that at least there was *someone* who could move her so, deserving or not. Many went through their lives without.

Three. She opened her eyes.

Nothing was any different. Magritte was as ordinary, as mundane as ever, and she felt no special reaction to it one way or another. Certainly she did not feel the presence of God.

"I don't think this is working," she tried to say. The words did not come. From the corner of her eye, she saw Tory wiping clean his facepaint, shucking off his jumpsuit. But when she tried to sit up, she found she was paralyzed.

What is this maniac doing?

Tory's face loomed over her, his eyes glassy, almost fearful. His hair was a tangled mess; her fingers itched with the impulse to run a comb through it. "Forgive me, love." He kissed her forehead lightly, her lips ever so gently. Then he was out of her field of vision, stretching out on the grass beside the cot.

Elin stared up at the dome roof, thinking: *No.* She heard him strap the bone inductors to his body, one by one, and then a sharp click as he switched on a recorder. The programming began to flow into him.

A long wait — perhaps twenty seconds viewed objectively—as the wetware was loaded. Another click as the recorder shut off. A moment of silence, and then—

Tory gasped. One arm flew up into her field of vision, swooped down out of it, and he began choking. Elin struggled against her paralysis, could not move. Something broke noisily, a piece of equipment by the sound of it, and the choking and gasping continued. He began thrashing wildly.

Tory, Tory, what's happening to you?

"It's just a *grand mal* seizure," Landis said. "Nothing we can't cope with, nothing we weren't prepared for." She touched Elin's shoulder reassuringly, called back to the crowd huddling about Tory. "*Hey!* One of you loopheads—somebody there know any programming? Get the lady out of this."

A tech scurried up, made a few simple adjustments with her machinery. The others—still gathering, Landis had been only the third on the scene—were trying to hold Tory still, to fit a bone inductor against his neck. There was a sudden gabble of comment, and Tory flopped wildly. Then a collective sigh as his muscles eased and his convulsions ceased.

"There," the tech said, and Elin scrabbled off the couch.

She pushed through the people (and a small voice in the back of her head marveled: *A crowd! How strange.)* and knelt before Tory, cradling his head in her arms.

He shivered, eyes wide and unblinking. "Tory, what's the *matter?*"

He turned those terrible eyes on her. *"Nichevo."*

"What?"

"Nothing," Landis said. "Or maybe 'it doesn't matter,' is a better translation."

A wetware tech had taken control, shoving the crowd

back. He reported to Landis, his mouth moving calmly under the interplay of green and red. "Looks like a flaw in the programming philosophy. We were guessing that bringing the ego along would make God such an unpleasant experience that the subject would let us deprogram without interfering—now we know better."

Elin stroked Tory's forehead. His muscles clenched, then loosened, as a medtech reprogrammed the body responses. "Why isn't anyone *doing* anything?" she demanded.

"Take a look," Landis said, and patched her into the intercom. In her mind's eye, Elin could see dozens of wetware techs submitting program after program. A branching wetware diagram filled one channel, and as she watched minor changes would occur as programs took hold, then be unmade as Tory's mind rejected them. "We've got an imagery tap of his *weltanschauung* coming up," some nameless tech reported.

Something horrible appeared on a blank channel.

Elin could only take an instant's exposure, before her mind reflexively shut the channel down, but that instant was more than enough. She stood in a room infinitely large and cluttered with great noisome machines. They were tended by malevolent demons who shrieked and cackled and were machines themselves, and they generated pain and madness.

The disgust and revulsion she felt was absolute. It could not be put into words—no more than could the actual experience of what she had seen. And yet—she knew this much about wetware techniques—it was only a rough approximation, a cartoon, of what was going through Tory's head.

Elin's body trembled with shock, and by slow degrees she realized that she had retreated to the surface world. Tory's head was still cradled in her arms. A wetware tech standing nearby looked stunned, her face gray.

Elin gathered herself together, said as gently as she could, "Tory, what *is* that you're seeing?"

Tory turned his stark, haunted eyes on her, and it took an effort of will not to flinch. Then he spoke, his words shockingly calm.

"It is — what is. It's reality. The universe is a damned cold machine, and all of us only programs within it. We perform the actions we have no choice but to perform, and then we fade into nothingness. It's a cruel and noisy place."

"I don't understand — didn't you always say that we were just programs? Wasn't that what you always believed?"

"Yes, but now I experience it."

Elin noticed that her hand was slowly stroking his hair; she did non try to stop it. "Then come *down,* Tory. Let them deprogram you."

He did not look away. *"Nichevo,"* he said.

The tech, recovered from her shock, reached toward a piece of equipment. Landis battled her hand away. "Hold it right there, techie! Just what do you think you're doing?"

The woman looked impatient. "He left instructions that if the experiment turned out badly, I was to pull the terminator switch."

"That's what I thought. There'll be no mercy killings while *I'm* on the job, Mac."

"I don't understand." The tech backed away, puzzled. "Surely you don't want him to suffer."

Landis was gathering herself for a withering reply when the intercom cut them all off. A flash of red shot through the sensorium, along with the smell of bitter almond, a prickle of static electricity, the taste of *kimchi.* An urgent voice cried, "Emergency! We've got an emergency!" A black and white face materialized in Elin's mind. "Emergency!"

Landis flipped into the circuit. "What's the problem? Show us."

"You're not going to believe this." The face disappeared, and was replaced by a wide-angle shot of the lake.

The greenish-black water was calm and stagnant. The thrust-cone island, with its scattered grass and weeds, slumbered.

And God walked upon the water.

They gawked, all of them. Coral walked across the lake, her pace determined but not hurried, her face serene. The pink soles of her bare feet only just touched the surface.

I didn't believe her, Elin thought wildly. She saw Father Landis begin to cross herself, her mouth hanging open, eyes wide in disbelief. Halfway through her gesture, the Jesuitical wetware took hold. Her mouth snapped shut, and her face became cold and controlled. She pulled herself up straight.

"Hans," the priest said, "push the button."

"No!" Elin shrieked, but it was too late. Still hooked into the intercom, she saw the funny little man briskly, efficiently obey.

For an instant, nothing happened. Then bright glints of light appeared at all of the condensor units, harsh and actinic. Steam and smoke gushed from the machinery, and a fraction of a second later, there was an ear-slapping gout of sound,

Bits of the sky were blown away.

Elin turned, twisted, fell. She scrambled across the ground, and threw her arms around Tory.

The air was in turmoil. The holes in the dome roof—small at first—grew as more of the dome flaked away, subjected to stresses it wasn't designed to take. An uncanny whistling grew to a screech, then a scream, and then there was an all-encompassing *whoomph,* and the dome shattered.

Elin was flung upward, torn away from Tory, painfully flung high and away. All the crater was in motion, the rocks tearing out of the floor, the trees splintering upward, the lake exploding into steam.

The screaming died—the air was gone. Elin's ears rang furiously, and her skin stung everywhere. Pressure grew within her, the desire of her blood to mate with the vacuum, and Elin realized that she was about to die.

A quiet voice said: *This must not be.*

Time stopped.

Elin hung suspended between moon and death. The shards and fragments of an instant past crystallized and shifted. The world became not misty, exactly, but apositional. Both it and she grew tentative, possibilities rather than actual things.

Come be God with me now, Coral said, but not to Elin.

Tory's presence flooded the soupy uncertainty, a vast and powerful thing, but wrong somehow, twisted. But even as Elin felt this, there was a change within him, a sloughing off of identity, and he seemed to straighten, to heal.

All around, the world began to grow more numinous, more real. Elin felt tugged in five directions at once. Tory's presence swelled briefly, then dwindled, became a spark, less than a spark, nothing.

Yes.

With a roaring of waters and a shattering of rocks, with an audible thump, the world returned.

Elin unsteadily climbed down the last flight of stone stairs from the terraces to the lakefront. She passed by two guards at the foot of the stairs, their facepaint as hastily applied as their programming, several more on the way to the nearest trellis farm. They were everywhere since the incident.

She found the ladder up into the farm and began climbing. It was biological night, and the agtechs were long gone.

Hand over hand she climbed, as far and high as she could, until she was afraid she would miss a rung and tumble off. Then she swung herself onto as ledge, wedging herself between strawberry and yam planters. She looked down on the island, and though she was dizzyingly high, she was only a third of the way up.

"Now what the hell am I doing here?" she mumbled to herself. She swung her legs back and forth, answered her own question: "Being piss-ass drunk." She cackled. *There* was something she didn't have to share with Coral. She was capable of getting absolutely blitzed, and walking away from the bar before it hit her. It was something metabolic.

Below, Tory and Coral sat quietly on their monkey island. They did not touch, did not make love or hold hands or even glance one at the other—they just sat. Being Gods.

Elin squinted down at the two. "Like to upchuck all over you," she mumbled. Then she squeezed her eyes and fists tight, drawing tears and pain. *Dammit, Tory!*

Blinking hard, she looked away from the island, down into the jet-black waters of the lake. The brighter stars were reflected there. A slight breeze rippled the water, making them twinkle and blink, as if lodged in a Terran sky. They floated lightly on the surface, swarmed and coalesced, and formed Tory's face in the lake. He smiled warmly, invitingly.

A hand closed around her arm, and she looked up into the stern face of a security guard. "You're drunk, Ms.," he said, "and you're endangering property."

She looked where he pointed, at a young yam plant she had squashed when she sat down, and began to laugh. Smoothly, professionally, the guard rolled up her sleeve, clamped a plastic bracelet around her wrist. "Time to go," he said.

By the time the guard had walked Elin up four terraces, she was nearly sober. A steady trickle of her blood wound through the bracelet, was returned to her body cleansed of alcohol. A sacrilegious waste of wine, in her opinion.

In another twenty steps, the bracelet fell off her wrist. The guard snapped it neatly from the air and disappeared. Despair closed in on her again. *Tory, my love!* And since there was no hope of sleep, she kept on trudging up the terraces, back toward Hans's rathskeller, for another bellyful of wine.

There was a small crowd seated about the rock that served Hans as a table, lit by a circle of hologram-generated fairy lights. Father Landis was there, and drinking heavily. "Tomorrow I file my report," she announced. "The synod is pulling out of this, withdrawing funding."

Hans sighed, took a long swig of his own wine, winced at its taste. "I guess that's it for the Star Maker project, huh?"

Landis crossed her fingers. "Pray God." Elin, standing just outside the circle, stood silently, listening.

"I don't ever want to hear that name again," a tech grumbled.

"You mustn't confuse God with what you've just seen," Landis admonished.

"Hey," Hans said. "She moved time backwards or something. I saw it. This place exploded — doesn't that prove something?"

Landis grinned, reached out to ruffle his hair. "Sometimes I worry about you, Hans. You have an awfully *small* concept of God." Several of the drinkers laughed.

He blushed, said, "No, really."

"Well, I'll try to keep this—" she leaned forward, rapped her mug against the rock, "fill this up again, hey?—keep it simple. We had analysts crawl up and down Coral's description of the universe, and did you know there was no place in it *anywhere* for such things as mercy, hope, faith? No, we got an amalgam of substrates, supraprograms, and self-metaediting physics. Now what makes God superior is not just intellect—we've all known some damn clever bastards. And it's not power, or I could buy an atomic device on the black market and start my own religion.

"No, by *definition* God is my moral superior. Now I myself am but indifferently honest—but to Coral, moral considerations don't even exist. Get it?"

Only Elin noticed the haunted, hopeless light in Landis's eyes, or realized that she was spinning words effortlessly, without conscious control. That deep within, the woman was caught in a private crisis of faith.

"Yeah, I guess," Hans scratched his head. "I'd still like to know just what happened between her and Tory there at the end."

"I can answer that," a wetware tech said. The others turned to face her, and she smirked, the center of attention. "What the hell, they plant the censor blocks in us all tomorrow—this is probably my only chance to talk about it.

"We reviewed all the tapes, and found that the original problem stemmed from a basic design flaw. Shostokovich should never have brought his ego along. The God state is very ego-threatening; he couldn't accept it. His mind twisted it, denied it, made it into a thing of horror. Because to accept it would mean giving up his identity." She paused for emphasis.

"Now we don't understand the why or how of what happened. But *what* was done is very clearly recorded. Coral came along and stripped away his identity."

"Hogwash!" Landis was on her feet, belligerent and unsteady. "After all that happened, you can't say they don't have any identity! Look at the mess that Coral made to join Tory to her—that wasn't the work of an unfeeling, identity-free creature."

"Our measurements showed no trace of identity at all," the tech said in a miffed tone.

"Measurements! Well, isn't that just scientific as all get-out?" The priest's face was flushed with drunken anger. "Have any of you clowns given any thought to just what we've created here? This gestalt being is still young—a newborn infant. Someday it's going to grow up. What happens to us all when it decides to leave the island, hey? I—" She stopped, her voice trailing away. The drinkers were silent, had drawn away from her.

" 'Scuse me," she muttered. "Too much wine." And sat.

"Well." Hans cleared his throat, quirked a smile. "Anybody for refills?"

The crowd came back to life, a little too boisterous, too noisily, determinedly cheerful. Watching from the fringes, outside the circle of light, Elin had a sudden dark fantasy, a waking nightmare.

A desk tech glanced her way. He had Tory's eyes. When he looked away, Tory smiled out of another's face. The drinkers shifted restlessly, chattering and laughing, like dancers pantomiming a party in some light opera, and the eyes danced with them. They flitted from person to person, materializing now here, now there, surfacing whenever an individual chanced to look her way. A quiet voice said, "We were fated to be lovers."

Go away, go away, go away, Elin thought furiously, and the hallucination ceased.

After a moment spent composing herself, Elin quietly slipped around to where Landis sat. "I'm leaving in the morning," she said. The new *persona* had taken; they would not remove her facepaint until just before the lift up, but that was mere formality. She was cleared to leave.

Landis looked up, and for an instant the woman's doubt and suffering were writ plain on her face. Then the mask was back, and she smiled. "Just stay away from experimental religion, hey kid?" They hugged briefly. "And remember what I told you about stubbing your toes."

There was one final temptation to be faced. Sitting in the hut, Tory's terminal in her lap, Elin let the soothing green light of its alpha-numerics wash over her. She thought of Tory, of his lean body under hers in the pale blue earthlight. "We were meant to be lovers," he'd said. She thought of life without him.

The terminal was the only artifact Tory had left behind that held any sense of his spirit. It had been his plaything, his diary, and his toolbox, and its memory still held the Trojan horse programs he had been working with when he was—transformed.

One of those programs would make her a God.

She stared up through the ivy at the domed sky. Only a few stars were visible between the black silhouetted leaves, and these winked off and on with the small movements she made breathing. She thought back to Coral's statement that Elin would soon join her, merging into the unsettled, autistic state that only Tory's meddling had spared her.

"God always keeps her promises," Tory said quietly.

Elin started, looked down, and saw that the grass to the far side of the hut was moving, flowing. Swiftly it formed the familiar, half-amused, half-embittered features of her lover, continuing to flow until all of his head and part of his torso rose up from the floor.

She was not half so startled as she would have liked to be.

Of *course* the earlier manifestations of Tory had been real, not phantoms thrown up by her grief. They were simply not her style.

Still, Elin rose to her feet apprehensively. "What do you want from me?"

The loam-and-grass figure beckoned. "Come. It is time you join us."

"I am not a program," Elin whispered convulsively. She backed away from the thing. "I can make my *own* decisions!"

She turned and plunged outside, into the fresh, cleansing night air. It braced her, cleared her head, returned to her some measure of control.

A tangle of honeysuckle vines on the next terrace wall up moved softly. Slowly, gently, they became another manifestation, of Coral this time, with blossoms for the pupils of her eyes. But she spoke with Tory's voice.

"*You* would not enjoy Godhood," he said, "but the being you become will."

"Give me time to *think!*" she cried. She wheeled and strode rapidly away. Out of the residential cluster, through a scattering of boulders, and into a dark meadow.

There was a quiet kind of peace here, and Elin wrapped it about her. She needed that peace, for she had to decide between her humanity and Tory. It should have been an easy choice, but—the *pain* of being without!

Elin stared up at the earth; it was a world full of pain. If she could reach out and shake all the human misery loose, it would flood all of Creation, extinguishing the stars and poisoning the space between.

There was, if not comfort, then a kind of cold perspective in that, in realizing that she was not alone, that she was merely another member of the commonality of pain. It was the heritage of her race. And yet—somehow—people kept on going.

If they could do it, so could she.

Some slight noise made her look back at the boulder field. Tory's face was appearing on each of the stones, every face slightly different, so that he gazed upon her with a dozen expressions of love. Elin shivered at how *alien* he had become. "Your need is greater than your fear," he said, the words bouncing back and forth between faces. "No matter what you think now, by morning you will be part of us."

Elin did not reply immediately. There was something in her hand — Tory's terminal. It was small and weighed hardly at all. She had brought it along without thinking.

A small, bleak cry came from overhead, then several others. Nighthawks were feeding on insects near the dome roof. They were too far, too fast, and too dark to be visible from here.

"The price is too high," she said at last. "Can you understand that? I won't give up my humanity for you."

She hefted the terminal in her hand, then threw it as far and as hard as she could. She did not hear it fall.

Elin turned and walked away.

Behind her, the rocks smiled knowingly.

Never Love a Hellhag

By Alfred Bester

1

Circe, the Hellhag, got busted for Mope One. I'm making a madly free translation from the Alien of anno Circinus $3 + g/G$ into our Terran of anno Domini 2020 which we boasted would be "The Year of Perfect Vision." Whether it was I leave to you.

Yes, Circe was found guilty of Mopery in the first degree and was condemned to be zombied. All cultivated senses were to be wiped, leaving only the crudes necessary for minimal survival; sight, sound, smell, taste, and touch, plus an imbecile I.Q. of 247. It was Draconian, and Dodo, the Duckface Boy, had to spring her before the execution because this neoCirce still owed him six transformations already bought and paid for.

Woe to thee, O Bedlam which we call Mother Earth! Dodo goofed and added the Circinian Circe, to the rest of us inmates. Circinus is a teensy-weensy constellation in the

Milky Way and a neighbor of Centaurus who couldn't care less. The original Circe (Sur-see) was a sorceress who turned men into beasts, and you can read all about her hanky-panky in Homer's *Odyssey*. This modern Circe didn't fool around with wolves and swine; her concept of bestiality was based on the psychopathology of the unconscious.

It was easy for Dodo to spring her. In the Circinian cluster they imprison themselves and let the alleged perpetrators roam at large, hoping they'll vamoose forever. But Dodo was never bright to begin with and he got rattled by the snatch. Instead of putting the Hellhag into his getaway craft targeted for his stash, he got mixed up and shoved her into the craft alongside, which was programmed "to hell and beyond." He was too flustered to notice that its hull was plainly blazoned: CIRCINUS MOBILE AURAL MAJORITY. It was a robot missionary mission.

The craft carried its incomprehensible aural sermon and Circe through a dozen populated systems. Most of them boarded the ship to explore and loot. They pirated objects meaningless to us but evidently precious to them. Some tried eating a piece of the Hellhag—"absorbing" would be a more apropos image—and apparently didn't relish her. Some left graffiti that looked like Rorschach inkblots. All of them were too smart to dream of capturing the craft; they had enough headaches of their own without adding alien complications, but not us Bedlamites. Oh no! We're the smartasses of the universe.

Anyway, this religious number was spotted by our radio telescopes just inside the asteroid belt. They picked up its AM, FM, and PM broadcasts which sounded like a convention of cicadas arguing about rules of order. Then the opticals observed the aural simulcast which flickered like a convention of fireflies, also in dispute. Actually this was the Majority message which translates roughly as, "Why don't you all do everything *our* way, which is the *right* way, and find salvation? Free brochure inside, but offerings welcomed."

The discovery generated the same explosions ignited by gold in California and diamonds in Kimberley. The adventure crowd drooled over the possibility of fantastic alien treasure. The AMA warned about deadly plagues from outer space. The Arabs denounced dangerous new energy sources which might supplant safe and sane oil. Communications hollered that the intruder's broadcasts were lousing satellite relays. And naturally the Pentagon and Kremlin were contending for far-out alien weaponry which might settle the neutron stalemate in their favor.

The only thing the adversaries agreed on was that the drop-in from space was not to be explored until they'd all come to an agreement. Any unauthorized investigation was threatened with summary execution by electrocution, hanging, guillotining, keelhauling, the garrote, trampling by a very large elephant, or worse.

We figured that by the time everybody agreed to agree the Spacewagon would be through our Solar and halfway out to the stellar boondocks, so Amby and I heisted the Langley Research ship. By '20 scores of spacecraft were owned and operated by the industries and institutions that could afford them. We used our clout as distinguished members of the staff, plus lies, bribes, and blackmail, and went up to snoop knowing we were taking one hell of a risk; but no scientist can fight the passion of discovery.

"Anyway, you'll be taking the rap," I told Amby. "If we're busted I'm going to plead like I'm an absent-minded perfesser which was suborned by Amby, the felonious footpad."

"Won't do any good," Amby said. "They'll execute us both with Chinese tawchuh."

"They won't make me whine. A Vostok can take anything

Fu Manchu can hand out."

"I've been meaning to ask you, Jeff," Amby said. "You're listed as Jeff Vostok, Director of Parabiology. What the hell kind of name is that? Vostok's a Russky town."

"And that's where my folks come from. The name was Vostokowitz originally but they shortened it."

I knew all about her name. She was Amby Zedilla from Anthropology, Zedilla being the diminutive of Zeta. She was a Greek; a big woman with black hair, black eyes, and ivory-white skin. She was also a raunchy bull-dyke who didn't give a damn for the morality of the Langley Research Institution. Neither did I, and that brought us together on a friendly sort of man-to-man basis. She was pleased that I was a straight (lesbians and gays hate each other) and sometimes hinted at introducing me to her twin sister, who was hetero and very lonely, but she never explained why, and she piqued my curiosity when she said she'd taken the job in Anthro so she could be near her and support her.

How I came to be Director of Parabiology at Langley is even curiouser; it was the last thing I wanted. When I was a kid around three years old, my Uncle Morris came to our house mad as a hornet. It seems his cab driver shortchanged him by ten dollars through some sort of sleight of hand.

"I didn't get his name," Uncle Morris said, "but I did get the cab number, 1729, if I can remember it. Jeff" — he turned to me — "get a pencil and paper so I can write it down."

"You don't have to, Uncle," I said. "1729 is easy to remember. It's an unusual number."

"It is? Why? A famous date?"

"No, Uncle Morris. It's the smallest number expressible as the sum of two cubes in two different ways."

My uncle and father stared at me.

"My God!" Uncle Morris exclaimed. "Only three years

old! This kid's another Einstein."

But I wanted to be a chef.

This was fine with the men in the family who had visions of freeloading in their relation's classy restaurant but my mother raised hell. She wanted to be able to say, "My son, the doctor."

She won, of course, but I cheated a little. I didn't take my doctorate in medicine but in molecular biology. This was a happy solution. It meant that she could boast about her son, the doctor, and he could cook *DNA mit Kartofles* or *Nucleoli Goulash* in the laboratory. I was hoping I'd brew something celebrated and make the whole *mishpokeh* admire her, but I never dreamed it would be as dazzling and destroying as Circe, the Hellhag.

So up Amby and I went in a spaceshuttle piloted by Commander Marv Merkin. We linked up with the Startrespasser and this is what the experts in Parabiology and Anthropology found. Make what you can of it.

Miniature craters in the deck which bounced you up when you walked on them.

The same in the bulkheads which blew you back when you came too close.

Ceiling looking like an Indian punkah; you know, dozens of swinging horizontal fans. They seemed to be giving transfusions to each other or maybe vampiring.

Kaleidoscopic illumination from a strip which squirmed up and down like a cobra being serenaded out of a basket by a fakir.

Six opaque crescents which might have been portholes, only when I tried to look out I saw Amby Zedilla's face. When I turned to see if Amby was still inside she was at another crescent seeing my face.

A pile of what seemed to be red rock candy.

About a hundred dodecahedron solids that floated and

shuddered light when they bumped against you.

A Gordian knot of transparent tubing containing tiny flames chasing after each other like commuters trying to catch a train.

A pick-up-sticks stack of orange rock candy.

A mosaic right triangle in constant realignment. It seemed to be demonstrating the square of the hypotenuse being equal to the sum of the squares of the other two sides.

Rorschach images everywhere, not only drawn on surfaces but also in the forms of floating smoke, mist, liquids and gel.

A jumble of yellow rock candy.

Have you ever seen a Möbius hourglass with no inside and no outside? Of course not. What kind of time could it keep? Was it meant to keep time?

What looked like a handful of giant paramecia which had been tossed up and never came down. They weren't mitotic.

A heap of green rock candy.

Something crimson and gold, about the size of a doormat. It undulated like the amazing marine creature of the coral reefs nicknamed, "The Spanish Dancer."

(By the way, everything I'm describing moved anywhere from slow-motion to speed-up. It made us dizzy.)

There were other things and whats and wows defying description. I'll tell you; put "One, two, buckle my shoe" into a blender along with a chess problem and sixteen bars of punk rock, churn at low speed, and try to describe what pours out plus its use. Now you've got the picture. Now you know what "alien" really means.

We'd promised each other that we wouldn't disturb anything and certainly not pinch anything; just examine and photograph without touching to get a head start on future research. We kept our word faithfully, but while Commander Merkin was piloting us on the homejet to Terra,

Amby suddenly let out some sort of Greek exclamation and began feeling around frantically.

"What? What?" I asked.

"Wait! Wait! And don't move."

I had a sinking feeling that a giant tarantula from outer space was poised on my back sharpening her jaws. Amby found the first-aid kit, opened it, and snatched out an empty hypodermic syringe. That didn't reassure me. She pulled the plunger all the way out of the barrel, clapped the open end of the barrel against my back and tapped my suit smartly. Then she held the syringe up and inserted the plunger again.

"There," she said. "Got it safe and sound."

"Got what, for God's sake?"

"It must have rubbed off on your back when you were exploring. Look, Jeff."

Inside the sterile syringe was a crystal of white rock candy. I won't keep you in suspense; it was a piece of Circe, the Hellhag, but it took days of tough research to spring that surprise on us.

2

Para is a prefix meaning "beside" or "beyond" and sometimes implying "alteration" or "modification." The daredevil Parabiology Department I headed worked in all these directions, juggling and challenging nucleic structures and using all the disciplines, which meant that I had to be a versatile polytech. So I set out to do a quantitative and qualitative analysis of this crystal of rock candy the size of a jellybean.

No sweat because I was used to working small. No, what made the job hell was the fact that contaminants can ruin results, and the same stringent sterile conditions which Amby tried to follow in the shuttle must be obeyed at all times.

Just to make life easier, a top-level inquisition on our appropriation of the Langley craft for unauthorized, unspecified use was gathering like thunder over China 'cross the bay. If we were lucky we'd get off with ruined careers and a lawsuit for the cost of our excursion. If the Feds found out where we went, it'd be the elephants for sure. A high price to pay for a Socratic reconnoiter but we lucked out . . . at least I thought we did at first.

Running hard in opposite directions we collided on the walk between Zoology and Anthropology. Since I'm a light-weight (130 lbs) and she's a light-heavy (160 lbs) it kind of took the will-to-win out of me. When I got my breath back I gasped, "Hot news! I was coming to tell you."

"Me too," Amby said, waving a large envelope.

"What day is today?" I asked. "I've lost count."

"Wednesday, I think."

"What time is it?"

"Sixish."

"Great. Jumpin' Joe's saloon must be open. Come and celebrate the triumph of Jeff Vostok, superscientist."

"My triumph can lick your triumph any old time," Amby said and batted me with the envelope.

Vodka-tonic, easy on the ice, for me. Screwdriver for the Grik. After ten minutes of silent, internal *k'veling* and a second round, I said, "Me first, then you'll talk."

"No. Me."

"I outrank you, staffwise."

"The E.R.A. will hear of this. All right. Go."

"Roger and over, Tom Swift." The triumph in me burst out. "First I ran a qualitative on a chip from the crystal. Among other results came up alpha-amino acid."

"So? Why all the excitement?"

"It's one of the essentials in protoplasm."

"My God!"

"Easy. Easy. So far only a signpost pointing to who knows what."

"*I* know what."

"You do? How?"

"Wait for it. Wait for it. Go ahead."

"Then I shaved a microslice and had a look under a field mike at 20x. Lo and behold, graptolites!"

"Grapto-whats?"

"From Invertebrate Paleontology. Grapto — written. Lite — stone. Written on stone. A class of fossils that look like pencil marks on slate."

"Do you know *all* the disciplines?"

"I have to in my business."

"Man, you are one smart little boy."

"I think that crystal nodule may be what they call a 'coal ball.' "

"What's that?"

"Concretions they find in coal. They're fragments of petrified life sort of rolled up into a doughnut."

"So?"

"I sliced more sections and put together a three-dimensional picture. The graptolites sketched an unmistakable cell wall. Amby, we've got an animal or vegetable fossil."

"Fossil, hell!" She was beside herself. "Bless you, Jeff, your genius has given me the one piece of evidence I needed. That ain't no fossil, son; we've got a fragment of dead derma that's been sloughed."

"What?"

"Like peeling after a sunburn."

"That's crazy."

"One picture is worth a thousand words. Here, look at these and use your memory."

She opened the envelope and took out a pack of glossies.

They were blowups of the shots she'd taken inside the Space-wagon. I went through the stills twice, then looked up at Amby. "Yes, I remember all this."

"Thank you, Jeff." She was victorious. "It took me three days to notice. Now I don't feel like such a fool."

"Notice what? Have I missed something?"

Amby nodded. "You've missed something that's missing. Now that I've clued you in, try again."

I went through the glossies twice again. Something I missed that's missing? Something missing? Something? Then the hundred-watt bulb lit up over my head. "The rock candy! Heaps, piles, stacks, red, orange, yellow, green, all over the place. Where are they?"

"Right here." She pulled up a giant blowup, part of a shot. "That's from you making eyes at the Spanish Dancer. What's behind your back?"

No doubt of it. One edge of a mound of white rock candy was just visible. It seemed to be touching my back.

"And that's how that crystal got attached to you," Amby said. "Must have been love at first sight."

I waved a feeble hand; this was no time for jokes. At last I managed, "This is a bit much for me, lady. Is it what I'm afraid to think?"

"Damn right it is. Motility. Spontaneity. Life. That single heap was shifting around, changing colors, and we thought we were seeing more than one."

"Life? Alive life?"

"Alive. Maybe just barely after a stretch in space. Maybe dying life. That sloughed derma may be the product of a living *or* dying process. No matter which, it means danger."

"That's what I was afraid to think. We've got to get it down to earth as quickly as possible for an all-out examination before it's too late."

"How can we get up again to bring it down?"

"We'll need official cooperation from the U.N. and they still can't decide who's on first and what's on second." I tried to smile. "And that means a full public confession with no guarantee that they'll let you and me run the show."

She gave me a sour grin. "You got it, turkey. It's a dead end."

We sat in silence and suffered.

Then this image of Amby Zedilla came up to the table; black hair, black eyes, ivory skin, white teeth flashing in a friendly smile, but it was a duplicate in miniature. I've said that Amby was a light heavyweight. This image was a flyweight, under 110 lbs, and it was like looking at Amby through the wrong end of a telescope. Absolutely amazing. I stared.

"My sister, Moe," Amby said, brightening a little.

"I thought you said she was an identical twin."

"A story goes with it."

"Later." I shoved over and patted the bench. "Hi, Moe, I'm Jeff Vostok. Join the funeral party. What are you drinking?"

"She can't hear you," Amby grumbled. She motioned, and her sister sat down alongside her, opposite me, smiling into my eyes.

Fascinated by the miniature beauty, I mouthed to her, "I. Am. Sorry. Moe. I. Am. Jeff. Vos. Tok." The girl nodded and winked. Enchanting.

"She can read lips but she can't answer."

"What? A mute? Complete?"

"Complete."

"Dear God, what a shame! What a waste! But how? Why? An identical twin, only you're twice her size and have all your faculties."

"That's the story. Some sort of localized placental trauma in Mum cheated her, which is why she's smaller and a deaf

369

mute. But don't underestimate her, Jeff. Moe has all her marbles; more than me, I think, more than most, and maybe even you. She's a brilliant adult living in the Big Lonely Silence."

"What. Is. Your. Real. Name. Moe?"

Amby made a face and answered for her. "Mum was obsessed with the Grik shtik and gave us names out of mythology. Amby is short for Ambrosia, the food of the gods. Moe is short for Moly, with a long 'O'. That was the magic flower of Hermes."

"What flower?"

"It's in Homer. When Circe turned Odysseus' crew into swine, he had to rescue them. Hermes gave him the magic Moly flower to protect him against Circe's witchcraft."

"So why did your Mum give that particular name to your sister?"

"Because she was Old World superstitious. When she saw the strange difference between her twin daughters she was convinced it was witchcraft. She wanted Moe protected from any more sorcery and gave her the name of the magic flower."

When I managed to tear myself away from the silent chemotropism generating between Moly and me and get back to the dilemma of our discovery with Amby, the smaller version watched my face intently, reading my lips, obviously sympathizing with the despair I was expressing. Then, under the table, Moly's knee touched mine.

It was no accident. It was a deliberate pressure that said, "I'm with you."

My knee answered, "Thanks."

Her face asked, "Can I help?"

My shrug answered, "I don't know."

And her body said, "Come and find out."

"Thank. You." I mouthed while Amby was addressing

Jumpin' Joe on the lunacy of bureaucracy. "Can. You. Kill. Me?"

She smiled, aimed a finger at me, and shot me through the heart. Then she shook her head and uttered a long, low, "Ohhh-ehh."

That startled me. I turned to Amby. "I thought you said Moe was a mute."

"She can make sounds but that's all," and Amby continued her denunciation to poor Joe.

Moe differed from her sister a hell of a lot more than mere speech and size. She took my hand and motioned with her head toward the door. Amby started a protest but one imperious look from the *petite* quashed her.

Now I know you're thinking that I escaped from myself in bed, but you're wrong. It wasn't the bed, it was the awesome discovery of this girl's answer to her own disaster that challenged and restored my courage. In fact, if it hadn't been for that, there wouldn't have been any bed at all. A man without hope remains limp in all respects.

Moe had a one-room skylight apartment in the top floor of a quasi-loft building, a walkup. Books everywhere. Art and graphics everywhere. Pullman kitchen behind folding Venetian doors set in one wall. A queen-size studio bed against another. Bathroom, of course, and, *mirabile visu,* a sophisticated sound system interfaced with a computer display screen. Completely out of place for a deaf-mute.

Moe saw the incredulity on my face. She laughed, went to the system, and switched it on. She picked up the microphone and made unintelligible mute wauls into it. Print appeared on the screen:

HELLO JEFF

It took me half a moment to twig the electronics. Some

genius (perhaps Moe herself) had managed to transform the impulses of a terminal keyboard into her rudimentary mute articulations. In that case the screen should be able to display any articulation. I grabbed the mike and said, "Hello, Moly." This is what showed:

$$0)(0(0)0$$

Moe took the mike:

NO NO SPEAK SLOWER
AND DEEP AS YOU CAN

Many small guys like myself have deep voices — I suppose it's nature's way of compensating — so I placed mine down in the cellar and out printed:

HERWOE MOOYEE

And we both broke up.

I pulled a fat hassock around. We sat on it, close, cheek to cheek so that we could keep the microphone before our lips and with a full view of the screen. We began to chat, barely able to keep the conversation going, we were laughing so much at what the transmission was doing to my words, which really weren't on its wavelength. I won't give you the distortions, just the talk itself.

"I don't think Amby cared too much for the snatch you put on me, Moe."

"But she likes you, Jeff."

"Yes, we're good friends, but she's protective of you."

"I know."

"And I think maybe you made your commitment just a little too fast for her."

"And for you?"

"I'll be honest. Ordinarily I'd have backed off, not that I'm chased that often, but between us it seems to be spontaneous combustion."

I've had my fair share of get-acquainted scenes with girls but none so unusual and delicious as this. So naturally, while we talked and laughed, so close, it turned from cheek-to-cheek to kissing cheeks and lips and then to the queen-size bed with Imperial-size communication in it. Words are overrated. Our bodies spoke for us without the hide-and-seek of speech and the camouflage of semantics.

Hours later Moe kissed me for the umpteenth time, got up, and went to the Venetian doors. She opened them and gestured to the Pullman kitchen like an emcee. I took my cue—evidently she knew about my chef dream—and checked the tiny fridge. The makings were there so I gave us *Croque M'sieur Roquefort* with coffee for breakfast. Then she demonstrated further lovely concern for me. Alongside my plate she smacked down a huge volume titled, *The Development of Legal Institutions*.

I took her advice, which is why later that day Amby and I appealed to Webb Bohun, pronounced "Boon," known as "The Houdini of Juries." His batting average of hung juries and acquittals was over .600. It's believed that he could have gotten Genghis Khan off with a warning. He was clean-shaven. Big thatch of iron-gray hair. Thrusting nose. Mouth like a grouper.

We told Bohun the truth, the whole truth, and offered our life savings as a retainer. He pronounced two crushing words, "Morons. Salvage." He contemplated us. "Here you are, potentially rich, presumptive public heroes, and you whine about public confession."

Before the two astonished morons could say a word, Bohun continued, "It is established law. There is ship and/or cargo salvage at sea. There is also life salvage. Three distinct categories: ship, cargo, life. Any one of them entitles the rescuer to a fair reward. All together entitled him to all. You have all. Have you any notion of the exploitation potential of that ship and cargo?"

"N-no, sir."

"It is a Comstock Lode. You allege that there is a form of life aboard the craft. Splendid. You have brought back, that is, rescued a moiety of said life. That clinches it. In essence you have saved a member of the crew."

"But it was —"

"You are about to tell me, Dr. Zedilla, that the fragment was not living. Already aware of the fact, thank you. Immaterial. You salvaged life. If it died before or after said rescue is no concern of the Admiralty court. The *res* is the rescue."

"But it wasn't —"

"You are about to point out, Dr. Vostok, that the event did not take place on the high seas. Already aware of the fact, thank you. It is established law that salvage is not limited to the high seas. It can take place in rivers, bays, estuaries, even at a wharf. Then why not space? This will be the first, the leading case. It will be a prolonged court battle and it will be historic. Our perpetual fame is assured."

"Yeah," I grunted. "Prolonged court battle, *if* we can afford it."

"You can afford it, as I shall presently make clear."

"And meanwhile our research subject dies on us," Amby said, "if it isn't dead already."

"It will not die on you, as I shall make clear if you have *quite* finished interrupting me."

We both shut up.

Bohun gave us a warm, paternal smile and went on, "You may keep your life savings. My fee will be twenty-five percent of the gross salvage revenue. Now, tactics. I require your undivided attention."

We both looked attentive.

"You will contribute fifty percent to the Langley Research Institution, thus ensuring its distinguished support and defense against angry governments."

"No trampling elephants, Amby," I whispered.

"*Undivided,* Dr. Vostok. We will retain Studs Fortay, public relations, computerized solicitations, lobbyist, fundraiser, political consultant, the best in the business. Fortay will represent you, along with me, and you will do nothing—repeat, *nothing*—without our advice and consent. Understood?"

We both nodded.

"Fortay will write your speeches, stage your public appearances, and shepherd you through press interviews. He will probably demand fifty percent of the gross but I'll get him down to twenty-five."

"Hey! Wait a minute. Wait a—"

"You have, through your arithmetic genius, Dr. Vostok, just calculated that that leaves nothing of the Comstock Lode for you. I congratulate you on your acumen. However, you and Dr. Zedilla will have the one thing you really want."

"What?"

"That alien life form for examination. I can see that you're not really interested in wealth; you have your sights fixed on distinguished awards, including the Nobel prize."

"True, but how will we get the alien out of the hands of wrangling courts?"

"You won't have to, as I promised to make clear when you interrupted me, Dr. Zedilla. You will return to the salvagee, rescue the entire creature, and bring it back to earth. I will defy any and all attempts at replevin and your Langley will lend its powerful support."

"But—"

"But how will you return to the salvagee, Dr. Vostok? Already aware of the perplexity, thank you. Certainly not by purloining another shuttle. No. However, a client, the gigantic Cosmic Cartel, Inc., will provide you with their craft in return for the exclusive merchandising of all products derivative from the discovery. I will arrange that."

"Aren't they the people who've been combing the moon, looking for something to sell?" I asked.

"Quite, and without success so far, but now we're offering a blue-chip exploitation and they'll be delighted to cooperate. You will leave immediately and secretly to make the rescue. That will give Fortay time to promote an enthusiastic worldwide reception for your heroic return with the mysterious, glamorous alien from the stars. Public confession! Bah!"

I could understand how he overwhelmed juries.

3

Headlines from Studs Fortay's office files:
COURAGEOUS SCIENTISTS RIVAL NASA MISSIONS
AMBY AND JEFF: BRAVEST OF THE BRAVE
SEXY VISITOR FROM SPACE
SPACEGUY OR SPACEGAL?
EXPERTS ALLEGE ALIEN IS GIANT DIAMOND
DIAMOND AL OR DIAMOND ALICE?
NOT MAN NOT WOMAN I AM A SPACE PERSON — THE ALIEN
AMBY AND JEFF REFUSE HOLLYWOOD
CONTRACTS
"ALL FAME AND FORTUNE GO TO SCIENCE NOT US!" — JEFF
DIAMOND ALIEN REFUSES BROADWAY STARRING ROLE
HOME DECORATION IN SPACE — BY AMBY
ZEDILLA
HIGH FASHION IN SPACE — BY DIAMOND ALICE
SYMBOLS FROM SPACE: ART OR GRAFFITI? — BY DR. J. VOSTOK

Fortay had had extra time to propagandize, not because Cosmic's mission control wasn't ready for instant liftoff but because their *apparat* group needed it to prepare an airtight, wide-mouthed, reinforced twenty-gallon Dewar flask — giant thermos bottle to you — the size of a water cooler but obeying a tough weight constraint. A basic rule is that a living specimen must be transported in its original environment, which in this case meant a near-zero vacuum.

Remember shooting galleries? Targets that traverse, revolve, pop up and down, now you see them now you don't? That damned candy-crystal-diamond-demented heap was a whole shooting gallery. It was almost as though it knew we wanted to capture it and didn't like the idea, which was preposterous. It took us twenty minutes of swimming through null-G, swearing and sweating inside our suits, to trap it into the flask. That thing was motile, all right, which meant that it was alive . . . living and intransigent.

We put down at Cosmic's Kansas spread where they'd turned a square mile of flat cornfields into runways, and were met by a discreet group (our whereabouts was still hush-hush) headed by Bohun and Studs Fortay. In addition to the Cosmic brass there were two silent men who accompanied the four of us and the space package on the charter plane back to D.C. Bodyguards.

We couldn't understand that precaution, and were even more bewildered when we got the flask back to the Institution and discovered that Zoology had been turned into a fortress with barred windows and armed guards everywhere. Bohun, Amby, and I had to show ID before we were admitted and permitted to go up to my lab.

"All this with the consent and aid of Langley," Bohun told us.

"Why?" Amby asked. "Are we prisoners serving time? Punishment for this?" She tapped the flask.

"Not at all. Langley is proud of you, grateful for the tremendous fame and fortune you've given them, and they're celebrating your return with a gala reception. Studs is arranging full media coverage now."

"So why the prison bit?" I asked.

"It was deemed necessary for protection."

"Why do we need protection?"

"Not you, Dr. Vostok, Diamond Al." Bohun smiled. "Or Alice, as the case may be. Studs felt that 'alien' was too off-putting. People couldn't warm to it."

"An unknown thing needs protection?"

"Pay attention, both of you. Fortay has done a magnificent promotion creating worldwide enthusiasm for you and your find, but a side effect has been hostility and threats against this alien."

"You have to be kidding."

"No. Consider. The Right-to-Life zealots."

"They're hostile? Why?"

"They're opposed to abortion, fertilization in vitro, sperm banks, intraspecies implantation, all things they judge unnatural. Your life form is alien, unnatural, and may be a threat to life on earth as God created it."

"Meshugah!"

"The Mafia and other criminal types would do anything to get their hands on a twenty-pound diamond. And what about the frenzy of collectors' mania?"

"If it *is* diamond."

"Studs has made the world believe that, Dr. Zedilla. Have you any concept of the reckless greed aroused by ten kilos, fifty thousand carats, of diamond? Have you any concept of the dismay of the Diamond Syndicate and the steps they would take to prevent your find from destroying their control of gem prices through strict rationing? Now, consolidate these dangers and—"

"I'll take the elephants," I said.

" . . . and you can understand why this building has been turned into a fortress. Now get to work and don't be surprised by anything."

But we were.

Langley, now all sweetness and light, no more inquisition, installed one of NASA's high-vacuum subzero test chambers, borrowed from Goddard, and the Dewar flask was offloaded in an environment approximating that of the spacewagon where we'd found it except that no sermon from the AURAL MAJORITY was serenading it.

The attack was launched while Fortay was shepherding me through a press interview in the main building conference hall. It didn't come from any of the candidates Bohun had predicted but out of left field by the "Forward Trust Front." Never heard of them? No one ever had, which is why the FTF attacked. Simply another new terrorist group that didn't give a damn about unknowns from space; all they wanted was publicity and this was *the* headline target of the century.

They prepared it very well. They assembled a contraption of shiny auto and plane parts, seven feet high, senseless and indecipherable, but it sure looked scientifical. They got into jumpsuits, put on faked Goddard ID tags, put the contraption on a dolly, and wheeled it to the freight elevator of Zoology.

The four FTFs took their decoy up to the top floor and wheeled it down the front corridor, one man to each of the four sides. At the Parabio lab the guards stopped them to check, but the contraption masked the entrance and the FTF concealed on the door side of the hodgepodge went into the lab with a hand bazooka. They knew that Amby and I with our assistants were at the giant press conference and thought the lab was empty. They didn't know that Moe Zedilla was there waiting for her lover to return.

She took one look at the bazooka aimed at the test chamber and began throwing anything she could get her hands on at the gunman. She was as fast as the FTF and her barrage broke his aim. The bazooka went off with a kazowie accompanied by assorted crashes. The guards burst in and that was the end of the attack.

When word was whispered to me in the conference hall I took off like a shot. I tore into the Parabio lab, which is the size of a basketball court and filled with benches, tables and desks, all cluttered with gear. There were the guards holding three FTFs; the fourth was writhing on the floor. There was Moe, sitting composedly on a stool, smiling as ever. I took a lightning scan of the shattered ceiling, fire damage, and smashed lab equipment. Then I ran to the test chamber.

Quick look through the viewport. Rock candy seemed to be okay. Quick look at the gauges. My heart sank. The attack hadn't touched the chamber but the kazowie had disrupted the maintenance systems. Vacuum pumps and refrigeration shaken and laboring. Air pressure inside the chamber up to a quarter of an atmosphere and rising slowly. Temperature, minus fifty centigrade, which is a hell of a climb from minus two hundred Kelvin, and also rising. God knows how long before it would be a lovely spring day inside the chamber and there goes our whole damned Nobel examination. Tragedy . . . Misery . . . and I ran to my phone, dialed, and hollered for Goddard techs.

While I was blurting out the crisis and trying to explain what was needed, Amby and the assistants plus Bohun and Fortay charged into the lab followed by some Langley brass and assorted press.

"Amby!" I hollered, "take a look. Is the rock candy still okay?" On the phone, "Yes, yes, vacuum and temperature. Tell'm to bring what's needed for repair or, goddammit, bring new maintenance gear. On the double!"

From the viewport Amby shouted, "It's gone!"

"What?"

"Gone. Disappeared."

"It was just there."

"It's nowhere now."

"Oh God!" I dropped the phone, muscled through the clamoring crowd, and joined her. She was right. Gone. Disappeared.

I was frantic. "It's got to be in there somewhere. If it could shuffle around in that spacewagon and fool us, it can do it again." I caught the eye of one of our assistants. "Break out the space suit. I'm going in for a search."

Goddard had supplied me with space gear so I could go into the chamber and run tests on Diamond Al or Alice in its space environment.

"What are you going to look for?" Amby demanded.

"How the hell do I know? If that thing can change color it can probably change into anything." I started climbing into the armor. "Ships and shoes, cabbages and—"

"We could see them through the viewport."

"All right; paint, flooring, walls, dust, dew . . . you name it. What I've got to do is notice anything I know doesn't belong in that sterile chamber."

"And then what?"

"We play it by ear."

The Goddard techs poured in, panting and loaded with tools and added their contribution to the assembled noise. The helmet went over my head, the air-tank valves were opened, and I lumbered to the entry hatch. I swung the lock wheel and pulled the heavy hatch door open. I was in the air-lock chamber. I didn't bother safing the outer hatch behind me; it was too late for that.

I opened the inner hatch and started to crawl in, on the alert for anything that didn't belong in the test chamber. I was ready for anything except what actually happened. At a quarter of an atmosphere inside you'd expect the normal air pressure outside to go hissing in, the way it does when you open a can of vacuum-packed coffee. No way. A hurricane-force blast hit me and knocked me back, clear out of the airlock, to land sprawling on the lab floor.

It got noisier and crashier as I came rocketing out. The crowd yelled and ducked for cover, smashing almost as much equipment as the squall which had whipped into the lab from the test chamber. They all hid, and the only one who came to my rescue was Moe, who got me upright and lent a hand as I took off the helmet and started shrugging out of the suit. To her questioning look I could only shake my head. I hadn't the faintest notion about anything.

After I was out of the suit and had my wits together I looked around fast and nervous and I saw nothing, *niente, rien, nichts,* nothing. The wind squall had died down and I heard nothing. The crowd was still crouched behind benches, desks, tables, and invisible. But the Hellhag was there; Circe was most grotesquely there.

One of her sophisticated Circinian senses (of which she'd been condemned to be deprived) was psychception. We all know body language, the silent somatic tongue that speaks volumes to those who perceive it. Circe sensed psych-language, the buried impellants of our unconscious yearnings, and she could answer them in kind and thus inspire transformations.

She wasn't psych-appearing or psych-speaking to me, yet, but she was appearing and speaking to each of the rest of the crowd in my lab. Heads were poking up and eyes were peering, staring, fascinated. I don't know what psych-language she was speaking to them or how she appeared and appealed to what was inside them, but transformations were taking place.

Amby Zedilla suddenly leaped up and shouted, *"I am the ambionic woman!"*

She didn't look any different but she sure acted Herculean. She grabbed an Erlenmeyer flask and squeezed it until it shattered in her hands, cutting her palms badly. She ignored it; evidently she believed she was bionically impervious. She made for the door and it was obvious she thought she was moving faster than the eye could see. "I'll get my Biogirls together for you, *Wonder Woman!*" she called. *Wonder Woman!* So that's how Circe appeared to her.

"And JayC, Holy Mother!" This in the overwhelming voice of Webb Bohun. He was on his feet. He'd taken a ringstand off a bench and was holding it behind his back with the ring over his head like an improvised halo. *JayC! The Virgin Mary!* Talk about *chutzpah!*

By now the place was a madhouse. The Goddard techs were proclaiming themselves "The Panzer Division" and smashing themselves against walls to show how armored they were. Some of my assistants had stripped off their clothes and were running around displaying themselves proudly. Superstuds. There were snarls and growls from the press; Black Jaguars and Alaska Grizzlies.

Fortay wriggled out of his clothes as if from a straitjacket, and began juggling beakers and test tubes which crashed in all directions. Harry Houdini. One of the institution brass was folding filter papers and trying to sky them, insisting, "My aerodrome *will* fly some day." Probably identified with the original Professor S. P. Langley, founder of our Institution back in A.D. 1900.

The FTFs who were still on their feet were bellowing, "We're the Jacks! We're the Rippers! We're social justice!" And their guards were turning their uniforms inside out to disguise themselves, and concealing their guns under their belts, now that they were steely-eyed counterintelligence agents.

Then the transformees departed. All walked, swaggered,

ran, got the hell out of there, always in character. Moe and I were left alone. We looked at each other, at the chaos around us, and at each other again. All I could think of was a line from *As You Like It,* "O wonderful, wonderful, and most wonderful wonderful!"

But Circe was loose and the bedlam began.

4

It was as though half our world had been turned into a lunatic asylum where the inmates run wild without restraint. We all have secret kinks and quirks and fantasies concealed inside us. Circe didn't create them, she simply hyped them and forced them to erupt into action. There were the old familiar antisocial outrages, of course, but many of the Hellhag's magnifications were bizarre. Circe was also a catalyst for the strange, the odd, the downright hilarious.

The Panzer Division staged a Survival Jamboree featuring survival contests for their iron men on Venus, Luna, Mars, and Pluto. It was held in the Kwik-freeze Cavern of the Bird Brain TV Dinner Company. The only protection the Panzers wore was their own skin.

The James Bonds sauntered into the top-secret contest, all suave and exquisitely dressed in white tie and tails. Their chief introduced himself as "Double-Oh-Seven-teen, with license to voyeur," and warned the Panzers not to resist the invasion On Her Majesty's Secret Mission because the James Bonds' impeccable white ties, silk shifts, and tail coats concealed deadly weapons, poisons, and lethal gas. Then each began to raise an eyebrow at the girl spectators who also wore only their skin.

Houdini's Magicians began shoplifting in drug stores across the country. It was their belief that they could create the legendary Philosopher's Stone which, among other marvels, could prolong life, by baking together one gram of every known element and feeding the resultant to a Galapagos Tortoise. Said Tortoise would then excrete Philosopher's Stones. A battle broke out when a splinter group calling themselves The Merlins insisted that it would excrete gold and silver nuggets.

The Ivy League instituted a fundraising "Permanent Prom" in the U. of P.'s giant Palestra. Music by Columbia. Decor by Brown. Catering by Cornell. Accounting by Harvard. Stag line by Princeton and Dartmouth. Security by Yale. All went profitably until the Ambionic Woman denounced it as male chauvinism and launched a ferocious attack with the Biogirls she had enlisted.

JayC had gathered a corps of Angels who put on seethrough blouses, checked miniskirts, black net stockings, and Joan Crawford pumps, and began soliciting on street corners in a campaign to entice, entrap, and arrest criminals and clean up the city. Unfortunately their only johns were the Superstuds, who provoked a bitter battle when they refused to pay the Angels. They claimed they were doing the girls a favor.

Circe's hype wasn't limited to humans; all were susceptible. A retired cavalry horse tried to join the American Legion. Three wolves tried to audition for the Metropolitan opera. Frosty, a zoo panda, turned up missing one morning. After a frantic search Frosty was found elegantly figure skating in a rink. He had already applied for admission to the Olympic Winter Games. An octopus, wearing an aquatank, stole a taxicab. A thousand mice marched on the White House.

A thieving magpie stole the contents of a radio shortwave chassis, piece by piece, which it reassembled in its nest to pick up police APBs. A colony of wasps turned their hive into an acupuncture clinic. A brown bear lumbered into Floyd's Fish Market carrying a double armful of ripe poison ivy. It nodded to a whole salmon on a slab and then gave the poison ivy bomb a little warning heave. Its threat was clear. The customers screamed. "What the hell," Floyd said later. "At least it wasn't a chinook."

I brought a TV set up to Moe's apartment and we caught the news on whichever channel made sense at the moment. Circe had corrupted broadcasting, of course. Once we caught the soap opera, "Lost Horizons" changed to "Lust Horizons," which was pretty wild but not in a class with a live cooking show demonstrating how to carve a cannibal roast on a skeleton probably stolen from some medical school. That was tasteful, I thought. They might have pinched a cadaver.

Moe could understand the location news coverage and whenever possible she read the newscasters' lips. When she couldn't, I reported via her microphone and display screen, I'll leave out that intermediate step and just give our exchanges as straight dialogue.

Moe said, "She seems to be infecting everything."

"He, she, or it," I said. "Almost."

"And everywhere."

"Practically."

"How?"

"Well," I said, "Webb Bohun loves to control people, plan, lay down the law, run the world. So what does he transform into?"

"He thinks he's Jesus."

"And your sister. We both know she's a tough lesbian and she makes no bones about it. What would Amby want most to be?"

"A man."

"So she transforms into the Superwoman role, which is

about as close as she can come to it."

"And the others?"

"Circe hypes their secret fancies."

Moe was perplexed. "Why?"

"We don't know."

"Is she doing that to us . . . and we don't know it?"

"Not yet."

"Why?"

"We don't know."

"Then it's a mystery," Moe printed.

"Yes."

"But what does she want?"

"We don't know. It's a dead end so far."

This conversation parenthesized on-the-spot news reports of burnings, lootings, muggings, and murder, but when they filmed a character in gorilla drag trying to climb to the top of the Empire State Building with a Barbie doll in his hand it was too much for me. I began to shake with laughter. Then I sobered. It suddenly occurred to me that a not-so-funny character might climb into my apartment and that I'd better get home to make sure that it was as secure as possible.

So I made Moe swear, Scout's honor, cross her heart and hope to die, that she would stay barricaded in her loft and let nobody in but me, and I skulked through the streets back to my place feeling like someone wanted dead or alive. Apartment still secure. Naturally I turned on the tube for more lunatic news the moment I was safely locked inside.

I kept putting Moe's question to myself. "What does Circe want? How can she be stopped? Is there any fundamental rationale, ours or alien, or is it simply a case of a rotten kid running wild until her Mum catches up with her and whales the living daylights out of her?" And meanwhile I was watching more dementia.

The "Alaska Grizzlies" spent hours breaking into a warehouse to steal a packing case of aluminum containers, nothing more.

The "Langley Aerodromes" descended by hang glider onto the roof of the Peerless Plating Company and heisted fifty pounds of cadmium metal usually used to put a shiny finish on cheap souvenirs. No sense to that unless they were manufacturing miniature mementos of the first successful flight of The Founder's first aerodrome on May sixth, 1896.

The "Ripper Jacks" (formerly the FTF) demonstrated the Dialectical Materialism of social injustice by stealing two truckloads of Portland cement. That was easy to figure; they were going to throw the "system" into Chesapeake Bay with its feet encased in concrete.

The "Gala Gays" stole pounds of deadly dangerous sodium metal, volcanic stuff that no sane man would want to mess around with. I concluded that they had confused "sodium" with "sodomy."

A flock of turkey buzzards swooped down on the yard of a coke furnace and flew off with hundreds of graphite bricks. It was speculated that they imagined they could hatch them. Myself, I thought, "Ah-ha! Graphite as in a pencil lead. They're going to improve Mount Rushmore with graffiti." Then I realized that the madness I was watching was beginning to rub off on me. Enough already! I quit.

I went to bed, thrashed for half an hour, got up, took a double dose of tranquilizer, got back under the covers, and drifted into a narcotized limbo flickering with flashes of the dementia I'd seen. Then a warm, silken nude silently slipped under the covers alongside me. She made no move but it was unmistakably my Moe. The familiar sweet breath and scented skin; unmistakably Moe, even in the disruption through which I was floating, and then she murmured, "I had to come. I love you, Jeff. It's like the first time I've ever loved anyone."

And I whispered, "It's the same with me, sweet love."

But then cold thoughts began dropping into my warm soufflé:

Didn't Moe promise to stay home?

How did she get into my place?

Did I give her a key?

I don't remember.

I don't remember her voice being so sultry.

Voice? Moe?

Moe? Moe! My God, Odysseus and the magic Moly flower!

I lurched up in bed, turned on the lamp, and looked down at her. She smiled up at me, the image of my love. Score points for alien psychception. Score demerits too. She hadn't perceived that my magic Moe flower was a mute. I grinned down at the enchanting imitation.

"D'you know who I am?" I asked. "I know who you are."

"Don't be silly, Jeff. Of course we know who we are."

"Do we? If you're my magic Moe, why aren't you all over me, as you always are when we're in bed together? Come on, love, love me.'"

"You're acting so strange, Jeff," Circe said, not moving.

"What? No touch? No caress? Not even a kiss?"

She didn't move.

"Last chance to fake it. You must have psyched the act of passion from me. Give me a reasonable facsimile."

"You're talking in riddles, Jeff."

"Only to you," I laughed, and I admit I was close to hysteria. "It's no riddle to me because I've figured you out. Yes, you've sensed the love and lust I have for my Moe but you can't fake it because it's unknown where you come from."

"Don't be silly, Jeff. I come from nowhere but here, your

adoring Moly."

"Only a lovely copy. Actually, in real life, you're King Kong's daughter."

"Oh, really!"

"No? Then maybe Godzilla Girl. Yes?"

"No more, Jeff. Please!"

"Right. Right." Fury suddenly generated in my loins and crept through my body. "No more laughs. You're the alien pile of rock candy we shanghaied off that ship, the creature I think of as Circe."

She shook her head solemnly, the image of a lovely, denying Moly. She was a magnificent mimic.

"It's been fun and games with us for you," I said, "and I resent it. I'm sore as hell about it."

"I can't understand what you're saying," she protested. "What fun? What games?"

"So now I'm going to play games with you, and I'm going to start with your first lesson in love and lust. I'm going to drill your imitation ass off. Here on earth we call it a grudge-fuck."

And I tried and it was as insane as everything else she'd corrupted. Oh, she faked her best on the basis of what she'd psychsensed from me and my fellow Bedlamites but it really was nowhere.

And yet, despite that, Circe ensorcelled me anyway, for she'd sensed my not-so-secret deep desire to make an important discovery. She combined that with lust, turning the sexual encounter into the challenge of one of those electronic games in which things try to shoot things down or gobble them up.

So I was bewitched by the challenge of winning a physical response combined with the challenge of discovery, and damn if she didn't hook me the way you see addicts hooked in bars and arcades playing the machines for hours. Can you imagine how powerfully they'd be drawn if the excitement of beating the game was combined with a sexual challenge?

We talked, part psych, part body, part speech; many questions from me that must have bewildered her, many answers that bewildered me. It was through this *macédoine* that I learned what little I've been able to report about Circinus and Circe, and finally discovered what she wanted from me although not why she wanted it. I translate into the Terran equivalent.

"I must leave."

"You're going back to Circinus?"

"No, I must change."

"Into what?"

"Myself."

"I don't understand."

"You will when you help me."

"And that's why you came to me?"

"Yes."

"What do you want?"

"An armored truck."

"You can't be serious! You paid this price for that?"

"Yes."

"You sold yourself cheap. I can rent a truck for you first thing tomorrow."

"No, it must be one particular truck. You will steal it and drive it to one particular place for me."

"My dear, demented alien, that doesn't make sense. I've seen you in action. You can do anything you please with us. You can bewitch a truck from driver and guard and drive it wherever you want."

"No, I can't. You've seen but not understood. I can appear. I can magnify what's inside you into action, but I can do nothing physical myself."

"But . . . But our lovemaking?"
"It was all in your mind. It never really happened."
Bitch! Witch! Harpy! Hellhag!
And again you know what "alien" really means.

5

She had to leave me dramatically. She had to ensure my
help with a bribe. She psychsensed my deepest buried secret
which no scientist could possibly reveal, that I have a devout
faith in Animism.

I believe that natural objects, natural phenomena, and
the universe itself possess souls and consciousness. So Circe
transformed into the most beautiful wonders I've ever seen,
inspiring me with a devotion to cling to her and see all the
rest of her enchantments.

She became a miniature summer storm; tiny black thun-
dercloud, tiny lightning bolts flashing through it, a minus-
cule shower of rain falling into a haze the size of a powder
puff.

She transformed into the fog creeping up San Francisco
Bay to envelope the Golden Gate Bridge in her lovely white
embrace, and I was that bridge.

The rainbows shimmering at the feet of great waterfalls
like daughters who can't be wooed away from Daddy, and I
was Daddy.

A silver moonbow I once saw over a northern lake that
seemed to be an evening gown for Morgan le Fey.

Sundogs guarding an Inca pyramid.

And most wonderful wonderful, she enlarged me. I didn't
feel like a little guy anymore. That hangup was gone, wiped;
I was as big as the universe.

I hightailed it back to Moe's place and code-rang (there

were lights linked to the bell) until the flashes caught her attention and she let me in. I poured out an edited report of Circe's epiphany and our exchanges.

"I was only able to see her because she wanted something from me," I said; all this via screen.

"Yes, I can guess. You fair white bod."

She was jealous, by God, and I was flattered. "Forget that, Moe. They don't know the meaning of love and lust in the Circinian cluster."

"And how did you find out?"

"Easy. She was trying to convince me she was you. She looked the part perfect but didn't act it. She spoke. That was the giveaway. And not once did she offer a kiss or caress. They probably reproduce by budding, like the hydrapolyp."

Moe seemed to believe me. I let well enough alone and continued, "Now this is why she came to me, this is what she wants, and I can't figure it out."

"What does she want?"

"An armored truck."

"What!"

"One specific truck, Brink's 101, ICC license 9DC369. Driver and two guards. Leaves Washington tonight at midnight. Takes turnpike bound for New Hope Island, arriving at dawn. I'm to heist it and drive it to the Jersey Astro Resort International. That's a gambling casino."

"But . . . But that doesn't make sense, any of it."

"I told you I couldn't figure it out."

"Why does Circe want that particular truck? What's in it? Why drive in the middle of the night? What's on New Hope Island?"

"I couldn't get any of that out of her."

"And take it to a gambling casino? What's she up to?"

"Which brings us back to square one. We don't know, yet. We may find out after we deliver the truck."

"You're not going to steal it!"

"It's the only way we'll ever find out what Circe's really after. Then maybe we'll be able to purge her and her madness pandemic. Now watch the screen patiently, please."

She nodded.

"Circe's turning the world lunatic because she's a psychogenic catalyst, but after her appearance to me because she wanted something I have the conviction that some of the madness she's generating isn't chance. No. She wants things. She hypes us into getting them for her."

"Yes," Moly agreed, "but stealing a Brink's truck may be as senseless as carrying a Barbie doll to the top of the Empire State Building."

"That's a chance we'll have to take. Now how do we hijack Brink's armored truck number 101 from the driver and armed guards?"

Moe whistled softly.

"I've thought of crazy gimmicks like digging a giant pothole in the turnpike, a phony detour, blocking a tunnel, me playing a fake sheriff . . ."

"Wait, Jeff. Why not use me?"

"You? How?"

"A decoy. A fake accident victim. That ought to bring the troops out of the truck if she's naked, her clothes ripped open by the—"

"No way! Never! No naked! Not even half-naked!"

She burst out laughing. "Now I really do want to believe your story, but after that reaction I couldn't care less about what happened between you and Circe." And she gave me a long delicious kiss.

Dammit, she had my number; I wasn't fooling Moe. Best to drop it and get on with the strategy and tactics of a truck heist. After a long discussion we came up with a plan:

We rented a Peterbilt forty-foot trailer truck with blank

body. I insisted on one built low to the ground.

Bought an electric paint sprayer.

Bought five gallons of Alzac Mylar paint.

Calculated that Brink's 101 would pass the Durham Road Access to the turnpike at 2:00 A.M. approx. (We had to explore via chopper to select that particular spot.)

Drove trailer truck by backroads to Durham and reached turnpike access at 1:30 A.M. It was a black night, no moon, no stars, rotten visibility. Perfect.

Drove trailer onto turnpike and jumped it across the low island separating the opposed lanes so that it halfblocked both.

Connected electric paint sprayer to truck battery.

Sprayed both sides of trailer with Alzac Mylar and ran like hell for cover under the bridge which was the Durham Road overpass.

Then we waited, but not long.

The spray dried to a brilliant mirror finish, turning both sides of the trailer into reflectors. The few cars dribbling up and down the turnpike at that hour saw their own headlights reflected. All thought some damn fool drunk was coming at them the wrong way on the wrong lane. Horns howled, tires screamed, crashes, roars of rage, and more kept coming with the same results. By 2:10 A.M. Brink's 101 arrived at the scene of a spectacular tie-up, a circus of headlights, yellings, and fights.

The three guards leaped out, leaving the doors open, and ran to investigate the uproar. I really couldn't blame them for being careless because another attraction had been added. Kneeling, half-fainting and helpless on the roof of the trailer, was the quintessence of a skin magazine centerfold. Her clothes were ripped open at exactly the right places and the only word for her physical assets was prodigious. Circe, of course, and I had to give the Hellhag points. She'd read me, read my plan, and was lending a hand.

The reason I'd picked that particular spot to stage the "accidents" was that the turnpike was flanked on both sides by flat farmland. So while any possible opponents to the heist were busy fighting and climbing over each other to be the first to rescue the naked beauty in distress, it was relatively easy to weave Brink's 101 across the fields onto the Durham Road exit and head for Jersey and the Astro Resort.

I'm convinced that all gambling resorts are cloned from the Great Mother Casino. Enormous porte-cochere before the entrance spacious enough to accommodate an invasion of tour buses. Small lobby with minimal seating; they don't want you loafing out there, they want you inside for the action. Gigantic gambling hall the size of an armory, brilliantly lit. Aisle after aisle packed with slot machines, roulette tables, blackjack, craps, and elbow-to-elbow gamblers. That was the Astro Resort International. Was. Now Circe and her slaves had taken over.

Evidently the troops had been alerted and were waiting for *my* glorious epiphany. When I drove the Brink's under the port-cochere, a demolition squad of Panzers armed with sledgehammers came charging out and attacked the rear doors of the armored truck with an Anvil Chorus. Although I was perishing to know what they were after, I knew it would take some time to batter the doors open so I helped Moe out of the cab and took her into the casino for an exploratory.

To repeat one of my favorite-type images; put a Mardi Gras, Mummers' New Year Parade, College Hell Week, and London Guy Fawkes' Day into a blender, churn along with clanging hardware, and pour it out. You have what was inside Circe's casino; a Busby Berkeley production number with music by Yankee Stadium.

They were all there; the James Bonds, JayC's Angels, Houdini's Magicians, the Alaska Grizzlies, Amby and her Biogirls, the Ripper Jacks, Superstuds, Gala Gays, and a gaggle of new ones. They were spread all over the great hall in a frenzy; yanking at slot machines, dancing on the crap tables, romancing on the roulette wheels, fighting artillery barrages with coins and chips from the cashiers' cages, screaming, shouting, singing, dancing.

Center, a space the size of half a tennis court had been cleared by ripping back tables and machines, and in their place stood a dark cube maybe twenty feet high. It looked like the sacrosanct Kaaba in the Great Mosque at Mecca but it wasn't any shrine, as I discovered when the Panzers came puffing in lugging a heavy load from Brink's 101. It was a wooden crate containing a massive leaden case. I knew because the crate was stenciled: U.S. DEPT. OF ENERGY - PU^{239}.

Plutonium. The fissionable isotope. No wonder Circe had conned a scientist into hijacking it. With 20/20 hindsight everything fell into place.

Dear God, I thought, of course! Graphite bricks and a concrete surround. Cadmium metal rods to control the process. Molten sodium to regulate heat exchange. Aluminum containers for the plutonium in the core. It's a goddamn nuclear reactor. That's what the Hellhag's been after all along, a fission bomb to blast us into a nova so the bitch can break free from the Solar and go on her merry way. If you can't leave 'em, wipe 'em. Christ! She's got to be stopped!

Moe couldn't help. It'd be impossible to communicate and make her understand the crisis without the display screen. I looked around. No Circe. Her lunatics all playing, brawling, wild. No help from them. Then I had a flash. I left Moe and tore out to the Brink's in the porte-cochere. Just what I'd guessed; doors battered open and four sledgehammers lying where the Panzers had dropped them.

I sprinted back into the casino with two hammers for me and my gal; target for tonight, one nuclear reactor. I wouldn't have to explain to Moe; she'd follow my lead when I started battering the pile to pieces, but she wasn't where I'd left her. She was standing before the reactor going through a crazy combination of calisthenics and semaphore. It looked like a St. Vitus's dance in slow-motion.

The insanity's rubbed off on her, I thought, making for the pile, and I'd better get the demolition finished before I come down with it, too . . . Unless I've got it already.

I squared off in a half-batter's-half-golfer's stance with a heavy hammer poised. Then I heard a long, sustained chord of music, teasing and promising, that sounded like a dawn, and sounding through it was a sweet sunrise voice speaking on a single note, "Don't, love."

"What? What?"

"Don't smash it."

"What? Who's this?"

"Your Moly."

"Talking? My Moe? Damn you, Circe, not again!" I swung the hammer savagely but Circe/Moe shoved hard. I went off balance and dropped the hammer.

She grabbed me and looked into my face. The single sunrise note came again. "It's me, Jeff. She's helping me talk to you."

No!"

"Please listen, Jeff. I've been talking sign language with her and now she's helping me hear and speak words."

"Impossible!"

"She says on Circinus it's supraception."

"And I say on Earth it's horse manure."

"It's paraliminal; how Circinians can communicate with

all aliens. It's how she was able to talk to you."

"As you are now, you damned Hellhag. What scam d'you want to con me into this time?"

"Jeff, it's really me speaking, Moly."

"The hell you say."

"Have you ever heard a paraliminal voice like this?"

"You can fake anything, you bitch."

"If I'm Circe, why don't you see me?"

"I'm seeing you, imitating my Moe again. Listen, my para-rockpile, you've maneuvered me into helping you put together a reactor for your fission bomb. Am I supposed to stand by and wait for you to blow us to hell and gone? Not bloody likely."

I bent down to pick up the sledge. A cannon shot exploded against the back of my skull. There was a dazzle of fireworks and I went black.

6

When I woke up, there was Circe/Moe weeping over me most realisticlike. I grunted. "Thought you couldn't do anything physical, girlie. What'd you use on me? Crowbar?"

The sunrise music again. "A gold ingot. From the casino display."

"That's your style. Nothing but the best."

"For mercy's sake, Jeff, it's me, Moly. Can't you believe that? My God, I've never hit anyone before. I was afraid I'd killed you."

"Sorry to disappoint. Care to try again?"

"I had to stop you, Jeff. I had to."

"From what, as if I don't know."

"Yes. Destroying the reactor."

"Why?"

"Because she's inside."

"What!"

"Circe's inside with the plutonium."

"Inside? The reactor?" I sat up. "This is insane!"

"I can explain what she told me, if you'll only let me."

I was beginning to believe that this really was my Moly. "You saw her? That means she wanted something from you."

"Yes. She gave me the hearing and speech I've prayed for all my life because she wants me to speak to you and stop you."

"What did she look like to you?"

"An egret. A beautiful crimson and gold and purple bird singing the song of the rising sun, the voice she gave me."

"You do sound like that, but—"

"It was the only way she could show me what she really was."

"Which is?"

"The Phoenix."

"Phoenix? The legendary bird that lives for five hundred years and then burns itself to rise from the ashes young again?"

"Yes."

"But that's a myth."

"She said you're a scientist and wouldn't believe her. That's why she wanted me to persuade you to help. She said to tell you something that might convince you."

"What?"

"That it's probable our Earth was originally settled by Circinians and that she would never dream of harming her own people."

"Then why the reactor? Why the fission bomb?"

"There won't be any bomb. It isn't a fission pile, it's her fission pyre. She's burning herself for the rebirth."

That gave me pause. At last, "One of the last things she said was that she'd be leaving to change into herself. Now it makes sense. The legend says the Phoenix lives for five hundred years, then it enters a temple and burns to ashes on the altar. The young new Phoenix emerges from the ashes and flies away. That could be how the Circinian reality degenerated into myth here on earth."

"And how seven eras of evolution turned into seven days of creation in the bible."

"The Fundamentalists won't like that. Now look, I know now that you're really, truly, my dearest Moe." And I clinched her hard and long. "I apologize for my goofs and I'll make it up to you, I swear."

"It's not your fault, Jeff. Circe turned the world into a funhouse with trick mirrors."

"All the same I owe her. She gave you this sunrise speech and hearing. No more display screen."

"But it may not last after she's gone."

"I'll still owe her. I've got to see her through the rebirth. She's inside the reactor, which is in operation. Did she tell you who got it all together?

"The Langley Aerodromes and the Ripper Jacks and the Superstuds and — and a lot more she was controlling. She told them what to do."

"Evidently this isn't her first rebirth. Did she say how long the burn would take?"

"No."

"Then we'll have to wait it out. Let's get as far away as possible from the reactor. No telling how solidly Circe's dingbats insulated it. It's even possible that a Circinian has no concept of the dangers of radiation to Terrestrials. Come on."

I convoyed Moe through the bedlam to a low balcony at the far end. It rimmed what had once been a bar, restaurant, dance floor, and bandstand. Now it had been taken over by Houdini's Magicians and it was a shambles. They were still trying to generate the Philosopher's Stone and were ransacking the bar and kitchen, dumping everything from kirsch to ketchup into a kettle drum on the bandstand. They didn't seem to have a Galapagos Tortoise handy.

But these dedicated alchemists, most of them unfrocked druggists, weren't bothering anybody so we paid no attention. We sat on the balcony balustrade with our legs dangling and concentrated on the reactor. I put my arm around her and hugged hard. I was extraordinarily happy.

Moe gave me as good a hug and then the sunrise voice, "How long do you think we'll have to wait?"

"Three days, six hours, and twenty-five minutes," I said with tremendous assurance.

"You're not serious."

"Of course not. I really have no idea."

"Then we don't know when the death-birth will happen?"

"All we know is where."

"How will we know when it does happen?"

"We will hear a tremendous trumpet voluntary," I said with tremendous assurance.

She laughed. "Then we won't know. Actually, all I'm really interested in is what the reborn Circe will look like."

I nodded. "But we may be disappointed. She's been colored rock candy, a summer storm, an egret, a gust of wind, you, et cetera, et cetera, et cetera. Suppose she emerges from her ashes invisible?"

"I was hoping for something fabulous."

"Keep your curiosity crossed. But to be serious, you're falling into the trap of terramorphism. Most imaginative people do."

"How?"

"Well, when they try to create something fabulous, a

monster or whatever, they merely take familiar terrestrial forms and recombine them; a man with two heads, a frog with one stork's leg, a snake with a woman's face, a cave with a human mouth, a bass baritone volcano that sings Mozart, and so forth."

"That's true."

"I've described the alien objects in that ship to you, utterly incomprehensible. Suppose the reborn Phoenix emerges from the ashes similarly incomprehensible?"

"Such as?"

"Darling, you're asking the impossible! My parameters are terramorphic, too. All right, I'll try. She emerges as the ultimate prime number, as something centripetal, as antimatter, as antitime, as a black hole, as $X^n + Y^n = Z^n$—"

I broke off because the Langley Aerodromes had climbed on top of the reactor and were shoving the cadmium control rods back into the pile to kill the fission process.

"What is it?" Moe asked. "What's the matter?"

"I think the burn is finished," I said slowly. "They've stopped the reactor. Stand by. Circe must be ashes. Anything can happen now."

"I'm scared. You?"

"Petrified."

I was anticipating anything except actually what took place . . . Silence. Deafening silence. I looked around in amazement. Circe's lunatics were silent, motionless, standing, sitting, lying in a stupor, eyes open, expressions frozen, looking like subjects waiting for the hypnotist to count to three and snap his fingers.

"She's died and left them all," I muttered. "They're on their own again." Then the full implication hit me. I turned to Moly in terror. "You too? Can you still hear me, love? Can you speak?"

The blessed sunrise chord sounded again. "Yes."

"Still with you? Thank God. Or is it the new Circe needing us? Let's find out what she looks like and what she wants."

We threaded through the zombies to the pile. When you visualize a nuclear reactor, think of a solid four-sided letter H. The cadmium control rods are thrust down through the roof into the core. The four sides of the H are the insulating walls. The central crossbar of the H is the horizontal experimental passageway to the core. It was through this that the plutonium isotope and Circe had entered and through this that the newborn Phoenix had to fly out.

I swung the heavy hatch of the passageway open. I leaped to one side, yanking Moly with me. I was expecting anything to shoot out, from Old Faithful to Leonardo de Vinci. Nothing. No action. No sound. No trumpet voluntary. Not even the chirp of a fresh-hatched chick. I took five, sort of crooked around and peered in, then dodged back just in case something inside started shooting. No flying objects. I took another quick look and ducked back.

"Well*llll!*" Moe asked in a tone peaking with suspense.

"There's something inside."

"What something?"

"Something that glistens."

"Glistens!"

"Stay back. I'm going to take a good long look, and I don't want you hurt if I'm blown to pieces."

I took the good long look with my fingers crossed. I couldn't believe what I saw.

No ultimate prime number.

Nothing centripetal.

No antimatter.

No black hole.

Not even the square root of minus one.

I saw hard porn glowing in the core.

Hard porn.

It was a crystal statue, maybe ten inches high, of a man and a woman in one of the *Kama Sutra* copulation positions. He was down on one knee, the other raised. She was seated on his raised knee with her legs around his waist. Both nude, of course, but what made it particularly bizarre was the fact that she was pregnant. Her belly bulged, almost ballooned against his.

I stared so long in fascination that Moe had to push me aside to see what had hypnotized me. Then she stared as long as I had. At last she pulled back from the hatch and turned to me. Her expression was incredulous. "That's you and me," she said.

"What?"

"He has your face and she has mine."

"That's crazy!"

"Pull the statue out and you'll see."

Too much! Too much! I used the tongs to bring the statuette out. She was right; my face and Moly's.

"Why? How? Why?" I wondered helplessly.

After a moment Moe said, "I think she needs our help. I think this is her way of telling us. And that's why she's still with us. Please analyze what she's saying."

Moe was right, I tried to do a visual analysis. Query: Why had Circe gone to all that trouble to produce this, and what was it?

"Probably silicon dioxide," I told her. "A pure quartz, transparent and opalescent. You don't often come across it so flawlessly crystalline, not even in the most expensive jewelers."

"Does that tell you anything?"

"In a way. The first time I saw Circe it was in the form of a heap of crystals. Now the Phoenix rebirth is a crystal statue. It hints that organic life on Circinus may have a silicon rather than a carbon base."

Moe was gazing at me with an approval that made me feel even bigger.

"I'm no art mavin," I went on, "but I can see that the sculpture of this love duet is almost photographic in detail except, of course, for the advanced pregnancy. I wonder whether we can deduce why Circe—"

I stopped short because something in the female figure's balloon belly had caught my eye, something that shouldn't, wouldn't, couldn't be in a work of art. It was a giant micropyle. A micropyle is the minute opening in an ovum through which a spermatozoon can enter.

I looked closer and closer now that I knew what to search for, examining and wondering as my inspection revealed clue after clue. At last Moly had to tug my arm.

"What is it?" she asked. "Have you found something?"

I'd been holding my breath. I let it out in a burst that was half a laugh of exasperation and half of ecstasy. "That damned witch, bitch, harpy, hellhag! She always throws a curve. She razzle-dazzles and then, at the very last moment, she lets you discover what it's all about."

"What d'you mean?"

"You want to know why this Phoenix caper ended in a statue of me banging a pregnant you?"

"Of course. You know?"

"Everything. I'll tell you, but I'm warning you that it's wilder than anything I predicted."

"How?"

"Listen. We'll never know what the reborn Phoenix will look like."

"Why?"

"Because Circe isn't born yet."

"Then what's this statue?"

"A chorion."

"A what?"

"A chorion." I spelled it. "A shell, and entomologists have come across some beautifully sculptured, strangely shaped shells covering—now hear this—covering and protecting eggs."

"Eggs!"

"Yes, lady, eggs. That balloon belly is a chorion shell protecting a giant, macroscopic ovum. If you look closely and know what to look for, you can make out the—"

"Please, Jeff, you're going so fast . . ."

"Sorry. In simple terms, the Phoenix metamorphosis isn't finished. Circe isn't reborn yet. She's become a virgin egg waiting to be fertilized."

Moly was shaking her head dazedly, trying to take it in. "But—but that shell—What's it called again?"

"Chorion."

"Is it unusual here on earth?"

"Not at all. Rare but not unusual with some species. And three cheers for terramorphism."

"Wait, Jeff. I still don't understand. Does the chorion look like us because it's her way of asking us to protect her until she's fertilized and reborn?"

"You got it. She left an unmistakable message in Terran terms."

"How did . . . does . . . she know we'll do it?"

"Because the bitch has my number. She knows that my prime compulsion is scientific discovery, and she knows how to manipulate it."

"So she's adopted us as her Mum and Dad?"

"Right again, which means that her gift of supraception will stay with you forever."

"Why?"

"Because she'll need us and we'll have her on our hands forever."

"Again, why?"

"Because there's nothing here on earth that could possibly fertilize her."

"How do you know for sure?"

That stopped me cold. "My God, darling, you give me a *kvetch!* You think it's possible?"

"Why not? An armadillo maybe, or an aardvark?"

"And when the egg hatches?"

"Then it's your Nobel prize for sure."

I laughed. "No, it'll more likely be me hollering, 'Moly! Their monster and our monster are fighting again.' "

She laughed with me and cried and smudged me with her wet face.

"So come on already," I said. "Pick up the virgin and let's get the hell out of here. Circe's lunatics are beginning to revive and they'll be rotten hung over. They'll be ashamed and whining, 'But it wasn't my fault,' and looking for someone to blame."

"Probably you," Moe giggled.

"Uh-huh. I'll be branded as the Judas Iscariot who sold civilization down the Milky Way, and this will be remembered as The Year of the Fink."

It was at that moment that a robot mission from the parallel counter-universe burst through a black hole near Krüger 60, the M3 star some twelve and a half light years distant from our Solar. The countercraft from reverse space was emblazoned with a slogan which translates literally as, SEVAS GNIKUF. It was an arsenal of mreps.